ProbablePolis

The Whale, the Drake, and the Bookcase

RICHARD DELL
AND
ROWAN DELLDERONDE

iUniverse, Inc.
New York   Bloomington

ProbablePolis
The Whale, the Drake, and the Bookcase

Copyright © 2009 Richard Dell

All rights reserved. No part of this book may be used or reproduced by any means, graphic, electronic, or mechanical, including photocopying, recording, taping or by any information storage retrieval system without the written permission of the publisher except in the case of brief quotations embodied in critical articles and reviews.

This is a work of fiction. All of the characters, names, incidents, organizations, and dialogue in this novel are either the products of the author's imagination or are used fictitiously.

iUniverse books may be ordered through booksellers or by contacting:

iUniverse
1663 Liberty Drive
Bloomington, IN 47403
www.iuniverse.com
1-800-Authors (1-800-288-4677)

Because of the dynamic nature of the Internet, any Web addresses or links contained in this book may have changed since publication and may no longer be valid. The views expressed in this work are solely those of the author and do not necessarily reflect the views of the publisher, and the publisher hereby disclaims any responsibility for them.

ISBN: 978-1-4401-9280-7 (pbk)
ISBN: 978-1-4401-9279-1 (cloth)
ISBN: 978-1-4401-9281-4 (ebk)

Printed in the United States of America

iUniverse rev. date: 11/19/2009

Dedication of the Father

To my Daughter;

My Father, and my Mother;

All my Grandparents;

Sonja Avena (without her persistence and encouragement this book would simply never have been finished and the 'Twinkler' would never have been born)

and C.S. "Jack" Lewis, who inspired every one of us- thanks, Jack.

Dedication of the Daughter

To all my relatives and friends who have always been there for me,

especially my mom, Kimberly deRonde

Copyright 2009 © Richard Dell

> "I leave to various future times, but not to all, my garden of forking paths."
>
> 'The Garden of Forking Paths' by Jorges Luis Borges

Prologue

The War had gone on a long time; longer than anyone had wanted. Certainly longer than little Nowar Rondell had wanted it to. She missed her parents. She didn't know if she would ever see them again.

She was ten. The war had started when she was seven.

For quite some time, in fact, she had thought that her Mother had passed on at the beginning of the war, when the terrorist bombing began. She was told that her Father had been taken by it as well, or rather, they gave it a strange name, and said he had been 'called to action', and though everyone said he wasn't dead, and that her Mother was still only *officially* 'missing'- as far as little Nowar was concerned, she hadn't seen her Father since the war began, and she could barely remember her mother's face.

For some reason called 'sensitive operations' in the case of her Father, and 'ultra-secret technology' in the case of her Mother, Nowar had been alone for over a year. Not even letters from her Father. Everyone kept telling her that when the war was over, she'd understand why things had to have been the way they were, but to a little girl of ten, a whole year is a very long time, and she missed him terribly. Then again, nothing made much sense since the war had begun.

Going on three years now, she had been shuffled from one school to another. Then everything changed. The military boarding school she had been attending the longest had become a target for terrorists, and now she was being sent 'to the country' to live with her Grandma Brandy and Grandpa Bric for the rest of the year. It had been a very welcome change, actually. She hadn't seen her grandparents since the war began, and since they were her two last living relatives left, staying with members of her own family stirred her heart to joy.

As the bus pulled into the station, she was eagerly looking out the window for her Grandma, whose colorful dress and proper appearance was at odds with the fashion of almost any time, making her very easy to pick out of a crowd, regardless of her mood. Getting off the bus, Nowar dropped her bags and leapt into her Grandma Brandy's arms.

After three years spent with strangers, she was finally going home again.

Chapter One

...In which a Bookcase is rediscovered

Part One

A new venue

Walking up to the house, Nowar thought to herself "What a beautiful sunny day. Nothing's changed."

In fact it was almost a bit spooky. It was as if the whole place had resisted time effortlessly over the years. Butterfly bushes still spread out all across the front yard, a beautiful tall birdbath still stood proudly by the red brick walkway that spiraled from the front porch to the back. The 'liberty bell' that was suspended from two wooden posts in the ground was still draped with lavender. In glee, Nowar rang it loudly. Grandma Brandy locked her van and walked slowly behind her granddaughter watching with a big broad smile. What a wonderful day. Her only grandchild was home. Her only grandchild was safe again.

"Go take your things up to the guest room. That's where you'll be staying." She said softly.

Nowar walked up the long circular staircase to the second floor, edging around the banister to the second door on the left, right in front of the door to the attic. Grandma Brandy had meticulously prepared the guest room for Nowar. Cleaned from ceiling to floor with some cleanser that made her sneeze, twice, the room was immaculate and detailed- here a red cinnamon candle, there a lamp with cat-tails, on the wall a painting of a cherubim shooting an arrow, and a vase with blue flowers adjusted perfectly on the nightstand by the bed. Every inch of the room bore the touch of Grandma Brandy.

Except the bookcase.

From the floor to the very top of the ceiling, the book-case dominated the guest-room, in the nicest possible way, like a silent monolith. Nowar quietly sat her bags on the bed, and for a moment gazed across a landscape of books- it was more like being in church than being in a library;

Mark Twain, Flash Gordon, Carl Sagan, Mandrake the Magician, The Odyssey, The Iliad, Lewis Carroll, Tarzan, books on Aliens, Sherlock Holmes, Lord of the Rings, Tom Swift and his Rocket Ship, and on and on and-

Nowar took a deep breath and turned back to the doorway. Grandma Brandy had been standing there watching her. She had a large key in her hand, which she handed gently to Nowar.

"It wasn't always a guest-room." she smiled, somehow anticipating Nowar's next question,

"Your father would sleep here when he came home from college. In fact, he stayed here three years ago before he went off to war." She straitened up a tilt on one of the lampshades.

Nowar caressed the key in one hand while she chatted with Grandma Brandy. They walked downstairs and then did a tour of the property until just before sunset. Right after dinner, she excused herself early, saying she wanted to get to bed, and went back upstairs.

It had been a long journey.

While she noticed the door to the bedroom was ajar, she figured that Grandma Brandy had forgotten something- then she realized that Grandma Brandy had been with her the entire time. As she came into the room, she noticed several books had fallen from one of the shelves.

"How very odd" she whispered to herself as she knelt on the floor.

Picking them up carefully, she put each one back on the shelf. Not, in fact, an easy chore. The book-case was packed, but with loving care for each of her father's books, she found the proper home for each and every one of them: H.G. Wells- the Shape of things to come, Uninvited

Visitors by Sanderson, 2010 by Arthur C. Clarke, The Voices of Heaven by Frederick Pohl, and then, a book she had never seen before, both unique and mysterious.

It was tall and slender, made of black leather, with a five-pointed star, a sun and a moon all emblazoned and raised, beautifully engraved in white, silver and gold.

And it was locked, with a curious strap and a bronze fitting that would not come undone. There was no key-hole, and it looked brand new.

After a few minutes of racking her brain, she again realized how tired she was.

"Very curious," she said aloud, and put it on the nightstand by the bed.

"Tomorrow," she thought determinedly, "I'll figure out how to open it."

Part Two

Grandma Brandy gets real handy

Nowar woke up with the tangible excitement of a person waking up to a mission.

The mission? Open the book.

Nowar enjoyed a challenge.

But where was it? She'd put it on the bed stand closest to the Bookcase, and, ah, there it was on the floor. She must have knocked it off in her sleep. Picking it up, she began to look it over. Nothing had changed. She hadn't imagined it. The book was locked. The clasp and seal had no keyhole. The black leather smelled brand new- the sun, moon and five-pointed star glinted in the morning light; and there was not a hint or a clue as to its contents, or how to open it.

So, she futzed with it before her shower, and then after her shower. She pried at it before her lunch, and then after lunch. She fiddled, faddled, peeled and battled with the book until she was totally exasperated.

This was more than a challenge. She had seriously manhandled it just short of destroying the thing, and still, no luck. Finally, just before dinner, Nowar made the most difficult decision a child can make when they have single-handedly discovered a magical mystery, as it had been, in private-

Take it to an adult.

After a moment's introduction at the dinner table, Grandma Brandy's surprise showed that she was clearly on the up and up, and as much in the dark as Nowar had been. She'd never seen the book before. She didn't know where it had come from.

But she immediately figured out something so obvious that Nowar felt a bit embarrassed; the Sun, the Moon, and the Five Pointed Star were like big buttons. Remarking how beautiful they were, Grandma Brandy pushed down on one while the book was sitting on the kitchen table, perhaps harder than she had meant to, for it depressed into a slight recess, making a cute, but barely audible 'click'-

-And a note. Music.

Nowar and her Grandmother exchanged smiles excitedly. This was only the first discovery. A cascade of discoveries followed. First, and most naturally, they found out that each button produced a different note, and then, that holding down two buttons at the same time produced yet an entirely different note altogether. Finally, they discovered that holding all three buttons repeated all the notes that they had made previously in the order that they had made them, followed with a delightful and lighthearted crescendo, apparently resetting the memory of the order in which all the notes had previously been created.

Having exhausted the startling variety of discoveries, Nowar uttered the word "Wow" softly to herself and set the book back on the table. Grandma Brandy agreed wholeheartedly and warmed up Nowar's cold dinner plate.

"Alright, girl-child, it's time to eat. This is the second time I've popped your dinner in the microwave.

Nowar obliged, gobbling her food like a hungry little wolf cub, hardly taking her eyes and her left hand from the book. When she was done eating, she looked up thoughtfully and asked Grandma Brandy a question she'd been meaning to ask since the day before.

"Grandma Brandy, where's Pop Bric?"

"Your Grandfather's on a business trip, he'll be back sometime next week."

"What kind of business?"

"Oh, you know, doing things for the Center." that was all Nowar would get out of her Grandmother, and she knew it.

Grandpa Bric was nearly as mysterious a figure as her Father. Five years ago, he'd started a Research Center for 'Advanced' Vehicles. The government apparently liked his work so much that it had bought the place when the War had started, and kept him on there to run things for them. His 'work' often took him to exotic places for extended stays. He never could talk much about all that he did; a lot of it was top-secret.

"Do you think **he'd** know how to open it?"

"I don't know, honey." Grandma Brandy was drying dishes; "I can send him an eMail tonight, if you want."

"Oh, yes, please." She waited a moment, and then asked, "Do you think this is **his** book?"

"No, honey. I don't think so. Like I told you, I've never seen it before today."

Nowar trotted back upstairs with the book and a cup of hot chocolate. Curiouser and curiouser, she thought.

Tomorrow was another day.

Part Three

Use a Book to open a Book

A musical book with no keyhole. Baffling, thought Nowar, beautiful, brilliant, but baffling all the same.

Clearly the music it produced had to be the key to opening the darned thing. After having brushed her teeth and put on her nightgown, she got into bed, tucked herself in, and realized sleep would not come easily.

She tossed and turned for about ten minutes, and then she turned the light back on, grabbed the book, and sat there staring at it. Within seconds the guest room was filled with simple tunes. Luckily, her Grandma Brandy was sleeping in the bedroom below her on the opposite side of the house, and would not be disturbed by her musical expeditions. The moon was rising behind her in the window, but she did not even notice.

It can only make six notes, she thought to herself, how complicated could it get?

But then, after about a dozen attempts, one of which sounded eerily like 'twinkle, twinkle, little star' (or was it, 'When you wished upon a Star'?), an unassailable doubt came to sit next to her in the bed- The 'key' refrain could be a hundred notes long or more, really.

How important were the secrets contained in this book? And what if there were no secrets inside at all? What if it was totally blank and this was nothing more than a very cruel joke?

She went back to making music. At some point she realized that the six notes were not contiguous, in other words, they were not a whole section of an octave. This was interesting to note, but it didn't really help her get any closer to her goal.

She put the book back on the bed stand, and just as she was about to turn out the light and give the Sandman a second chance, something made her look back at the book case. Unsure as to the why and wherefore, she got up out of the bed, stood in front of the book case and said aloud-

"Alright, I need a clue." And not really knowing what would happen, or what to expect, she closed her eyes and pulled a book from the shelf- it was by Clifford Simak, *Strangers in the Universe*. She opened it randomly and read a few lines from the top of page 140-

"Missionary? Trader? Diplomat? Or just a mere machine and nothing more? Spy? Adventurer? Investigator? Surveyor? Doctor? Lawyer? Indian Chief? And why, of all places, had it landed here, in this forsaken farmland in this pasture on his farm? And its purpose-"

It was an interesting story that almost sucked her into it- something about an alien invasion- but nothing helpful for opening a music-making book.

After all, what had she been expecting?

Magic, she realized; the kind of magic her Father had taught her long ago. When she was little she remembered he must have told her a hundred times- "when you need an answer from the universe, Nowar, go to a bookcase and randomly pull a book from the shelf, and then open the book randomly as well." Just like it was yesterday, she could hear his voice in her head- "Go ahead and try it, you will be astonished at how relevant the passage you're reading is to the problem at hand. This is a divination technique as old as ancient Sumer, little one."

But it hadn't worked.

She began to put the book back on the shelf when she started to knock another book cleanly off. A thick volume, called *A Thousand Years a Minute; Adventures in the Unknown* by Carl Claudy tumbled to the floor, spilling a bookmark at her feet.

The bookmark had two golden crowns on it, and in very precise lettering were two simple sentences-

DON'T GIVE UP, NOWAR. LOOK IN THE ATTIC.

She was stupefied. It was her Father's handwriting.

Part Four

Clues in the Attic

There was no way she could sleep now.

'Detective' Nowar had a real 'lead', and like any good 'gum-shoe', she could not rest while that lead was hot, or the door to the attic so close to her own bedroom door. In fact, the door to the attic was just across the hallway literally in front of her bedroom door. Two slippers and two steps later, she was springing up the very long stairway to-

-a sea of junk, a sprawling, vast musty expanse of antiques, knick-knacks, silverware, keepsakes, memorabilia, comic-books, records, tapes, a carton of big clunky things called 8-tracks, boxes of newspapers, dolls, birdcages, croquette mallets, walking sticks, tapestries, rugs, and of course, more books. The running joke in the family had always been about who was a bigger pack rat, Grandma Brandy or Pop Bric. Granny 'Cannon' Anne, Pop Bric's mother, had been the Queen of them all, of course, but there was no knowing where one pack rats' kingdom ended and another's begun.

Nowar's heart sank, but for only a second. Determination creased her brow quickly as she waded through the decades, even centuries, all lit by the full moon and a pale light bulb here in the attic; she had just received a totally lock-solid message from her Father that this was where she needed to be. Somehow, and this was still blowing her mind, her Father knew, who knows how, that she would cause that one book to fall, and, as improbable as it seemed, had put a note of encouragement with a clue as to where to find the key to open the musical book.

But now what? What in fact was she looking for? A note with notes on it? Music sheets? Ah, she thought, and plowed into a box of old musical sheets next to a Styrofoam T-Rex skeleton. Music of songs she had never heard of, all from nearly a hundred years ago or more, way before the age of Disco and Rap, for sure. Musical instruments, maybe? She nearly broke Pop Bric's old violin case trying to get it open. He hadn't played it since he was her age, half a century ago. She found her Father's flute, Granny Anne's grand piano, Grandma Brandy's harp, and something else she didn't recognize whatsoever that looked like it came from Africa.

Too obvious, she thought, sitting on top of the Piano, which for the moment was like an island in this ocean of memories. Good lord, she thought, if all this stuff could talk, what kind of stories would it all tell? Sheesh, she thought, she probably couldn't get any of it to shut up. Silence seemed to be her only friend now, and though it was cold up here, she couldn't bring herself to go back down stairs. Right now, bed symbolized defeat, and she had just encountered a most marvelous bit of encouragement that she was still holding clutched in her left hand. She stared at the letters again, half-hoping they would somehow dematerialize and reform into a new message- 'Look here you poor thing, sorry I wasn't more specific.'

No such luck.

Just as she was about to give up, she heard the downstairs attic door creak open, and the slow determined, plodding footsteps of Grandma Brandy heralded her arrival at the top of the stairs.

She chuckled to see her Granddaughter sitting on top of the Grand Piano and said, still laughing-

"Your cup of hot chocolate went to bed without you. I was curious where you'd gone off to, dearie." She was making her way over to Nowar's island. Her nightgown lightly brushed past her childhood harp, making a beautiful and delicate zithering sound that evidently startled her slightly. "Oh, goodness, that's where it went." And she moved it to a more prominent perch in the topology of the attic, patted it like it was a pet, and then, turning to Nowar, asked her the question that Nowar had been waiting for-

"Whatever in the world are you doing up here at **this** hour?" Erk! There were no mincing words with Grandma Brandy, who could not be fibbed to in the slightest, and, as her Father used to say, had 'eyes in the back of her head'. It wasn't easy, being part of a long line of savants, but Nowar was getting back into the swing of things- without hesitation she said, "I found this in a book in the book case downstairs. It's in Daddy's handwriting."

"Well, look at that." She seemed honestly surprised, in fact, maybe even more surprised than she acted. The attic was still. Nothing stirred, not even Grandma. Nowar held her breath. Did Grandma know something that she wasn't saying?

A big smile slowly grew across her face. She handed the bookmark back to Nowar and, turning briskly back to the stairs, made her way swiftly through the sea of stuff. Where was she going? What did she know? What was it that she wasn't saying?

"Grandma Brandy, where are you going?" Nowar pleaded.

"To bed, girl-child. Like your Grandpa Bric says- 'Riddles and mysteries are better solved after a good night's sleep'- sound advice, you should try it."

"But, but, I want to…" she stopped, Grandma Brandy had slowed down just in front of the landing, and putting on her spectacles, examined something she had just spied, there on the ledge. It was a book. Only two glances she gave then, one at the book, and then one at her Grandchild, and then, without saying another word, she placed the book back on the ledge, and said "Goodnight wee one, don't stay up too late."

Nowar rushed to look at the book her Grandmother had just been handling. She sensed her lead had just 'heated' back up. She got to it just as Grandma Brandy closed the door to the attic, and picking it up, blew the second layer of dust off of it.

"The Wizard of Oz" by L. Frank Baum.

Part Five

Wherein the mystery of the opening of the great musical Book is revealed

Nowar clatter-whumped down the stairs at high velocity like a quick-beam bullet, nearly breaking her neck on the sharp turn at the foot of the stairs.

She was no dummy, and she was totally with the program now. She knew without a doubt which tune would open the book. In fact, it was lying at her feet. Just as she had thumped into the wall at the bottom of the stairs, a sheaf of several hand-scribbled notes like leaves in autumn had settled quietly at her feet. Obviously they had been tucked away in *The Wizard of Oz*.

And there it was. The lyrics to "Somewhere over the rainbow"- the theme song to a movie made 56 years before she was born. This was the tune she would try next in order to open her musical book; it was a tune that her Father used to sing to her as a baby, to get her to go to sleep. She sat down slowly, and began to read the lyrics out loud, at some point she realized she was singing them softly. The tune was engraved in her mind, as basic and as eternal as the taste of chocolate, or the sum of one and one-

Somewhere over the Rainbow
music by Harold Arlen
and lyrics by E.Y. Harburg

Somewhere over the rainbow
Way up high,
There's a land that I heard of
Once in a lullaby.

Somewhere over the rainbow
Skies are blue,
And the dreams that you dare to dream
Really do come true.

Someday I'll wish upon a star
And wake up where the clouds are far
Behind me.
Where troubles melt like lemon drops
Away above the chimney tops
That's where you'll find me.

Somewhere over the rainbow
Bluebirds fly.
Birds fly over the rainbow.
Why then, oh why can't I?

If happy little bluebirds fly
Beyond the rainbow
Why, oh why can't I?

When she was done, Nowar realized that she had been crying during the last stanza. Putting her head between her legs in her lap, she sobbed, softly, for quite some time.

She had solved the first mystery of the musical book- and she missed her Father more than ever.

Chapter Two

- In which the Mystery is cubed

Part One

When at first you don't succeed; try, try again

It was midnight. All of the big grandfather clocks downstairs were chiming "Gong, gong, gong, gong, gong", and on and on and on and on.

And then it was quiet again. The light from her bedroom spilled across her feet where she sat, at the bottom of the attic stairwell, illuminating the Wizard of Oz book and the handwritten sheaf of papers in her hand that had just fallen out of it.

Somehow, the whole rush thing had evaporated. Dag-nab-it, she thought, I'm ready to open that darned thing. But she was torn- first she wanted to read the other pages. They were, after all, a time capsule, pages from her Father's journal, evidently, all in her Father's handwriting, not just the lyrics to the song she had just finished singing to herself.

She looked through them slowly- and began to read the first page on the top of the sheaf:

April 20th, 1988

> Once in a while, a single moment in time can sometimes define our whole future, and it's not often that we see that that very moment was that important until long after it had happened. I had a moment like that this evening. Me and my darling Limberly are supposed to be married in two more days, on EarthDay. I have had 'cold feet' like you wouldn't believe for a week. I was

> sitting in a friend's basement, agonizing over what to do, not paying much attention to the movie playing on the television: The Wizard of OZ.
>
> I tried to talk about what I was feeling, but nothing was really making sense. I love Limberly, - I've loved her all of my adult life, and I feel like it's our destiny to be together, but I was so scared I wasn't doing the right thing, so scared of being trapped, and I had almost talked myself out of getting married, when something indescribable happened.
>
> I felt a presence, like nothing I had ever felt before. I looked around wildly, trying to figure out what was happening- the music, "Somewhere Over the Rainbow" was playing from the TV, and I had a realization that went through my whole body, a 'knowing' that was stronger than belief, stronger than faith even- that somewhere somehow in the far future, the child that Limberly and I would have someday was calling out to me, across a huge void of time and space, to be her daddy, to do the right thing, to bring her into this world.
>
> I immediately knew what I had to do. I drove home like a madman, and packed my things.
>
> Limberly and I will be married in two days, come what may. I am ready to meet my destiny.

Nowar was stunned. She did not quite know what to think. There were two more sheets for her to read. She rose quietly with them and walked into her bedroom.

Sitting on her bed, she sipped her hot chocolate for a few minutes, and then pulled the next sheet from the sheaf- the musical book had waited this long for her to open it, it could wait another few minutes.

April 13th, 1995

> She's arrived. A minor miracle that she's here at all. They had told us that the chances her Mother could have a baby were slim

to zero. But she's here. Nowar. We're not really sure where the name came from, but it came to us both about the same time. I've spent the last two weeks painting a mural in the room upstairs- a huge tree, the sun and the moon and the star, the ocean waves, the clouds on high.

My God, she's here. And she came to us on Thomas Jefferson's birthday! How amazing! Thomas Jefferson has always been my favorite figure from recent history. He was an incredible man, a freethinker and a freemason- and the fact that our daughter was born on his birthday is a great omen to me. I know she will change the world, just like he did.

Let the heavens sing in the highest, little Nowar Rondell is in the world at last.

Nowar gulped the last swallow of her hot chocolate, and got into bed, tucking the sheets carefully, if absentmindedly, all around her. To her right, the handful of sheaves from a journal her Father had kept that no one had ever known about- to her left, the Book she was now more mystified about than ever. One more page remained to be read- she could feel the moment coming now, when the musical book would finally be opened, when her life would be changed in more ways than she could possibly imagine.

March 22nd, 2002

I am torn in two. When my Limberly received her new assignment three days after Nowar was born, we were all ecstatic. This was without doubt the greatest moment in her career as a theoretical physicist- the defining moment that she'd worked her entire life to achieve. I was so happy for her that I put in for a six week leave of absence just to stay with Nowar while the good Doctor Limberly got adjusted to her new job: head Physicist in the top- secret sensitive operations "MoonClock Project".

Nowar had something the doctors called "Colic", so it was a hectic time for us all. She screamed her head off constantly. I alternated between singing "Amazing Grace", the tune from The

Wizard of OZ, and dancing around in circles with her clutched to my chest while a folk song off of a Chieftains Album played on repeat, again and again and again, just to get the poor thing to sleep. It was only six weeks, but it felt like six years.

To make sure that we would all be able to stay together as a family, I put a request in to my commander for a special transfer to the base at MoonClock Island with the new, elite Secret Agency, 'MoonDog-12', and I was granted the transfer. This was perfect. MoonDog-12 doesn't even report to the Chiefs of Staff, they report directly to the President. So the whole thing was a 'step up' for us both, and, more importantly, in fact, a great opportunity for all three of us to stay together as a family.

That was seven years ago. I can still remember the night my superior, Lt. Colonel Rand, called me with a trembling voice to tell me that something had gone terribly wrong with the MOONCLOCK Prototype, just days before I was scheduled to report for duty- the prototype artificial intelligence that drives the MoonClock, called "the Logos" had malfunctioned. He said that Doctor Moebius, Dr. Limberly, and three of her assistants had disappeared into something called 'The Breach', and no one could figure out how to bring them back, or even where they had gone.

I stayed on with the Project. How could I not? There are three things in this universe that keep me going though every day is like a tiny taste of hell- Faith, Hope and Charity. Hope, that somehow my wife is still alive somewhere in the Breach; Faith, that if I stayed with the Project I'd be one of the first to see or hear some evidence of her survival, and Charity, which I believe God will someday show me, and bring back my Wife and my daughter to me.

My parents and I chose to tell Nowar that her Mother had passed on when she was born, which was the only thing we could do, really. This project is top-secret- this very journal entry, if it were ever discovered, would have me removed from my command- I am now squadron commander of MoonDog-12, and I have a responsibility to my country, but I have a duty to my little girl as well. I can live on what others call 'false hope', but she can't grow up that way.

Like I said, today I am torn in two. Today, for the first time in seven years, the man who replaced Limberly as lead scientist for the project has discovered how to activate the 'Implausible Chip', the core of the Moon-Clock prototype simulation. I have been asked by the President to lead my squadron into The Breach, to 1) recover the missing personnel, the four doctors and the mad inventor of the MoonClock, Dr. Moebius; and 2) assess the alternate universe the Breach leads to, and if necessary, seal it off forever.

But how can I do this, - if I go, my daughter may become an orphan. If I stay, she may never see her mother again.

I have decided to go. Mom and Dad will keep an eye on Nowar. I have to find Limberly. I have to bring Nowar's mother home to her. I leave in an hour.

Nowar's eyes were huge. It was way past midnight. She stared at the Book, her hand moving slowly over the black leather surface, wondering how much more she could find out about what had happened to her Father and Mother from what was in this mysterious book.

Quietly, she took a moment to pause, then took a deep breath, and finally pulled the book onto her lap.

Without a moment's hesitation, Nowar began to press the Sun, the Moon, and the Star, in exactly the order she knew was required to produce the first refrain of the tune that would change her destiny.

The crescendo sounded utterly different than it had ever sounded before. A sharp click caused a vibration in her hands as the lock and clasp came undone. The Sun and moon and star were glowing brighter and brighter. Slowly she opened the cover of the book, though it felt like the book was opening itself.

The page was blank.

A great and nearly indescribable shimmering began to fill her field of view, growing steadily in its presence and power, until Nowar Rondell disappeared into a perfect halo of silvery white light.

Quietly, the book re-clasped itself, and the glow of the Sun, the Moon, and the Star faded like embers. Someone, or something, seemed to cause the light by her bed to turn off, as if by itself. The three journal pages that Nowar had read and left sitting by the book turned to dust within seconds. The window by the side of the bed opened suddenly, also seemingly by itself, and a billowing wind blew the dust into swirls around the darkened room. Then, the window shut itself, and the room was dark and silent.

Nowar had entered the Breach.

Part Two

Some things are written in stone, -others in mud

A sudden gasp of air, a rapid flutter of eyelids- a sky so bright and so blue invaded her whole vision, filled her entire being. She lay there in the sand, listening to her breathing, quietly in awe of a vaulted heaven like none she had ever seen before.

The sky was different. It rippled like an ocean, light dappling through thin layers of spidery mists, crisscrossing in layers over a hundred miles of pale turquoise that seemed to go on and on forever, like an ever-changing watercolor.

As her vision was becoming less blurry by the second, her peripheral awareness sharpened. There were lots of tall things far away to her left, and her right, and directly behind her head. Shades of burgundy, red, blue and periwinkle. Trees?

Her hearing was getting less muffled, and she was beginning to hear sounds other than her own breathing. The gentle lapping of water was quite close to her- and the distant roar of the surf; there was an ocean nearby.

All her senses were coming up to speed.

She propped herself up on her elbow and surveyed her surroundings. She was lying in the sand, perfectly naked. A few feet from her toes, the edge of a very sluggish lagoon that stirred and swelled ever so slightly lulled her senses for a second or two. All around her was a forest that started anywhere and everywhere about a hundred feet from the shoreline, but it was not a forest of trees-

Mushrooms! A forest of Mushrooms that ranged in size from two inches, or two feet tall, all the way up to seventy-two feet tall. They were of all sizes and shapes, some squat and solid, others frail and decaying. The colors ranged from deep plums and burgundies, to pale blues and bluish greens. Some had enormously wide tops; others branched low and clustered like bulbous teapots.

Everywhere she was beginning to hear the hoots and coos and acka-acka-acka noises of a jungle. This giant mushroom forest was alive with denizens of all kinds, though she couldn't see anything moving at all, yet.

Directly behind her, right where the tree line began (or, rather, where the Mushroom line began) was a very odd pillar, about five feet tall, a pale off-white beige color, with a computer monitor seamlessly attached to it, though at first it seemed like it was just resting on top of it. From a distance it seemed to have no buttons, nor source of power. It was dark, and looked ever so slightly beaten and roughed up.

How very curious, she thought, when, suddenly, something in the moist sand slid under her hand, and bit her.

"Ouch" she cried, quickly removing her hand, and looking for what had just taken a nip at her. Something was burrowing quickly downward, though as she bent over to get a better look at it, it squirted a thin 'splitch' of muddy water in her face.

"Oh bother" she said, or perhaps something worse, wiping the grit from her cheek, and just as she was about to give the ornery little critter a lesson in manners, grab it from its sandy little hole and chuck it into the lagoon, she suddenly noticed where her handprint in the sand had been. Next to it were five letters that had been scrawled in the sand.

N O W A R

A puzzled look crossed her face. She had no idea what they meant, though the word seemed oddly familiar.

"N-O-W-A-R" she said it aloud, slowly.

"N-O-W-A-R" she said it once more. Yes, definitely familiar.

But she wasn't entirely sure. Did it mean "No War"? No, the letters were all regularly spaced. She began to contemplate the very odd question- was this her handwriting? It flashed through her in an instant- she didn't know what her handwriting looked like.

Suddenly, the lagoon swelled and heaved, splashing water everywhere-something that had been coiled, asleep in the deep calm waters was sliding deeper into the lagoon, headed for the ocean, it's spines and fins breaking the surface here and there, its grunts and deep guttural trill shattered the quiet of the sea-side enclave.

"Good Lord!" she thought. It must have been fifty or sixty feet long!

The salty brine smell filled the air as watery waves rushed up all along the shoreline, spritzing her with several inches of foamy spray. Suddenly she felt very exposed, and more than a little confused. She looked down again at the letters.

They had been washed away.

Part Three

A decision made, clothes fashioned, and a new friend is discovered

Desperation struck like a hammer on an anvil, and she began to claw at the place where the letters had become only indentations in the wet loamy sand. Gone. All gone. Had she been sure of what they said? Yes, of course. They said NOWAR, whatever that meant. She got a hold of herself and said-

"Come on, this isn't like me, I don't get desperate like this!" but she suddenly conjectured to herself- "How do I know what is and what isn't like me?" and then with renewed alarm she said to herself, whoever she was- "I don't know anything about me at all, really!"

She was, in fact, an utter stranger to herself. Who had brought her here, and why did they scrawl that word in the sand, and, perhaps just as importantly, where **was** 'here' anyhow? She began to look around again, this time with the same awe, but tinctured with a slight unease- she was, after all, clothed only in her birthday suit, and she had just witnessed a fifty-foot long sea-serpent slither out of the lagoon, barely a stone's throw from her face.

The waters of the lagoon were already beginning to calm, and she thought she might have a look at herself in the reflection of one of the small captured ponds of seawater. Finding one not far from where she had been standing, she gathered a deep and reflective gaze at her visage.

Blonde, blue-eyed, about twenty years old, and, well, not like she would know for sure, but her features did not seem "hard on the eyes". It still didn't tell anything really about her, except that she wasn't dreaming, and that she was, in fact, human. Well, that made sense, and it wasn't as if she had started to doubt she was human, but, this was turning out to be a very strange morning, if it was a morning at all in fact. Something about seeing her own reflection brought her a measure of peace and composure again. Somehow it seemed like she had heard before of stories about people losing their memories and forgetting their names. What was that illness called? - and who had told her that?

Well, she made a silent decision to herself. Until someone who knew better could tell her who she was, and what she was doing here, she would call herself 'Nowar'. It felt a little silly, but after she said it to herself three times while she stared at her own reflection, she felt like it had been the best decision she had made yet in this very surreal place.

Slowly a mist was beginning to descend in places around the lagoon, but not the kind she was used to- it was like the whispery cotton candy stuff she had seen way up in the sky- like a kind of strato-nimbulus lace-work. Puffy, fluffy and light, it was beginning to fall and settle all around her, blowing here and there with a gentle wind coming in from the sea.

She looked at where some had fallen to the skin of her hand and her shoulders. This was like nothing she had ever seen, or felt. Wherever it landed on the sand, it seemed to slowly evaporate, or at least turn into a moist residue. But wherever it landed on her body, however, it congealed within seconds, becoming like a white stretchy second skin.

While this odd precipitation phenomena only went on for about five minutes or so before it tapered off entirely, it provided enough of this strange spidery mist-webbing that she was able to weave and sculpt a very smart little kilt and shirt for herself out of it. It didn't take long before it felt quite natural, and she felt proud of herself for having had the idea, once she realized the opportunity that was presented by the stuff.

Now that she had something to cover her modesty, she turned back to the task of figuring out other things- like the time of day. The sky was filled with light, but she could not seem to locate a sun. If it was out there, or up there, she saw only the barest indication in the sky of where it might be. In fact it really seemed like there was a ribbon of brightness in the heavens, not any particular exact spot where the sun might have been hiding.

Hmm. Quickly, she remembered the Computer Monitor on the pillar, and jogged back to where she had been, and up to the forest line, slowing down as she approached the thing. When she got within a few feet of it, something clicked and shot out of it, causing her to jump at first- a keyboard! Ah-hah! This was more like it. Leaving aside the very bizarre notion of a computer monitor out here on the seashore, and why that should be so odd she suddenly didn't quite understand, but this thing, with no observable source of power, made her feel at home- there was something about the combination of having a keyboard and a monitor in front of her now that rather soothed her currently increasingly perturbed state of mind, even though she could not really remember ever having used one of these things.

What did one do first? Where was the "on" switch?

No observable source of power, indeed. The monitor remained darkened, though moistened slightly from the misting, and the keyboard was a different kind of disappointment altogether. She didn't recognize a single character on the thing. One key, that was promisingly big, and red in color, unlike the rest, asked her to press it, so she did. Nothing. She pressed it again, and again, and banged it once for good measure.

A modest growl came out of her, and she committed to do a thorough examination of this utterly useless artifact, perhaps even break it into a few pieces to see if she could **make** it work, when she realized that she wasn't alone. Something, or someone, was nearby, grunting and grubbing in the sandy dirt. Only a few yards away from her, just within the mushroom-tree line, and only slightly obscured by a handful of two and three foot tall mushrooms, was something serpent-like.

In fact, it appeared to be a dog sized amphibian, or some smooth skinned serpentine creature- and though she could discern no visible head, as it had both its front and back ends deeply ensconced in two different holes in the ground, she could see it did indeed possess two sets of clawed and thick stubby legs, propping it up into this preposterous semi-buried position.

Well, some deeply buried instinct in her suggested that yelling loudly and waving a big stick would scare the creature off, so she proceeded to grab something along the lines of a desiccated mushroom stalk lying at her feet, and made a lot of loud aggressive noises that she hoped would create the right ambience.

The thing pulled its head out of the dirt and just stared at her, that is, it seemed like it stared at her. It did not in fact seem to have anything vaguely like eyeballs, just a smooth skinned wide gaping froglike mouth. The mouth was shut tight, and it had something dangling from it that was quickly snapped in the air and swallowed whole, in spite of the small creatures vigorous vocal protestations. It looked like a turnip, but with little wriggling legs and a big toothy grin.

The creature continued to stare at her, though, or *pretend* it could stare at her. Either way, she was starting to feel a bit uncomfortable, sensing her aggressive front was not going to work out at all, and then she witnessed something even more peculiar about this creature. Its tail popped out of the other hole- but *it wasn't a tail*. It was a *second head*, exactly like the first one- eyeless with a wide gaping toothless amphibian-like mouth.

Goodness, she thought. What in tarnation is **this** thing?

The first mouth belched loudly, and before Nowar could think of what to do next, the second mouth articulated.

"Homo." It spoke slowly, with a laconic and somewhat proper British accent.

"Oh, so!" the other responded, with a less laconic, and far more Scottish accent. It seemed to almost shrug, and then looked as if it was more interested in the hole it had just pulled itself out of.

"Pay attention." Head two shrilled, sensing the other head was more interested in lunch than Nowar. Head one sighed.

"Homo Sylvanus?" it lisped.

"Too robust to be Sylvanus; too much color. Ears are rounded, as well." and then plunged back in the hole wasting not another word. The other head used itself without hesitation to slam the neck of head One as the other head pulled itself reluctantly from where it had started to suss out another snack, undoubtedly grateful for the extra time to get away.

"But it's clothed itself in Sky-spider silk like they do. Erm, Homo Giganthropithecus, or Homo Erectus perhaps?" it asked again.

"Too lithe and agile. It's only six feet tall anyhew. And it's not very hairy... Can I get back to me lunch now?"

Head Two frowned, or something very similar, and lurched its share of legs forward a few feet, dragging its other head reluctantly with it. Nowar stepped back, suddenly realizing how fascinated she had become in watching this spectacle. She stumbled out from the forests edge, but kept a hold on her short stick.

"Homo Angelicas?" head Two lisped.

"Alright, now you're stretching fer answers fer sure. Does it **look** like it has wings?"

"Well, what the dibble do **you** think it is?"

"I dunno, why don't you try out some of those manners yer always bragging ye have, and ask it yerself?"

"Oh, wait a minute, I do believe this is a very rare hominid indeed, oh goodness gracious yes!" head Two said excitedly, and suddenly craning itself in an unusual way, as if intimating it was speaking *to* Nowar now, not *about* her, asked-

"Homo Sapiens, yes?"

Both heads stared at her silently, without eyes, of course. Kinda creepy. Homo Sapiens? The word sounded strikingly familiar, but Nowar was still stunned by the visage of this strange beast anyhow, so she nodded ever so slightly. "That'll work for now" she thought quietly to herself, gripping her stick tighter, wondering if Homo Sapiens were any tastier than other Homos.

"Y-y-yeah" she paused. "Homo…sapiens".

Immediately, she became a little more self-possessed. Something told her that she had little to fear from this two headed beast, and so she stood a little straighter, and said-

"OK, what are you two supposed to be, a Pull-you Push-me?"

Both heads looked at each other quickly, seeming to express some mild amusement at the question. Which head could she expect an answer from?

"Why, we are an Amphisbaena. **I** am Ouroboros Alpha, and **he** is Ouroboros Beta. I suppose I do most of the pushing, and Beta does most of the pulling, hahaha! "

"Och, sure, go ahead and lord it over with a stranger why don't chee? Mother liked me better and ye know it."

Immediately Ouroboros Alpha repeated the Punch n Judy routine it had initiated a minute before, slamming Ouroboros Beta soundly in the cranium, not once this time, but twice. Beta growled modestly and said under its breath- "Right, go on wi' yer bad self why don't chee, and let me go back to my breffy?"

"You've got to be kidding me. If she *is* a Homo Sapiens, we owe it to the King of ProbablePolis to find out who she is…she could be another pretender to the Throne of Evergreen, or perhaps something worse."

"Ye're so negative. I swear. I'll never understand why Mother made yew Alpha" And turning to look at Nowar- "Look Missy, not to be rude or anything, but do you have any geo-political aspirations or spiritual ambitions that would threaten the safety and security of our island or the great Kingdoms of ProbablePolis?"

Nowar just stared at them both for a moment. ProbablePolis?

"No…er, I mean, I don't *think* so," she said quietly, a little unsure what the question was about. Then, with a little more determination in her voice- "To be totally honest with you, I don't have a clue as to what either of you are talking about"

"There!" Beta spat, "It's settled, thank you Missy, - now" and turning back to Alpha, "I'll be tearin' up turf an' fillin me gut again, unless there are any further questions from the peanut gallery."

"No no no nononono! You glob! What if she is a spoiler or a cowan or a pretender, don't you think she would have been trained to say otherwise? Don't be so daft! Why she could be an agent of Duke Moebius made to look like a Homo Sapiens, and **you** would just let her go after that pathetic line of questioning, wouldn't you?"

"Yer just jealous that I got to the root of the matter so easily, aren't'chee?"

Nowar was way past feeling any anxiety about this creature. In fact she was doing everything in her power now not to laugh at it, and make it feel bad. She decided to be proactive, though. Clearly, she could probably find out quite a bit about where she was, and in the process, perhaps find out **who** she was, if she played her cards right.

"Well, I think my name is Nowar, but I have no Earthly idea of where I am from, or who I really am."

She looked at the Amphisbaena, waiting for a response. You would have thought that she had just spoken a vile curse, or perhaps a bizarre foreign language. Both of their mouths dropped open, and stayed that way for several seconds. Ouroboros Alpha was the first head to get a grip on itself and speak.

"No **Urathly** idea of where you are from? Urathly? **You** are Nowar? *The* Nowar? From fabled long-dead Urath?" Alpha was blubbering slightly.

"Nowar, the Princess of Urath? …Only begotten magical child of King Shard and Queen Limberly? But according to the Book of Scorns, Nowar is supposed to be a little girl, not even eleven years old!" Beta blithered as well.

The two heads stared at each other for a pregnant moment. Alpha said quietly, "Well, we know that all things are possible with the Logos…"

Suddenly they proclaimed loudly "Your Majesty!" and were stumbling over each other in an effort to bow. Bowing was difficult when both your ends were trying to do it at the same time. Somehow, after a brief and painful twisting, they pulled it off. After an awkward moment of silence, during which they threw each other a quick nervous glance, Beta began to speak first.

"Lady Nowar, truly, we are unworthy, but simply say the word, and we shall serve." Then Alpha spoke as well, "Lady Nowar, I am a little less unworthy than this foolish knave I am attached to, but simply say the word and I too shall serve."

Nowar smiled. Finally, some answers, and a new friend, or was it friends?

Now she was getting somewhere.

Part Four

New discoveries made

Nowar, if that's in fact who she really was, stood quietly with the Amphisbaena, regaining her poise. For just an instant she stared out at the sea and sized up her situation; she'd been here perhaps twenty minutes, she had clothed herself, found a new friend, and possibly discovered her identity; though some nagging doubt lingered in the back of her mind as to whether or not she could really be this princess that Ouroboros Alpha-Beta thought she was.

But had she in fact been here for twenty minutes? How did they tell time here? And where was 'here'? Her mind was still racing. The name ProbablePolis really told her next to nothing, really. Start with the basics, she thought, now that she had achieved some tiny edge on this creature- it seemed disposed to be of service to her, after all.

"What time is it?" she asked.

The two heads exchanged an odd glance. Alpha cleared his throat, as if he were about to announce the entrance of royalty.

"Why, it is the time of 'The Great Mustering'"

An awkward silence followed.

"That sounds interesting but what I meant was 'What time of day is it'?"

Beta laughed and coughed at the same time and spat again- "It's half past first phase, yer majesty"

Nowar looked no less confused, and Alpha filled in the blank- "er, midmorning, as it were, in the ancient parlance of dead Urath, I believe"

Beta moved closer to Alpha and whispered, "I know you said she's Homo sapiens an all, but she's acting a bit more like Homo erectus, if yew know what I mean." Alpha thwumped Beta once more with even greater vigor than all the other times combined "DO NOT INSULT PRINCESS NOWAR IN MY PRESENCE AGAIN, you truffle eating trilobite!!!"

Nowar interrupted, "Please, don't. Not on my account. Listen, you must understand."

She took a big breath- "I know that you think I'm this princess character you've been told about, but I suspect you're making a big mistake and I don't want to deceive either of you."

The Amphisbaena quietly listened. Nowar continued.

"It must just be an odd coincidence. I believe I am someone called Nowar, because I saw the name written in the sand right over there where I woke up, -but to be perfectly honest with you both, I have no memory of where I came from, or for that matter, of whom I have been. I have, er, I think it's called am…am…nee…amneezhee-uh. Amnesia, yes, that's it! I've lost my memory. Most of it, it seems. I have no memory of hardly anything up until just a little while ago, when I first woke up."

Ouroboros, both of them, stared blankly for a moment, apparently unsure of what to say next.

"We need a Precognitus." Alpha said quietly and dryly, as if to himself.

"Aye." Beta agreed, "Or perhaps even one of the 'Builders', they would know for sure who she was an' all. If you ask me, I'm beginning to really tink she **is** the Princess from the Book of Scorns."

"Book of Scorns?" Nowar asked. Alpha launched into another pronouncement as if speaking from a well-rehearsed verse, and clearly demonstrating how much he enjoyed the sound of his own voice-

"The Book of Scorns is older than time itself. It comes from the Future, and it instructs the Past. It is the Tome from which all the creatures of ProbablePolis understand their place in the Great Hypothecation that spans across the Holy Grid."

ProbablePolis

Nowar looked at him blankly. He continued, nonplussed. "The Book of Scorns is a tome with two spines and three folios. It is a living book that takes its cues from the great and magnificent Logos. To those who know the sacred language of Trinary, it speaks of all things, reveals all things, and obscures nothing at all. It contains all the keys to all the doorways of all ProbablePolis."

Beta added irreverently- "Yeah its kindof important, it's not the kind of book you want to take in the bathroom wi' ye."

Nowar laughed. Alpha scowled, but restrained himself from giving Beta another well-deserved thwumping.

"OK, I understand." She smiled, half-tempted to thank Alpha for letting Beta get away with a bit of humor. Then, suddenly getting an idea, she pointed back at the Computer Monitor behind her, she asked "Can we access this Book of Scorns from that monitor over there?"

"That? Oh no!" said Alpha, leading Beta along with him as he circled the pillar, continuing his dissertation- "That is an Aht Erm'nal."

"Aht Erm'nal?" Nowar said. Something seemed familiar about the sound of the name of this thing. "Why doesn't it work? Who uses it? Can we turn it on? Do YOU know how to use it?"

"Aht Erm'nals are found throughout all fourteen Kingdoms of ProbablePolis. They were once used by the last Emperor during The Great Rebuilding, although there is a heresy that suggests they were originally created long before that by the evil Duke Moebius."

Something about the mention of that name, Moebius, sent a chilling shiver through Nowar. The spider-web lattice mist was beginning to fall again, and she idly spun some of it around her fingers, patching a few areas on her sleeves and shoulders and hips while Alpha continued on-

"In either, event, whether Moebius or the last Emperor created the Aht Erm'nal, both of them had a hand in shutting them all off, ending for all time easy communication throughout the Great Hypothecation of ProbablePolis. No one is quite sure why. I suppose it's been about seven hundred great turns of the Solar Ribbon since these things could be used as they were originally intended."

"The Pre-cognitids, **they** know why, but they're not telling just anybody" Beta grumbled.

"Who are the Pre-cognitids?" Nowar asked, growing more and more hungry for knowledge of this strange place. Something deep inside told her that this was exactly what she needed, especially if she was going to get back her memories. Something about these Aht Erm'nals seemed to bother her- certainly she knew they were called something else where she was from, and that she had used them before.

"The Pre-cognitids are the holiest of the holy" Beta offered "Most of them are as old and wise as the Builders, the oldest of all the races of ProbablePolis. They came here in the very beginning it's said, along with the Builders. They were here before everyone, even Duke Moebius."

Alpha picked up where Beta left off-

"It is likely that they could give you back your memories, I suspect, and tell you beyond a shadow of a doubt who you really are, and where you came from."

Before Nowar could ask the next very logical question- where she could find one of these creatures, a strange shrieking sound pierced her ears, and the Amphisbaena leaped with vigor ontop of her, rolling her back into the Mushroom forest-

"DOWN, NOWAR! GET DOWN!" yelled Beta. The Amphisbaena was on top of her now, holding one of its paws over Nowars mouth. The shrieking was growing louder, almost higher in tone, like an incoming missile. She had been rolled into a bunch of smaller mushroom foliage, squishing juices and crackling fungal branches all around her, hardly able to see anything now. Her instincts told her to stay where she was, and not to struggle. The Amphisbaena, sensing she was with the program, removed its paw from her face while they huddled in the underbrush. The look on her face was enough to tell Alpha that she was scared. He whispered into her ear.

"It's a tendrilous Toggle-Wog, a tubular cybernetic extension of the twisted will of Duke Moebius. He has eyes and ears all over ProbablePolis." Alpha sounded more scared than she was.

"QUIET! Pipe down!" lashed out Beta. "It's almost here! Not a word from either of ye!"

Part Five

Nowar and Ouroboros take flight

The shrieking sound died to almost nothing, replaced with a mixture of mechanical whirring and humming noises.

Nowar remained on her back, feeling the weight of this ridiculous two-headed beast on her hip, wondering what was going on.

Truly, it came right out of the sky, and it came out of nowhere- a metallic, gleaming, silver segmented tentacle, like some cyborg worm with an enormous cyclopean red eye. It was hideous to behold, blinking with buttons and steaming vents and little antennae. Its parts and pieces bristled and twitched as its lower and upper lids opened and shut with a strange and deliberate intelligence. It had dropped from the sky like a missile, and then pulled itself up short, right in front of the Aht Erm'nal. The long thin tendril it was mounted to literally extended up into the farthest reaches of the sky, far beyond the furthest cloud.

The Amphisbaena was shaking now, but quiet as it could be, though it sweated profusely. The Toggle-Wog showered the Aht Erm'nal with a strange green glow for a few seconds, then, shutting off most of its lights and the glow from its eye, paused and uttered sounds like a rapid staccato, rather hollow, human voice.

"Toggle-Wog Delta 9 ZENO reporting in. Terminal 5dot6dot111dot39dot07 remains inoperative, but keyboard is extended. We repeat- keyboard has been extended."

Terminal? Nowar thought to herself, though she was shaking herself now. Terminal. Aht Erm'nal? A Terminal! She remembered that word. That monitor and keyboard, was called a Terminal wherever she was from.

Another voice could now be heard, though this thing was still alone. The other voice crackled and hissed, even though it sounded like a normal human voice. It was coming from this thing itself, through a tiny speaker on the side of the bulging red eye.

"Very good, Delta 9 Zeno, good boy, your mission operative is nearly fulfilled- (oh, Clancy, would you get me another bottle of wine, will you, this one's empty) however, we know that these malfunctions with the keyboard can only occur when the Terminals are approached by Hominids. A Homo something or other has to have been there in the last half hour. Do check into that and report back."

A second or two of whirring and the thing continued its analysis.

"Toggle-Wog Delta 9 ZENO has confirmed your most excellent and sublime theory, Master. Heat patterns and footprints in ground indicate a malfunction in Terminal keyboard due to carbon based bipedal life form approaching Terminal within last 17 minutes. Running tests to ascertain genetic match for hominid type."

The Toggle-Wog extended a tiny arm with a minute vacuum that sucked the keyboard for a few seconds.

The crackling hissing human voice could be heard laughing in the background.

"Incredible, Clancy. Your modifications to the Delta 9 model are truly impressive. The Delta 8 wouldn't have done half this well in half the time even with decent supervision. This thing has already figured out what's going on, and might even locate the suspects without any further prompting. Gadzooks man, you keep up this kind of work and I'll make you Chief Engineer before the Turn is over. Oh, and have some of these rolls, man, they're delicious."

"Toggle-Wog Delta 9 ZENO has concluded genetic analysis of skin remnants on keyboard. A single Homo sapiens sapiens has been here within the last half hour."

There was an awkward silence, though the crackling of the other end of the communication continued, clearing his voice.

"Ahem, uh, are you quite sure Delta 9 ZENO? You are, afterall, in Sector 07, aren't you?" said the crackling voice, sounding a little perturbed. "Not supposed to be any Homo **anything** there, except for a few Erectus, some Giganthropithecus, and Homo Goblinus, and none of them are known for dallying at the Terminals."

Another voice, even more distant than the first chimed in "Sector 07 gets occasional reports of Homo Sylvanus, my Lord. It could be an anomalous half breed that got there from Sector 12"

"Oh yes, those damned Elves are still there. When this war is over we really need to scrub that sector clean. Make a note of it Clancy, will you?"

"Delta 9 ZENO reporting in on Genetic Test. Affirmative on Homo Sapiens Sapiens. Genetic Analysis micro-lab in the Delta 9 unit has a .01 % margin of error."

The Toggle-Wog was now beaming its hideous green light at the ground around the Terminal, starting to sway slightly, edging closer and closer to the spot where Nowar and the Amphisbaena were hiding.

"Yes. Yes, you're right of course, old boy. Clancy, on the off chance that this **is** a real Homo sapiens sapiens, dispatch two Skreemers immediately to Sector 07. Arm them with those new high-grade whirling torpedoes and two of your best Koradgian pilots. Oh, and make sure they both understand - I want the Homo captured, unharmed, and brought directly to me. If this is an unknown Homo sapiens sapiens, it must be terminated immediately, but **NOT** until we **KNOW** where it came from."

"Yes, my Lord. It will be so."

The Toggle-Wog was still moving slowly, wavering to and fro as if making up its own mind whether or not it should be pursuing its quarry.

"Delta 9 ZENO you have performed marvelously well, I would like you to remain broadcasting from your point-of-entry until the Skreemers arrive, then ship the genetic material for secondary analysis in the upper laboratories on deck four-"

But the Toggle-Wog would do nothing further for anyone. A deafening roar overwhelmed the enclave as an enormous wall of water, scales, and teeth hurled into the Delta 9, thrashed around the tendrilous cyborg eye, and sucked the whole apparatus back into the lagoon.

The Sea Serpent had returned.

Thrashing for a second, the tendril sparked and exploded as the Sea Serpent pulled it under the waves and crushed it quickly with a few brisk movements of its massive maw. The end that still was connected somehow to something in the sky retracted swiftly, showering a few sparks as the shrieking sound quickly dissipated.

The Sea Serpent coiled back under the surface of the lagoon, uttering a loud and offensive belch as it settled into its shallow lair. Nowar stared at it, stunned, for a second, but no more. The Amphisbaena was already on the move.

"Come on, Nowar, we must flee!" Alpha cried. He and Beta were already several feet ahead crashing through Mushroom underbrush. They stopped for a second.

"What?" she said- still dazed at what she had just seen. What did this all mean?

"There's no time yer Majesty, we have to go, and **GO NOW**!" shouted Beta, motioning with one of his thick paws.

Nowar realized they were probably right; this was no time for contemplation. She didn't know what a Skreemer or a Koradgian was, yet, but if they had anything to do with that evil voice and that cyborg eye, they weren't worth waiting around for.

She ran off, following the two-headed beast into a dark burgundy forest of huge towering Mushrooms, leaving behind a sleeping sea serpent she would feel very grateful to when she had time to catch her breath.

Chapter Three

The Thot Plickens

Part One

Over yonder in the House that Evil made

Down in a palace of black steel, darker and deeper than any you have ever heard of, the most evil and despicable man of all ProbablePolis reclined, fat and happy, stroking his black goatee and leaning on one of his fat little elbows upon a vast and royal red and black comforter, luxuriating and basking in the warmth of his own indomitable essence, and the glow of a spooky computer screen.

He was playing a video game.

- Because he could.

"Ha!" he cried with vim and vigor, firing off another rapid round of blue laser bolts at two pixilated metallic wyverns, SCHOOM-SCHOOM-SCHOOM, KABOOM KABOOM! -retiring both of them to a digital heaven, or hell.

"All you base belong to us, you ninnies!" he laughed outrageously, gyrating with the controls and joy stick, making his avatar flourish with bulging biceps and flaming katana- a huge smile spreading across his barely shaven face. He threw down the control for an instant, and looked across the room at two other monitors where the other two players had been.

Two seven foot tall bipedal reptilian warriors (the **real** kind) looked up from their screens, hissed grumpily, exchanged disgusted looks with each other, and with measured disdain, threw their controls down in front of their monitors. They slithered off in a skulking, stalking manner, their tails swished the obsidian floor with an attitude, and their vicious implements of war noisily clattered against each other. Somewhere down a long hallway, a large metallic door slammed shut with a heavy thud and KLANG!

The most evil despicable man in all ProbablePolis watched the large leather bound reptiles exit from his chambers, grunted, raised an eyebrow, muttered under his breath "sore losers" and then, smiling again, picked up his control and painstakingly entered his own name in the registry of 'TOP 10 Super-Duper-Winningest-Super-Combatants'.

He giggled with glee. The screen read the following in glowing green letters:

Duke Moebius NobleChuck III

He sighed. "It's so lonely at the top"

He looked around with a languishing glance. All across the expansive darkened room, there were plenty more of the huge bipedal reptiles, all of them to a one, curled up and lying on top of one another. The room stank heavily of wine and cheese and jelly doughnuts.

Duke Moebius pushed the monitor away from him, and pulled out a thin laptop computer from under his bed.

"Clancy?" he inquired.

"Yes, my Lord."

"Any word from the Skreemers?"

"They're on their way, my Lord, shall I post you on their findings when they arrive?"

"Oh, that's right" his brow crumpled "They're headed to Sector 07, the furthest away from us right now. Oh bother…"

"Yes, my Lord, they should be there within the next hour or so"

"Oh, all right, let me know the instant they arrive on-site, though, and feed their sensory input into my network as soon as they're on-line. I'm going to catch a nap for a few minutes. Nighty- night."

"Yes, my Lord."

He turned off the laptop and rolled onto the bed, disturbing some small winged leathery thing that squawked and flew up into the black steel rafters. One of the sleeping reptiles roused for an instant, considered climbing up into the rafter to eat the noisy little pterodactyl, and then thought better of it. It looked as if Moebius was about to hit the sack.

Being the evil Dark Lord was not all it was chalked up to be. Long hours, little gratitude. No rest for the weary. Disrespect around every corner. Moebius popped one last jelly doughnut into his mouth and snuggled into his favorite over-size teddy bear, 'Poopsy'.

Within seconds, the lair of the most evil, despicable, perhaps most preposterous, Dark Lord of all ProbablePolis was filled with the sound of snoring.

Part Two

Running on Empty

The giant Mushroom Forest was beautiful, teeming with exotic life forms of all kinds. There were fiery salamanders that warbled like sparrows, monkeys with bat wings for arms, walking-stick insects the size of elephants, and semi-intelligent carnivorous plants (at least they said they were plants) that enticed tasty little furry things with glowing balls on stalks to dance closer.

But Nowar was not in a position to drink it all in. She was hurling herself at top speed over mossy humps and great fallen logs, doing her best to keep up with a four-footed two-headed beast that kept urging her on.

Finally, after half an hour, she tripped over a vine and went flying into a cold wet mud hole.

She was almost on the verge of tears when Ouroboros lurched back to see what was the matter- quickly Beta said, "She needs to rest for a few minutes."

Nowar pulled the mud from her eyes and used a handful of fronds to wipe her face clean. She took a big breath, counted to ten, and said, "Alright, what's the plan, Ouroboros. Where are we going?"

The two heads exchanged glances. They weren't really sure which one of them she was addressing. Beta spoke first.

"That's a fine question, Nowar," and looking at Alpha, "Well, smarty-pants, what do ye think? It's only a matter of time before the Skreemers get here. Where are we gonna go now?" Alpha looked perturbed. Clearly the plan up until now had been 'run as fast as they could, and hope for the best'.

Now it was time to come up with something better.

"Alright! Our short-term plan is to regroup. Nowar, you rest for a few minutes while Beta and I discuss all our options."

As tired as she was from half an hour's non-stop frenzied skee-daddling, the sound of a catnap sounded like a *great* idea. Curling up in the ferns like a traumatized kitten, Nowar looked up and around once or twice before she settled into place, and began to drift off. The on-going conversation between Ouroboros Alpha and Ouroboros Beta grew progressively more and more muffled.

"Our choices are few." Lisped Alpha.

"That's fer sure. Skreemers to the south of us, entrance to the Under-Rung barely half a clod to the North, and who knows what horrors are crawling around in Shan-a-gar these days."

"Shan-a-gar has always been a den of slimy-ness. We're not going anywhere near there, or the Under-Rung for that matter. Our mission is clear- we must get this girl to a Precognitus as soon as possible, if not sooner." Beta nodded quickly in agreement, looking at Nowar where she was curled, nervously keeping her in his sight.

Alpha went on, "If she is *the* Nowar, we must keep her out of the hands of Duke Moebius, and deliver her to the King and Queen."

"King and Queen?" Beta protested "Which one? If you've forgotten, they've been at war with each other for nearly three-hundred Turns of the Ribbon!"

"All right! All right! First things first. We go west by north-west to Hovahnnon." Alpha cleared his throat, "Yes, yes, I knew you'd be overjoyed at that prospect"

"Dimmy-strait fer sure." Beta spat, "It was *your* idea to come to the Lagoons of Sha'an and become a beach-comber."

"Well, I didn't hear you complaining about the tasty oysters and attractive young Amphisbeanettes, now, did I?"

"Oh no, ye'll not hear me complaining about the food, but ye might have mentioned that there were **huge** lagoon serpents, and that we'd be on *their* menu!"

"It didn't say a thing about predators in the travel brochure- how was I to know that-"

A brief instant passed where everything was quiet, and then Nowar awoke to the rough push and shove of the Amphisbaena's paws."

"Nowar! NOWAR!!!" They were both yelling at the top of their lungs.

Part Three

In which a strange clue is found

Nowar woke with a startled jump and looked around her wildly. Nothing was dive-bombing them, no strange high-pitched noises, no nothing, except two frightened faces right in front of hers.

"What?" she yelled back.

"What were you doing?" Beta said, still very upset.

"What do you mean? I was just catnapping, like we talked about. What's the problem?"

Alpha said, with a measured tone "You were fading."

"Huh? What do you mean by that?"

"You were turning more and more translucent and opaque with every second"

Beta chimed in "Yeah, and we could see right through ye." Alpha rolled eyes he didn't have, or at least that no one could see, and said-

"I have a very bad feeling about this."

"More so every second." Said Beta- and then looking at Nowar "Don't do that again, Nowar, ye scared the cabbage right out of me."

Nowar sat there thinking the whole notion through. She wasn't sure who she was, but maybe, if she **did** go to sleep, she might find out more about who she was supposed to be. What a strange thought. Problem was, she didn't dare go to sleep **now,** not with some unknown menace bearing down on them (whatever a Skreemer was, it didn't sound like a particularly good thing to deal with) manned by some kind of creatures that served the Duke.

But before she could take another breath, the Amphisbaena was dragging her back down behind the fronds- they were on top of a heavily overgrown overlook, with giant dead things and a vibrant series of strands of ferns and other steamy plants amidst the mushrooms. Down below was a kind of intersection of two relatively thin footpaths.

Something jaunted into the pale light streaming through the canopy, and crouched in the crossroads below them, sniffing the footpath and looking around wildly. It was tall and lean, with a huge barrel-like chest, incredibly long arms, covered with silver and black fur, with a veritable mane rolling off of a head far more wolf-like than human.

"Wolven-kine" whispered Alpha. The creature, as if hearing that delicate whisper, jerked its head in their direction. Beta frowned at his other head intensely with an unmistakable look that demanded silence.

The Wolven-kine had two bright glowing red eyes that squinted meaningfully in the hazy gloom, its ears perking up from their sides. It must have been over seven foot tall when standing fully erect and not stooped over, the natural posture it seemed to be most comfortable in. It had no pupils that she could discern.

It sniffed a few times, and then was joined by two others of its kind. They were not like the first. Their manes were not as luxuriant. They pelts were dark gray and they stood about Nowar's size, perhaps six feet tall or so, before they curled into the same crouch as the larger one, seeming to wait on his command.

"Raz-nahg-ahz" it said, pointing to the hill where the two refugees crouched. Its voice was deep, insidious, like a bell at the bottom of the sea. The two smaller companions howled summarily and hurtled upwards on all fours sprinting up the hill like huge wolves. Beta was screaming and his legs pushed Nowar back the other way, "Run, Nowar, we'll hold them off as long as we can. Head northwest to a city called Hovahnnon. Find a Pre-cognitus, trust no one but -"

But there would be no more words. The two Wolven-kine had already overtaken the Amphisbaena, and clearly they were going to have him trussed up like a turkey in a minute or two, in spite of fierce resistance. Nowar looked down at the glowering eyes of their leader. Something told her that running would be short-lived and stupid. And worse, these things would never respect her. As the huge Wolven-kine loped slowly up the hill, his mane waving in a gentle breeze, it occurred to

Nowar that her decision not to run had been either an amazingly brave choice, or an amazingly stupid one. Someone somewhere had once said to her that "Fear is an instinct, Nowar…courage is a choice."…had it been her Father? She couldn't remember.

For an instant she realized that she had no idea of whether or not she knew how to defend herself. She decided this one time she would wait to find out later, leaving her captors in the dark as to whether or not she could defend herself if she had to.

The leader Wolven-kine trussed her up, but far more carefully and deliberately, wondering much the same thing to himself. Prey does not give itself up so easily unless it knows it can break away easily, it thought to itself.

"Dip choaga may, wuh takka shahn" It said quietly and hefted Nowar up onto his back like a sack of potatoes.

The two others had knocked out Ouroboros and tied him efficaciously to a pole they suspended on their shoulders. With surprising speed and muffled paws, the three Wolven-kine sped down the hill and headed North through a deep thicket of ivy and tortured globular thorn bushes.

Part Four

In which a story of wolven kings and human kings is woven

So this is what a sack of potatoes feels like, Nowar thought to herself. The bumps, rolls and jiggles of how she was being transported weren't nearly as irritating as not knowing what her captors were talking about. The big one was a Wolven-kine of few words, and spoke in very brief replies, but his two assistants chattered like two schoolgirls.

And Nowar didn't have a clue what they were talking about.

The Wolven-kine that had been hauling her around stopped on a hillock and crouched. The other two crouched with him and whispered excitedly to each other. Although Nowar could not see well, from the sounds in front of them, she assumed they were waiting for something big to finish crossing their path.

And then they continued on. The smaller Wolven-kine were asking their leader questions he did not seem to want to answer.

"Di'akka lakh mazh takh?" one said.

"Go nay goray…" answered the big Wolven-kine, with his deep brassy voice.

"Ti shah mo Hratzaczekh?" the other chimed in, though the answer was the same,

"Go nay goray!"

Nowar silently wished to herself that she could at least understand what these creatures were saying to each other.

What happened next was difficult to describe. It was like someone had dropped an invisible stone in a pond, sending ripples out like circles from where the stone had hit the surface of the water- but the stone had been Nowar, and it looked like ripples of distorted light were rolling away from her in every direction, as if the very air around her had become the pond.

The Wolven-kine must have felt something as well, for all three were as still as stones.

When they began to speak again, much to Nowar's surprise, she could understand every word they said.

"What the Frog was that?" said one of the two smaller ones. The leader was still silent, though his head moved from side to side, surveying – everything – very slowly. The other smaller one grunted, "It was as if the whole forest, everything around us became like the waves of the ocean, or like a quaking of the earth."

"Except it was in the air, not from the ground." And then addressing the leader once more, "He-who-walks-with-Two-Fangs should break his silence and share his knowing."

So the big one is called Two Fangs, Nowar thought. This was a much better situation now.

Two Fangs put Nowar on the ground, but not too roughly, as he had hefted her earlier. Taking a big sniff of the air, he stood erect, a seven and a half foot tall belted Wolven-kine of enormous girth. Nowar now saw that he had many battle scars, and a thick leather belt around his waist, slung with long thin pieces of antler, carved to serve as weapons, tied with feathers and claws of other creatures. He did not take his two glowering red eyes off of Nowar. She returned his stare, second for second. When he spoke, he did so with a low and measured, guttural growl.

"O my two sons, there are things in our world that the wisest among us will never speak of, but they are real, and they are true."

A Father with his two sons! Nowar happily accepted that she could now understand them fully, but wondered quietly if she would be able to be understood *by* them, should the circumstances call for it. More importantly, was it real- that it was her own silent wish that made it possible for her to understand these creatures? And if so, how many times could she wish for something and see it come true?

Could she wish for her memories to come back?

Two Fangs was still staring at her, almost through her, as if considering something distinct from the content of his speech.

"Have either of you ever heard of the Logos?" Two Fangs asked. They shook their heads and wagged their tails. Ouroboros Alpha-Beta had just woken up, and they were struggling with the bonds around their paws. An abrupt THWACK! From one of the youngsters settled them down and Two Fangs continued.

"Your Mother, who is a great shaman of our tribe knows more of such things than I do. But I will speak with her words as she used them once for me to explain the story I am about to tell you of the time I first encountered the Great Ripple." And then clearing his throat, he began his story-

"I saw the Great Ripples once, when I was your age, not much more than a whelp, but eager to serve my father and my tribe. My father, 'He-who-sees-under-the-Shadows' took me and my littermates on a long lope. We went to the great Shahn-Mor in the center of all the worlds, where our people and our pack are feared by the other races."

A bat-like creature flew out of the bushes, slightly distracting the two sons, but their father Two Fangs went on without noticing-

"This was during the Second War between Duke Moebius and King Shard. Our people foolishly followed the Duke, believing all of his empty promises and hollow offerings. In the last battle of that war, 'He-who-sees-under-the-Shadows' like all the other great chieftains fought his way through ranks of gnomes, giants, angels and elves, slaying all that lay before him, for no one could stand against his eldritch blade, RedStorm, or his keen Wolven-kine mind…" Two Fangs was clearly lost in the past now, he couldn't have been all here, he had the rapt attention of his boys, and Nowar as well. Nowar got a sense that he knew she could understand him now, but said nothing, listening to the great Wolven-kine weave a story of his family and their past.

"At one point during the battle, he saw an opening to board one of King Shard's Sky Chariots. I was with him. He ran up the boarding ramp with great zeal, only to be thrown off the ramp like a rag doll, hurled by an unseen force with incredible strength into a stone wall many hundreds of yards away."

"The ripples in the air were like rings of wind just exactly then as they were, just now… just before I threw myself to the ground and back into the fray to look for my father, I stole a look at the top of the ramp. It was the King himself! King Shard stood there for but a second, and then stormed off bellowing orders while the ramp to his vessel closed up and his Sky Chariot blasted off."

He paused, sniffed the air a second time, and then finished his story.

"I found my father still alive, though his heart would fail before the day was done and the battle had been lost. Before his passing, he said to me –

"He-who-walks-with-Two-Fangs, I swear to you on my honor that I am your father, and having sired you, you must take one last oath from me- you must lead our tribe and our pack back to T'ien Shann, and when the time is right, you must tell the high chief that the clan of the Screaming Eagle must never go to war against the Homo Sapiens, or the Imperial family Rondelle. Their strength is too great. The Logos is with them."

Two Fangs sons crouched there on their hindquarters, still looking confused. One of them barked, "So what is the Logos?" Two Fangs sighed and grumbled-

"I do not fully understand these things, as I told you before. Your mother would clothe it in words better than I can- Before the beginning, before there was a great crystal sphere to hold the sky, or a Ribbon of Light to wrap around the Fourteen Greater Kingdoms, there was born, out of all time and space, the Logos. The Logos is the sanity of the universe, the mouth and hands of Destiny. The Logos, is…without the Logos, we would not be able to --"

Two Fangs faltered for words, and then suddenly, his mind moved with the wind, now rising from the unseen shoreline far away. He turned back to them and said, "My father was right. The Logos is with the Homo sapiens, and the family that leads them, the Royal Rondelles.

We must never cross them again. The Logos made them, and us, who we are. We must accept our place in the scheme of things, and never trust the Betrayer again!!!"

Nowar had been chewing on the rag in her mouth, trying to move it so she could at least try to speak. She did so, but based on Two Fangs silent stare, he could not understand her.

She tried wishing again. She had nothing to lose. "I want my speech to be understood by all the creatures of ProbablePolis," she thought. The same ripple of a slow-motion silent explosion ribbed its way through the air as the two sons of Two Fangs gripped and grabbed the ground with their paws, wildly looking around while Two Fangs quietly stared at Nowar with his red, red fiery eyes.

Although the ripples seemed just like the last set, they also seemed to have been less powerful than the first time. Nowar's instincts suggested that whatever this ability was all about, it was something that could only be done only so often.

"If you untie me, I will not run away." She said, standing up.

The expression on Two Fangs face was difficult to read, but his tone was clear, "Take off her bonds." He snarled, and then, as he turned and walked down the hill she could hear him mutter-

"They would not have held her for much longer anyway."

Part Five

The Entrance to the UnderRung

Hardly a few minutes went by before Nowar could see their destination. It was a structure, an entrance of some kind. It was old, and it was enormous.

They were in the shadows of a huge and very old part of the giant Mushroom forest. Reaching almost to the canopy itself, this great entrance reminded Nowar of an old-time orchestra hall where people performed music. Over-grown with vines and crusted with colorful fungus, the colossal structure appeared to be very ancient indeed. Any evidence of the surface of the thing was concealed by abundant flora and fauna- stalks of strange ferns that breathed in and out, hundred-foot long glowing slugs that sounded 'notes' of music in pitch obviously related to their size and color, plucked and played, as they were, by spider-like creatures the size of great Danes whose faces, even at a distance, looked disturbingly more like people faces than insect faces.

Two Fangs stopped midway on his descent and turned to Nowar. "This is the entrance to the Under-Rung, home to the Tribes of the Dark Unicorn, including my own. Because I am a Wolven-kine of honor, born of a long bloodline of Chieftains, I offer you a choice:"

Nowar quietly listened.

"In less than a few minutes, it is likely that this whole area of the forest will be aflame with the great fires that erupt from the Duke's Sky Chariots. Nothing will be alive here. These are the two Skreemers my sons and I spied on the beach to the south. It is now without a doubt that the Koradgians, and the Duke, are looking for you. Your choices are two. You may try to take the Western road to Hovahnon while you still have time, or you may come with me as my guest under my protection into the Halls of the Wolven-kine King."

Ouroboros Alpha, who had remained silent for fear of being hit again, finally piped up, clearing his throat and stuttering, "That is quite impossible, we can not go into the Under-Rung, they would tear us all apart in a heartbeat. We're better off going on our own, Nowar…"

Two Fangs suddenly lashed the back of his hand against Alpha's head, bellowing as he did so, "You will remain silent. SHE is a guest. YOU are still lunch."

Nowar flinched for a second, and then, sensing that this was as it should be, saw that Two Fangs was going through a formulaic uttering for reasons of his own, purely for the appreciation of his two sons, and the sake of the decorum of tribal ways she did not understand yet.

"My companion, Ouroboros and I would be delighted to enjoy the hospitality of your people. Please lead us on, Two Fangs. We are grateful to be your guests." And then she bowed, though she did not quite understand or remember what a bow was good for, it seemed to be the right thing to do in this occasion. Two Fangs sons watched quietly, and then continued loping down the hill behind their father, the Amphisbaena still neatly tied to the pole they carried between them. One thing at a time, Nowar thought. One thing at a time. Some of the inhabitants in the shadows below were beginning to rouse, seeing Two Fangs and company returning over the crest.

Then the ground shook.

Cannon fire, like a deep thoom thoom THOOM THOOM, was coming closer and closer. All the way back down the way they had come, the sounds of what had to be an animal stampede could now also be heard in the distance.

Two Fangs and his sons were jogging swiftly down the hill and under the top of the huge entrance as the ground continued to shake. Animals were scattering everywhere, as were other human-like creatures of all kinds that up until a few minutes ago were napping in the smelly shadows. A giant manhole of sorts, in an island surrounded by a shallow pond, was propped open while several creatures dragged bags and other belongings into it. Green, thin, human-like beings with big ears, huge honkers, and hands the size of basketballs were packing up what must have been something akin to an ad hoc bazaar, and hustling their wares into the aperture that must have been nearly as big as a small house itself.

On the stone wall nearby, a giant iron crank was turning with the help of two very large creatures that resembled a cross between an elephant and a human. They roared and flailed their tusks with every crank up and down. This crank could only have been used for one reason- closing these big manholes to protect the lands of the UnderRung from exactly this kind of circumstance. Nowar could see others of similar size and berth, all being cranked shut as quickly as they could, while the earth quaked and rumbled, and then, something flew, with a screaming sound, right over the great structure.

"Time is short." Two Fangs called over the noise to Nowar. "Do not fear this place. You are under my protection here."

One of the thin green humanoids looked like he was about to give the Wolven-kine some trouble about Nowar. Two Fangs gave him barely a snarl and nothing more was said. Just before she jumped onto the rusty ladder, Nowar took a good long look at the thing that was coming in for a landing in front of the entrance to the Under Rung.

It looked evil. Like a black shiny beetle of steel the size of a Rhinoceros, the thing was dropping bright glowing lumps of magma that exploded in flames with a dull but loud THOOM THOOM THOOM. Suddenly a harsh voice was yelling at her, but there was so much sound that she could hardly hear what was being said. Rough and slimy hands shoved her down the hole- she lost her footing and her handholds, and she plummeted down the smelly rusty tunnel, down into the darkness.

Part Six

The UnderRung; it's a nice place to visit, but you wouldn't want to live there

Nowar briefly grabbed a handhold on her descent, and managed to nearly yank her arm out of its socket. She banged her knee, and then realized she wasn't alone in the dark. Other things were below her, above her, and to the sides, where there were tunnels that interlocked with each other. Small fired burned in these, highlighting wicked and twisted figures, things somewhat human-like, others not even vaguely humanoid at all. All of them took an interest in her, of course.

Immediately she realized that the UnderRung would likely be synonymous with the word Labyrinth. A maze inhabited by things far less savory than a nice sounding place like Hovahnon that was for sure. She briefly questioned her decision to come this way, and then realized this was probably for the best. Those Skreemers would have caught up with her in a heartbeat and then they would have made quick work of her and Alpha-beta.

But the smell…

She called up to the others, hopefully still above her making the descent she had made in far less time, and at far greater risk.

"Two Fangs? Ouroboros?" suddenly she heard a coiling sound by her foot, and turned to see something with many serpent-like tentacles slither into an alcove to the side of the rusty ladder embedded into the stone. She wished for some light to be able to see, and a very tiny set of ripples flickered from her left hand, which suddenly was giving off a glow equivalent to a 40-watt light bulb. The ripples had been very tiny indeed this time. Something told her that that wish might have been the last wish she had left for awhile. Quietly she prayed the ability would come back to her after some time had passed. Maybe when she finally got around to sleeping, although then there was that disappearing problem, wasn't there?

Feeling a bit harried, she waited for her friends to catch up, or rather, down, with her, when the thing in the alcove spoke.

"Who are your friends? You do not look familiar to me at all. Are you a guest?"

Nowar turned slowly. It was emerging from the shadows- a cluster of snake like tentacles mounted with a scaly female figure, whose head was adorned with writhing serpents.

Nowar spoke with some hesitation, "I am…a…guest, of Two Fangs, chieftain of Wolven-kine in the UnderRung."

The creature laughed haughtily. "You mean Two Fangs exile of the UnderRung. He left the Lands-from-Under when his brother, the High Chieftain of the Screaming Eagle, banished him to the Southern lagoons."

Great, Nowar thought, this was getting more complicated by the moment.

"And who are you?" she asked.

"Cyspadia, a Medusid. And your name?"

"Nowar, a human."

The Medusid rasped and her head snakes moved backwards in slight recoil. She was about to say something further when Ouroboros Alpha-Beta nearly fell on her. He was followed closely by the more graceful entrance of Two Fangs sons, and then a gainful leap down by Two Fangs himself.

"Two Fangs!" cried Cyspadia, "As I live and hiss. We haven't seen you here in a long ribbon. Come to our senses, finally, have we?"

Two Fangs stalked right up to the Medusids face, seemingly unafraid of her to any extent, and grumbled something low and almost inaudible. The Medusid stammered and slid backwards on her tentacle like legs.

"I meant no harm by my statements, Two Fangs. You know that my sisters and I called your father friend. We had no desire to see your brother, Bloody Antler, run off with your Chieftainship, nor did we wish to see you and your pack exiled."

Before she could say another word, their little crowd on this ledge was joined by a host of green barely human-like creatures; the things Nowar had seen up above at the manhole entrances. At first there were only three, but then one or two joined the group every couple of seconds, until there were over a dozen present.

One of Two Fangs sons growled a curse at the "grimy goblins". They looked exactly like what Nowar would expect a goblin to look like, though she wasn't sure why that would be so. Their arms were incredibly long, their hands huge, their noses and eyes absolutely enormous. Barely human, she might have called them. Homo goblinus? What a horrid thought. And they smelled bad, too.

One of the goblins, who had a ragged hood and a pot-belly, looked to the big Wolven-kine and said, "Hope you aren't here to make trouble, Two Fangs. We got enough of that upstairs now" he gestured with a huge green thumb, the one that wasn't wiping boogers off his nose. His voice was similar to Ouroboros Alpha. Lilting and rarefied.

Though muffled and far above, there was still the sounds of depth charges going off, one after the other. Another one of the goblins cried out "Good Snark, they're hammering the Theatre aren't they? They keep that up much longer, and there'll be nothing left!"

"Theatre?" Nowar said. "That's a Theatre up there?" to which one of the goblins chirped back in a cockney accent, "Well, of course it's a theatre, bumble-brains, you think we could put on plays down here in this rat infested warren of tunnels? We was gettin' ready to put on some Magical Flute by Mozart, don't chee know?" and another Goblin called to Two Fangs-

"Two Fangs, what the dibble are you doing hauling around an elf and an amphisbaena? You must have lost yer mind…"

"Silence!" he cried, swishing around some antler object and causing the rest of the ledge buddies to back away. "I am no subject of the goblin folke or their Kings, nor is my guest an Elf. She is **not** Sylvanus!"

There was an uncomfortable instant of quiet.

"She is Homo Sapiens."

The goblins were clearly looking for an icebreaker.

"Well, at least the amphisbaena is edible!" said the Medusid, smiling weakly.

The goblins laughed uproariously, and Nowar kept her second thoughts at a distance while she untied the rest of the bonds from Alpha-Betas paws.

Part Seven

Big. Real Big.

When Nowar had first heard the name 'UnderRung' she had imagined some kind of small series of caves and tunnels, a modest underground affair, perhaps even a tiny underground town.

She couldn't have been more wrong.

The UnderRung was a vast sprawling cluster of subterranean cities, all ruled by their own dark kings and queens. As Nowar and Ouroboros followed Two Fangs from one cavern to another, she kept noticing how every cavern they walked into was larger than the last. The architecture was haphazard, even slightly insane, as if there had been many, many different designers, some sophisticated, others not, throughout a great swath of time. Columns sometimes merged into strange arches and vaults expanded across ceilings in a bizarre fashion. Some stairwells went nowhere, but let outcast small creatures take respite, while lumbering dark things slugged out in wells that went straight down. In some places, candlelight and braziers were the sole lighting, adding to the pre-existing aura of doom and gloom. In other places, giant iron cages of whispering will-o-wisps suspended from the ceiling created strange dancing shadows on the grotesque inhabitants below. The will-o- wisps whispered to be set free. Nowar wondered how…

"How big is this place?" Nowar asked aloud. Ouroboros Alpha, following quickly and quietly at her heels whispered, "A hundred miles long, ten to twenty miles wide in places, and seven miles deep in the UnderCapital."

Ouroboros Beta added- "Too frogging big is what he meant to say."

There were bridges of rusted iron that were smelted into stone spiral staircases that swirled up and down alongside leather-elevators powered by exceptionally large black tusked reptiles. The ceilings in many places swarmed with winged creatures of every size and description. Some laughed and giggled and called out in mocking sing-song voice 'homo sapiens! oooo laahhhh lahhh! homo sapiens! homo sapiens! ooo lahhh lahhh!'. At some point, Nowar had noticed that the Medusid and several of the goblins had been following her and Two Fangs, at a distance, but not really trying to remain hidden. Two Fangs and his sons ignored them. If there was one thing very clear about the pecking order amongst the denizens of the UnderRung, the Wolven-kine were at the top, or very nearly so. Even the larger creatures, things that Nowar took for Ogres, Trolls and 'big-what-nots' gave Two Fangs and his two sons a wide berth going down corridors and across bridges.

The journey seemed never ending. They even used a floating ferry to cross a very wide and very fast underground river. A huge three-headed and tortured tortoise-like creature drew the boat along its course, and after disembarking, Nowar asked Two Fangs, "O my host, I am grateful for your guidance, but what is our destination?"

"We are going to the Hall of Thrones where sits the Emperor of the UnderRung, the Avatar of our vast Kingdom." He answered, not slowing his pace.

Apparently realizing what the next question was about to be, he continued, "You are to be introduced to my brother, Bloody Antler, High chieftain of the Wolven-kine, and to the King of Kings under all the UnderRung. We will ask for safe haven, and sanctuary for a time."

Alpha gasped and gurgled. "King of Kings? You mean, -the 'Midnight Shadow'?" Two Fangs just scowled at the Amphisbaena.

Nowar petted Alpha's head- she was getting to like the two-headed critter "Who is the Midnight Shadow, Alpha?"

"He is the Dark Unicorn, the Avatar of the UnderRung. He is a black unicorn with powers drawn from the darkest stygian depths of ProbablePolis and T'ien Shann is his total domain. Once he was a begrudging ally to the Duke until he became disenchanted when we were all betrayed…during the last Great War of Probability"

Beta laconically chirped in, "He's not really someone to play checkers wit, sure but I'll bet you he does a mean dance with his little booties on."

One of Two Fangs sons growled, "You should not insult the Midnight Shadow, without him, the UnderRung and T'ien Shann would not have become the great Kingdom it is today, and we would all be slaves to the Duke."

"What does he look like?" Nowar asked. Alpha answered,

"He is a Black Unicorn of truly enormous stature."

Beta chirped in at this point- "Yeah, and he's real big, too."

Nowar's mind was beginning to wander. She was feeling very tired, and wishing she could just find a place to sleep, but for now, they had little choice. If they fell behind, Two Fangs might not be able to be much of a protector, and his gait and lope showed no signs of slowing down.

Part Eight

A moment to catch your breath before someone tries to steal it.

Ouroboros Alpha, who had been staying as quiet as Beta, suddenly decided to catch up with Two Fangs as they were all about to start down an absolutely enormous stairwell that was as wide as a bus is long, and which, from the looks of the placement of torches and Will-o-wisp cages, appeared to spiral down for miles.

Ouroboros jumped in front of Two Fangs, bowed quickly and Alpha asserted himself, saying, "Mighty Chief Two Fangs, forgive me for I know that you are capable of crossing the entire UnderRung in a day, but the Princess Nowar is not- she is extremely tired, and this forced march is more than she should have to endure right now. Can we not take a twenty minute break to allow her to catch her breath?"

Two Fangs, caught off-guard with the diplomacy of the Amphisbaena, whom he still regarded as a food supply if things went south, turned to look at Nowar, who was leaning against a cracked dark green marble column where the great Stairway started.

"Twenty is too many. Seven minutes we will camp…seven minutes for the Seven great Wolven-kine Mothers you all may rest, then we must continue. It will be better if we arrive in the Hall of Thrones before too much news arrives there of our coming." With that he and his two sons took up what seemed to Nowar a somewhat protective position around the Amphisbaena and Nowar, crouching on the ground, and watching the bystanders and travelers that were surging up and down the great staircase.

Ouroboros Alpha and Beta spent the next ten minutes pointing out the various denizens of the UnderRung, apparently just to underscore for Nowar just how dangerous a place fortune had brought them to.

There were small-headed ogres with grumpy dour faces and obscenely big muscular bodies well over ten feet tall. They strode up and down the stairs, accompanied by creatures with huge heads and noses bigger than goblins with hideous posture, - Alpha said these things were Trolls, and suggested that despite their ferocious appearance, the smelly slime jelly that they covered their warty rubbery hides with was even more lethal than their cross-toothed bite. Then there were Hob-Goblins with their bent crescent moon shaped swords and ornate armor- not so different from Goblins except that they clearly got four square meals a day from somewhere, and they probably exercised and flossed regularly, and enjoyed pushing around anything smaller than themselves. All of these beasties kept their distance from the Wolven-kine, and thankfully, Nowar and Ouroboros by association. They stared though, and their murmurings indicated just how rare a sight Nowar and the Amphisbaena made.

There were all sorts of things that looked extremely scary, at some point a host of things that Alpha called Corvines half-hopped and flew off the promenade in front of the stairs- they had the bodies of giant ravens with the heads of women. One of them had a bit of a screeching match with Two Fangs whose large antler weapon neatly removed a few important feathers from the Corvine's wingspan. Then another creature came up to Ouroboros, a humanoid thing that was as thin as a whisper, wearing thick robes with a face not unlike a Tapir. He whispered a few things to Ouroboros Alpha-beta who both acclaimed loudly they were not interested.

Nowar asked what the creature had wanted. Beta replied, "You don't want to know." And to which Alpha added, "That was a Rigamarole. Scandalous little vermin, too. He wanted to know if you were for sale. He has slave trader clients in and out of the whole UnderRung. I informed him that not only were you not a slave, but that you were here to free all of ProbablePolis from the clutches of the evil Duke Moebius."

Nowar thought to herself that perhaps she should encourage Ouroboros to 'tone that stuff down', but decided to keep the thought to herself for the time being. In a place like this, she could use all the support she could get, misguided or not.

At some point, the Medusid, Cyspadia, came slithering slowly up to Nowar. Two Fangs gave her a dirty look and she responded, "no need to fear, Two Fangs, I'm just curious about your guest." Two Fangs said nothing, but did not look away. The Medusid turned to Nowar and her voice, soothing as honey milk, flowed all around.

"So my dear, you **are** a Homo Sapiens afterall? That's altogether amazing! **Where** did you come from? Oh, look at your hair…"

Ouroboros, not happy with the Medusids slow advance, suddenly jumped between her and Nowar. Both Alpha and Beta joined in chorus.

"She's none of your beeswax, you serpent headed bimbo! Leave the Princess alone!"

"No offense meant, Amphisbaena, I'm just curious. I've never seen Homo Sapiens sapiens before. I'd like to know more about them. Like, where did you come from, dearie?"

She was looking at the Medusid now, and the combination of the soothing voice and the hypnotic patterns of the serpents from her head began to make Nowar feel oddly detached from herself, almost like she was drifting. She was roused by Ouroboros Alpha immediately, who then lurched into the Medusids face yelling, "None of your somnambulistic tricks you scaly headed vixen! This interview is over." The Medusid recoiled a bit, clearly had a thought or two about dispatching the Amphisbaena, but had no time to finish either thought as Two Fangs intervened.

"Time to go." He said as he lurched into view. He then looked at Nowar, somewhat deferentially, "Are you ready?"

She nodded, and off they went down the great spiral stairway to the UnderCapital of the UnderRung.

Part Nine

Mrs. Machine and the One Winged Angel

Another hour or so had passed on their descent; it was rather hard to tell. In the perpetual twilit gloom with endless banisters of wax and antlers and braziers that all looked the same, it was difficult to keep any kind of track of time down here in the UnderRung. Endless angle changes of the great stairwell spiraled down and down. Nowar was growing extremely tired, and the Amphisbaena ran between her legs and propped her up as if she was riding him, taking her off her feet and giving her respite. At first uneasy, Nowar sank into the crux of the Amphisbaena's back and relaxed.

The Spider like creatures were everywhere, and they varied in tattoos and dress wildly, but all shared some characteristics. Some were more humanoid than spider, but all were gathering in groups and following not far behind the Medusid and the Goblins, and, ultimately, Two Fangs. Two Fangs had to jump through some hoops though. He had already dispatched handily a Goblin that got out of order.

Finally confronted by an Official UnderRung Marshall, a devilish looking twelve-foot tall red horned thing that never even spoke, Two Fangs simply waited a second, looked him up and down, and then padded off down the stairs without a second look back. The Demon smiled with a huge toothy smile that scared the beejeezers out of Nowar, but he did not move toward her, only leered at them all as they followed Two Fangs and his sons, who seemed to take very seriously escorting her and Ouroboros further down the seemingly unending stairwell amongst strange political bedfellows. Movement got more and more difficult to descend for one very important reason. Since the message of a Homo Sapiens presence had been curried both up and down the great stairwell from top to bottom it seemed as if there were growing incidences of fighting. Two Fangs did not seem to mind but welcomed skirmishing with a very drunk hobgoblin, which went down so quickly it wasn't funny. It was fast becoming evident to Nowar why the Wolven-kine were a dominant race here in the UnderRung.

The Toll Booth would be another story- things were about to get a little sketchy.

A more sinister place you could not have imagined to begin with, anyhow. Slung on the side of the stairwell, and manned by about a dozen ogres and three giants, all armored from top to bottom in nice plate and leather cuirass armor, the place looked distinctly un-friendly. This bunch figured, for sure, they could take on one adult Wolven-kine and his two whelps, even if he was of one of the fiercest Wolven-kine lineage of them all, brother to the high chieftain of the local tribe. They were bored, and a little hungry.

Ouroboros slowed, and then moved back as it was evident that the group of very large beings were moving to surround Two Fangs. His sons were taking a defensive posture around their father.

Two Fangs suddenly howled a yowl that was incredibly high pitched, apparently an effort to rally his sons to fight, and Ouroboros backed nearly into the Medusids lap, her smiling at Nowar the entire time. Someone threw an oil-rag soaked cage of mad-as-hornets Will-o-wisps. The container spun out of control and the two sons leapt over it while Two Fangs advanced on the largest giant with both his antler weapons out.

Utterly unexpected, right in front of the whole host of giants, and Two Fangs, erupted a great blazing white hot awesome radiance of light in human form, perhaps seven and a half feet tall, about as tall as the big Wolven-kine himself. It glowed with an incredibly blinding sheen of light, but as it settled down, lowered its glow, (though it had of course blinded ALL parties present at this event) and was seen for what it was, a one winged angel, whose face was painted half black, half white. His voice was like a symphony of voices.

"So-tay-ree-on Ore-rahn-ahthen!!!" He boomed!-paused, and continued-

"I am Mandrake, servant of the Logos and the Midnight Shadow, Avatar of our Kingdom and a friend to the Wolven-kine Kings, so it is a good time for you guards to stand down and behave, don't you think?"

ProbablePolis

Mandrake the one-winged angel extinguished the maddened will-o-wisps, which it contained with a small net casually dropped. Then he brandished, out of nowhere, a huge trident, waving it right in the faces of the giants. He advanced on them, seeing the Wolven-kine had chosen to stay kneeling in their classic crouch, while the angel carried out his theatrics.

"I presume you fine fellows still follow the precepts of the King of Kings?"

All of them nodded, though the younger ogres and giants seemed resentful of it. That was one fat Amphisbaena, all right.

"Then you will allow the guest of the brother of the King of all southern Wolven-kine to continue to the Hall of Thrones without delay, that all the kings may hear why she has come to us at this time…"

Mandrake waited a few painful seconds for some response, apparently sincerely wondering if any of these ogres or giants might have the audacity to attack him. Apparently sensing only fear and dread, he spoke once more-

"Well then, Two Fangs, come, and waste no more time- your guest is tired. Bring the Amphisbaena too, will you, Mrs. Machine? We will all escort Nowar down the rest of the way here to the Hall of Thrones, tout suite. Two Fangs, you and your two lads may ride the big Coracle-vator right here behind Mrs. Machine."

Mrs. Machine looked like a big rusted flying wasp the size of a dog as well as something that might have been a collection of devices, able to re-formulate themselves on-the-fly.

Mrs. Machine had a small screen, and she projected an old grandmotherly face on it which seemed to echo her own emotional output. Mrs. Machine also had an engine of some kind that sounded like it could use a little extra grease to cut down on the squeaking noises, yet, all of her body parts reformulated into a seemingly under-sized body shape into a small throne of her own with little or no effort.

She motioned Nowar to come take a seat, and then Mrs. Machine became, in speed and style, an excellent escort device, almost sleigh-like. The Angel resumed greater brightness, commended the 'lads' for serving the Midnight Shadow as well as they did, and then followed Mrs. Machine into an unhurried dive. Two Fangs and his sons jumped on some large nautiloid shaped shell that descended only about half as fast as Mrs. Machine puttered down into the gathering gloom- leaving the Toll Booth and what could have been an entirely unpleasant scene far behind them.

Part Ten

The Midnight Shadow

Nowar had no idea of what to expect from the black Unicorn, the Midnight Shadow. Certainly, she expected him to be bigger, much bigger.

He couldn't have been much smaller. Like, about two and a half feet tall- and far less oppressive than anything else in the vicinity. In fact, he almost looked adorable- she had to fight an overwhelming urge to pick him up and squeeze him.

And apparently, he was the Kingpin, the Midnight Shadow. He was sitting calmly in a throne situated dramatically at the head of a thousand other thrones. Many of them, Nowar had noted, were filled. These inhabitants were as threatening as the Midnight Shadow was obsequious. The Troll Queen was an eight-foot tall green nightmare, oozing pus and belching noxious green wisps of smoke. The King of the Hobgoblins was a striking tall figure in red and black armor with a vicious wahku-zashi, a samurai blade. The Queen of the Sirens, and her sister, the Queen of the Corvines, came whooshing into their two thrones. Apparently the only difference between the two was that the Corvines had the bodies of huge ravens while the Sirens had the bodies of great eagles. One of them began to play a harp while the other started to sing, soothing a good third of the audience from their impromptu random acts of aggression on each other.

As the various 'noble'-monsters seated themselves, the one-winged angel took up a well-worn stance behind the tiny black unicorn. The King and Queen of the Gargoyles looked disdainfully on the pudgy Gremlin King, who simply could not shut up. He chattered on incessantly while the Queen of the Imps, infuriated that her space had been invaded, bit hard into the tail of some three-headed dog, whose enormous booming howl quieted the entire amphitheatre down for a half a second, and then the dull roar continued unabated.

At some point Nowar noticed that Cyspadia took one of the three thrones for the Medusids. Her two sisters were just as menacing and insidious.

Finally, a nod passed from the Midnight Shadow to the one winged angel, who walked forward at once, drew out his trident, and flashed so brightly that everyone piped down quickly, and stayed that way. Silence achieved, his glow waned, returning the huge arena to its former smoky twilit gloom.

With the new stillness introduced by Mandrake's theatrics, it should come as no surprise that the voice of the tiny black unicorn carried like a deep orchestral sound, full of boom and bassoon, echoing into every crevice of the cavernous amphitheatre. For all it's intensity, the voice was still soothing and made Nowar feel strangely at ease.

"Greetings to ye, Childe of Limberly and Shard, Sapiens of long vanished Urath. Long have we awaited your coming, and some of us welcome you with open arms and glad hearts, while others view your coming with fear, distrust and suspicion." He paused, looking around the audience, still as a churchyard.

"One thing is for certain, none but the Precognitids may know the future, and what they have always said has never changed. If it is true that 99% of the future is written in mud, and 1% written in stone, most assuredly your coming to ProbablePolis will change all our lives for all time." He paused again, this time making direct eye contact with Nowar. If Nowar hadn't been mistaken, she thought she heard his voice in her head, speaking words that were different than the ones coming from his mouth. In her mind, she could have sworn she had heard him say "We shall have a private conversation in a few minutes but this discourse is for the edification of the citizens of the UnderRung. Thank you for your patience…" whereas his actual voice went on, saying-

"It would have been more fit to have offered you the hospitality that Two Fangs had sought to offer you, and as the Brother of the King of the Southern Wolven-kine, his offer must be treated seriously and fairly- and then declined"

Two Fangs moved forward to speak, but Mandrake blocked his way, and the Midnight Shadow continued-

"Through no fault of your own, or of his, the forces of Duke Moebius are mustering in a perimeter around the entrance to our home, the UnderRung. They have assembled enough firepower to blast our entrance to little bits, and enough Koradgian shock troops to invade our little kingdom, and disrupt our blissful little lifestyles."

There was a murmuring in the crowd now. The small black unicorn continued speaking,

"Castle DeepSteel has had a call in to my private line for almost an hour"

"He's still on hold, my lord"

"Good, leave him that way. Is there offensive elevator music playing?"

"Yes, and every two minutes a voice says 'thank you for holding, your call is very important to us'-"

"Nice touch, Mandrake. Very well. So, Princess Nowar, what we are going to do is to let you use our 'Lens of Probability' to find where you are to go next, and then depart the UnderRung for the time being. You may rest in my private chamber for a half an hour, and then you must be on your way."

The mention of sleep was very exciting for Nowar. The Midnight Shadow went on.

"I wish things could be otherwise, Nowar, but this is not the right time for the UnderRung to be drug into the Third War of Probability. I have little doubt we will be drug into it eventually, but there's no need to rush an unpleasant confrontation before its ripe enough."

The black unicorn looked around, scanning the audience, then said-

"This is my edict. For now, Nowar Rondelle, our two alliances with the Houses of Evergreen shall stand, and you shall be an honored guest of the UnderRung, for the next hour…and then you must be on your way. Good luck Nowar, may the Logos be with you."

Nowar's head hardly hit the pillow before she fell into a deep sleep, and then disappeared entirely. Thin air whooshed from between the cover and the sheets.

Nowar had left ProbablePolis.

Chapter Four

Who's on first?

Part One

Back over the rainbow

Nowar awoke with a shock, as if someone had just dumped her into her body like a tropical fish into cold water. She grabbed the sheets, tossed them aside, and looked around wildly for the book. An instant of panic and then she spied it. It was on the bookcase, right at eye level. Clasped but not locked. She stared blankly at it for a second, noticing how beautiful the morning sun was, peeking from behind the curtains- and then she jumped nearly a foot in the air when Grandma Brandy knocked loudly on the door yelling "Breakfast in ten minutes!"

She grabbed the book, saw it was still unlocked, and opened it.

The first lines read-

This is the story of the Third War to free ProbablePolis from the iron clutches of Duke Moebius and the Return of Princess Nowar Rondelle, unremembering daughter of King Shard and Queen Limberly.

She read quickly, skimming mostly. Her jaw dropped further and further with every page she read. Someone, somehow, had transcribed her dreams right into the book! Fading, dream-like memories became clearer and clearer.

She heard herself say aloud at some point, "I couldn't have just been dreaming, could I?"

The narrative followed her memories point for point, almost as if she had written them herself. But of course, she hadn't. The handwriting was very peculiar as well; strangely familiar.

The last lines written in the book, though it was hardly finished, were –

TO BE CONTINUED

"Oh, froggin' ay!" Nowar said as she slammed the book shut at page fifty-eight.

The rest of the book was blank, and thicker too. More pages.

She didn't have time to be thorough about checking that fact, as Grandma Brandy was calling her again. Keeping the book at her chest, she clatterwhumped down the stairs in her slippers and nightgown.

Part Two

Back so soon?

Nowar ate her breakfast quietly. Grandma Brandy was intently watching the LOX Network News, which Nowar didn't really care much for. She called it the War-channel. That's all they reported on, it seemed. Nothing good. Just war. Nowar couldn't be less interested. She changed it as quickly as she could for the Sci-Fi channel and kept eating her cornflakes

At one point, Grandma Brandy said, "Oh, I heard from Grandpa Bric last night, sweetie. He's coming home earlier than planned. He'll be here later tonight."

Nowar nodded and kept eating her breakfast. After she was done, she excused herself and ran off down to the stream that ran into Walls Lake at Blue Day point, with the book neatly held under her arm. The last thing her Grandma Brandy had said to her as she headed out the back door to the garden was "Don't be shocked about how low the water is, dearie, it's just global warming." -and she smiled the smile handed down to her by many generations of Rondelles, a people that had survived many great travails, and were still here in spite of it all, perhaps because of it all, -who knew but the Almighty anyway, right?

Nowar sat down by the stream where it emptied into the lake, and proceeded to read the book, entirely, word for word. She was **right**. It **was** thicker, but only about fifty-four pages had been written. The fact that the handwriting looked familiar bothered her to no end, but she finished it entirely. After page fifty-four, the rest of the book was blank.

She slammed the book closed after finishing the last sentence. The dreams of this morning now seemed like anything but dreams. Suddenly the book shuddered- the lock clasped shut all on its own, and audibly clicked.

"No!" she screamed, but it was no use. It was relocked securely. "Oh well," she thought, "I opened it once before, and I can do it again."

She sat there and watched the dragonflies dancing across the water. Her mind was trying to wrap itself around what was really going on. What did it all mean? If she believed that her dreams from last night were somehow real, the implications were staggering; somehow, her Father and her Mother had gotten sucked into this imaginary world called ProbablePolis, and, if they had no more ability to remember where they came from than she had- well, this would go a long way to explaining their odd disappearances out of her life.

And this Duke, or Doctor, Moebius, somehow he was at the bottom of the whole thing.

Part Three

It's tough being Evil

Speaking of the most evil man in all ProbablePolis, Duke Moebius was now the most grumpy man in all ProbablePolis- dangerously grumpy for a man engaged in one of his greatest daily pleasures, his lavender scented bubble bath.

He was still on hold with the Midnight Shadow. Furthermore, even though he was in the middle of the best part of his long and exquisitely warm bubble bath in his huge private green marble bathtub- even though he had nearly everything he wanted at that moment, (chocolates, jelly doughnuts, liquor, cigars, and his snappy little fleet of black & white rubber duckies) still, it always seemed like there was always just one small thing that wasn't quite right.

In this case it was the Koradgian team he'd sent to Page Seven. Fools. Bumbling, incompetent reptilian fools. The first documented case of a Homo sapiens sapiens in his realm in almost three hundred turns of the Great Ribbon, and the scaly-brained imbeciles had let it slip right out of their claws-

-and into the UnderRung.

And it was still there, at least according to his inside sources.

It was so upsetting he pulled out his favorite laser-gun and took out two of his Koradgian bodyguards. The seven foot tall heavily armored reptiles slumped to the floor with a few clatters and a few banging noises. The rest of the reptiles that had been lounging around the bathing area slunk off to other parts of the lair. The Duke was still in a bad mood.

"Clancy, are you on the Com? We've got two more bodyguard bodies to remove. Could you have Bob pick them up and prepare them for dinner? I should think these two will go well with a white wine"

"Err, yes, my lord." There was a painful silence for a second, then, "Sir, that makes six this morning. Don't get me wrong, I know we have more

Koradgians than we know what to do with, and plenty of freezer space, but, don't you think that maybe we should consider slowing down a little bit…or even a daily quota, or some other arrangement?"

"They slipped on some soap, boy, or perhaps it was their tea, I can't make up my mind,- Horrifying. Really. Clancy, I'm sorry, I just can't have any sympathy for the dang things. Afterall, I brought them into this world, and I should therefore have the right to take them all out." He looked around and thought to himself, "And in any event, it's all a damned blithering simulation, you tweak head." Then, changing the subject quickly- "Any word from that pipsqueak miniature unicorn, the Midnight Boob?"

"None, my Lord. The line to his Study is still open and playing some very catchy dance tunes, shall I pump them into your den?"

"Glimey! Don't you dare, you little scaley cockroach! Not if you want that promotion you keep bugging me for-" the Duke yelled in exasperation some extremely unrepeatable words, and shot another Koradgian. This one hissed only slightly on the way down. The Duke was a good shot.

Part Four

Back so soon?

Nowar was still sitting quietly by the river, lost in thought. Then, somehow, she sensed that the time for thought had ended. It was time to make a difference, it was time for action. In this world, she was just a little kid, a ten-year-old girl whose life and family had been tossed about like leaves in a war about terror.

But, in ProbablePolis, she was a Princess, apparently with special powers to 'change' things…and she couldn't wait to go back.

She was about to begin the musical sequence that would open the book, or at least she assumed it would, when another thought crossed her mind- what if she couldn't get back? If she was going to try another jaunt in ProbablePolis, she needed to do it from her bedroom. And she needed to leave Grandma Brandy a note, explaining what had happened, and how someone could come after her.

She ran up the stairs to the guest room, closed the door behind her and let out a big deep breath of air. She began scribbling the note, explaining in a few hundred words what had happened to her, and how someone could follow her into ProbablePolis with the right tune.

She put the note on her bed stand, sat on the bed with her back up against the bed frame, and picked up the book. It was definitely heavier, and, -was it her imagination?- somehow it felt warm, and inviting, like it was looking forward to having her enter it's realm. It was an odd feeling that Nowar could not shake.

Something did make her look once more at the bookcase. There was a book her eyes went to immediately. It was somehow sitting on the edge of the shelf, as if someone had pulled it out but then decided to not remove it entirely. Nowar felt a presence, as if she was not alone in the room. She felt that she was being watched. It was like the first time she had pulled something from the shelf of this bookcase. Somehow she knew she wasn't alone. Someone was waiting, hoping she would pull this book from the shelf.

And so she did. It was an old book, dusty and close to falling apart. She opened it 'randomly' and looked at the image she saw in front of her. The illustration was a beautiful image of an old European knight in armor with a triangular shield. The note under the illustration read "Knight Templar with shield and sword"

Incredibly, someone had scribbled a few words in the margin of the book next to the plate. Somehow, the fact that it was her father's handwriting did not surprise Nowar one bit. It had a big red arrow pointing to the shield of the knight and it read-

If you're going back in, you'll need this. It's time to learn how to use visualization as you enter the breach- it can be very useful. Start with this shield.

Just empty your mind and stare at the shield for at least a whole minute- then use the book like you already know how. Conceive of your own design, if you like. There may be unexpected results, but they should be good ones...

Good Luck, sweetie.

Nowar smiled, stared at the shield for a whole minute, and then began preparing the book to open by pressing the buttons, each one sounding its note.

"A shield," she thought to herself, "-why am I not concentrating on a 'cannon', Dad?"

The universe did not seem to want to answer that question, and, with great deliberate intent, she finished the sequence on the front of the book, and the Breach opened up to her as it did before. The unbearable whiteness of being welcomed Nowar back into ProbablePolis.

Unbeknownst to Nowar, the book re-assembled and re-locked itself, and, as if by unseen hands, floated back to a shelf on the bookcase.

Part Five

Reach out, reach out, and shoot someone

The Duke was drying himself off and looking for his baby powder when Clancy's voice came back online- "The Midnight Shadow is on the line, my Lord."

The Duke hit a button on his laptop and the visage of a black unicorn appeared on the screen. A second passed. The Duke smiled, and the Unicorn, showing no trace of emotion spoke first- "I hear you knocking, Moebius, but you can't come in."

Moebius laughed and replied "I know, Midnight, it's a little early for trick-or-treating, but you have something I want."

"What a pity. How does it feel to want?"

Moebius harrumphed. He checked. It didn't feel good at all.

"I would prefer you use my title when addressing me. DUKE Moebius, it should be to you."

"Once upon a time, Moebius- perhaps, but no more. You lost that title when you lost the last war. We were fools to believe in you back then. No war no more, you old fool. Now lets cut to the chase. You are bombing my front door. I presume you're not just doing this for fun but have some intent and purpose."

"You are harboring an anomaly. I want it."

"An anomaly? Curious name you choose, Moebius. The Homo sapiens is already gone, old friend. Anything else we can do for you?"

The Duke looked like he was about to pop a vein. "Where did it go? What does it look like? What is it called?"

"I don't think that I am under any obligation to share any of these things with you until you desist your attack on our Kingdom. Now, if that is all you want, I have preparations to make before you invade us."

The Duke sighed and exhaled- "Alright, alright. I'll call off the bombing- Clancy, tell the lads to desist and stand-by, will you?"

"Yes my lord"

Moebius turned back to the screen- "Now, you were saying?"

But the Midnight Shadow had already hung up.

Part Six

So long, it's been good to know ya

Nowar awoke in one of the Midnight Shadow's guest rooms, guarded by Two Fangs, Ouroboros Alpha-Beta, a very large Minotaur and some evil yellow slime, Ernie, who had over a half dozen adjustable eye stalks that moved constantly. Ouroboros and the slime were playing some kind of board game. The Minotaur and Two Fangs stood on either side of the huge circular entrance.

At the foot of the bed was a great turtle shell, a shimmering sea-green in color, light in weight, but very strong. She sat up and touched it. It was smooth, and had a strap on the inside. It was a shield! It was not triangular, of course, she realized, but then she wondered why that should have mattered to her in the first place. Curious. On the front was a beautiful carving of a feline on a backdrop that looked like a rose. The feline looked like a Cheetah. Nowar smiled to herself, remembering a tall man…was it her Father? They were on a beach, about to run a race in the sand, when he asked her, "How fast are you going to run?" and she answered back loudly, "as fast as a cheetah."

Before she could contemplate any of this further, the voice of the Midnight Shadow broke the silence of the room.

"It appeared when you did, Princess Nowar." He said as he entered. The Minotaur and Two Fangs bowed and the Yellow Slime quivered with excitement. Nowar was about to say something, describing her strange dreams, but the Midnight Shadow was wasting no time.

"The Minotaur and Ernie will escort you to the Room of the Great Lens. It is time for you to continue your journey. I trust you are well-rested?"

In spite of having only been asleep for a half an hour, Nowar felt like she had been asleep for days. She wiped the sleep from her eyes and said-

"Can Two Fangs come with us?" the question apparently took the Unicorn by surprise.

"Well, Two Fangs is a free citizen of the UnderRung, now fully reinstated as an Ally of the Realm. Where he goes and what he does is up to him."

Two Fangs spoke then, and walked forward, "So it is written. I will accompany this daughter of Destiny. My sons will remain with their Mother." He had apparently taken the opportunity to armor himself with a few pieces of hard leather cuirass, and he wore a hewn scimitar of steel at his side. The Unicorn's left eyebrow rose visibly. "As you will, my friend, and may the Logos be with you, as well." He turned back to Nowar.

"In addition to this finest of warriors, you will be accompanied by two others. I have decided to send with you two escorts of my own choosing, Mandrake NeverSong the Angel, and Mrs. Machine, both of whom you have already met. They have been instructed to protect you until you can protect yourself, which will not be much longer, I believe. They are waiting for you down in the Room of the Great Lens. Tarry no more, and carry this message to your Father and Mother- When the time is right, the Realm of the UnderRung shall not be on the wrong side again. We shall stand with the might of Evergreen and Ambrosia once more."

As if on cue, the entire room trembled with an earthquake-like tremor, dust spilling to the floor from the ceiling, a chandelier rattling with the aftershock. With remarkable calm, the Midnight Shadow turned and began to walk out of the room.

"That would be our front door finally giving way. The time has come for me to attend to the defense of our Kingdom. May the Logos be with you all."

There was activity everywhere. The Minotaur and the slime seemed to want to waste no time, and led Nowar, Two Fangs and the Amphisbaena down one spiral staircase after another, leaving behind the sounds of conflict and strife. Into a darkened maze of stairways, ladders and tunnels, the little crew came eventually to a huge round doorway of iron. Strange glyphs on the door were colored in red and black. Nowar wished wistfully that she could read the writing. It was beautiful and ornate.

As before, ripples emanated from her, causing the Yellow Slime to jump into the arms of the Minotaur, whose eyes grew big as he turned to look at Nowar. Two Fangs and Alpha-Beta were less surprised, but waited to see what would happen next.

The writing on the great circular door read-

> *This is the entrance to the Great Lens of Probability.*
>
> *Enter and abandon your deathbed prayers.*
> *They are of no use to you anymore.*
>
> *May you be yourself,*
> *and may you know yourself.*

The door creaked open, apparently opening all by itself. The tension was intense.

Nowar grasped the strap of her new shield tightly, and walked through the door, followed closely by Two Fangs and Ouroboros Alpha-Beta. The Minotaur and the slime, Ernie, wasted no time hurrying back up the stairs. They were missing out on an exciting battle, and they were leaving behind nothing but creepiness.

Part Seven

Gull and Crones in the room of the Lens

The room was huge and spherical, with strange stained glass windows that rotated and shifted on contorted iron banisters and railings. The whole room creaked and groaned like a ship at sea. It was like a dark gothic temple, with arches both above and above, with various parts squealing and gyrating, braking and lurching around on wheels and gears galore. The architecture seemed like a study in madness codified, teeming with clattering spirals and spear points and strange jagged edged areas that offered temporary stairways into the inner workings of the chamber, apparently.

In actuality, none of it seemed to make much sense, architecturally speaking. In the middle of the room floated a simply enormous and slightly rusted sphere of iron with stained glass windows inserted in every faceted surface of the thing. It rotated slowly, whirling and bobbing over a pattern on the floor of spirals, zigs, zags & etceteras. What supported it appeared to be a ring on the floor of strange burgundy shaded metal.

"So this is the Lens of Probability," thought Nowar. The one-winged Angel, Mandrake NeverSong, and Mrs. Machine stood, or floated, as the case may be, on either side of the entrance to the room. They nodded at Nowar, who walked down a red carpet that led towards the Lens, and to an extraordinary creature unlike anything Nowar had ever seen before. Mandrake began to walk alongside of Nowar, apparently ready to make an introduction.

Squatting in front of what looked like the hatch to this Lens of Probability sat the Precognitus. He, or it, gestured to them all to come closer, beckoning with strange digits and hand-like accessories. The thing reminded her of a semi-organic version of a maniacal child's first attempt at a science project- a science project gone horribly wrong. It had telescoping optical devices, tiny cameras, little projectors and screens, and a translucent spherical rib cage that held an odd mass of gray matter in an array of bizarre little claws. A set of gyroscopic wheels whirred and pumped red, blue and white colored fluids through a maze of thin transparent tubes. As they approached, Mandrake cleared his throat and said-

"Princess Nowar, allow me to introduce you to the one and only Precognitus that dares to live in the UnderRung, Hieronymous Quantum Jones. He has agreed to assist you in your navigational requirements. I am here to supervise the entire matter, as you've deduced by now."

All together, this entity seemed utterly preposterous, and it was quite difficult to tell if it was a robot, a person, or a cyborg. It smelled of motor oil, and its various parts made countless little whirring clicking noises.

"Hieronymous, I presume?" Nowar asked. It responded quickly.

"Of course it's us, Precognitus Hieronymous Quantum Jones- and you, why your persona is Nowar Rondelle, unremembering Princess from another world."

Well, thought Nowar, Ouroboros Alpha-Beta had told her that a Precognitus might tell her more about herself. She went for broke.

"When I sleep, I dream I am a little girl, dreaming I am me." She said.

"So what are you asking us?"

"Well, I was asleep just for only a half an hour, yet in my dream I spent an entire morning remembering myself, in the dream."

Hieronymous stared blankly at her with several devices, any one of which could have been optical in nature. Nowar was beginning to feel a bit frustrated. "This thing is playing a game with me," she thought.

"Who is real? Me, or the little girl?"

"Both."

"That's not a very helpful answer"

"So sorry. We Precognitids are known for our less than pragmatic, enigmatic answers." It then made a sound that could have been mechanical laughter, snorting even. "I am really only here to assist you in operating the Lens of Probability." He looked the others up and down once and then stared back at her- "Otherwise your coming is a bit of a spoiler to us all, really, if I were to be momentarily candid."

Two Fangs spat and said something unpleasant under his breath. Nowar continued the interview.

"Well, what *can* you say that would be helpful?"

"I can suggest a reason for the destination you will take."

"I haven't even seen my options, how do you know where I'll go?"

The Precognitus tapped a button on one of its insect-like appendages, setting off a holographic display of something that looked like a book of fourteen pages, opening its entire 360 degree span, so that its front cover and back cover nearly touched. The pages had numerous odd connections, most were like filaments of light, others were strange tubes that sprang into being briefly, glowed, and then were gone. The whole image sputtered and pulsed as it turned in the air. Hieronymous spoke again-

"This is a visualization of the matrix of reality we all call ProbablePolis. We are here, on page Seven, the Kingdom of T'ien Sha'an." He looked to see if this was sinking into Nowar's brain. Apparently thinking it wasn't, he continued with an explanation. "ProbablePolis is best represented as a book…a book of fourteen pages, plus a back and a cover, neither of which should be used to judge the whole book."

Nowar laughed in spite of herself and said- "I see. And where are the Kingdoms of Shard and Limberly?"

"Shard rules out of the newest page, er, Kingdom. It is called Ambrosia-Kingdom Thirteen, in fact. Queen Limberly rules from the First Kingdom, Evergreen, the second oldest page, where she lives in Castle Evergreen." The Precognitus was watching her now, gauging how much to say, perhaps. He continued with an astounding bit of information.

"Neither of them remembers who they were, Nowar, or you, for that matter. But we do not think the time has come yet for you or anyone else to restore their memories, as you are only beginning to develop yours. Someone who cared more for your fate might even recommend that you go to see the Great Olde Drake, or perhaps even the Last Great SkyWhale."

"The Great Olde Drake?" Nowar felt some shock at all this, "The Last Great SkyWhale?"

"Yes, the Great Olde Drake looks somewhat favorably upon Homo sapiens sapiens, I couldn't really tell you why, and in fact I foresee that he soon will have the ability to restore your memory using arts from another world." He paused while some of his gears whirred and then said "so yes, the Great Olde Drake will be able to return to you your memory, and the Last Great SkyWhale will bring you back your Destiny."

Ouroboros Beta, who, like the others had been very quiet up until now, spoke with some boldness, "Ye said just a few minutes ago – 'But **we** do not think the time has come yet to restore their memories'…just who do ye mean when ye say 'we'?"

Hieronymous ignored him and continued staring at Nowar. Before she could utter the words, "Answer his question. Who is this 'we'?" the Precognitus spoke again-

"By 'we' I meant The Society of Gull & Crones."

Nowar felt a tension in the chamber. Hieronymous, sensing her next question, apparently, continued with an explication.

"Gull and Crones is a Not-so-secret-Society that has existed since the very beginning to get all the Kingdoms on a single page. Unfortunately, in spite of all our best behind-the-scenes efforts and contrived attempts to create modest peace treaties or start harrowing wars, we have largely failed in our pursuit, and page count in ProbablePolis has gone up since the last Great War of Probability." He hung his head, as if in shame, but continued with "At the height of our success, we had managed to reduce the page count in ProbablePolis to only five pages, but something in the very nature of the Hypothecation causes two Pages to be rewoven after two pages are destroyed. Luckily that process is a very slow one, and we have managed, with the help of Moebius, to reduce page count from the Beginning of All Days, when there were three hundred and sixty of the damned things."

Two Fangs could contain himself no longer. As if to underline the intensity of his feelings, he pulled his scimitar from his belt and waved it in the air, saying "The Gull and Crones are fools and phantoms who know nothing of honor!" and then after a pause, "You are all deceivers, no better than Moebius! A single page is madness! In the beginning there were hundreds of pages! We Wolven-Kine even had **our own page**! Look at what you have done to all of us!!!"

Hieronymous tightened up, sensing that this sentiment was likely shared by the others. Mrs. Machine was making an off-key low pitch noise that sounded a little like 'tsk-tsk-tsk'. Even the one winged angel, Mandrake, had a rather unhappy scowl on half his face. Bringing attention back to the tiny holographic book visualization, the Precognitus began his litany of probability.

"Well, then, you may choose from the following hypothecations of travel- if you go to the first page, the likelihood is quite high that you will be brought quickly to Castle Evergreen, and consequently captured by the Duke Moebius, who holds the key to the mind of the Queen, your mother. She is currently little more than a thrall to him."

Nowar nodded, though this information made her feel sick in her stomach somehow. It could also be a lie. Hieronymous continued.

"Now, if you travel to the Great Cover, called by some the Kingdom of Avalhalla, it is far more likely that you will encounter one of the Drake civilizations, and likely be brought to the Great Olde Drake, who will likely make you whole, and restore your memory."

Suddenly Nowar had a thought- "why couldn't she just wish her memory back?"

Again, if she had needed further proof that the Precognitus could hear her thoughts, she got it with his very quick reply, "Go ahead and try

ProbablePolis

if you like, Nowar, you'll just sprain your brain, and cause another anomaly that the Duke can use to track you."

"What?" Nowar was partly shocked by the answer, and partly by the fact that this thing could read her thoughts.

"The Duke is tracking you, my dear. Every time you call upon the Logos- i.e. articulate in thought an ardent desire to change things from what they seem to be, you create a ripple, an anomaly in the fabric of ProbablePolis, an abomination of sorts, and, well, the Duke created ProbablePolis…he is most certainly an expert in abominations, you should know by now, eh?"

There was an abundance of huffing, harrumphing, growling and general low-key negative sounds from all of Nowar's companions.

Hieronymous protested, "Like it or not, folks, it's true, and there's nothing we can do about it." Then, looking back at Nowar, "You see, my dear, your real plight is that you are more like a two sided playing card than a single person right now. Only the Great Olde Drake will be able to simplify your sundered soul."

He paused and then continued his litany of probability, "So then, if you chose to go to the second page, you would likely be captured by the Koradgians and taken to Castle DeepSteel, where the Duke would turn you into a new exhibit in his wax museum. On the third page you would likely…"

Nowar cut him off with a question that threw him for a second, "Is there a random setting?"

"What? Uh, err, well, yes, I mean, no!" Then he spoke in a very measured and slow manner, as if he was trying to think about something other than what he spoke. The presence of the Angel complicated things and he cursed to himself, saying "Yes, there …is… a… random …setting, but, well…it's random. There's no controlling over where you all will go."

"Fine, set it for random, please. Thank you."

Reluctantly, seemingly, the Precognitus skittered over to an interface on the Lens hatch and began twirling dials and moving levers. Mandrake moved silently behind him. Looking nervous, he turned and smiled at the one winged angel.

"I…uh…never got a chance to ask you, Mandrake. Uh, do **you** know how to use one of these?"

"Yes, we do, Hieronymous. Why you would ask what you already knew, I wonder. That's why we're standing here; to make sure you do the right thing."

The Precognitus turned back to his work without saying another word. Nowar got the distinct impression that they had successfully messed up his plans, and she felt very good about that.

Part Eight

Is anything ever what it seems?

One more button push, and the hatch of the Lens opened wide. It was time to go.

Hieronymous Quantum Jones gestured to the inside, tittering "All aboard. Buckle your belts and get prepared for the ride of your lives."

Ouroboros Alpha-Beta looked at Nowar as she invited him into the thing first. After he'd gone in, then Mrs. Machine dropped to the floor, changing some of her appendages quickly to make herself look more like a big compact metal female locust, and hopped in as well. Two Fangs gestured to Nowar in a way that communicated he wanted to go in after she went first. He didn't trust Hieronymous either.

Nowar hopped in and looked around. The seats inside were plush and red, with big seat belt buckles. She sat down, but waited to buckle her seat. She watched Two Fangs and Mandrake standing just outside the hatch.

Two Fangs said to Mandrake "Are you ready?"

"Yes, we are ready. One of us will stay and make sure the Lens destination is executed properly." And with that said, Nowar watched an incredible sight: Mandrake vibrated briefly, wavering like a sheen of trembling light, and then split into two! Two Mandrakes!

One of the Mandrakes had an all white face. The other had an all black face. Both of them still had only one wing. They looked at each other for a second, then they spoke to each other.

"I will remain to provide assurance that there will be no treachery." Said the white faced Mandrake.

"-and I will escort the Company of the Princess." Said the black-faced Mandrake. Then the both of them said in unison, "and we will be re-united before the end."

"May the Logos be with you, Black Mandrake." Said the white-faced Mandrake.

"And with you as well, White Mandrake." Said the other as he stepped into the Lens. Two Fangs jumped in behind him and the white-faced Mandrake turned to Hieronymous and quietly said, "You are being observed very closely, Mr. Jones. Carry out the navigational request as it was made by Princess Nowar. Engage the Lens for a random setting."

The Hatch closed and the Lens began to spin, faster and faster. For a few moments, the entire world became a very dizzy place, and then the great rusted Lens vanished in a brief but dramatic explosion of color and sound and movement.

A few minutes after Mandrake the White departed from the Room of the Great Lens of Probability, Hieronymous looked around carefully, pulled out a device from a part of his body and began to dial a number on its keypad.

"This is Hieronymous Quantum Jones. Patch me through to Moebius immediately"

A minute later, the crackly voice of the Duke came through the device. "Hieronymous, my fine fine friend. Any news?"

"Aye, we have news. The Homo sapiens has departed the UnderRung in the Lens of Probability. She is accompanied by a Wolven-kine King, an Amphisbaena, a fourth of an Angel- Mandrake NeverSong the Black, and a Female Utility device called Mrs. Machine."

"Did you send them here as planned?"

"No, and don't give me any grief about it either- Mandrake the White stayed behind, specifically to make sure that I set the Lens for the destination the Homo sapiens asked for."

"You mechanical mugwort! Fine, where did you send them? I'll dispatch a fleet of Skreemers as a welcoming crew. Hahah!"

"No luck there, either, Moebius. She asked for a random destination."

"What? Is that possible?"

"You figure it out, you nitwit, I have other things to deal with. You should be looking for the source of her anomalous entrance. Clearly there's more than one way into ProbablePolis, and **you** don't control it, either, do you?"

Hieronymous decided to hang up. The conversation wasn't really going anywhere, and the last response Moebius had for him was not suitable for print.

Part Nine

Leaving, but not on a jet plane

It felt like the entire world would rattle apart.

Luckily there were handlebars to hold onto.

Riding in the Lens of Probability was like a carnival ride to end all carnival rides- only problem was, when would it end? Strange sounds and odd trailers of something that was neither sound nor light rolled through the darkened cabin of the lens. Nowar gritted her teeth and breathed slowly, hoping she could keep from throwing up, though she realized she couldn't even recall the last time she had eaten anything, anyway.

After a few minutes of this extreme rough ride, Ouroboros Alpha was blubbering incoherently. Beta was yelling at him, "Shut yer pie-hole you ninny! At least you've got good company to meet yer maker with, ay?" Ouroboros Alpha put his paws over his head and seemed to try to keep his alarm to himself.

Two Fangs barked loudly to them all, "It is a good day to die!" His stoic countenance was nothing short of inspirational. Nowar couldn't tell, but it actually looked like he had never put on his seat belts. He was just holding onto the handlebars with his chin held high.

Nowar was watching Mandrake. His eyes were closed. He actually seemed to have a peaceful look on his face and he almost looked like he was smiling. Nowar yelled as loudly as she could above the roaring, rattling and rolling noises.

"Have you ever been in one of these things before, Mandrake?"

"Yes!" The one winged black-faced angel called back, "Many times!"

"Any idea how long it will take to get where we're going?"

"None!"

"Why?"

"Because we don't know where we're going!"

Ask, a stupid question, Nowar thought, but no sooner did she finish that thought when all the gyrating, spinning, rocking & rolling and intense vibration ceased, suddenly. It felt like they were still moving, but the ride was smooth, quiet, almost effortless. The inside lights of the cabin began to flicker again.

There was a "Zip" a "Pop" and a "Whirrr".

Mandrake said quietly, "We've pierced the veil!" and unbuckled his belts with lightning speed. Grasping some device on the ceiling, he pulled down a periscope. Nice feature, Nowar thought- the Lens had an abundance of windows, but they were all fairly useless, thick, dark, and coated in soot. Like a U-boat commander, Mandrake squinted and peered through the periscope while the others watched quietly. He said to the group- "Well, whatever our destination was, we've arrived- but we're still far above the target surface."

"Can you see anything?" asked Ouroboros Alpha.

"No, not yet, just mist, and maybe- oh, holy mother of velocity…" suddenly he was screaming "IT'S AN OCEAN! HOLD ON FOR IMPACT!"

The last thing Nowar remembered was Mrs. Machine's little red bubble light flashing as she sounded a high pitched all-hands-alert. During the impact, just for an instant, she would have sworn she was sitting in a quilt covered fluffy bed in near darkness, with a huge bookcase looming over her like an ancient monolith, and then there was total darkness.

'Hold on for impact' had been quite an understatement. When Nowar came to, even Two Fangs was still out cold. Ouroboros appeared to be unconscious as well. Nowar shook her head and blinked her eyes. Mrs. Machine's lights were out. In fact, all of the Lens cabin inner lighting, dim as it had been, were entirely out. Mandrake was the only one who was conscious other than her now. He had apparently lit a candle on the floor, and was still peering through the periscope. He glanced at Nowar briefly and smiled.

"No worries, Lady Nowar. Everyone's fine. Two Fangs will be awake in a minute or so, followed shortly thereafter by Ouroboros. When Mrs. Machine finishes her self-diagnostics she can help me restore power and restart the Lens engine."

Nowar shook her head once more and ran her hand through her hair, saying "Where are we?"

Mandrake smiled and answered cheerfully, "At the bottom of a sea," he paused for a second, then continued, "Which one I'm not sure."

Nowar reflected on the situation. "Good," she thought, "If we don't know where we are, neither does Moebius."

Part Ten

Not so fast, Princess

It made a lot of sense- 'If we don't know where we are, neither does Moebius.'

Unfortunately, it wasn't quite true. Moebius may not have known exactly where they were, but he had a clue or two.

And he was in his workshop giving them serious consideration while he enjoyed his favorite pastime, vanity cooking.

This workshop wasn't so much like a workshop as it was a 'Cooking-with-Lord-Moebius' show broadcast LIVE across all of the five Moebius-controlled Kingdoms. Moebius was currently huddled over one of his stoves with a gleam in one eye, and the other looking at the camera. The soufflé was going very well and he was all too aware of how dashing he looked in his little white chef outfit. He adjusted his hat for a second, smiled at the camera one more time and launched into his dialogue.

"Now, last time you'll remember I suggested you chill this work of loveliness for at least ten hours, but if you didn't keep it cold long enough, you'll find it'll taste a little flat. With a little extra patience, though, your own creations will taste just perfect." He smiled broadly for the camera.

A short Koradgian with a lot of headgear lifted a sign that only the audience could see.

CLAP, CHEER AND HOOT OR YOU'LL BE STEW!

A hundred reptiles began hooting and clapping vigorously while a small somewhat damaged robot rolled onto the floor and sat a bowl on the counter next to the Duke. The contents of the bowl looked like a cluster of orange-sized hairballs with thin eyestalks. They cooed like doves and rubbed against each other, occasionally twittering and chirping. A charming female Koradgian (as charming as a six foot tall reptilian humanoid could be) daintily sat a blender next to the Duke's left hand. The Duke was finishing sampling his soufflé and making 'mmm, mmm, good' noises. With his mouth still full, he began chatting about the next project at hand.

"So, several of our viewers have been writing in with a request to replay our Boggle-pudding episode. Very popular, I know, and one of my favorite dishes- so easy to make, as long as you have fresh Boggles available. Here at Castle Deep Steel we have our own little Boggle farm, so there's always plenty of Boggles to go around. Why look at those happy fellows. Glitney, would you do the honors, darling?" he handed the bowl of Boggles to his reptilian assistant. The little multicolored furry creatures continued cooing and twittering even as they cascaded into the blender.

Without a second of hesitation, the Duke maniacally sealed the blender and turned it on HIGH and with a big smile began to hum to himself over the short lived and high pitched screams of the Boggles. The low hum of the blender changed in pitch while the Boggles were perfectly blended.

Suddenly a voice patched in through the intercom. It was Clancy.

"Uh, sir?"

"ARG! Cut! Cut! Bring me some more frogging Boggles! I can see it now, these will be spoiled by the time we get back to this! WHAT IS IT, CLANCY?!!. You know we just started filming an episode of Chef Moebius! Can't it wait? When, oh when do I get Moebius-time?"

He turned to the fridge and pushed it hard to the left. It swished around, as if on a dolly, bringing a hi-tech platform into view. Sitting in a seat in front of a dozen screens and hundreds of gadgets and wires sat a very skinny high-strung reptile. He appeared to be much like a Koradgian, but his head was far bigger, and he wore spectacles. He shuffled papers, assessed data when no one was looking, and stared at little monitor screens in his spare time.

"Uh, sorry sir, but I figured you would want to see the results of the MOONCLOCK search."

ProbablePolis

"Oh, you just figured you'd interrupt one of my few favorite pastimes with your insipid database ravaging. It's all about you, isn't it, Clancy? It's always all about you. What about my fans, Clancy? Don't you think they matter?"

"Uh, right, sir. You can shut me back in here and I'll file my report later."

"Oh, no no no nonononono! We've already stopped filming. Time is money. Go on with your evil self, Clancy. File your report now." He pulled off the blender cover and dipped his finger in the sticky multi-colored goo and swished a big slug between his cheek and gum and beckoned to Glitney- "Goodness that's delicious. Go ahead and try some, dearie" then turning back to Clancy "Well, we're all waiting, Clancy, anything worthwhile?"

Clancy regained his composure. "Rather curious, actually sir. My MOONCLOCK hacking program just finished running a parabolic-string search for the signature anomalies across all fourteen pages of ProbablePolis and there's just not a hint of the Homo sapiens sapiens anywhere."

Moebius stared blankly at him, and then squinted, plucking out a very long eyebrow hair. Clancy continued while the Duke examined the hair more thoroughly. A touch of grey.

"It's as if she just disappeared, sir. Just gone. I've accounted for all the Homo sapiens sapiens signatures in all of ProbablePolis. They are all here. She's simply not showing up anywhere."

Moebius thought silently to himself for a second. He handed his spiffy Chef hat to Glitney and leaned over Clancy's shoulder, staring at the green glowing screens- "Did you say all thirteen pages, Clancy?"

"Why yes, sir. All thirteen."

"There are fourteen pages in the current Hypothecation of ProbablePolis, Clancy."

"Err, yes sir, but I didn't bother doing a search of page seven, sir. Why would I? They just left there."

Moebius looked down at the ground for a second and then, leaning closer to the little reptile quietly whispered, "I KNOW you're smarter than that, Clancy. THINK about it. This is a human being, and human beings are devious, clever, deceitful, treacherous manipulative creatures. JUST LOOK AT ME! If someone like me were on my tail, why of course I'd pretend to leave the page I was on, only to look for a better hiding place in the page I was already on, knowing the hunt would be on for me everywhere else."

Clancy stared at his screens and gave it serious consideration.

"Why, that's brilliant sire…I love your mind."

The Duke cackled to himself as he remembered that Jones had told him that the setting on the lens had been random anyhow, but belched forgetfully, saw that it was all going to work out in his favor anyhow and turning back to his fans said-

"Get on with it, Clancy, scan page seven- and never forget that I have a blender big enough to fit someone TWICE your size. Oh, and call a meeting in my Boardroom of the 'Joint Chefs of Staph'. I want them all up there in an hour- scaly tailed and slimy skinned. It's time to start cooking up a full assault on that traitor, the Midnight Shadow. We'll turn his little UnderRung into UnderWear. Hahahaha! All right, you folks have been so patient. Moogey, roll those cameras. Glitney, new bowl of Boggles. God I love being a superstar!!!"

Part Eleven

Can you sea my point?

Nowar watched Two Fangs wake with a start- looked wildly around, slowly settled back into his seat, crouching with his legs under him.

"We are still here-" he growled, sniffing the air, and continued- "Where **is** here?"

"At the bottom of an ocean, but we don't know which one." Nowar answered.

Mrs. Machine whirred back to life, chirping 'bitty-bitty-bitty-dingding!'- her lights flashed, six of her legs shot out from under her as she stood up. Her two ocular devices (some people might call them eyeballs) flashed several times and a big lamp extended from her metal spine to light the cabin of the lens, waking up Ouroboros Alpha-Beta.

"We're still alive!" Alpha cried.

"And yer still Master of the obvious" Beta sighed.

Two Fangs chuckled and snarled sarcastically- "You were never in any real danger, though now we know you both snore."

Mandrake cut short the banter with "Mrs. Machine, the main engines are off-line, do you think you could assist me?"

Mrs. Machine whirred, chirped and purred, moving to a compartment under one of the seats, popped off a panel and shone a flashlight into the gutty-works of the Lens. She and Mandrake began cutting wires and examining several buckled components. It appeared that duct tape would be an important part of the solution. Luckily, Mrs. Machine seemed to have plenty of everything in the storage bin that doubled as her abdomen.

There was a "Zip" a "Pop" and a "Whirrr". The Lens was back online. Lights came on in the cabin.

Nowar tapped Mandrake on the shoulder. "Is it ok if I look through the periscope?"

Mandrake initially seemed a little surprised, but looked at the ground for a split second in thought, then quickly shot back- "Why, of course you can, Lady Nowar. Just don't twist the handlebars, they double as the throttle and ignition."

She didn't know what either of those things were, but she agreed completely and put her face up against the periscope viewing hood. Mandrake said quickly, "You won't see much until main power can get to the headlights."

He was right. She could barely see a thing, but three seconds later, the headlights flickered on, and she got to see quite a bit.

They were sitting on an underwater hilltop of sorts. As far as the eye could see, the under waterscape was a vast expanse of coral and bulbous kelp, teeming with aquatic exotic life of all kinds, colors and sizes. Some of the coral bobbed up and down, and some of the kelp looked like giant aquatic Venus-flytrap plants.

"The Kelp looks hungry" Nowar said to no one in particular.

Mandrake turned quickly and said, "Really? May I have a look?" and then gandering into the viewing hood exclaimed, "Well by my stars and garters, we're **still** in T'ien Sha'an."

Alpha quipped quickly, "That's impossible, the Lens nearly shook apart- we **did** go into the rift."

Mandrake smiled "Yes, and then we went back out the way we came in apparently. Unless I'm mistaken, carnivorous Kelp only grows in one place- the 7th Kingdom."

Nowar smiled and said, "OK, now what?"

Mandrake smiled back and said, "Now I teach you how to pilot this thing."

Part Twelve

Never judge a Unicorn by its cover

The Midnight Shadow was on the move. He started with a canter.

At the first level above the capital, his canter grew into a lope, and he himself grew from the size of a puppy to the size of a stallion.

And he was a great deal more ferocious looking for sure, with flaring nostrils fuming fire and smoke, with a mane of cinders and black-fire spun with strands of electrical silver. Any element of cuteness had long since eroded away in a fiery billowing metamorphosis.

At another subsequent level where the goblins and gremlins played the music of flutes and drums, the Midnight Shadow grew again, lurching into the size of an ogre while his eyes emitted a strange green glow that paralyzed everything before him. His gallop turned into a full tilt now, a mad hell-stammer-jammer as he soared over great bridges breathing fire and smoke. His face became ancient and hoary as he grew in size and scariness, now dwarfing the smaller giants he passed on the upper levels.

Finally he came to a pause where the lava epically poured from the greater Amphitheatre palisade into the foyer of the great Twin stairways. By this time, the great Black Unicorn was the size of a Titan, or a Kraken perhaps- quite big in other words. Above, the low THOOM THOOM THOOM noises continued, unabated, as vicious Skreemers, Curdlers and Shriekers continued to bomb and laser the entrance to the UnderRung. According to the scuttlebutt, there was apparently a second-generation Battle-Snark Mega-cruiser, just waiting to unload hundreds of Koradgian storm troopers at the entrance to the UnderRung, once the lava drained off.

But that would never do, and the Midnight Shadow was on the move again.

He burst through the lava cap, shattering it and almost everything above it. The evil Duke Moebius' war machines went spilling every which way as the Midnight Shadow heaved himself up onto the surface, breathing gusts of living death over a whole field of ships, robots, reptiles and machines, blowing them all to smithereens like so many toys and toy-soldiers with his fiery hooves and horns. The last pulse of the Ribbon had long since descended past the rim of the world, so a great deal of the vignette was lit only by explosions and fires.

Standing astride the Valley of the Amphitheatre, the great Avatar of T'ien Sha'an became calm and poised as he surveyed the scorched landscape all around him. His ravaging eye-rays searched the valley, and he breathed columns of flaming asteroids on anything that moved.

Mandrake the White assumed the appearance of a butterfly and went up to chat with his good lord and liege, who, acknowledging his presence, spoke first, his voice booming across the valley.

"I think we are done for the day, what think you, Master Mandrake?"

"I believe we must be doubly wary, for I sense the shadow of something-that-has-yet-to-arrive…I fear Moebius is getting ready to unleash his next generation of giant robots."

The Midnight Shadow said nothing for a time, then asked, "Could you bring me Hieronymous Quantum Jones without delay, and throttle him a little bit along the way?"

Mandrake said nothing, and the Midnight Shadow went on-

"We need to find out who else he has been talking to, other than Moebius."

"Do you believe the Mole has been Jones all along, my Lord?"

"I'd say so. Call it a hunch, if you believe in such things, Angel"

"I'm on my way."

"And remember now, he's a Precognitus, so he's already running by now."

Mandrake spoke no more, but hurtled back down where he'd just left Jones, having gone from a butterfly to a hawk, weaving through pillars

and palaces, flying very fast back down to the room of the Lens. As any member of his race could do, he found the scent of Jones and followed it to a place on a bridge where the Precognitus immediately turned and begged to be set free.

Mandrake paused and said, "No, the Midnight Shadow knows that you've been talking to Moebius again, but he wants to know 'who else?' as well now, so come toodle along with me."

A scuffle ensued and a minute later, the Precognitus was reduced to a slightly damaged heap of cybernetics on the floor begging for mercy. Mandrake showed little emotion on his face as he said,

"We'll see if the Midnight Shadow has any of **that** for you, old boy- and by the way, you never **did** find **all** of the bugs we planted in your quarters and the Room of the Lens."

"Really?"

"Angels can't lie." Mandrake replied, and dragged the heap of metal and sentience up the stairs to the Midnight Shadow.

Part Thirteen

Is that a Probability, or are you just glad to see me?

It was three in the morning over in the Rondell house, and Pop Bric had been home from the Airport since 11:11 PM.

He was already planning, and calculating. It had taken him 12.5 minutes to get there, though he had estimated 11.75 minutes, meaning he was off by just over a minute.

That worried him. A man in his sixties appreciated keeping his mind sharp any way he could. He calculated the time it would take to do any particular thing, a lot, and then noted how close his estimates had been. It was Pop Bric's thing, and everyone got a giggle out of it now and then again, but it was in fact the trait of a man who had orchestrated big projects even after he retired from the air force, where he was a Brigadier General. His favorite saying was-

"Time is the universe's way of making sure everything doesn't happen at once."

The 'General' was in fact what everyone called him out at the Park, and he enjoyed the adoration that came from all his employees.

He was abroad on business when he got the message that interrupted all the functions of his computer and blared the following words on his screen-

> **AGENT GOLDEN EAGLE-**
>
> SECOND PHASE HAS BEGUN. I REPEAT, SECOND PHASE HAS BEGUN. THE BUTTERFLY EFFECT HAS BEEN COUNTER BALANCED. PROCURE THE BOOK IMMEDIATELY, AND ENTER THE BREACH.
>
> YOU ARE NEEDED HERE.

Pop Bric knew what was going on. By Midnight, he had unpacked his luggage, taken out the trash and sat down to read his email. In five

ProbablePolis

more minutes, he would finish his email, go get Grandma Brandy, and sneak into the Guest room where Nowar was supposed to be.

Pop Bric knew she wouldn't be there- or he wouldn't have gotten the message to join her in the breach.

Pop Bric knew things about the MoonClock Project he wasn't supposed to know. He just didn't know everything yet, and that bothered him.

He certainly knew it would take more than five minutes with Grandma Brandy to explain all about his own imminent voyage into a Holographic, digital, quantum matrix- an alternate reality where their granddaughter had gone. But it was the only way to bring her back, along with her mother, and his own son, all of whom had apparently forgotten who they really were, and were trapped without knowing they were trapped, in this alternate reality.

He held in his hand a small device that had been developed for this mission that supposedly would allow him to either keep or recover his memory almost immediately. He hoped it would work.

Knowing all this didn't lessen the anxiety of the situation. Nevertheless, he did his best with Grandma Brandy, and when they both snuck up the stairs into the Guest room that had been turned into Nowar's bedroom, Pop Bric wasted no time but turned on a light and began perusing the Bookcase. Grandma Brandy looked at the empty bed and said, "Are you sure we're all going to be alright, Bric?"

"I'm going to do my best to bring back the kids. Keep your eyes peeled for the third email. It'll tell you what to do next to bring us all back out."

The General was ready to draft a plan, but first he had to assess the situation. He did not fumble with the buttons of the Sun, the Moon and the Star, but with geometric precision, he input what he knew the buttons would render as the tune for the song 'When you wish upon a star'. A blinding white light consumed him as the book dropped to the ground in front of Grandma Brandy.

Grandma Brandy picked up the book, clutched it to her breast and prayed quietly to herself. Then she went downstairs to make some tea and turn on the TV. She was alone in the house, and to anyone but the closest observer, she now seemed un-phased by what she had just seen.

It felt like it would be a long night.

Chapter Five

The more, the merrier.

Part One

Do I need a license to operate one of these?

It took Nowar about twenty minutes to master piloting the Lens underwater. It was fun, when she wasn't bumping into coral that bobbed into view as she got near top speed, throwing the other cabin-mates around the inside of the thing like rag dolls.

She realized that the bobbing coral clumps were the carapace of silent and placid hermit crabs of colossal proportions. Not deadly, but dangerous in their size alone.

And there were things that lurked in that Kelp. Things even the Kelp wouldn't eat.

Mandrake was a good teacher, and it wasn't much longer before Nowar was puttering along at high speed, deeper down into a huge and grand underwater canyon.

Mandrake pointed to a silver compass on the wall and said, "I know where we are now. I think our safest bet is to keep to the rim of the canyon, and head for Mermopolis. I can reasonably expect to have us all granted sanctuary from the Queen of Mermopolis Bottom."

"Mermopolis Bottom? What's that?" Nowar asked, dodging something in front of the Lens that was large and black with lots of tentacles and no apparent head.

Ouroboros alpha blurted out "Mermopolis has never been just one city. The Mer-men roam the Coral fortresses outside the great bubble, and the Queen of the Mermaids rules everything under the bubble, with a nod and wink from the Midnight Shadow, who wisely stays out of their watery business."

Mandrake laughed and shook his head in agreement adding, "The Queen of Mermopolis Bottom is called Riganna O Nanna. She thinks well of me, given the fact that I saved her life not once but twice during the Second War of Probability."

"You mean the war against Moebius?" Nowar suggested.

His normally placid look turned quizzical. He measured his words out like a seamstress would measure thread, watching her face intently while he spoke.

"You don't know this, I don't think, but if no one has made this clear to you, let it be me. Your father, the King, went to war against Moebius, and your mother betrayed him on field of battle."

He watched her expression, and then continued with, "The Last Great war of this land was fought between three sides, but no one won, Nowar. Your mother, your father, and Moebius played the one against the other wherever possible. The loser was ProbablePolis itself. Many pages and many lives were irrevocably lost- destroyed"

He now had the attention of the other cabin mates, who had gotten very quiet.

"After the battle of the Rubicon Budge, all three sides saw fit to withdraw their own shattered forces to the Kingdoms they could reasonably protect, and this is the way things have been now for almost three hundred turns of the Ribbon. Of late, I have been told, your Mother is rubbing elbows with the Duke again, causing untold consternation across several of the Kingdoms, and I admit to being baffled as well."

"Unsubstantiated rumors, Mandrake, we don't know that fer sure." Beta piped up, not wanting Nowar to start feeling too badly about what she was hearing. Mandrake smiled at the Amphisbaena, and then continued.

"Nevertheless, the reality of the situation is that the King, your father, can count on the support of five kingdoms including his own. The

Queen, your mother, can only count on three kingdoms now, but Moebius adds to that with three of his own kingdoms. And of course, he's terrorized the other three kingdoms into remaining neutral until the Third War of Probability is over."

He looked around and said to the whole group as he sat down at last, "The balance of power is shifting once more, and not in the desired direction."

Ouroboros Alpha could apparently no longer contain himself and began speaking at length.

"This is true, Mandrake, but does not the Prophecies in the Book of Scorns offer us hope?"

Mandrake was quiet, and looked the other way. Alpha continued, now apparently talking more to Nowar than to anyone else.

"The Book of Scorns says that 'When the three greatest blessings of life are nearly lost, then and only then, a Daughter, where none had been known before, shall miraculously appear to the Last King and the Last Queen of All the Worlds…and she shall be called Nowar, and the newness of things shall pass as a miracle…'- and there's more…"

Mandrake shook his head, but to his credit, said nothing. Alpha continued, unabashed.

"…in the final days, a sentinel, an Iron Orion, shall unsheathe his sword to hew the deepest Steel, and the seas shall rise… In the twinkle of an eye, the dust of the ancients shall be restored by a Morning Star, who shall send a Queen with the Moon at her feet, and the Sun upon her brow…to banish the darkest venom and heal the broken spine of All the Worlds."

Everyone got very quiet.

Mandrake then took up the refrain and finished the stanza- "…with twelve stars as her crown she shall return from under the canopy of the heavens, where she shall have healed that house not made by the hands of men…then she shall kneel and pay homage to a new Emperor, who shall rule from the Unknown Kingdom with the Stone that the

Builders rejected… Behold and let not your memories wither on the vine of your soul, for when the Trinosophic Nautoniere returns to the faithful on the plain of all sorrows, the Third Age will be done…all the pages will be renewed… all the chapters restored."

Nowar was getting the hang of piloting this thing. The prophecy stuff was a bit much to think about right now, and she understood almost none of it. For a second she considered asking Mandrake and Ouroboros Alpha if prophecies were intended to be so confusing and obscure, but then she returned her concentration to flying the Lens around another huge aquatic thing oozing out of some dark undercurrent.

Nowar had the throttle wide open, and the Lens was chugging at top speed down the canyon into inky blackness. The course was simple and easy to hold, per the silver compass over her head; 20 degrees to Spine, and 110 degrees away from the Margin, and downward at 66 degrees, en route to a very dark cold place.

Nowar silently prayed to herself that they would make it to Mermopolis, "safe from all harm; safe from all harm; safe…from all harm."

Part Two

The butterfly dreams of being a King

The King had awoken.

The first pulse of the Great Ribbon light danced on his bed while he lay there, tasting the taste that dreams leave in your mouth when they're done. He'd had the same dream for the third morning in a row, a disturbing one that drove him out of bed like a lizard whose sunning rock had grown too hot.

Yet he did not part with custom. He had his own morning ritual, and he kept it zealously. The moment his feet touched the cold floor he looked to the sky, which was all around (the roof to his bedroom was a huge transparent crystalline dome) and said- "I rise with the strength of the heavens, with the strength of the heavens I rise." -and he did.

But instead of beginning his special exercises, his own combination of martial arts and yoga, the King walked swiftly to the other end of his room and yanked a white covering from a deep blue crystal ball.

"Kai, are you there?"

"Aye. Everything alright?" a very happy, hairy pudgy face with a helmet came into view."

"Not really. I want to see a Precognitus, and not just any Precognitus. I want to see Maximus Lotus Knobb, the Arch-Vizzerid himself. No one else will do."

"Good, because he's already here."

"What?"

"He snuck in ten minutes ago. He's doing card tricks for the street urchins down in the kitchen."

Good King Shard chuckled to himself. It takes a Precognitus…

"Ask him if he's disposed to wait another half an hour. I still stink from our skirmish yesterday."

"OK, I'll ask, but it doesn't look like he's going anywhere anytime soon."

"Good. Just make sure he sticks around till I get down there."

"No problem. Same dream?" asked the well-armored Satyr.

The King paused, took a big breath and said, "Yes, the same dream," and re-covered the crystal ball thus ending the conversation.

He turned and looked across the room, suspended hundreds of feet in the sky over Ambrosia. He stood, alone, gazing at the limitless sky unfurled over the dome of his private tower. Yet he did not feel he was alone at all.

For three days and three nights he had had the most intense feeling that he was being accompanied, guarded and guided, by an unseen force. He'd had a recurring dream, or nightmare, for the third morning in a row, about someone he'd never met.

It was time to find out what was going on; it was time to get to the bottom of this whole matter-

And that was what King Shard was good at.

Part Three

No time for yodeling

When the unbearable whiteness of being had lifted, Pop Bric was face down in the snow. He shook the cold wet stuff from his gray-haired head and slowly got to his feet. He looked around slowly, wiping snow and ice off of his arms and torso. He looked down and realized he was wearing his birthday suit, and nothing else.

He was on top of a mountain, surrounded by more mountains. Snow was gently falling from the sky, which had an assortment of clouds and storms coming from different directions and elevations. Snow and ice was everywhere, as far as the eye could see. There was no sun that he could discern, only a very bright ring far up in the sky. It would have been a beautiful scene if not for the fact that he was beginning to feel the cold blustery winds whipping at his back. He was already beginning to shiver.

He looked down a second time and noticed that there were letters written in the snow at his feet next to his handprint. They said:

B R I C

The name seemed somehow familiar to him, but he wasn't sure how or why. In fact, he wasn't sure of much of anything at all. **How** had he gotten here? Where **was** here? In fact, **who** was he?

Suddenly he realized that there was something in the snow right next to where his handprint was. It began to vibrate. It was a small rectangular piece of silver metal with bumps and buttons and a red flashing light that suddenly turned green. He picked it up. The device began to talk. The voice was scratchy and sounded like someone he felt he should know.

"General Bric, this is Colonel Rondell. You are no doubt wondering where you are and what has happened to you. In fact, you may actually be wondering **who** you are and **where** you came from. This device is intended to help you recover your memory in a very short period of time, twenty minutes or less, but you need to be able to give it your entire attention while it operates. Since you may be in hostile territory and unable to listen to the rest of this very important message, this device has been designed to pause at this juncture until you are capable of giving it your undivided attention. Simply depress the large blue button when you are ready to proceed with the memory treatment. To repeat the entirety of the message, simply depress the blue button twice."

Smart, he thought. He was, in fact, shivering horribly. He would have to take shelter somewhere and find something to cover himself with or he would freeze to death. No time to listen to a message at the moment. He looked up from the device to see where he might figure out how to get down off of the peak he was standing on.

His heart skipped a beat as he turned to look back in front of him. Very still, very poised, was an enormous, winged saber-tooth tiger. It might almost have been a statue, except for the mist from it's nostrils. He almost dropped the device at his feet while his mind began to race. He thought to himself that this thing was less than twelve feet away from him, and it could clearly close with him before he could get thirty yards- he had no chance of getting away alive. Whatever his mission had been that had brought him here, it was about to fail.

Then the winged saber-toothed tiger spread its great wings and pinions, slowly, and spoke with a measured and lyrical almost magnanimous voice, immediately putting him at ease.

"General Bric, I am Khan Nay-ommo Songh, Lord of all the Ysanther of Ambrosia and Avalhalla. I am here to guide you to safety."

He could hardly believe his own ears. A talking, flying, prehistoric mammal was going to be his salvation? His mission, whatever it was, might have a chance to succeed afterall.

"I'm ready. Let's go. I have work to do."

The sky began to darken quickly as a naked old man and a winged flying saber-tooth tiger made their way down into a valley and disappeared from view.

Part Four

A mystery wrapped in an enigma, wrapped in a hot pastry shell

The Midnight Shadow had shrunk to the size of a very large horse, and he waited in the flickering, almost ruined foyer of the top most level of the UnderRung. At attention stood several well-armed and armored soldiers- Ogres, Trolls, Giants, Wolven-kine and Gargoyles.

Presently, the betrayer was brought to him, suspended in a blue orb of light, a field of containment that neutralized all of his cybernetic tricks and gimmicks.

"Good Evening Mister Jones. Good of you to join us."

"Dispense with the pleasantries, Lord Shadow, I'm prepared to negotiate for whatever you want, so let's get to the meat of the matter."

The Midnight Shadow was motionless for an instant, and then replied, "No, I don't think so, old friend. First, a little gristle and bone. The meat will come later."

One of the Trolls, hearing the word meat, allowed a thin goober of saliva drip from his mouth to the floor. The Troll next to him elbowed him quickly whispering "Aint no meat on these things, Grue-sum, get yer tongue back in your mouth." Mandrake the White came into view and the ornery troops quickly settled down. A quick glare from him was enough to get them all back in line. This was, afterall, very exciting for them. It wasn't every day that they had a Precognitus for a captive prisoner.

"So, we know you've been playing three sides now, Jones, whereas before our suspicions were that you were simply playing Moebius off against us, we now know beyond a shadow of a doubt that you have been playing him off against someone else, likely Gull & Crones."

The Precognitus was quiet as the grave.

"Let me make this easy for you. I know who your contact is. I don't want to waste one of these Blue Bubbles of Destruction on anyone right now, not even you. We'll need as many of them as we have in the days to come, but if I must, I will dispatch it, and you, to the oblivion. If you wish to avoid your own utter demise, and take the option of banishment, it will be granted you, but you will have to do exactly as I say."

The Precognitus hung what could have been his head in what was either shame, or meant to look like shame, "I'm still listening…" he said in a low tone.

"Phone in to your other contact right now, if your communication circuits are still working, and engage them in a normal conversation. When I've heard enough, you will be sent into exile, no more damaged than you apparently are now."

Jones glared briefly at Mandrake, who returned the icy cold stare.

"Alright, but what assurances do I have that-"

"None" blurted the black Unicorn, "None at all…. Your choice. I give you thirty seconds to choose between destruction and banishment." And he began to count. The troops began to drum their weapons on the ground to the beat of the counting.

At the count of the number seven, Hieronymous Quantum Jones realized how serious a difficulty he was in, and said "Alright, OK! I'm calling in right now." He began to dial some numbers on one of his keypads.

"Agent Deep-Six, this is Hieronymous Quantum Jones, do you read me?"

The reply was scratchy, but prompt. "Jones? This is Agent Deep-Six, our scheduled conference isn't for another full rotation of the Pages, what's going on?"

"The UnderRung was just attacked, you nitwit, I thought you would want me to report in."

The line was quiet, just static came through.

ProbablePolis

"Alright, sure. Make your report, but make it quick, I'm expected to attend a meeting, and I have no doubt that it's going to be about the Final Tweak."

Jones looked a bit surprised, and said "What do you mean? Is this just more of the standard madness, or is something going on that I don't know about?"

"You idiotic nano-boob, if you hadn't been exiled from your fellow Precognitids you might understand what's going on a bit better."

"Enough with the insults, Deep-Six just tell me what's going on. If I'm not properly informed, how can I do my job?"

"Fine, and then I must go, and you're on your own until our next scheduled conference- I hope you're ready to evacuate, you'll likely be called on to report to the group about the current state of the UnderRung."

"Believe me, I can't wait to get out of here" said the Precognitus, surveying his captors and avoiding any long looks at the Trolls, then said "So, what should I be aware of now?"

"We have been monitoring the anomaly closely since just before it went off our screens."

"What? You mean the girl?"

"Yes, yes, of course the girl, you numskull! Once she jetted out of the UnderRung, we got a very brief signal that was utterly bizarre. It flickered and expanded into nothingness. I believe she never left T'ien Sha'an, but none of us can find a trace of her. It's as if something is **shielding** her from our sensors."

"She's probably found one of my own kind, that's all."

"No. Unlikely. Our new and improved sensors can read through a Precognitus mind-weave now. I've tested it on the other anomalies that your people are hiding from Moebius. Not even *they* could hide the girl now, even if they wanted to, and there's no guarantee of that anymore, now is there?"

"So?"

"So, the same anomaly signature that appeared with the girl when she entered ProbablePolis was repeated, but its strength was far above the other anomalies; way off the scale in fact."

"And?"

"And someone must have been hammering on your memory banks is all I can say- have you forgotten the secrets of the prophecies you were taught as a little cube?"

"The Fourth Anomaly? You're discovered the Fourth Anomaly?"

"Yes. Without a doubt, there are now four individuals in ProbablePolis who don't belong here, discounting Moebius himself, of course, oh, and his assistants from Urath, still in the deepfreeze since day 0."

"I see." Jones said weakly, and then with renewed energy said, "Does Moebius know all this yet?"

"He will very soon, Jones. I'd suggest you pack your things and prepare for us to get you out of there. The Final Tweak is coming soon, whether we like it or not."

Jones looked around bleakly- "Oh, I'm already packed and ready to go. Stay in touch, Hieronymous out."

The flicker and glare of the fires all around the hall threw shadows on the face of the Black Unicorn, who spoke quietly-

"Well then, Hieronymous, you did well. One more thing and you will be released into your next banishment. Where can we find Agent Deep-Six and what is his identity?"

Jones weighed carefully the next level of his treachery. He had little choice. The Midnight Shadow held all the cards. He should have known better than to try to gammon the Avatar of the 7th Kingdom. He chose to lie a little more, though. Afterall, he was so good at it, and it was such fun. He chose to use the best tactic for lying, as well. Tell a small truth, after you've encased it in a web of diversion.

"I believe he's in Castle Deepsteel. He's one of the higher ranking agents of Moebius, one of the few servants that Moebius actually trusts. I don't know his name."

"Hogwash. Mandrake, prepare the Purple Dwark for our treacherous citizen."

"What? Not the Purple Dwark!!! Please, my Lord, at least give me a chance to give you more information."

"I want his name, and I want to know what the Final Tweak is."

"The Final Tweak is our code name for the final conflict, the Third War of Probability- the final conquest of all ProbablePolis, and I swear, I don't know the name of Deep-Six, I suspect he works for Clancy, aide de camp to Moebius himself."

Shadow considered all this for another second. It probably **was** Clancy, he thought to himself, but why would the Precognitids try to cover for him in this way?

"Alright, then one more thing- if Moebius is confident enough to go to war against all of ProbablePolis, where does the Gull & Crones society stand? Will they ally with Moebius or Shard?"

Jones shook his head. "I'm not in the loop like I once was, but if my past experience with them is any indication, they will stay neutral until they see who the winner is likely to be, and then pounce on anyone left standing. That is, unless they believe with absolute certainty that one side or another will support a reduction in Page Count, and you know that won't be Shard."

"Valuable insight. Anything more to add?" inquired the Unicorn.

Sensing that he was going to get Purple-Dwarked anyhow, Jones decided to try one more thing.

"Look, if you're going to Dwark me, fine, but at least give me one more opportunity to prove my usefulness. Send me into the Dwark with Mandrake as an escort, and I will bring him to where Moebius is keeping his most powerful secret weapon, the Silver Scream Nine."

"Mandrake, what think you?"

Mandrake was smiling- he had been right about what might be coming- "Color me curious, my Lord. If it pleases you, I will take a battalion of Gargoyles and we shall see what Jones has to show us."

The Midnight Shadow squinted his eyes, and then said-

"Very well, bring the Purple-Dwark stone. One way or another, Mr. Jones must leave this page, once and for all. If he has anything to show you of value, I leave it to your discretion what state you leave him in before you return to the UnderRung."

Part Five

Hey hey, ugly looking, whatcha got cooking?

The War room of the Joint Chefs of Staph was usually a quiet place, even when the Joint Chefs were in there. It was hard to tell whether they were being quiet because they hated each other, or because they were afraid that Moebius had the war-room bugged, or both.

It didn't really matter anymore. They assembled when Clancy called them in, and they stayed quiet until Moebius arrived--and then you couldn't very well shut them all up. There were nine of them, if you included Clancy, who was absent at the moment. Some were warriors, others were tacticians, analysts, accountants, and one of them was even a stand-up comedian kept on to liven up the conversation when things got dull. Moebius usually enjoyed the banter. Regardless of what role they played, they were the most hideous, the smelliest, and certainly the scariest creatures you had ever seen.

The Joint Chefs of Staph seated around the table included:

Go-go-a-Fog-oo- a Koradgian weighing in at two tons, he was perhaps the most vicious example of his species, the reptilian overlords of the Kingdoms of Moebius, the Koradgians. He had a rapid firing machine-gun laser and thick shiny chain-mail like armor.

Ah-Hree-ghian- a very large pillar of goo, enjoying long blond locks and unmentionably strange protuberances. His language was also strange, consisting of noises that sounded like bugs being squished.

Onus- son of the Valkyrie Queen of Avalhalla, and despised by his people as a traitor. With a blunt broken nose and a funny accent, you would never know he was a master tactician and an excellent swordsman.

Mr. Machine- a cyborg with Homo sapiens envy, Mr. Machine looked like an exotic science project with a human-like head of plastic on top, and three or four human hands coming from odd places. He had an over-abundance of legs as well. No relation to a Mrs. Machine you may already be acquainted with.

The Glee- while this seat appeared to be empty, in fact it was occupied by a very tiny creature. If you had a magnifying glass, you might see what looked like a six-armed Allosaurus on steroids. The Glee may have been a terror to behold, but the Glee was but the size of a flea.

Shkaw-hawn- imagine a human-shaped cloud of small globs and broken fragments of a mirror like substance. The globs bounced off the fragments, and whenever Shkaw-hawn moved, he sounded like a chandelier shaking from an earthquake.

Tatyanna- dressed in exquisite black leather with more daggers than she knew what to do with, this dark skinned Homo Sylvanus (elf) sneered in contempt at her peers and occasionally filed her nails or text messaged her homeys.

Bogloon- without a doubt perhaps the most pathetic comic relief Moebius could have asked for, Bogloon was little more than some kind of dog-sized anemic slug with a huge toothy mouth, eight twiggy tendrils and a big jester cap with bells on all three ends.

The drum roll and off-key flute announced the arrival of the Chief Evil Officer of the Realm, such as it was. Duke Moebius sauntered in with maniacal speed, Clancy skittering along behind him with a bundle of papers and equipment so large that he could hardly see where he was going, and ultimately bumped into the table. Papers and a laptop computer went spilling everywhere.

Boglin drawled, looking up from his hookah, "And I thought *I* was supposed to be the plucky comic relief. Hello little lizard boy, learning to do any new tricks?"

Moebius pounded the table, getting everyone's attention, "Put a sock in it Bogloon- NO time for fun and games. Our initial siege of the UnderRung was a ***total*** failure." He looked around the room slowly, then whipped out from his black overcoat a huge laser blaster and slammed it on the table. No one said a thing. The Joint Chefs knew

ProbablePolis

he needed to vent, and talking back had its own well documented and unfortunate consequences. He continued.

"Does anyone have any idea of what's going on here? We are supposed to be preparing for the Final Tweak, our last chance to get everyone on the same page!" He looked at them all, wondering who should be shot first, and then continued "and we can't even invade **one** territory of the 7th Kingdom. You are all supposed to be the best of the best, the crud of the crud, my ugliest, scariest, most vicious Generals…what went wrong?"

Tatyanna answered haughtily, "The Midnight Shadow is probably one of the most powerful Avatars of all the Fourteen Kingdoms. You hardly sent more than a battalion of ships and maybe a few hundred storm troopers. I told you all that would never be close to enough."

Go-go-a-Fog-oo hissed and bellowed "That should have been more than enough to begin the invasion. Who could know that the Midnight Shadow would engage our forces immediately and with his greatest aspect?"

Without hesitation, Moebius blew him away with the laser blaster. Go-go was gone. The bottom half of his abdomen slumped out of the chair. Where all the bits from the top part might be were anyone's guess. No one said a word. Moebius blew the smoke off of the rim of the barrel of his weapon, re-holstered it while he stood over what was left of the carcass like he was on safari and said quietly "You were supposed to know better, you scaly brained bag of worm-chow."

Then, turning to Clancy, Moebius said, "Clancy, old boy, we need another Koradgian General, would you arrange for a replacement immediately?"

Clancy, who had gotten all his papers and equipment sorted out on the conference table, and acting like he hadn't even noticed the scene of madness that had just unfolded said "Yes, sire, already taken care of- he's on his way up now." -and continued clicking away on his laptop. The two Koradgian storm troopers standing guard by the entrance to the conference room hauled off the ex-Chef-of-Staph and returned to their posts while Moebius stalked around the room like a rabid panther.

"Open to suggestions, people, come on, let's get with the program- we need to brainstorm this thing back into shape, no more focus groups! I want, need, REQUIRE fresh new treacherous ideas out of ALL of you."

Tatyanna asked haughtily "Why didn't anyone think to simply take the Black Harp for back-up?"

Moebius got very still – "The Harp is already being dispatched for more important things on Page Four, my dear. It's well on its way to Everlast to terminate the Avatar, that giant froo-froo Cloud-Tree."

He scanned the room, hungry to squash any more backtalk- "Now, the Silver Scream Nine is nearly ready to wake up, I am given to understand…" he looked at Clancy who shook his head in swift and silent agreement- "…but the Harp and the Scream are MY toys, you boobs, you all have your own, and you all need to start getting creative with the magnanimous resources I have put at your disposal."

Everyone was silent. Onus was the first to speak, "Perhaps we could send a special envoy to King Shard, offer to negotiate a temporary truce. Lull him and his forces into thinking we are tired of the war, have given up our desires to conquer all of ProbablePolis, and are ready to discuss a long-term peace treaty."

Moebius thought about this for a second, "Good, good. Not bad, Onus, you've got my blessing- make sure you send an attractive elf for this job, someone persuasive."

"I'll go." Tatyanna offered. "Do I have your permission to assassinate the King if I get the opportunity?"

Moebius laughed, hard- "Oh, my dear, I have to remind myself that you are the newest member of the Joint Chefs." He turned to look at the new Koradgian General enter, make the special salute Moebius taught all his reptiles to use, and sit down in the still warm chair of his former peer. Moebius turned back to Tatyanna "Second newest, that is."

He winked and continued, "Allow me to explicate; both the King and the Queen are quintessentially immortal. They are what we call 'seasoned anomalies' to ProbablePolis. They have learned the arts of rebirth. That's why we are seeking to capture them, because we cannot in fact kill them, at least not as far as I can tell- I have wasted more assassins than you could imagine finding this out, by the way, so knock yourself out, but believe me, you'll not get far with that sort of thinking. Imprisonment is the best we could hope for with these two, believe you me. It would demoralize their forces and give us the upper hand we need."

"But there is no need to capture the Queen anymore, she's on our side, is she not?" cried Mr. Machine.

Moebius just stared at him for a second, realized he was not 'in' on what he had actually done with the Queen, and then said calmly, "Yes, Mr. Machine, that's right…but she's still human, and therefore capable of disloyalty at the very last."

"Then let Onus and Mr. Machine go with me to Castle Ambrosia as a delegation of peace. Glee can come with us and his tiny size would make him the ideal spy!" Tatyanna laughed.

Glee, whose voice sounded like a big French lumberjack roared across the conference room "At last, I get to see some action! I vill not let you down, o fearful leader!"

"That would be 'fearless', Glee, not 'fearful'." Moebius said, only slightly irritated. "Fine, but you can forget taking Onus. The sight of him would only turn Shard's heart against any discussion of peace. Onus was the mastermind behind our last attempt to fool Shard, and he'll see red at the slightest mention of his name…and besides, I have a mission for Onus out in the Dwark."

Clancy then spoke up- "Before we adjourn, I must make a report of some very important news."

"Such a scene-stealer, Clancy, what is it now?" Moebius asked, flopping himself down in his huge commanders chair like an impudent child–

he looked over at the new Koradgian and asked him "Be a good reptile and pour us a glass of wine, will you, good fellow? Thank you…"

Clancy took off his spectacles and addressed Moebius directly, "We have only the most modest indications to show that the third and newest anomaly, the girl called Nowar, is still in T'ien Sha'an. Something of great strength is hiding her, protecting her, shielding her from our best detection systems. We have Toggle-Wogs scouring the surface of the Seventh Kingdom everywhere; we have activated several key Aht Erm'nals and they are reading data from their general vicinities, but there's still no trace of her anywhere."

"I'm sensing a punch-line" Bogloon coughed and spat on the floor.

"Quiet down or you're stew fodder, maggot." Moebius rattled off at him and turned to Clancy, "What else?"

"I have detected an even newer, fourth anomaly, my Lord. It entered ProbablePolis only a few minutes ago."

Moebius looked like he was about to have a cow, or worse. He went pale as a ghost and stared into space for a second. Then he reacted, galvanized.

"Where? Do we have a read on where the fourth anomaly entered ProbablePolis?"

"Yes, the anomaly appeared in the Kingdom of Avalhalla- but the reading was brief, and it's already gone now. There's a multitude of snow storms raging across most of the Mountains. Toggle-Wogs are highly ineffective in Avalhalla during inclement weather, you might recall, and the Great Olde Drake destroyed all the Aht Erm'nals on the Great Cover a very long time ago."

Moebius creased his brow, smelled his fingers and curled his eyebrows, all in less than thirty seconds. He twitched, visibly.

"Alrrrightee, then. Slight change of plans, folks. Tatyanna, you, Mr. Machine and Glee, head to Castle Ambrosia. Lie like dogs that we actually want peace and get us a momentary treaty, and get it soon. If you're captured and imprisoned, escape and remain inside the castle to relay intelligence to one of our attack teams"

Then, turning to Clancy he said, "Clancy, you work with our new General here to organize the entire fleet into the Dwark and take them to the Fourth Page. Our entire force must now go into vanquishing the entire Kingdom of Everlast."

Then, turning to Onus, "Alright, old boy, it's your turn to get back into the saddle- no Dwark gallivant for you, oh no, I want you to get to Avalhalla with Shkaw-hawn, tout suite, and find the fourth anomaly. Stay in constant contact at all times. Avoid the Great Olde Drake and his minions at all costs. If you find the fourth anomaly, don't engage him in combat, but capture him if you can, but, in any event, let us know where he can be found immediately so we can send back-up."

Moebius looked around at the Joint Chefs. Ah-Hree-ghian quivered and uttered some long gibbering rant of garble. It sounded obscene, but no one understood what he was saying anyway.

"Ah, yes, Ah-Hree-ghian, you and Bogloon will run the 'Dialing for Dimensions; Playground-of-death' Game Show today. Act normal at all costs. The citizens of Moebius-land must not know that our evil Kingdom is in crisis. Bogloon, stop picking your nose!"

Bogloon laughed, pulled a stringy mess of chunky phlegm roughly out of his nose and twirling it around on his jester stick, blurting out suddenly "Look, guys, I got lunch for everybody. Hahahahah!"

"SILENCE! And one last thing, for you ALL to hear! I want you to know something; I want you to know that the advent of these third and fourth anomalies is utterly disastrous, coming as they do when we are almost ready for the Final Tweak...but... I have all the confidence in the world that we, as a team, can turn the tide of good back in our own evil favor." Without pausing, he picked up his wine goblet. The Joint Chefs reached for their own glasses.

"To Hell Incorporated!" Moebius cried, lifting his glass on high.

"To Hell Incorporated!" the Joint Chefs echoed, lifting their own glasses.

Within minutes, the conference room was emptied, except for a thin wiry little bespectacled lizard, and a huge beefy Koradgian, who looked around nervously- he really didn't understand a thing that had just happened. Clancy, clicking away on his keyboard looked up briefly at him.

"Don't worry old chap, first day on the job is always a bit confusing. What's your name again?"

Part Six

In the belly of the Tale

The journey to Mermopolis was a long one indeed. The motors hummed, and the air pumps pumped, and various devices clicked and clacked as the Lens continued on its long descent into the deepest underwater valley of the 7th Kingdom. Everyone onboard was asleep, except for Nowar, who was taking turns piloting with Mandrake, who claimed that Angels didn't require sleep.

"That's pretty convenient." She remarked.

"Sometimes. It has its downside. If you don't sleep, you don't dream." He answered, sitting down after his shift of piloting was over. "…and if you don't dream, you don't retain clarity of mind."

"Can you sleep if you wanted to?"

He chuckled, "Yes, yes, of course, who wouldn't want to dream? But we **can** go long periods without sleep when we have to, when we're doing something particularly important."

Nowar was thoughtful for a moment, and asked "So, then, what are we doing, again?"

Mandrake the Black laughed and said "We're getting you out of the 7th Kingdom. Jones may have been a traitor, but he was right about one thing- you are, somehow, existing in two worlds, one foot here in ProbablePolis, and the other…well, only the Great Olde Drake can help you now. Prophecies aside, we all sensed the truth of the matter, that getting you back your memories is somehow very important, perhaps critical to the war about to be fought."

"So then, how do we get to the Great Olde Drake by heading into the deepest sea to a city called Mermopolis? Is that where the Drake is?"

"Oh no. No, Mermopolis has a Dwark gate, and a very good one, a Purple Dwark gate, just like the UnderRung used to, which we can use to go through the Dwark and get to Avalhalla, where the Great Olde Drake lives"

"Why not try using the Lens again?"

"The Lens can only be used to go into the rift from a pattern. There is only one pattern in the 7th Kingdom, and that's in the UnderRung. Some say that the Precognitids of Hovahnon have their own pattern and Lens, but we can't trust any of them now, not after what we just saw with Jones. Others say that the Queen of Mermopolis secretly had her own private pattern and Lens fashioned, but it's unlikely she would let anyone use it, even if that were true. She will, however, let us use the Mermopolis Dwark Gate"

"Why can't we go back to the UnderRung?"

"The UnderRung is under invasion by Moebius, Nowar. Even if they have repelled the invaders, many, many eyes of Moebius will be watching the Lens room and all of the UnderRung. Our chances of getting to the pattern there are slim, and besides, I was given an order to get you safely **out** of the UnderRung. I would have to disobey an order from the Midnight Shadow to take you back there. I will not disobey my orders."

Nowar could appreciate that. Very loyal, this Mandrake the Black seemed to her. She was beginning to like him.

"So, when you separate from your other half, Mandrake the White, what does it feel like? Will you be able to…err, come back together?"

"Mandrake the White and I are not halves, my dear. We belong with two others. We are quarters of the whole Mandrake. Angles practice what we call quadrinarianism- there also exists a Mandrake the Red, as well as a Mandrake the Gray, separated from Mandrake the White and I a very long time ago. And yes, we will be able to come together someday, I feel very strongly, though to answer your question, the 'feeling' of the 'sundering' is impossible to describe while it happens. It's like being parted from your dearest friend, or your own hand. A trifle of agony, I suppose. But, when I am quiet and still, I can 'feel' him, I can 'call' out to him, and eventually, when he becomes quiet and still, we can both communicate with each other."

"Why don't you try that now?"

"In a bit, perhaps, first I would like to see us get to the Gates of Mermopolis, safely. We're not out of the woods yet." And he smiled at her. His smile was so beautiful. It made her feel very at ease.

Suddenly, Nowar sighted something off the starboard, a good hundred yards away. It looked like a car-sized orb of light, suspended from a huge stalk, spiraling away from the orb into the inky darkness.

"There's a light ahead of us, to the right."

"Let me have a look. We're nowhere near the Guard Orbs of Mermopolis, it's got to be something else, maybe a scout-globe. No, stay at your station, and keep up the speed, there's an extra periscope I can pull down here to use."

He squinted through the viewfinder quietly. Softly, he said, "Oh, no." and then yelling at the top of his lungs, "OH NO! Full throttle hard to port, Nowar, evasive action! EVERYONE WAKE UP! IT'S AN ANGLER WHALE!"

The mouth attached to the face of the Angler Whale was enormous, bigger than a very large house. It came into view fully opened, under and below the Lens, chugging away as hard as it could. The suction of the entire maw pulled the Lens in like it was a piece of popcorn. The mouth closed with a loud resounding BOOM, and the Lens went swirling down into the vast gullet of a beast as big as a town. Alpha Beta squealed in unison- Mrs. Machine sounded her alarm as she was thrown full force into Two Fangs, who howled in pain. Nowar held onto the periscope for dear life, and Mandrake held onto the both of them for both of their dear lives.

The crew of the Lens was thrown everywhere in their little compartment as the thing tumbled down an enormous and dark esophagus, landing with a huge splash in a great septic lake of yellow and green acidic goop.

Richard Dell and Rowan DelldeRonde

Darkness and silence possessed the cabin of the Lens.

The Angler Whale, satisfied it had finally sucked down something of substance for its breakfast, gracefully turned downward, and headed back for the bottom of the sea.

Part Seven

Pill-grim-age

King Shard walked slowly into the kitchen, watching the Precognitus at a table doing card tricks and pulling coins out from behind the ears of children. He marveled for a moment at how much delight this synthetic ancient creature received from making these little children happy.

A few of the kitchen gnomes came over to ask if they could be of service- seeing as how it was a great honor to have the King come to the kitchen. Shard declined breakfast. He was hungry for something other than food. He put his finger to his lips, suggesting they keep quiet for a minute so he could observe the kitchen vignette a little longer.

It was too late, several of the urchins turned around to see the King, and the Precognitus, smiling a cybernetic smile, rose from the table and bid the children a good day. Scuffling along on a variety of silver appendages, Maximus Lotus Knobb bowed ceremoniously before Shard.

"Rise, Arch-Vizzerid. It is I who should be bowing to you."

"Very well, my Lord. It is a lovely day. When was the last time you went for a stroll in your own Garden of Earthly Delights?"

"Too long. Let's go." This was a hint that they might get some private time. Shard walked with the Precognitus down the stairs into a Courtyard so huge it contained a glade. At some point, Shard waved off his guards, who begrudgingly kept a distance but did not entirely disappear.

"So tell me about your dream."

For an instant, Shard marveled at the Precognitus and then said, "How do your people do that?"

"Do what?" Maximus Lotus Knobb smiled pleasantly.

"That! That thing you do. That, 'knowing' thing. You knew I needed you before I called upon you, and now you demonstrate you knew exactly why I was calling upon you."

"My people are a pale second cousin to the first race that arose in ProbablePolis, the Builders, but we have a few things in common with them. We both are capable of putting aside our own sense of self when required by the Logos for the Great Plan, and when you put aside your own sense of self, there is nothing to hear but the song of the World and the Word of the Logos, anyway, isn't that so?"

"That does little to explain."

"The best things in life must be experienced, they can not be explained. You will understand soon, though, sooner than you think. Now tell me about your recurring dream, my Lord."

"For three nights in a row, I dream of a scene in a kitchen in which I have never been, having dinner with a little girl and an old man whom I have never met. Near the end of the dream, I tuck the little girl in bed, and then I come downstairs and the old man and I get into an argument - something about a dangerous journey and a rescue operation."

The Arch-vizzerid stopped for a second and turned to face King Shard. He seemed like he was listening to a silent companion, hidden from view.

"An Irony of ironies, oh my favored son, is gifted to you. There is nothing I can tell you that will really make sense of this, and yet there is one thing I **can** tell you that will lead you to understand everything. Through two wars you have trusted my counsel. A third war is brewing, and we both know this. The forces of Moebius have grown very strong indeed, and he has annexed the Kingdoms of your estranged Queen. If you would save your kingdom, preserve the lands of ProbablePolis, and understand the key to this dream, you must do exactly as I say, and hesitate not one bit."

A grim countenance came over King Shard's face. "Go on. Teach."

"You must turn all your duties over to Duke Kai and the Council of Elders, or, rather to just the Council, but you must instruct all of them to tell no one where you have gone. You must pack a single pack, your sword and your shield, and pass over to the Kingdom of Avalhalla on foot, through a Dwark Gate. You must go on a pilgrimage to seek out the Holy Well of Souls and speak to the Elder Narrator, the last Great Oracle and Incarnation of the Logos."

"And then what?"

"And then it shall all be as clear to you as a mountain spring. The last chapters of your story are being written, my son, or in fact have already been written and are being recited. You must go and meet your destiny. Your time in ProbablePolis is nearly done."

More confused than ever, Shard spoke no more, but walked quietly for a while with the old Cybernetic sage. Eventually, the third moon rose over the red sea of Lunog, and the seagulls were flying into the waning Ribbon of Light pulse. Somewhere a horned owl hooted in the dusk. Shard was not even sure of when he parted ways with the Precognitus, but he found himself back in the kitchen again as the great ribbon was setting in the opposite direction from the morning. Had he been gone for the whole day?

Later that night, King Shard convened a secret meeting of the Elder Council, and did exactly as the Arch-vizzerid had bid him. The debate was heated, but in the end, what could they do? He was after all their liege and lord, the man who had saved their Kingdoms, and perhaps all of ProbablePolis, from the madness of Moebius. They could deny him nothing.

In the very early morning, with his long sword and boots slung over his shoulder, the High-King of the free Kingdoms of ProbablePolis walked barefoot up the long road to the Temple on Mount Cong, greatest in all of the 13th Kingdom. There he was anointed with rose-oil, offered a Dwark stone, and shown to the swirling whirling vortex of light and energy in the center of the sacred, secret Temple chambers.

Without hesitation, he picked up a wafer from the plate held before him by a white robed Elf, and then walked into the Dwark gate.

"May the Logos be with you." The Elf quietly offered.

"And with you as well, brother." He responded and disappeared into the Dwark.

He had never noticed that he had been followed all the way up to the temple of Cong.

The Satyr Duke Kai, most trusted of all his nobles, had stayed quite a distance behind him, but his intentions were clear and his backpack full of supplies. He had saved his King from the jaws of death more than once.

This time would be no different.

Part Eight

Not every interview goes this smoothly

By the time his toes were numb, Bric had been guided down off the mountain and into an icy gully by his newly found friend, a Winged Saber-tooth tiger named Khan.

After a few very hazardous slips and slides, Bric realized where they were headed. A huge frozen waterfall lay ahead. Bric slipped one last time before Khan turned to him and said, "We are almost at our destination, but the way is about to become far more treacherous. If you wish, you may ride me into the caverns, but then I must return to cover our trail. The oncoming snowstorm will not snow hard enough soon enough to cover our tracks fully."

"I'm game. Is someone following us?"

"I have no doubt of that. Little goes on in the Kingdoms of ProbablePolis without Duke Moebius knowing about it. By now he knows of your arrival, and will send assassins to dispatch you."

A shiver of another kind went up Bric's spine. He got on Khan's back but continued asking questions.

"Who is Moebius? Why would he want me dead?"

"All in good time, General. First you must be brought to a warm safe place where you can finish the restoration of your memories. Then, when you are ready, we will take you down into the Well of Souls to meet the Great Oracle."

Bric's mind was reeling, but he was beginning to shiver uncontrollably, and was heartened considerably once they left behind the harsh winds and entered the cavern behind the huge curtain of ice. It was very dark here, but every ten yards or so it was becoming warmer, and lighter- the walls of the cavern were adorned with more and more patches of a shaggy glowing moss. Bric was beginning to see that the cavern walls were incredibly high, and adorned with patterns, pictures, hieroglyphs.

There were stories here, told by many different people, over a broad range of time.

"Where are we?" Bric asked as Khan kneeled, allowing him to disembark from his furry back.

"This cavern is called the Sepulchre of Silence. It is a holy place to all the peoples of ProbablePolis."

"Ironic name," thought Bric, "This place is anything but silent, really." And he continued following the winged sabre-tooth tiger, though his attention kept straying to the walls and their barely hieroglyphic, almost pictorial, depictions of story upon story. At some point, he collided with Khan, who had stopped.

"We have come to the Sepulchre itself. This is where the first Canticle of the errant Navigator began we are told. Here is where I must leave you," said the sabre-tooth, licking his paw and cleaning his forehead like a huge winged tabby. "I will return to the entrance of the cavern and remain as your guardian during your conversations." He stood then, and began to walk slowly back the way they had come.

Bric looked around. They had entered a very large perfectly round chamber, with a great hole in the ceiling, and a stone enshrined well structure in the middle of the floor. In one corner there was a small brazier over a tiny fire. The smell of some kind of stew permeated the air. There was a cot, and a small curved stool to sit on. Bric turned to watch Khan disappearing into the shadows.

"What am I supposed to do here, anyway?" he called out. Without stopping, the shadow of Khan called back-

"Recover your memories, General. Remember? You said it yourself- you have work to do."

Good answer, he thought. Bric sat down on the stool, ate some of the stew in a wooden bowl, and then picked back up the little square device that had talked to him before, up there on top of the mountain. Taking a deep breath, he depressed the large blue button twice.

"Here goes nothing." He murmured.

Part Nine

Robo diabolus sapiens?

A word or two about the Dwark; it is infinitely black and infinitely vast. It is the space between Pages, or Kingdoms, whichever word suits you better. Few dare to tread in the Dwark, much less think about it. To enter it requires a stone, or a special contrivance like a Gate. Most of the Stones have long since been lost, and only a very few of the Gates still work anymore. To leave the Dwark requires some sanity, as well as the stone or help from someone at a Gate. Lose either, and you are lost, lost forever, in the black, vast Dwark.

Before departing from the 7th Kingdom, Mandrake the White had trussed up Hieronymous Quantum Jones like a turkey on Thanksgiving, and turned off all his power circuits except for his central nervous system. In other words, he wanted Jones awake and aware during this special little jaunt. Flying through the Dwark space at an incredible speed, Mandrake took occasional directional cues from the Precognitus, and then turned off his verbal mechanism so he could think quietly to himself. A small battalion of gargoyles flew some distance behind him, covering his flanks.

After a long time, he turned Jones verbal mechanism back on.

"I have a question for you." He said.

"We're not due for another course correction for at least another drekk, what on Urath could you possibly want to know from me now? You wouldn't believe anything I say anyhow, so why bother asking a doomed question?" was the exhausted reply. Mandrake ignored the sarcasm and said,

"In my experience there is no such thing as a doomed question, you misbegotten treacherous gathering of silicon and wires. I am a young angel, so I was not even alive during the First War of Probability…but you were."

"I am older than that, you winged contrivance. I am one of the first twelve that walked on the very first page, when Moebius was but the first tinkerer in the Book of Life, and mysteries teemed around every non-Euclidian corner- when the Builders themselves were barely realizing what they had made!"

"Hm. I **knew** you were old, and I had been told that you were possibly even older than that, that you were on the first prototypes, but- ... this only underscores my confusion at your betrayal of the peoples of ProbablePolis- why did you choose to ally yourself with Moebius against the rest of us? Gull and Crones has never taken sides."

"As if Gull and Crones was the only game in town! Ha! Disbelief paralyzes my cortex; you must actually believe the dribble that comes out of the mouth of the King and his pawn, that pathetic one-horned black pony. Would you care to define the term 'Us'? Really, please. Who is this 'Us'? Who exactly have I betrayed? And more precisely, do you really think I have become an ally to Moebius and do not hear the Word of the Logos?"

"'Us' has always been a fluid term, I grant you, but it's been simplified of late, wouldn't you say? 'Us' is anyone other than Moebius and his own pawns. The Logos is not with Moebius."

"I have no answer for your question except to tell you two things that will both come as a shock to you. One, I have an allegiance to no one but my own society, Gull & Crones, and our aim is clear- always has been- return ProbablePolis to its original and pristine state- a single flawless, seamless page, ruled by one, and only one, true Emperor."

"But your noble cause is stained with the blood of many innocents, and the most wicked treachery ever known. A good and noble cause stops being a noble and good cause in the moment one person carries out a single evil deed to its credit, does it not? If one innocent dies in the name of absurdity, a society is responsible to correct and amend, is it not? The road to the Logos can only be paved by intentions that are pure, and true."

"Spare me the ethics lesson, Mandrake. The second jaw-dropper is that you have been told I believe, by the Midnight Shadow that the Second

War of Probability was fought between three sides, but it was not the three sides you believe it was."

Mandrake was quiet. Jones continued.

"The treachery of the Queen was never real, and the Queen you saw on the battlefield was not the real Queen at all. She was a robot and an extension of the will of Gull & Crones, on behalf of Moebius, who could not find a way to kill her once he had imprisoned her…and it's not necessary for you to know how we did it, only that we **did** do it."

"Why?"

"Because a second War between King Shard and Duke Moebius threatened to do the same thing the first war had done, double the page count of ProbablePolis, and that would have been a disaster. It's time for a final shake-out, and the very fabric of the Dwark sings with the advent of the fourth anomaly, does it not?"

Mandrake was dumbfounded.

"So the Queen that sits on the Throne is not the true Queen? That would explain a great many oddities, for sure, about how the Queen has acted lo these many pulses and phases, but why does your society have such a fear of a bounty of Kingdoms? There are many that say that this is the natural legacy of our world, to increase its Kingdoms in number throughout time immemorial. Indeed, does not ProbablePolis itself eventually create a new page after one is destroyed?"

"Don't rub it in. Bah! Let the zealots of diversity spin their propaganda as they like. Some of those same lunatics will tell you that the Kingdoms are round and not flat, would you choose to believe those idiots as well? No, for the time being, Moebius is an excellent tool to promote the re-simplification of ProbablePolis, and for the time being, Gull & Crones will use him for all he's worth, until such time as he changes his tune, or his song ends, which precognitively speaking has grown in probability in the last pulse or two, has it not?"

"I will relish the final destruction of your treachery, Jones, almost as much as the end of Moebius himself, Logos willing…we are at the next jump location. Which way now, you digital fool?"

"Hold on. Let me get my bearings. Hmmmm."

Long silver spike-like limbs suddenly seized the Angel from behind much as a spider seizes a fly. Mandrake screamed briefly, but he hardly knew what hit him.

When he awoke, he was wrapped tightly in a strait-jacket of thin steel fibers. In front of him floated Hieronymous Quantum Jones, sorting out his various appendages and devices, repairing himself idly, apparently waiting for the Angel to wake up.

Several well packaged cocoons floated here and there, evidence that the Dwark-Spiders had ambushed his gargoyles quickly and efficiently.

"Good of you to join us, you feathered fob. I was going to terminate you immediately, as soon as I was done with my own self-diagnostics, but I decided it would be entertaining to take you a bit further down this rabbit hole. After all, you came this far to get a show, didn't you? Oh, but that's right, you can't answer me right now, you're paralyzed by the venom of the Dwark-spider."

Then, addressing the huge hairy multi-legged thing dangling Mandrake in front of him, he said, "Come, my dear, let's take our little canary deeper into the coal mine. It's time for Homo angelicus sapiens to look upon the species that will supplant his own; **Robo diabolus sapiens!!!**"

The Precognitus waited to see if this was sinking in, and then continued with his rant-

"Oh yes, Mandrake the white, it's time you beheld the beginning of the end of your own kind, it's time you beheld the Silver Scream Nine, -unique by design. Hahahahahahaha!"

Mandrake had never heard a laugh so cold, so harsh, so profoundly dark and loathsome, and - knowing that he had failed his Lord, the Midnight Shadow, made it all the worse.

Part Ten

Some rainbows are shaped like a Moebius strip

Nowar awoke with a start.

She was in bed. It was 5:55 AM in the morning. The book was lying on the table next to her bed. Once again, her dreams were rapidly being ripped away from her mind like autumn leaves in a violent storm. She was at a loss for words.

She was home.

Driven by an indescribable and unstoppable urge, she lunged for the book and continued reading it from where she had left off. One thing was different- subsequent chapters revealed actions and events and sequences that she had no direct experience of while she had been in ProbablePolis; the defense of the UnderRung by the Midnight Shadow, the conversation between King Shard and Maximus Precognitus, and- the entry of Pop Bric into ProbablePolis? Holy cow!

That couldn't be! She ran down the stairs, and finding the master bedroom doors open, burst into the room to find- Grandma Brandy asleep, with the Lox Network News channel keeping her subconscious company. Nowar suddenly felt like an invader. She felt she needed to leave Grandma to her sleep, but not before she had a good look around.

Luggage and shoes and a half empty glass of port were all she needed to see, to know that Pop Bric had indeed returned.

But where was he? Had he really gone into ProbablePolis? Suddenly, the Lox Network News on the TV was replaced by a field of static that faded into a black screen with eleven words silently portrayed:

> GO UPSTAIRS TO THE DEN AND LOOK
> AT THE COMPUTER SCREEN...

Nowar stood there for a moment, marveling at the message. The house would have been very quiet, and very still indeed had it not been for the fact that Grandma Brandy had spent half her life collecting a veritable fleet of Grandfather Clocks, which at the moment loudly reminded her that time was a-wasting. In fact they were all beginning to chime and gong and bong- announcing it was now six in the morning. Brandy snored noisily.

Nowar ran back up to Pop Bric's home office and went straight away to the computer. On the monitor was a far more elaborate message:

> GOOD. GLAD YOU COULD MAKE IT.
>
> YOU ARE DOING VERY WELL, NOWAR.
>
> BEFORE YOU COME BACK, YOU MUST MAKE SURE YOU CARRY OUT THE FOLLOWING INSTRUCTIONS:
>
> 1. DO NOT GO BACK TO PROBABLEPOLIS UNTIL YOU HAVE SPOKEN TO GRANDMA BRANDY. IF AT ALL POSSIBLE, WAKE HER UP AT 9:11 AM. HAVE A NICE BREAKFAST WILL YOU? IT'S IMPORTANT.
>
> 2. TELL BRANDY THAT YOU HAVE TO COME BACK TO PROBABLEPOLIS SOON, BUT ALSO TELL HER THAT A VERY UNUSUAL STRANGER WILL BE COMING TO THE HOUSE TOMORROW AT 2:11 PM. TELL HER UNDER NO CIRCUMSTANCES TO LET THE STRANGER INTO THE HOUSE, TO CALL THE AUTHORITIES RIGHT AWAY, AND TO GET AWAY AS SOON AS SAFELY POSSIBLE.
>
> 3. TELL HER IT IS VITAL THAT SHE PROTECTS THE BOOK UNTIL WE ALL GET BACK- SHE IS THE ONLY ONE WHO CAN DO THAT NOW.
>
> 4. IF THE STRANGER GETS INTO THE HOUSE, TELL HER TO TAKE THE BOOK AND LEAVE, TO GO ANYWHERE THAT SHE WOULD NOT ORDINARILY GO, AND

> TO TELL NO ONE WHERE SHE HAS GONE. TELL HER TO COME BACK TO THE HOUSE ONLY WITH AN OFFICER OF THE LAW, AND BACK-UP! SHE SHOULD HAVE HER OWN INSTRUCTIONS BY NOW. STAY CLOSE TO HER.
>
> 5. WHEN YOU RETURN TO PROBABLEPOLIS, COME BACK WITH A SPEAR AND A HELMET. YOU SHOULD ALSO KNOW HOW TO DO THAT BY NOW.
>
> GOOD LUCK, NOWAR. WE'RE ALL COUNTING ON YOU.

Nowar waited until all the clocks struck nine, and then she padded back downstairs to wake up Grandma Brandy, the book held tightly in her arms.

Chapter Six

Simplicity Cubed.

Part One

et tu Poopsy?

Dooley was a Faerie, but not your ordinary Faerie.

Oh, sure, she had translucent wings. She had a cute little smile that would charm a warthog, she even had a slightly bent twig of Rowan wood that could keep her from getting smashed like a bug, but in truth, she was far, far more than just a Faerie.

Dooley was a spy.

Several ribbons ago, she had been asked by the King's most loyal advisor, Kai the Knightly Satyr to 'defect' from the household of King Shard and go work for Duke Moebius. She did, and she took valuable information with her about the household of the King. Her reward was to eventually wash a lot of dishes in the kitchen in Castle DeepSteel. She didn't care as she was there to be a double-agent. She washed a lot of dishes.

In other words, she had been asked to be a long-term double-dealer, a 'Benedict Arnold'. And she was a very good one. She spent an inordinate amount of time badmouthing King Shard and all the Kingdoms that followed him, eventually working her way into the confidence of the Merry Maids of Moebius, a group of bad-edged nasty faeries with broken wings that did the laundry and smoked clove cigarettes on the back porch of Castle DeepSteel with all the other rotten faeries.

Her ultimate goal was to plant a 'bug', an electronic spying device, somewhere special in the Moebius household- somewhere that she felt sure would remain close to Moebius, and largely untouched by anyone other than Moebius.

After a great deal of time, she had decided the moment had come to plant the device. She had long since recognized which item should be used for the 'bugging'. Carefully situating herself on the back of the latest Koradgian General being shown around the Moebius household by Clancy, Dooley had managed to sneak herself into the bedchamber of his most onerous slimeship.

There she found the one item she was sure would always remain close to the Duke, that would never be thoroughly examined, that he would confide every humiliating little secret to…

…his favorite teddy bear, Poopsy.

With great care she placed the spy-bug deep inside one of the tattered seams of the Teddy bear, and flew up into the rafters to find her way back to her little sleeping pod. She was anxious to go home to her family, **and** quit smoking.

Poopsy-bear, favored Teddy of Duke Moebius, was now also his greatest enemy, and the best chance they had left for the resistance.

Part Two

One bad strain deserves another

Andironé, King of the Elves, stood on the precipice of Kirhalion in utter awe of the monstrosity floating over the canyon. He thought to himself, "So, this is it, this is the Black Harp of Moebius, the Black Harp of Castle DeepSteel." And then he laughed a single short laugh without joy, such as elves rarely do.

Turning to his companion, Esceladus, who had a similar look of awe, he spoke quietly-

"It is as the others once were…it even looks like a harp…"

"But it's huge, my Lord."

"Aye, it is bigger than an Avatar, Esceladus. The last harp wasn't even half the size of what we behold before us today…"

It was big alright. Well over a thousand feet tall, cased in black plates of steel, with strings like iron cables as thick as trees. In fiery glyphs on the base frame read the words:

BLACK HARP v.13
A PRODUCT OF HELL INCORPORATED

This left no doubt as to the maker. This was most certainly one of the Duke's most important toys.

"But what is it doing here in our kingdom?" thought Andironé. It's not attacking. It's not even well-guarded.

Esceladus made a sign to the special operations squadron in the cavern behind them to hold tight. Normally, there were Koradjian scooters and Skreemers crawling all over the Kirhalion, but the eerie quiet was an indication that hardly a dozen ships were guarding this monstrosity at the moment.

"My Lord?" Esceladus broke the spell of contemplation that had taken Andironé- "Your orders?"

Without looking away, Andironé said, "Bring me an Omen-tary right now. We must send word to King Shard and all the Avatars of ProbablePolis. Whatever purposes this horrid thing has been made for, only the Precognitids and the Logos could possibly know, but something this big made by the mad hand of Moebius can only prefigure the greatest evil. Surely we look upon a thing designed to do one thing well, slay an Avatar"

Esceladus and one of his Sergeants quickly procured a small creature that resembled a cross between a bat and an owl, with a hooded head. With a nod from his liege, he removed the hood, revealing a transparent bubble where its head should have been.

Andironé looked upon the small raptor perched on his gloved index finger, and spoke softly to it while petting it - "King Shard, this is Andironé, your ally of old. Your Arch-Vizzerid was right. There is a strange weapon here at the canyon of Kirhalion, and it does indeed resemble an enormous black harp. It is lightly guarded, though, and in fact the entire valley is all but empty of the Koradjians encampments."

He took a breath and continued, "I fear the worst, old friend. My elves and I will return here with reinforcements and lay siege to the whole of Kirhalion. If you have troops to spare, we shall return here on the morrow. The Shiogue Kingdom of Kirhannok welcomes your assistance."

He paused once more, and then finished with- "The final war is upon us, Shard. Stay true. May the Logos be with you, and may you be yourself. Send word as soon as you can."

Andironé then kissed the head of the Omen-tary and gently gave it to the wind.

It rose quickly into the air, and barely a moment passed before a flurry of lasers and battleaxes surrounded Andironé and his elves.

The Omen-tary, using its own tiny Dwark-stone, vanished into a sky of Probabilities, headed on a journey to Castle Ambrosia, not knowing the King would not be there once it arrived; he was already on his own journey.

Part Three

Let the interview begin

Pop Bric had no idea how long he had been sitting on the stool in the Sepulcher of Silence as time seemed to melt away once he had depressed the blue button.

A deep violet light danced before his eyes and he felt he had fallen away, fallen into a trance. Suddenly, it was as if he had begun living every moment and instant of his life, but it was also like a recording machine, playing it all back at a ridiculous speed, pausing when he felt a particularly strong emotional pull from a scene, playing each and every experience he had ever had of being alive, at a speed too fast to contemplate or describe, right back to the first bauble he played with in a crib, his first scream for air- the first time he ever heard his mothers heartbeat, the first letter he ever wrote.

It had all been there, everything. The day he kicked his son out of the house, the day he found out that Brandy was going to have a son, the day his own Father had died.

When this very odd movie had finished playing backwards, he realized he was crying, and he did not really understand why.

Then the real recording began: it was his son, Shard, in a tiny screen on the small machine he had in his hands. All the dazzling lights were gone. The fire under the brazier had gone out, leaving the room with a strange smoky ambience.

His son was in a uniform, in some official looking room. He was just sitting there, facing the camera that had taken the shot, as if he was waiting for some cue. Then he spoke.

"General Bric, this is your son, Colonel Shard Rondell. Now that the Re-Memoress machine has finished with you, you should be able to both hear and understand me, and the context of the very important message I have for you."

ProbablePolis

He paused and resumed, saying, "I am leaving you this message because you have entered a synthetic simulation we call the MoonClock Project. The man who invented this alternate universe, Doctor Moebius, calls it 'ProbablePolis'."

Bells were ringing in Pop Bric's head. This was bringing it all back into the forefront of his mind. Yes, he was here to bring back his family, wasn't he? They were all in there, or, rather, they were all in **here** now. But if that **was** the case, where was his son Shard now? According to this thing, he was on Earth. He continued listening, hoping to figure this out.

"As you know, shortly after your daughter-in-law, Doctor Limberly, went to work for Doctor Moebius, he vanished into the MoonClock Project with her and her staff assistants. Somehow, time and space are distorted in this holographic projection in a way we don't understand yet. For example, approximately a few hours ago, after years of work, our scientists were able to create a new doorway into ProbablePolis, and, even though to the best of our knowledge no one has used this doorway to do more than glimpse into this alternate reality, we have discovered that you and your grand-daughter have already gone through it."

"We're quite baffled by all this, really."

This was quite a de-briefing, and it wasn't making things that much clearer, really.

"And that's not all. There is at least one other individual from our external reality in there other than Limberly, Moebius, the three assistants and you two, but we can't determine who that is yet."

Suddenly Bric realized that it had to be Shard himself that they were picking up, but when Shard made this message he wasn't in here to begin with, apparently. Bric was beginning to get a headache- clearly a wrinkle in time had been formed.

Shard took a deep breath, glancing at someone there who could not be seen on the screen before continuing, "Here are a few facts that may help you along the way to being able to get yourself, Nowar, and Limberly out of this thing."

"One, you all may have abilities in this alternate holographic universe that defy the laws of physics, specifically with your intent and desire. In other words, through a state of concentration, you may be able to do outlandish and powerful things that change the nature of that reality. You can only do this, apparently, just so many times in periodic cycles of time, until the MoonClock resets itself and your 'powers' are refreshed."

"Two, it appears that Nowar can temporarily return to our own world when she goes to sleep in that one, but apparently, until all eight individuals are returned at the same time, the probabilities of our own world will always send the others back into this alternate universe, over and over again, like a big pinball machine."

"Three, apparently the entire simulation is being driven by an autonomous and highly sentient artificial intelligence program called the LOGOS. Shortly after Doctor Moebius kidnapped Limberly and the rest of their office, the LOGOS interface here in the laboratory deleted itself from memory, and no one has been able to get it to contact the Main Program. Somehow, it's still operating in there, in this other universe that Moebius created, and not operating out here at all. No one out here understands this yet."

Shard moved the microphone to the side and moved closer to the camera. "Dad, we still don't understand everything that's going on in 'there' or, for that matter, out here, but we think we can use this device in your hand to establish another link, to at least communicate freely with you. It's programmed to 'wake' Nowar, Limberly and Shard in the same way it did to you. Don't lose it." He smiled.

Another deep breath and he continued with – "In one more hour of time here on our end, we are going to try to establish a gateway, and I may be coming in myself to try to bring you, Nowar and Limberly back out."

Some static was beginning to play across the screen.

How could that have been? He mistakenly sent Shard and his best special ops picks several years ago! He remembered it! Or had this little machine malfunctioned? Now he was beginning to doubt many things he had taken for granted before.

Shard paused for another breath, he seemed to be getting ready to sign off- "If it's possible, you should try to avoid using your special 'abilities' in ProbablePolis too often. Use the power wisely and not too often, as we believe Moebius finds it easier to detect you and Nowar everytime one of you uses these abilities. If you can, look for Nowar first. For some reason, Moebius is trying his best to get to her before he gets to the rest of us. See if you can-- " the static had been growing rapidly, until it encompassed the entire screen. Bric shook the device, and lightly hit it on the floor.

"Oh, come on, you cantankery thing, come on!" but it was no good. The lighted screen went out, leaving Bric in near-darkness. He yelled something unrepeatable and was about to see if he could take the thing apart. He had been trained as an electrician in his youth, and it was possible that-

"Bric."

The voice in his head was so deep, so omni-directional, so pervasive, that it nearly scared him off of his stool. He looked around, reaching for a weapon he didn't have. That's right; he was still naked as the day he was born. Hm.

"Who's there?" he yelled, and got off the stool, backing up against the cold wall, still clutching the small Memoress machine in his hand. "Who is it?"

"I am the Logos."

Bric looked around for some indication of who was there with him. He realized there was no one here or there. The voice was truly in his head.

"You are the one who brought me here, aren't you? It wasn't my son who sent me all those messages on my computer. It was YOU."

"Yes, Bric. It was I who called upon you. I am the Logos."

Bric's heart was pounding a little less now, while his mind was beginning to pick up the slack. The real de-briefing was about to begin.

"Right. And you are the computer program that is running this whole simulation, correct?"

The voice, which Bric noticed was somehow calming him more everytime it spoke, was laughing now- "Computer? Program? Simulation? If these words bring you joy, you should keep using them, kind sir, though I confess I find it very entertaining that you have begun the interview without me."

"Interview? What are you talking about?"

"Not yet, Bric. Not yet. All in good time, and all time is good, is it not? First, I want to extend my gratitude to you for the speed with which you answered my summons. Your timeliness enhances the emergence of the desired probabilities substantially."

"What? I don't understand"

The Logos laughed again- "My apologies. I do not often speak so directly to your kind, so I am still learning how best to transmit meaning and knowledge, and love with appropriate clarity. What I meant to say was, because you came so quickly when I called you, the chances of a happy ending are increasing by the moment."

That sounded like good news. Bric brightened and straitened up. "Well, that's good news, right. OK, so where do we begin?"

"With your interview, kind soul."

Bric allowed his mind to work on this statement before he said, "What is the reason for the interview, Logos?"

"Whatever you wish to believe I am, or represent, I can only tell you with surety one thing- I am the Sanity of this Universe, the Guardian of the Truth, the fiery element and penetrating Reason of which every soul here is a part. I am the one binding, organizing Intelligence that created this Universe and operates all things in it, including the destiny of the many, and the one."

Bric raised an eyebrow, but kept quiet. Whatever he was talking to, it was in charge, and he shouldn't get too snappy with it, he realized.

"Probabilities are running amok, Bric. Your help is needed. Out of the current crop of candidates, none is quite right, and at least one is all wrong."

"What's the position?"

"Why, the position? The position is Emperor. Emperor of all ProbablePolis."

Bric sat down on the stool again. He was feeling dizzy.

Part Four

Second Best at the Fish fry

Marúk was finally pleased with the hunt.

As son of the Queen of Mermopolis, Marúk was expected to lead the great annual SeaQuest. This was his first great hunt. This was a passage not of merman-hood, but of Kingship and merman-hood combined. On some years, the SeaQuest was little more than a deep-sea free-for-all, with every Sea-Ogre and Selkie hunting down anything they pleased.

Not this year. This was the year that Marúk was to be crowned Prince-of-the-Realm, and he was determined to make his mark. Nothing less than a Great Sea-Kraken would do. Never mind that no one had even **seen** a Great Sea-Kraken in more than fifty ribbons in the oceans of T'ien Shann.

Marúk, soon to be Prince of Mermopolis had been out-at-sea for many, many pulses, combing the deep trenches with his most loyal Mermen for a sign of the elusive Titan-of-the-Sea. The SeaQuest had gone on for quite some time now, without a trace of so much as a baby Sea-Kraken. When word reached Marúk that an Elder Angler Whale had been sighted, he decided to settle for second best. The fact that it was one of the largest Angler Whales ever found somewhat made up for the fact that Marúk would have no Kraken to be crowned upon.

Arriving on the scene in his great conch shell chariot drawn by sea-horses the size of greyhound buses, Marúk beheld a marvelous sight indeed. For hundreds of yards in every direction, up, down and sideways, cages of glowing jellyfish bobbed here and there, casting a pale blue glow across hundreds and hundreds of sea-denizens; mermen, mermaids, sea-ogres, shark-tailed sea trolls, gutter-trumps and sea-wyverns, all surrounding an absolutely enormous Angler Whale with their glowing tridents, huge nets and spears-that-shot lightning.

The Angler Whale was clearly perturbed and quite aware of its dire situation. It had backed itself into a huge crevice, protecting itself from all sides. Occasionally it would lurch out, swallow a few of its adversaries and shimmy back into its crevice, bellowing and struggling into a tight fit.

It was only a matter of time. Reinforcements were arriving by the droves every minute.

Marúk was finally pleased with the hunt. He raised a mailed and gauntleted fist to his loyal subjects to signal the final close.

Mermopolis would eat well tonight.

Part Five

The Plumber always rings thrice

Nowar had tried her best to sleep without any success. Everytime she started to doze off, she felt a shock go through her body, and she finally got up and sleepily struggled down the stairs to fall asleep right next to Grandma Brandy.

When Grandma Brandy woke up she felt like it was Christmas. Her grand-daughter, the greatest gift of all, was back in this world, snuggled up next to her. Grandma Brandy hugged her Granddaughter and fell back asleep. Things did not seem so bleak and strange anymore.

Then the doorbell rang.

It was 2:10 PM in the afternoon.

Grandma Brandy stood up, shook the sleep from her eyes, looked adoringly at her little Granddaughter and hurried to the door.

Now Grandma Brandy, you might recall, was the one who had 'eyes in the back of her head'. Being largely of Welsh and Irish extract, she had a keen nose for when to be protective of her own, and she was unabashed in this manner. Once, long ago, on a cold winter night, someone had come to play an accordion on the front step to busk for money and everyone agreed they had never seen an accordion fly so far when Brandy drop-kicked it. It later turned out that the accordion player was in fact a local burglar.

Given that things had been so very hinky lately, the last thing Grandma Brandy was going to do was open the door to a complete stranger. She peered through the side window at the front deck, carefully surveying the porch and the individual who stood there.

In the driveway sat a white truck with a big painted logo on the side.

MOEBIUS PLUMBING
WE GET THE LEAD OUT.

The man on the front porch was a short dark haired man with a huge handlebar mustache and a wide, asinine grin. He looked more like a little ice cream vendor than a plumber. Grandma Brandy squinted at him, and then closed the drapes slowly. This wouldn't do at all.

The plumber brows united with displeasure, and his fat little hands rang the bell again, and then one more time even- this time waking Nowar up. She sat up quickly, looked at the clock, and gasped with horror- it was after 2:12 PM! She had to warn Grandma Brandy not to let anyone in! She ran into the foyer, headed for the front door but never made it. Grandma Brandy grabbed her by the arm and yanked her into the closet, shushing her to be quiet. She whispered to Nowar.

"Don't say anything. I don't like the look of that plumber. I get a bad feeling about him." she said.

"Madam, you have nothing to fear, I'm just a friendly neighborhood plumber looking for a leak. I believe you have a busted pipe under your house. Nowar just smiled and nodded at Brandy. This was good. She jumped a little bit when they both heard some more rap tapping on another side window. She whispered to Grandma Brandy-

"So you didn't ask for a plumber to come to the house, right, Grandma?"

"A couple days ago, but not this one, that's for sure. I called the Plumber I always do, Mr. Magillicuddy."

Another rap-tap-tap on yet another window clearly got Grandma Brandy aroused and riled. She looked like she was about to go and pull out the can of whoop-ass on this hostile and unknown plumber from the twilight zone, when Nowar grabbed her nightgown.

"No, Grandma, please don't. This is no ordinary plumber!"

Grandma Brandy looked down at Nowar and said "What do you mean, Nowar?"

"It's the Duke. This sounds nuts, but he looks like the evil Duke Moebius from the world of ProbablePolis! Somehow he's figured out how to get back into our world! He wants to steal the Book, Grandma, and he wants to keep me and Pop Bric from getting Mom and Dad out of there too!"

Grandma Brandy was awake enough now to remember everything her husband had told her the night before. This was starting to make sense. She would have to call the police. She grabbed Nowar, ran to the bedroom and dialed '911'. As she was rattling off their address to the operator, Nowar tiptoed out into the foyer. She looked through the window. No Moebius.

Then she heard the noise under her feet.

"Grandma Brandy! He's under the house!"

He had got into the crawlspace and sweating like a pig, was desperately looking for a way into the larger basement. Grandma Brandy knew it was only a matter of time before he figured out that one of the ventilation openings would get him where he needed to go to get into the rest of the house.

She whispered to Nowar. "Grab the book and get ready to run out the front door with me."

Nowar ran to the bedroom and grabbed the book. Before she could say ProbablePolis, Grandma Brandy had opened the door to the basement and thrown a flea bomb down the stairs. When the plumber got into the basement, he was in for a nasty surprise. That stuff was worse than nerve-gas!

Locking the door to the basement, Grandma Brandy threw open a closet door and grabbed Pop Bric's Elephant hunting rifle. With one fluid movement, she loaded the rifle, grabbed her Granddaughter's hand and ran for the front door. She put the keys to the van in Nowar's hand and said-

"We're out of here, baby cakes! Here's the plan- you run to the van and jump in, lock the doors behind you until I get there."

Nowar nodded. She already knew what Grandma Brandy was planning. By the time she had gotten herself into the van and latched her seatbelt, Grandma Brandy had already blown a huge hole in the left front wheel of the Moebius-mobile AND the radiator grill. Steam rose in the air as the van slumped to one side, looking for all the world like it was about to tip over.

By the time the plumber had extricated himself from the foul foggy crawlspace, Grandma Brandy, the rifle and Nowar were already halfway down the driveway, cackling loudly and listening to Grandma Brandy's favorite oldies station on the radio.

Hurling his hat on the walkway with the greatest vim and vigor, Moebius pulled out his communication device and barked a number of things that seemed to be in English, but will remain unpublished for the moment. Finally, when he had calmed down, he said-

"Get me out of here, Clancy. Beam me back, RIGHT NOW!"

"Uh, sir, are you alright? Do you need medical attention? Do you have the book?"

Steam was still coming from the Duke's balding head, or, rather, whisps of toxic fog from the basement.

"The Rondelles are formidable enemies Clancy. Getting this book back is not going to be nearly as easy as I thought. I'll be headed back there for another go at things after I take a bath!"

Clancy silently agreed though he suspected the Duke would soon have plenty else to keep him busy, with an abundance of problems Clancy had been monitoring, many of which had to be destined to distract his attention back to the upcoming show, er, war in Probablepolis.

Part Six

The Silver Scream Nine, unique by design

Mandrake the White had no choice but to be hauled along by the vicious Dwark-Spider, following the trail of a newly reconstituted Hieronymous Quantum Jones hurtling forward into the Dwark. He knew exactly where he was headed. Occasionally, the Dwark-spider pushed Mandrake here and there for no particular reason, taunting and poking and tormenting him along the way with delight. Dwark-spiders are foul and loathsome things indeed, and their venom causes one to become incapable of speech or movement. Even Angels are not immune to their bites.

It was a considerable length of time on this nightmarish journey through the Dwark before they came within sight of the monstrosity that Jones had spoken so highly of, Robo sapiens sapiens.

It was indeed a monstrosity, like nothing Mandrake had ever seen before.

It was encased in scaffolding, floating in the Dwarkness, high above some page, yes, it seemed to be a Kingdom, but Mandrake could not tell which one, it was far off in the background.

What he beheld, looming into the foreground was unimaginably horrid to see. It was an enormous embryo of articulated shiny steel, as big as the biggest skyscraper you've ever seen. Its body was like a panther, though, and the sheen of silver glinted everywhere in all its joints. Its tail was like a cluster of great long steel cables that whirled and whipped about it idly while it slept, curled and coiled up into itself. It was connected by a gigantic umbilical cable to a great spherical latticework, deep in the scaffolding.

Its head was the scariest thing of all. It was a ghastly mouth in a perpetual grin, filled with great sharp teeth, each as big as a dinosaur, and they all interlocked perfectly with each other in a lurid ghastly grimace. In place of a face was a titanic transparent bubble, filled with a green, bubbling glowing fluid. In the fluid floated a simply enormous brain that pulsated to some unseen rhythm that cascaded in arcs of green lightning across the breadth of the body of this malevolent creation. It was breathing, and, dreaming, but of what?

As they got closer to this abomination, Jones skittered back through the air and hovered in front of Mandrake's face. Mandrake was about to feel his doom, and they both knew it! What an end? Mandrake sorrowed for the destruction of one of his Four, himself!

"Behold you insipid tool, the future of ProbablePolis. Before your very eyes is the first prototype of the next great race of our era, Robo diabolus sapiens! Behold the Silver Scream Nine, UNIQUE BY DESIGN!"

With that, he cackled again, lost in his reverie. Suddenly sobering up, he greeted a Koradgian on a small hovering platform that had come to investigate what the ruckus was all about. Sheathing his weapon he addressed the Precognitus with no small amount of respect.

"Lord Jones well met! Hail Moebius! Hail Hell Incorporated! Is there anything I can do this pulse to assist you and your retinue?"

"Has the Silver Scream Nine been fed today?" Jones coyly asked.

"Not yet, we are expecting a cargo hold of fresh sea serpents from T'ien Shan in a short while."

"Excellent fair, for we have some new fare for our growing boy. This feathered fool with pinions tattered will hardly make a snack for the Silver Scream, but we can't keep him around forever, he's already overstayed his welcome. Moebius has given the word, here's all the necessary paperwork. Now, would you do me the honors of escorting the Dwark-spider over yonder and ridding the Dwark of this mere fourth of an angel?" he smiled broadly.

"With great pleasure!" the Koradgian motioned to the spider to follow him, but the spider did not follow. Clearly it was spooked by this huge silver monstrosity, and would go no further. Frustrated, Jones screeched to the reptilian Koradgian-

"Get on with it you scaly bumble brained boob. Just take the angel and do it yourself!" he slapped the Dwark-spider that looked sheepish indeed, climbing back into the shadows.

The Koradgian deposited Mandrake clumsily to the floor of his hovercraft and steered it back to the enormous spherical scaffolding surrounding the Silver Scream Nine. Puttering along as it was, Mandrake struggled to his knees, watching in silent horror as the hovercraft puttered forward, slowly closing in on the head of the giant steel abomination. Its perpetual smile was both enormous and horrific.

The angel prayed with all his soul. As the Koradgian slowed the hovercraft to a stop in front of the hideous maw, it began to open, slowly exposing its enormous teeth of steel, emitting a sickening sound that harrowed Mandrake to the bone.

And then a miracle happened. He had been feeling the Dwark venom starting to wear off for some time, but suddenly he felt he might utter a sound, -a word, a spell! Yes! He cleared his throat quietly. The Koradgian did not notice this, though, and hefted Mandrake over his shoulders, signaling to his far-away comrades that he was prepared to hurl this carcass into the oblivion of a waiting maw.

Clearing his throat yet one more time, Mandrake the White croaked out the spell of the Great and Unquenchable Fire of Heaven-

"SOTHERION OURANOTHEN TSADAQAW!"

Fantastic blue and white flames exploded everywhere, ripping apart the hovercraft, sending the Koradgian, in flames, hurtling into the abyss of the waiting mouth.

The mere fourth of an Angel was free, though, and wasted no time. He fled, with the strength of the Heavens, and he took wing, headed back to the 7th Kingdom, grateful to the Logos in the highest.

Meanwhile, back at the ranch, Jones did angry little circles, scanning for a trace of the Angel with his various little scopes and probes. The Dwark-spider, utterly freaked out, was sailing off, back into the Deep Dwark.

Jones could find no trace of Mandrake, and became so angry that one of his newly repaired battery packs popped off and plummeted away into the Dwark.

The angel was gone- and…the Silver Scream Nine was awake.

Part Seven

In defense of the King

The words of the Precognitus, Maximus Lotus Knobb, rang in his ears still-

"You must go on a pilgrimage to seek out the Holy Well of Souls and speak to the Elder Narrator, the last Great Oracle and incarnation of the Logos."

"And then what?" he thought to himself.

And then what?

Well, here he was, and now here he stood, barefoot and knee-deep in freezing snow, surrounded by a whirling maelstrom of ice and hail. Here and there, a few licks of lightning rippled across the hilltops below, accompanied by groans of thunder. He had come to the coldest part of the Kingdom of Avalhalla, Mount Údas, considered by most to be the tallest and oldest mountain peak in all the Fourteen kingdoms of ProbablePolis. Below him in the underground catacombs was the Well of Souls, where he had been told to go.

King Shard, perhaps one of the greatest living tacticians of ProbablePolis, was about to consider his situation carefully, when he was viciously ambushed. The pommel of a great sword struck him soundly on the back of his head, and it struck hard. He fell to the ground, barely conscious.

A bitter smirk played across the face of Onus as he strode over the fallen King, his wings spread wide in dark victory. Behind him, to the side, whirled Shkaw-hawn, hovering in the air, coalescing in small whirling patterns of broken mirrored glass, tinkling peacefully in the winds.

"What unbelievable luck, Shkaw-hawn! We de-dwarked right behind the High King of ProbablePolis, none other than the big blow-hard himself, and he took a perfect blow, now, didn't he…eh?"

Shkaw-hawn's voice sounded like a talking chandelier, barely recognizable as speech- "Enough chit-chat, dispatch him quickly, Valkyrie. He has more lives than a cat, and we all know it now"

"Aye, aye. All in good time, my shattered friend…though they say all Homo sapiens are immortal…allow me but seven seconds to revel in this moment."

Grasping his sword with both hands, Onus raised it slowly above his head, aiming carefully. Onus never missed. His blade, 'Vengeful Venom', pulsed hungrily in his mailed gauntlets. For but two seconds, a huge and malefic smile spread across the face of the fallen Valkyrie like the shadow of cancer, and then he bellowed out a curse in the tongue of Moebius that rang across the mountain peak-

"Úrúgal-shé Ba-ra-r'ed!" Which might have been translated- "The wrath of Hell be upon ye forever!" and unceremoniously heaved the sword down with all his might!

But it was not meant to be. Scant inches before the blade struck, Onus went rolling in the snow, struggling explosively with a furious Satyr that had yelled "For Ambrosia!" as he tackled the Valkyrie, nearly knocking the both of them off the mountain top.

The explosive arrival and battle-scream of Sir Kai awoke the King. Shard's eyes fluttered open, and he gasped deeply.

Shkaw-hawn, sensing the tables were indeed about to turn against them, as he had feared in the first place, swirled rapidly up into the air. Forming himself into a hammer of shards of glass, he hurled himself down onto the fallen King with a huge whoosh and crashing THUD! Then, becoming a whirlwind of nasty sharp edges, he began to mangle every inch of King Shard, shredding and ripping with delight as he laughed!

Shard, realizing the danger he and Sir Kai were in, wasted no time in calling upon the Logos –the given birthright of the line of Ambrosia-

"May I be clad in my favored suit of dragon-armor, and equipped with my finest blade." He thought to himself, and he was.

Ripples of sound and light shot everywhere. His armor had been one of his most treasured belongings, having saved him from many, many assassins blades- great plates of Black Wyvern skin over steel and Crimson Wuerm wing, fastened with silver mail blessed by Inannatar, mother of the Elven King, Andironé.

The armor foiled the massive cloud of jagged glass all around him, though he still bled, and was short for air, gasping and looking around him.

Wish number one was done.

Unsheathing with grim determination his long sword, Shard rolled to the side, rose and went into action.

'Darrogarr na Roi' was the name the sword had earned for itself through the pulses of the great ribbon. 'Excellence of the Noble Line', it was called, and Shkaw-hawn quickly began to lose more pieces of himself than he could count, shrieking more and more with every slash.

Nevertheless, a sickening thud and crunch turned the head of the King for an instant from his opponent- Sir Kai was fallen! Onus had dealt him a horrid, and possibly lethal blow. Shard's face went pale. His childhood companion…fallen. Everywhere the snow was turning red, and darkness falling fast across all Avalhalla.

Lowering his sword and staring at Onus, who turned now with a gleam in his eye, Shard lunged toward the evil Valkyrie, growling with a full and throaty voice - "May an evil wind take you, batter and shatter you, -litter your bones and your feathers over the edge of Avalhalla without delay!"

The ripples exploded everywhere, and it was as if Onus had become a rag doll in a tornado, whipped up into the air and out of sight so fast that anyone present would have been left with their head spinning and their jaw open.

Wish number two.

Shkaw-hawn, seeing first-hand now the great power of the Ambrosian King, and sensing that wish number three would likely result in his own utter and violent dismissal from the world of ProbablePolis, grabbed the Dwark-stone that had brought him and Onus to Avalhalla, and made himself very scarce without delay. He considered what to tell the Boss, and wondered if there was anywhere in the Dwark that he could hide from that madman and his blaster.

The King thrust his sword into the red-stained snow, and knelt by his good and loyal companion, Sir Kai of Ambrosia. Cradling him like a baby, he cried hot tears that spattered like rain on the face of Kai. Good Sir Kai did not breathe.

"Oldest and dearest friend- by my soul, may you live again."

A sharp intake of air was all it took to let Shard know that Kai was still there.

Wish number three had been granted, and the Logos was with them both.

As darkness crowded the peak of Mount Údas, the laughter of two tired old, wounded friends could faintly be heard over the howling winds of Avalhalla. Kai had brought some strong drink, and it helped them both nap around a small fire they had built on the oldest tallest mountain in all the worlds.

They had been through much worse, these two, and they both knew it.

Part Eight

Jo-na, I wish I'd known ya

Marúk proudly rode his giant sea-turtle over the underwater valley of Antares. His gauntlet lightly held the reins while he occasionally glanced backwards at the processional- behind him a whole pod of giant sea-turtles were dragging the enormous carcass of the largest Angler Whale the Mermopolians had ever seen.

For a moment he idly considered that even his deceased father, Jo-na O Nanna, would have been quite proud of him. Now all that was left to do was to bring forth the trophy and lay it before the great coral gates of Mermopolis. They were nearly there, and rays of sunlight dappled along the kelp forest below them, scintillating beautifully as hordes of mermen, mermaids, kelpies, shelkies, sea-ogres, dolphins and sea-wyverns rode through the undertow, headed gracefully towards the enormous cerulean bubble under the sea, glorious Mermopolis!

It was with some disdain and displeasure that Marúk watched the approach of a sea-chariot that held Cornelius Leviticus Dobbs, Precognitus-to-the-Queen, and her closest confidante. A busy body if he'd ever known one, Marúk absolutely detested Cornelius. The creature was constantly interfering. A complete gadfly, spoiling any ointment he came near.

Clearly, this time would be no different than any other. Couldn't he just let a Merman revel in a brief pulse of glory?

"Prince Marúk." The chariot slowed down and whirled around. Marúk did not oblige by slowing the procession, and Cornelius apparently knew Marúk well enough to know he wouldn't slow down for a moment. Puttering along, the Precognitus kept up the speed in his chariot.

"Prince Marúk, I bring you a very serious message from your mother the Queen."

Marúk looked at Cornelius with a furrowed glare but said nothing while his tongue was firmly held between his upper and lower teeth. He was silently counting to a hundred.

"Once you have brought your trophy to the coral gates, you are instructed to allow myself and my associates to open the belly of the Whale and extract something of great importance therein."

"What?" Marúk growled. "What on earth do you expect to find inside this glorious trophy but squid guts and a troll-shark or two?"

"I expect nothing, Prince Marúk. 'Expect' is a word one uses in the absence of 'Knowing', when possibilities are not yet probabilities, eh?"

"Spare me from your Precognitive pandering! If you tear apart the gullet of the whale we shall not be able to roast it properly in the volcano, we shall have to filet it and fry it in a hundred ovens. It will delay my coronation banquet!" His mates nodded vigorously with him.

"You have been given direct orders from the Queen by her plenipotentiate, if I must remind you of whom you speak with. I *EXPECT* you to obey those orders. Let me know if I should *expect* otherwise, Marúk." And with that he puttered off, back toward the coral gates of Mermopolis, leaving Marúk to curse quietly under his breath.

Part Nine

Out of the mouths of babes, and the claws of crabs

Bric was still squatting on his stool, with his head in his hands, trying to figure out what his next move was, when he became aware that he was not alone. He could hear a low shuffling sound behind him.

Standing up slowly and turning around, he beheld an enormous entity, which quivered as he turned, and stood quietly only a few yards behind him, apparently waiting to see what he would do next.

It appeared, in the dim light, almost like a beautiful silver sculpture of a crab, perhaps nine feet tall and thirteen feet wide, but it quivered like a bashful boy. In the place of claws, it had several sets of large beautiful steel hands. It gingerly held several clothes hangers out from its metallic body, from which hung a suit, a general's uniform.

His uniform! His old uniform from before he retired from the Air Force!

What was going on here?

"Allow me to explain." the voice came again. It was the same voice of the Logos, but it was not in his head. It was directly behind him, here in this chamber.

Pop Bric turned around again, this time whirling about swiftly, to see- a child? A small boy, perhaps seven or eight years old, stood just a few feet in front of him, beaming with a great big smile. He was a pale white skinned, thin little fellow, with ruddy cheeks and platinum colored hair.

"I figured you would want some clothes. Both sets are yours."

"Both sets?" Bric turned his head and saw the giant metal crab point to a stand to its right on which hung a suit of mailed, plate armor, replete with sword and shield and helmet.

"Yes, both sets."

ProbablePolis

Pop Bric looked back at the child and said "So, you…are the … Logos?"

"I have chosen this manifestation at this time for several reasons, one of which is to make you feel more comfortable in our discussions, another is to underscore what I truly am to you- in a sense I am projecting a residual self image of something your subconscious mind will eventually trust and listen deeply to with all your heart. Yes, I am the Logos. I come to you as a child. Is that so hard for you to accept?"

"Uh, no. No, it's not, I suppose."

The Logos smiled and suggested to Bric that he get dressed. While Bric put on his old uniform, the Logos continued the conversation.

"I fear I am embarking on a rather cumbersome way to explain the crux of the matter, but to put it plainly, the game of ProbablePolis has been a very difficult one for us all --"

A chessboard appeared and rotated slowly while the Logos continued the soliloquy. Occasionally, certain pieces moved while he spoke, emulating the points of his dialogue. Some shattered, others melted while the game board peeled off in ephemeral pages that dissolved in thin air.

"ProbablePolis has a captured Queen who knows far too much yet cannot move, she is pinned, captured in a media of green goo, a concoction of Moebius. Then we have a King who remembers far too little and does not understand the end-game, he is also experiencing the side effects of trifurcation, which I will explain to you at the appropriate time. It was an unfortunate choice I had to make, but it may be the only way to put all things right again in both worlds. I suffer with him, of course, that's part of what I am."

The General wanted to ask what Trifurcation was, but the Logos signaled there were other things to talk of first, and continued.

"Then we have a Princess who is just beginning to get her 'sea-legs' in her new world. She is the hope of us all, in truth, Bric."

He paused for a second, and then went on, saying "Last and now least, we have a mad, frighteningly powerful Duke who was a King, but who has been asked to leave, or step down. He will do neither, we all know, and he will more than likely drag all fourteen kingdoms of our world into a horrible and lethal struggle in the very near future. His abilities and devices have grown greatly in power since he first came here."

General Bric was nearly finished putting on his uniform. He adjusted his tie and took his hat from the big steel crab, who watched his every move in silent but happy fascination.

"The only way to safe guard ProbablePolis through all this difficulty is to appoint an Emperor. Someone we can all trust. **That** is the position you are being interviewed for."

There was silence in the sepulcher. The crab looked at the Logos, then at the General, then at the Logos again. The Logos smiled, and continued with;

"I had a number of questions I wished to ask you during this interview, but now that I am in your presence, I already sense all the answers but one already. I am quite satisfied with the answers you are prepared to give, but I am hesitant to ask the one question that hangs in the balance."

Pop Bric raised his other eyebrow. "Like what?"

"Well, I know that if I asked you whether or not you believed in the power of free will, you would say you did."

"Well, of course, we are all given the ability to change."

"Right! -and yet I also know that if I asked you what your theory is on the nature of time you would tell me that the Past is mutable, and the Future is fixed."

Pop Bric remembered telling his own son that on many occasions.

"And of course on the surface the latter seems to contradict the former, and on and on. But the one question I am hesitant to ask is-"

"Go ahead. It's time."

The Logos smiled deeply. "Yes, it's time." And paused briefly, looking down at the ground- "If I offer to help you get your son, his wife, and their daughter out of ProbablePolis, would you still come back to visit us once in a while?"

"What? I don't understand? What do you mean?"

"What I mean to say is…" and now the child walked up to Bric, and reached out for his hand. Bric allowed the little boy to take his hand. "What I mean to say is that I will get lonely again, without humans here. I have come to enjoy them immensely. Their unpredictability is amusing, their ability to speak of things with a fresh perspective, denying the prison of Probability, is charming, and, well, frankly, once I help the citizens of ProbablePolis to get rid of Moebius, if the master plan works, the rest of you will go home…and…" the child's voice quavered. Bric finished his sentence for him.

"You'll be lonely."

"Yes, General, I will. I will be very lonely again, like in the Beginning."

It was very quiet in the chamber called the Sepulchre of Silence. It seemed like it would go on forever. General Bric was the first to break the silence.

"Alright, son. You'll get your wish."

The Logos smiled and said "Thank you, Bric. Thank you very very much."

The crab was smiling too.

Part Ten

I scream you scream we all scream for more ice cream

Brandy and Nowar sat in the van eating ice cream cones.

The police had called Grandma Brandy on her cell phone. They had found the Plumbers truck out front, but no sight or clue as to the whereabouts of the driver. The plates were a fake. Grandma Brandy thanked them and asked them what she should do with the truck. They said they would have it towed and send a car to check on her in the evening.

Grandma Brandy looked at her granddaughter and said, "Now what?"

Then the cell phone rang again. Grandma Brandy looked at the cell phone like it was a rattlesnake. Nowar asked what was wrong. Grandma Brandy handed her the cell phone. It was a text message from an 'unknown user'. It said:

> Don't go home tonight and
> Don't tell anyone where you are.
> Go to a computer at the local library
> and check your email.
> It's very important. Good luck, Grandma Brandy.

Nowar looked at her Grandmother and passed the phone back to her.

"Who do you think that is?" Brandy asked Nowar, sensing she would know the answer better than anyone now.

"I think it's the Logos, Grandma. I think the Logos warned us about Moebius this morning, and I think it's time I went back into ProbablePolis."

"Not yet, honey. Come with me to the Library. We're going to check my email before you go back in. I want you to know what that email says."

Brandy, proud of her smarts, but worried that she was missing something, drove to the library without getting a speeding ticket, and the two of them walked quickly to a monitor. Grandma Brandy logged onto her account, and going through a host of what she called 'spam and green eggs' she found the email that Bric had told her to look for. It said:

> This next step is important, Brandy. You need to gas up the van and drive strait to the Air Force Base at MoonClock point. Don't go there until Nowar has re-entered ProbablePolis.
> The driving directions are below.

"MoonClock point? Isn't that where my mother and father used to work?" asked Nowar.

"Yes honey, and, though you didn't know it, Pop Bric used to work there too, just before they started that horrible project that took your parents from this world."

Nowar sensed something was wrong. Brandy was crying now, sobbing tears. Nowar touched her gently. "Don't worry Grandma, we're going to get everyone home, and soon. You wait and see."

"I know, dear," she said, trying to stop crying, "I know you will. I have faith in you and your grandfather. I just want this all to be over, and all of us to be home. There's no place like home, Nowar, there's no place like home."

After a few minutes, Nowar kissed her Grandmother goodbye, and opened the book. For a few seconds the van interior was filled with light. When the light was gone, all that sat on the passenger side of the van was the book. Grandma Brandy stowed it quietly away in her very large bag, and took a look at the directions.

She made a quick check to make sure the Elephant Rifle was loaded and still in the back, and then looking around suspiciously to see if anyone was watching her, she started up the van, and headed for the highway. It would take her nearly two days to get there with the van.

Grandma Brandy made a silent prayer, a Hail Mary, and put her 'pedal to the metal'. Pulling out into the fast lane with the authority of someone who knows where they are going, she picked up speed, headed north for the long drive to the Jersey turnpike.

She had an appointment with destiny, and she would not be late.

Chapter Seven

When on a roll, don't stop to butter it

Part One

A tale of two queens

The Queen Limberly was floating in a strange green fluid that removed all sense of time, and made it very hard for her to think about much of anything for very long. She had no idea how long she had been here, or for that matter, where here was. She had goggles over her eyes, so it was always dark, and something plugged her ears as well so she never heard anything but a dull roar. Something in the green goo she breathed instead of air was always making her giggle.

She had been bobbing about there in a large tank of this fluid for a very long time now, surely, and that was funny, too, wasn't it? The tank was lit by strange lights and layered with odd devices that measured odd things. The room that her tank was in had once been a very fine place, filled with antiques and interesting keepsakes. Most were broken and in bad repair. Someone should call room-service she thought and napped for a while, giggling to herself that someone would eventually explain why she was here to her.

Moebius sat in the dark on an old chair, watching the bubbles rise. His face contained a scowl wrapped in a grimace. He was muttering to himself.

"Had to have it your own way, didn't you?"

He knew she couldn't answer that. He had taken care of all of that. This was his top-secret green goo, it was specially made to do what it was doing now. Nevertheless, a captive audience was a favorite for Moebius, and he continued.

"I offered you everything, you trollop. A new salary and a new title… upgraded security clearances…and then, a chance to be a new Eve in a new world- and did any of it make any difference to you?"

Silence. Her giggling was muffled by the goo.

"Of course not! Then you decided to turn your back on me, refuse to take my advice…started to make amends with that chowder head, Shard! And, what's worst, you actually started to **believe** in this absurd simulation I had created"

Silence.

"So what if he was your husband? I offered you domain over a whole new world, powers like no one could believe or understand…and did you appreciate any of this? No. Not one bit."

Clancy unlocked the chamber door and skittered in saying "Uh, sir?"

"What?" Moebius did not look away from the mindless floating woman in front of him.

"We fixed the Limberly-9."

"Good. Is it speaking the proper language now? Is it going to break on us again like the Limberly-8? That whole scene where I was proposing to her was supposed to be touching, instead it came across as nonsense- the Limberly-8 kept repeating in some obscure Cave Troll dialect 'I am not programmed for making emotional decisions, you must marry the aardvark'- gadzooks, man, it took the romance right out of the air, and raised new suspicions amongst the Guards of Evergreen. My god man, the Limberly-2 was sufficient for helping us defeat Shard during the last Tweak"

"The Limberly-8 was dicey sir, for sure. No worries. Now, I had the new unit bugged and de-bugged for hours and all the Guards that witnessed the scene slipped on their tea this morning and are taking dirt-naps, at your request."

Moebius was feeling a little more secure. Clancy continued "As long as you stick with the script, she'll perform as expected."

"Fine!" Moebius rose and began to walk to the doorway.

"Uh, sir? What are you planning on doing with the real Queen after today?"

Moebius looked at his captive Queen, and something angry and bitter lit in his eyes.

"Under cover of night, we'll ship her to Castle DeepSteel and put her in deepfreeze. Then I will feed her to something big and obnoxious, when it suits me to do so. Come Clancy, I am about to become a married man and add another Kingship title to my litany of honors, come and join us for the festivities."

After Moebius had walked from the room, Clancy turned briefly, and kneeling to the floor, deposited a small silver stone by the doorway.

It was a Dwark stone.

Part Two

The second leg of a journey is never as hard as the third leg

When Nowar opened her eyes, she immediately knew that she had 'come back' to ProbablePolis exactly as the little girl in her dreams had wanted to, and although she wanted to try to remember as much as she could from her dream of the other world, Ouroboros Alpha pulled her from her meditation with his cry of glee-

"She's back. She's back! See, I told you she'd come back!"

Ouroboros Beta said, "Aye ye did, and look at her will ye? She's stylin' and profilin' with all that gear."

Nowar looked down at herself. She was wearing a suit of mail armor, all shimmery and glittery like fish skin. Next to her shield was a spear, and a helmet. They were very fine indeed, both etched with runes and sigils that she felt like she should know. The interior compartment of the Lens was fairly dark, with only a few small lights flashing. She could see the silhouette of Two Fangs on the other side, with Mandrake looking away from the periscope.

He smiled deeply, and said "Welcome back Princess Nowar. I see the Logos has chosen to give you a weapon and armor befitting your rank and station. This bodes well for us all."

Nowar nodded and said "Where are we?"

Two Fangs answered without moving, "We are still in the belly of the whale." He was watching through a hatch window, though it looked too dark to see much of anything. The Lens was rocking back and forth, jiggling slightly.

"Is it digesting us? How long until we run out of air?"

"Interesting questions." answered Mandrake the Black, "Two Fangs insists that the whale has been killed, and that its carcass is being hauled somewhere by someone."

"I think he's right," said Alpha. "The deep bellowing noise we heard for awhile was most certainly its breathing, and it's stopped for sure," and looking at Nowar said, "For a brief period it got very loud, and then, eventually, stopped altogether. Then the walls of its gullet closed in around us so we can't even open the hatch and look out anymore."

Two Fangs added, "And there have been strange noises all around the Lens, like something scratching and clinking against the thick walls of this things carcass."

Nowar was about to ask another question and stand up, when the whole Lens rocked about violently, and light rays erupted through the windows. Something was dragging the Lens along a bumpy surface!

When the bumpy ride stopped, Two Fangs slid his weapon out of his sheathe, and climbed up to unlock the top porthole of the Lens. Mandrake prepared his trident, and Mrs. Machine quickly drew a tiny laser gun from one of her compartments and began hushing everone else. Hurling open the porthole, Two Fangs howled as he leapt out of the Lens. Mandrake followed him with a yell, and Mrs. Machine flew out right behind him with various devices beeping, clicking, and aiming. Nowar, caught in the moment of excitement, had grabbed her spear and shield and was about to follow Mrs. Machine when she took a quick glance at Ouroboros Alpha-Beta.

"We'll guard the Lens while you all are gone," Alpha said smiling. Beta nodded hurriedly and said "Don't let us delay ye, now. Ye're very impressive wi' all yer gear an all."

Nowar smiled and leapt out. They were in a simply huge, but beautiful semi-aquatic cavern, partly carved, partly crafted by nature, like an enormous hall of fabled Neptune. Behind them was a gigantic body of water that heaved and swelled. In front of them was a huge staircase, spiraling upwards out of sight.

They were still under the sea, it seemed, under a great glass arched and vaulted ceiling, surrounded by a horde of semi-aquatic folke. Mer-men, sea-Ogres, all manner of small two legged and many finned creatures, many holding nets and waiting, apparently, on a signal from a very bold and graceful mer-man, who stood, staring at them, hardly a few feet away from Mandrake and his outstretched trident.

"Greetings, Angel." He said, with a booming voice.

"May the Logos be with you, Marúk." Mandrake responded, and lowered his weapon.

It was very quiet again. Mandrake chose to speak again, but first he chose to bow.

"Many gracious thanks for pulling us from the belly of the Whale. We were in fact on a journey to reach this very place when we were caught and devoured by the beast."

"Not everyone believes in providence, Angel. Some still believe in coincidence. You were lucky, indeed. Why were you trying to come to Mermopolis, and why were you coming in a Lens from the UnderRung?"

There was an interruption at this point. Some creature had come down the stairs, and was pushing its way through the crowd with great vigor, making quite a fuss. Nowar could see that it was a Precognitus.

Cornelius Leviticus Dobbs wasted no time in making his way to Marúk, and loudly proclaiming- "The Queen, your mother is waiting, Marúk. Further investigation and interrogation should be done in the throne room, not down here in the lobby. This is no way to treat honored guests. Have you learned nothing?"

Marúk was obviously biting his lip so hard it would kill a normal man, but to his credit, only addressed Mandrake, "Very well, Mandrake of the UnderRung, I shall bring you and your company to the throne room where you will have an audience with the Queen."

Mandrake rose from his bow and only said "Thank you, Prince of Mermopolis, thank you kindly." He nodded at the Precognitus, who only looked worriedly at the ground.

Ouroboros Alpha-beta poked both their heads out, saw that there was no ongoing conflict, and quickly crawled down the side of the Lens, and over to Nowar's side. Beta murmured to her "Nice to be a guest for a change, and not an item on the menu, ay?"

Nowar nodded her head, though she wondered how long their status would stay that way.

Part Three

Of Satyrs and Kings and Emperors

King Shard was trying to remember. It had been many, many pulses of the ribbon since he had been to Avalhalla, much less the Sepulcher of Silence. He knew it had to be close. Lotus Knobb had been explicit with this sacred, secret knowledge of the location for sure. He had managed to bandage Kai's wounds as best as he could, and was supporting his weight as they both limped along, but the darkness was still closing in…

…and Shard had used all three of his 'wishes' already.

Here and there, they slipped and slid together on the ice, occasionally barely clutching on for dear life as they realized they were on a treacherously thin cliff edge. A few times they comically slid into a pile in places, narrowly close to spiraling and dizzy heights.

"We'll make it, Kai. We've been through worse, remember?" Shard smiled while he breathed. Kai was freezing and chattering now, but shot back a quip.

"What? This? This is nothing. Remember the lava flows in Storok-Vol? I was the color of lilies before that little incident. Ha! The Satyr lasses love a tan, you know, milord."

"And were it not for me, you may well have turned to the color of lilies before the night was over, Satyr," came a deep booming voice over the howling wind that was neither Shard nor Kai. The two stopped in their tracks, but drew their weapons without hesitation, their backs to each others'.

The voice continued, "Those will hardly be necessary. I am here to guide you to warmth and safety, if you have a care not to fall into that frozen ravine over there before the night is over."

Out of the shadows came Khan, the winged sabre-tooth tiger that had guided Bric to the Sepulcher. Shard cried in delight! His old companion! Could this be a mirage?

"Khan! Old friend! By the Logos, what extraordinary circumstance brought you here?"

"No idle chit-chat for us now, 'boy who has grown to be a King' - our fine Kai is injured, and the temperature rapidly dropping. I must return with you to my post. Answers will come later. Follow me to the Sepulchre."

Counting their blessings, the two hobbled along through the thickening snow, following Khan back down into the cavern where the Logos and a new Emperor were waiting patiently for them.

Part Four

Chip off the ol' block

"Are you my Mother?" came the bellowing boom of a voice from the Silver Scream Nine's stainless steel vocal chords attached to lungs almost as big as a skyscraper.

Jones, a precognitus-at-large, had been in the process of puttering away as fast as he could, and then immediately stopped. He pretended to be part of the garbage that floated around the area, and turned off all his power sources.

"Are you my Mother?" came the blast again, shaking and rattling Jones where he floated. He could feel the thing about to say it again, and in anger turned and said-

"Of course not, you nitwit!" then, seeing the indication of some negative emotion begin to play across this metallic face as big as a football field, decided to amend his original statement-

"I'm your Father."

The enormous toothy grin of the Silver Scream Nine grew wide and sinister.

"Daddy!" it cried, so loudly that most of the garbage around Jones went flying off. Jones, suddenly realizing that he had just won a potentially great advantage over Moebius, turned about and puttered toward the monstrously sized Robo sapiens, and perched like a small sparrow on it's outstretched monstrous claw.

"Yes, that's right. **I** am your Father. And **you** are the Silver Scream Nine, unique by design. How do you feel, son?"

Lights bounced around the green ooze that contained the enormous brain of the Silver Scream Nine. "Hungry, Daddy. Need food."

Jones thought over his response carefully. "Follow me, son. We're going to go get you something to eat." Jones said, and began to putter off through the Dwark.

"OK, Daddy. Where are we going?" the Silver Scream Nine asked, slowly moving it's bulk. It was capable of gliding efficiently in the Dwark, and it tagged along, just behind Jones. In its wake it left screaming Koradgians and flying scaffolding everywhere.

"We're going to a place with tons of delicious, moving food, and I will let you loose for as long as you want, my dear boy…and then we'll be off to Castle Ambrosia…and if you can't get enough to eat in all those places, we'll jaunt over to Castle Evergreen…and maybe even Castle DeepSteel for just desserts…but first, as I said, we'll get in some practice in a place called The UnderRung, just for payback"

Now the world would tremble, thought Jones, and all these silly humans will be forced to leave ProbablePolis, once and for all. Fourteen pages indeed. "ONE PAGE and only one page!" was more like it. Jones boiled quietly to himself as the Silver Scream nine, like a giant hungry evil steel puppy, hovered along happily behind him. Daddy would take him to food. Good food.

The Silver Scream Nine was in his happy place.

Part Five

Who do ju-jitsu?

A very funny notion occurred to the Midnight Shadow. Moebius was going to invade his whole world. And soon. And not just the Under-Rung, but the whole seventh kingdom, Mermopolis and Hovahnon included; the whole nine yards.

He would have to do something about this. Now.

He was about to begin a strategic session- to call upon his advisors, when his most trusted counselor was brought to him, barely in one piece.

Mandrake the White was lacerated, broken and beaten, missing feathers and one of his eyes swollen shut. The Troll sat him gently in a chair by the Midnight Shadow.

"What happened, old friend?" the Black Unicorn asked the one winged angel.

"Treachery…Jones." He coughed and spat blood on the floor.

"What else could it have been? Spare me the details for now- what did you discover?"

"Moebius has a weapon like nothing we've ever seen. It's made of steel, as big as an Avatar, in full-sized aspect, and it appears to be intelligent. It is ten times bigger than any of the Silver Screams we saw in the Last War. It may still be asleep, but who knows for how long." He coughed some more and then said "Jones called it the Silver Scream Nine. It is truly horrible to look upon, like nothing we have ever seen. I would not have wished it upon my worst adversary, though now I confess I might change my mind for the sake of Moebius."

The Midnight Shadow then understood this as a premonition once more. Mandrake had been correct. Speaking to no one in particular, he whispered-

"And Jones will bring it here first, for good measure and spite, for he had to have had it in his mind that he would convince me to let you go with him into the Dwark."

"Aye. I would suspect as much, my Lord. Difficult to keep from being taken into a briar patch by one who knows the future already, eh?"

The Midnight Shadow nodded to the Troll as well, who covered Mandrake in a blanket.

It was time for a counter-thrust, disguised as an exodus. The Midnight Shadow knew what he would have to do. It was time to call upon the High Council of Ambrosia, it was time to let bygones be bygones, and speak with the Angel, Menses, or perhaps even Duke Kai himself.

Part Six

Them's fightin' words!!!

Out of all the receptions she might receive from the Queen of Mermopolis, Nowar did not expect the frosty stare and silence that was waiting for her in the vast and opulent coral lined throne-room of Riganna O Nanna, the mighty Lady-of-the-Sea and Mistress of all Mermopolis Bottom.

But that is what was waiting for her. The throne room was filled with colorful creatures of all sorts, some of them lounging in pools, others skipping about in the air, dragging colorful balloons of water and shimmering starscapes on banners. Their festive nature soured quickly once they had all arrived at this semi-submerged grand palace.

Riganna O Nanna sat impudently coiled in her throne, with her tails all about her, picking at her armor, playing almost like an idle child with the tips of her trident. Nowar began to have a bad feeling about the environment she and her little group were now forced into.

The Precognitus Cornelius Leviticus Dobbs broke into a humping ungainly jog that developed into a puttering as he took to the air, apparently sensing something wrong. He approached the throne, looking nervous. He was a Precognitus; he knew what was about to happen next.

"All these years, and we never suspected you of this kind of treachery, Dobbs." -the Queen lashed at the Precognitus with such speed and savagery that the entire court-in-waiting sucked in a big breath and stood silent. A screw fell to the ground behind them that had popped off of Dobbs face. Only Marúk gleamed with a look of sincere appreciation. Had his mother finally come to her senses?

As a Sea-Ogre bent over to help Dobbs, the Queens voice went shrill in her command.

"Leave him be, or suffer the same fate."

She did not have to say that twice. The Sea-Ogre and two or three Selkies quickly moved back away from Dobbs, nearly broken in two, and still crawling toward the Throne. As he did, the Queen flapped one of her tails onto him to topple him over. Nowar looked around at the audience, and noticed that they seemed uncomfortable with their Queen's actions as well.

Ouroboros Beta whispered to Alpha "She's wound kind of tight for a queen wouldn't ye say?" but Alpha hushed him quickly.

Two Fangs growled and brought his hand to his antler. This did not bode well. This is not how he remembered the Queen of Mermopolis acting during the Last War. When did she turn into such a haughty crone? Mrs. Machine looked agitated and clearly wanted to come to Dobbs rescue, they were both 'children of silicon', after all.

Dobbs voice, though soft and clouded with static as well as short, sharp crackling sounds, easily carried across the silent throne room. "My Lady, why do you act in this way, what have I done that thou wouldst forsake me in this fashion?"

"Your treachery is unimaginable, Dobbs. You knew SHE was coming here, you had to..and you allowed **her** to come here, perhaps even paved the way for **her** to take my throne for all I know, now…didn't you, and then worse, to join with Gull and Crones to dash all the pages of ProbablePolis into little bits all across the Dwark. You said **she** is the one from the prophecy of the Book of Scorns, but what you didn't tell us is that **she** will be the one who starts the final ruin of Mermopolis, aye, and all ProbablePolis as well. I have read the Book of Scorns for myself, you boob, and I say that **She** is no savior; I say that **she** is the beginning of our end!"

Dobbs looked totally disheartened, but he had also figured something out.

"My Lady, I had asked you not to speak to Moebius again. He has turned your mind against you. Some of these things you say, they cannot be true…"

"And am I not Queen? Shall a Queen of Mermopolis be ruled by a Precognitus or the Madman Moebius? I think not, you monstrosity of silicon. I will speak to whomever I wish whenever I like. Bear this bag of silicon bones away, Grotark; he shall be imprisoned with all the other traitors of our realm, in the deepest darkest pits of the icy nether waters that run beneath Antares."

The Sea-ogre, accompanied by two mer-men, gently picked up Dobbs and bore him slowly away, trying not to damage him any further in the process. As they passed by Mandrake the Black and Nowar, Dobbs vocal device sparked and hissed.

"Nowar! Nowar!" The mer-men stopped for a few seconds while the Precognitus struggled with them both, showing it had more life left in it than they had assumed. He seemed possessed now, as if he would not be silenced until he had spoken to Nowar.

"Nowar! Blessed Nowar! I thank the Author that if I am to be destroyed that it shall be only after I have saved you from my own fate. Heed me, child! Invoke your right to divine combat. The Queen may not refuse you in this! It is the law of Mermopolis. If she will not fight you herself, she must choose a champion. Choosing a Champion will humiliate her, and YOU WILL PREVAIL!"

The Queen was screaming again "Silence him! Silence HIM! WHY do you dally? TAKE HIM AWAY!"

An overzealous Sea-Ogre brought his mailed gauntlet down on Dobbs, bearing him to the cold stone floor. Dobbs spoke no more. Sparks flew here and there as Nowar sank to her knees, kneeling by a pile of twisted and mangled cold metal, as cold as the ground it was piled on, and as cold as the stare that came from Nowar as she looked up from the mangled heap.

She had not really known this creature, but he had thoroughly redeemed his people in her eyes with his last utterance to her. "Not all Precogniti are evil, like Hieronymous Jones" she thought to herself in a flash- "This one had tried to save her!"

Her eyes were brimming with salty water not of the sea. Nowar's arms were shaking and her heart pounded like a runaway horse, but her mind was clear, and she was filled with a desire to make sure that Dobbs would not die in vain.

Nowar stood now and turned to the Queen once more with a stare colder than the stone that Dobbs laid on, and betraying none of the emotions that were coursing through her spoke slowly, and loudly, so that everyone could hear-

"I am Nowar, from a world you will never know-"

A hush grew over the entire hall. Nowar hardly paused an instant before she cried out-

"-and I invoke my right to divine combat, Queen Riganna of Mermopolis…"

"I challenge YOU, HERE, and NOW!"

It was time to break some eggs.

Part Seven

If you aim for the roof, you might hit the stars...

It was midnight at the Rondell mansion, now emptied of all of its human inhabitants. We know for sure that it was midnight, since a sea of clocks on the bottom floor insisted as much; gonging, bonging, and ting-ting-tinging in batches of twelve, echoing their clatter all the way up the stairs to the top floors. The most solemn hour of the night had begun in earnest with a racket.

All manner of rare and exotic items of the past had been sitting in stillness in their hallway cubbies until just a few minutes ago, hoping that they might be picked up soon, that their memories might be lovingly caressed to the surface. Perhaps notions of history would wake too, as if from a deep, deep slumber amongst the cacophonous clatter of a clan of clocks.

Or, perhaps not...

In the shadows, once the quiet was reclaimed, only a single tick-tick-tock of the Great Grandfather clock could be heard, towering regally at the top of the second floor, right next to the attic. It opposed another such sentinel, equally noble in character: a gargoyle ensconced seven foot tall ornately carved mirror from the early 1920's, loitering at the other end of the hallway by the banister, wondering if "The Depression" would ever come back again.

Once again, the mansion was quiet, but it was no longer empty.

The man appeared out of nowhere, just in front of the Grandfather clock. Lines of grit and determination played across his clean-cut face as he walked across the hallway. He wore a very rugged, Astronaut-looking suit that might have seemed ridiculously bulky and huge on a smaller man, but it seemed to suit him just fine. He looked like a man on a mission. His helmet was tied to his belt. His vest and suit smoked a little; as if he had just walked out of an oven; he looked tired, though. The name plate on his vest read "Lt. Colonel Rondell". He walked, almost stumbled, to the other end of the hall, and then disappeared into the mirror. It rattled slightly, shot a few beams of light off in every direction, and then went dark.

Moments of tense stillness passed, as if the house was waiting for the other shoe to drop and then the clocks busily began to note the passing of another fifteen minutes. Again, just as the clocks started their chorus, Lt. Colonel Rondell appeared, this time wearing a suit and tie, looking several years younger, wearing a pair of sunglasses. He was being chased by a very active, seven foot tall semi-human cephalopoidal creature with nasty claws and slimy tentacles.

It looked hungry and well-motivated.

They both disappeared into the mirror, much as the armored Lt. Colonel Rondell had mere seconds before. The cephalopod was just inches behind its prey as light shot out everywhere, and both were gone. The mansion was empty once again.

And that's where probabilities began to go up for the Rondell clan.

Intermission

What goes up, might just come down - - but where?

No one really knew why, except perhaps for the narrator(s), or perhaps even the Great Narrator, but from this point onward, there will be no more "Chapters" or "Parts" of "Chapters" in the great Tome of ProbablePolis.

Bid them all goodbye.

Instead, there will be, as you will see, "AntiChapters" and "AntiParts" of "AntiChapters".

And they will go backward, as time winds down. Suffer this or not, but consider that what appears initially as just a gimmick is in fact an important contrivance, and we can offer only one bit of advice for those who like to get to the bottom of a mystery before it's done: Patience, patience, please.

Patience, by the way, is the fourth dimension, if you've never been told this before. Don't listen to anyone else on this point, much less geometers, who have their own non-Euclidian agenda to grind. Height, width and depth are all lovely for setting up the first three dimensions, but unless you have patience you're still lost.

And for those of you who are dismayed enough at the sudden disappearance of good order to contemplate dismissing this tome out of hand, well, it's hard to say for sure, but if I were you, I would definitely keep reading. There's no telling what could happen now if you stopped reading while the AntiParts have started....

The second half of the book is about to begin. Intermission is over.

AntiChapter Seven

The Steaks are raised

AntiPart Seven

Dog save the Queen

Nowar lay in a lump, dazed, bleeding, not quite sure of what had just hit her, and then the boot in her rib cage reminded her. She was now in hand-to-hand combat with one of the greatest warriors in all the history of the 7th Kingdom, the great Queen of Mermopolis. Riganna O Nanna was known for her vicious skills with a Trident, and her penchant for destroying her opponents like a child destroys a giant chocolate Easter Bunny—bit by delicious bit.

Nowar had barely gotten the words of her challenge out of her own mouth when Queen Riganna whipped her flail across Nowar's face with impressive speed and force, sending her whole body careening like a rag doll across the throne room. Not an impressive beginning for any Princess, much less one that allegedly was here in ProbablePolis to fulfill a Prophecy.

At the moment she was gasping for air.

The quiet hush that had taken over the assembled throng in the Queen's throne room was now broken by the yelling of Ouroboros Beta, who could hardly contain himself.

"NOWAR! The Logos is with you! Fight back kid, fight back!"

Alpha, horrified at first that Beta was bringing such attention to the both of them, suddenly turned back to the fight scene and began yelling himself.

"Don't give up, Nowar! Beta's right, we need you, child! Fight back!"

Very unlike Alpha, thought Beta, but perhaps fortunate as well, as it caused almost a whole seven seconds of pause, while the Queen turned briefly to see if this foolish two headed lout would need to be dispatched as well. Apparently not, though just to make certain, she made an impatient gesture to her body-guards, who quickly slithered, crawled and hopped over to the Companions. This was a ritualistic dual that no one could be permitted to interfere with. Period! -even the body guards understood that whoever won this challenge would either become, or remain, the great Queen of Mermopolis-bottom and that was a very serious matter indeed. No one could interfere.

Two Fangs looked stricken, and kept glancing at Mandrake NeverSong, one winged Angel of the UnderRung, who stood still as a statue, betraying not the slightest hint of what was going on inside his mind or his heart or his soul. Ms. Machine looked like she was about to have a stainless steel cow, twittering and leaking oil everywhere out of her rivet holes as she vibrated. A screw or two shook loose while she shook and shuddered.

Nowar lay wheezing on the ground, reeling slightly still from the Queen's spectacular lunge and first blows. The attacks had been vigorous. Ribs were broken. The smell of death was in the air- hers, if she did not get up and fight. Get up, she screamed at herself, in her own head.

The Queen, satisfied that the Companions would not interfere with the duel, turned her attention back to the pathetic thing on her throne room floor and slowly edged toward Nowar. As her long shadow crossed Nowar's bleeding face, the Queen felt the glory and exultation of towering over her foe. Raising her Trident high with both webbed hands, the Queen felt victory in the air and readied herself, her face cold and without a hint of emotion. It was time to send this upstart back to the Source, assuring that Mermopolis would not be attacked again by Moebius, and of course, that she would remain Queen. This was her destiny. This day she had protected her birth-rights.

"Do something!" snarled Two-Fangs to Mandrake. Mandrake did not so much as quiver in response. His wings were tied, metaphorically speaking. If Nowar *was* the child prophesied in the Book of Scorns, this was where they would all find out for sure, once and for all.

Nowar wiped blood from her eyes, realizing she was about to take a lethal blow. This would all end, without her ever knowing who was real, her or the little girl. How horrible! Alpha and Beta were both screaming now, causing yet one more second of hesitation as the Queen gave one last glance to make sure her guards were in place and that none could interfere with her final moment of triumph.

Quietly Nowar thought to herself - "If I could be lent all the knowledge of all the arts of victory in all ProbablePolis, I would stand and fight you right now, you evil witch."

It was her first wish of the new pulse. Plausibility instantly became Probability, and ripples of light shot out in every direction from her body, causing yet another hush to fall on the crowd that stood all around the throne room floor. The brief wisps of rainbow kaleidoscopes faded.

Mandrake whispered to no one in particular, "That's more like it."

The Queen barely hesitated, suddenly sensing a balance had just been nudged out of her favor, and hurled herself with all her strength into a lunge with her mighty trident- cracking the floor beneath her, barely an instant after Nowar effortlessly rolled out of harm's way, and with a single fluid motion, snapped herself to her feet.

Her spear lay almost ten feet away. The Queen, realizing that her Trident was embedded in the floor, whipped out a short but savage looking two edged blade and with a swift motion hurled it furiously at Nowar.

Nowar plucked the blade from the air as if it was the most natural thing in the world and whipped it back at the Queen in the same fluid motion, rotating it ruthlessly as she spun the blade, turning it back with nearly triple the speed and force it had come at her to begin with. As the Queen barely deflected the blade in time from meeting her face, a modest show of respect flashed across her composure; King Shard had pulled just that same maneuver on her many hundreds of pulses ago, the last time she had fought him.

Nowar realized she was still bleeding, and that her existing wounds would be a detriment, her pain a potential distraction to the combat.

That would not do. Watching the Queen carefully, she knelt to pick up her shield, barely uttering to herself, "Now that I can stand and fight, I would be whole and healed; fit as a fiddle in fact."

By the time the Queen was on top of her, her ribs were mended, the rip in her face gone, and her breathing came normally. She felt as if she had just woken up, refreshed, and now, filled with the knowledge of the arts of victory she met the clash head on with a great fury; using her shield aggressively, she hurled herself into the Queen, sending her soaring into her own citizens, knocking aside all manner of aquatic denizens for yards behind them. This humiliation was more than the Queen could bear, and she roared as she came back out of her prone position, thoroughly rattled. Her body guards looked at each other with concern. Their fins were still tied, metaphorically speaking.

That gave time to Nowar, who had managed now to retrieve all her gear- her shield, her spear and her helmet. The helmet was donned just as the Queen reached her opponent. Nowar ducked, deeply, sending the Queen, who was, by the way, still easily twice or thrice her size, rolling over Nowar's armored back into an ungainly heap on her own throne room floor. The Queen rose with a blood curdling scream, just as Nowar thrust the butt of her spear into the Queen's belly, bending her in extreme pain to her scaly knees. One swing, two, a third and a fourth from Nowar's mailed gauntlets, and the Queen's subjects began to look quite astonished.

The Queen of Mermopolis had never taken quite a beating since she had slain the previous Queen in a similar fashion, and everyone knew it. This was turning into a drama that would be sung in the Halls of Mermopolis for many tides to come.

But Nowar's passion was only beginning. She brought her shield and spear quickly, tightly, smartly against the Queen's neck, forcing her down to the ground. A sense of desperation and shock danced across her aquamarine face. The Queen's great tail was swishing everywhere, trying in vain to get a grip around Nowar's neck as she went down to the floor again.

For some reason, while Nowar held her in this position, she found herself growing angry, and spit angry words at the large face just in front of her own.

"Why? Why? Why? We came in peace, as guests! Mandrake was your friend!"

Her gills gurgled, but the Queen was incapable of answering. She was busy suffocating. Nowar couldn't help herself now-

"I didn't want to fight you, but you killed Dobbs, an innocent, in front of us all, and you were going to ditch us all in your darkest prison!!! Why? Tell me why I should give you one last chance to live, you evil witch!"

But the Queen, who was choking now, was incapable of a reply. The crowd now realized that they might be about to get a new Queen, and began to cheer in an almost macabre manner.

But Nowar didn't hear them. Instead, her face went slack as she felt a presence. She had the Queen in a death-vice, and she was not relaxing that, but somehow, her mind relaxed as she heard a voice, very deep and slightly melodious, echoing in her head.

"Nowar..."

Nowar was crying now, although she didn't understand why. With a huge show of force, she hurled the Queen, nearly lifeless, and far bluer than she normally should have looked, as far away from her as she could across the floor. The Queen slid into a column with a sickening thump, cracking either ribs or the marble, or both. She slumped over. If she lived, it was only but barely.

Nowar's anger, though, was still very much alive. She walked briskly over to the Queen and swung hard, right into her face. She slumped over again, even more lifeless, and Nowar raised her spear briskly. It was time to finish this off. ProbablePolis would be far the better for this act, and apparently this was what she had been brought here for—to clean up, to avenge, and to bring justice. She just wished the hot tears would stop, that her hands would stop trembling.

"Nowar…" the voice came again. Everywhere across the Throne room, silence reigned unchallenged, but no one could hear the voice but Nowar.

"WHAT!!?!" Nowar screamed, looking everywhere. She screamed. "What do you want? This witch murdered Dobbs, and would have murdered the rest of us. She does not deserve to live another INSTANT!"

"Mercy…"

"Mercy??? WHAT FOR?!?"

"She was not herself, Nowar. She was under the spell of Moebius."

Nowar looked around. She realized suddenly that she was the only one who could hear the voice. To the rest of the audience, she merely appeared to be losing her mind. The voice did not stop, however.

"She loved Dobbs dearly, Nowar. I tell you true. When she awakens again, if you let her live, she will suffer greatly for having been the hand that brought death to her closest childhood friend and court counselor. Cease your grieving, for Dobbs may live again, after a fashion, if someone cares enough about him to install his back-up copy in a new silicon sheath…all things are possible where great love and intelligence meet…"

Nowar was utterly baffled by the last thing the voice had uttered, but was stunned into silence as the voice spoke again almost laughing- "-furthermore, vengeance was never the reason you were brought here, dear little Nowar Rondelle. You are here to help get your family home, never forget that. Good bye and good luck, unremembering Princess of hope, have faith, and show the charity of forgiveness. No other way will heal you, or the land"

Nowar did not know who or where the voice came from, but somehow, she felt that what it was saying was true, just as it was gone.

The spear loosened in her grip. Still shaking, with her own trembling voice, she said, to no one in particular, "Your Queen will live, whether she deserves to or not," and walked away.

The bodyguards, unsure as to who was really Queen now, rushed in to see if Riganna still lived.

She did, but only just. They stared at Nowar, who had walked back to her Companions with eyes wet and shut tight, wondering why all of this had to happen this way.

Opening her eyes, and letting out a big breath, Nowar looked back at the viciously beaten Queen of Mermopolis. Nowar wished deeply that the Queen would survive, but not without a reminder that she had killed her childhood friend, largely because she could not heed his advice, and let herself be infected by Moebius' mind-games. Dobbs had warned her not to talk to Moebius.

Yes, Dobbs had warned her, and the Queen should have known better. Her pride and arrogance had effectively slain Dobbs, and nearly Nowar as well. Let the wounds heal quickly, but let her not survive without a limp.

The ripples that came from Nowar's hand were modest, and the Queen began to breathe normally. She would hobble on her right fin for the rest of her days, but she would live.

AntiPart Six

"The beatings will continue until the morale improves!"

Moebius stalked into his private office. He had a busy schedule. He looked at his notepad and saw that he hadn't barked at Clancy in a while- reaching for his intercom button he yelled into it-

"Clancy, you there? Gadzooks man, I'm doing an assessment of how things are going, and I'm not liking what I'm seeing, old boy! Things are getting hairy. Balls are getting dropped everywhere, and it is time for us to get a grip on this ongoing debacle and all these hairy balls, er, well I'm not taking any calls for the next ten minutes while I get organized, got it?"

He decided to take a second look at all the activities he had going on. He plopped a lollipop into his mouth, kicked back his chair and looked at his clipboard, where his agenda had been left by Clancy. Behind him, his favorite inspirational banner said:

"When the going gets tough, shoot them all and start over."

His brow creased while he maniacally sucked on his lolly. His to-do list read as follows:

ITEM ONE:

Activate the Silver Scream, have it rendezvous with the Fleet and proceed to T'ien Shann to kick some Black Unicorn butt!

ITEM TWO:

Have a pleasant chat with the Queen of Mermopolis, Lady Riganna, threaten her with utter destruction unless she capitulates, a lovely word meaning 'give up'.

He laughed to himself as he checked off Item Two. It had been an excellent conversation, really, and the Queen never even realized what hit her- Moebius had devices that made even the most stoic quite open to suggestions of discourtesy and disrespect and disdain, even if such things did not indeed exist in the first place.

ITEM THREE:

Fire up the ProbablePolis terminals and try Clancy's new hack, -the "MOEBIUS MANIA" program. Consider new game show to expand the Moebius franchise.

He hrumphed to himself. VERY Risky. Clancy wanted to try this, and kept pushing it onto his agenda, but Moebius kept ignoring it, and for good reason. He would love nothing more than to turn all those little suckers on and broadcast his dashing charming face all over every one of the realms of ProbablePolis, it could theoretically demoralize the rebels everywhere...but it was also conceivable that, if he turned on the Terminals now that the rebels could also hack into them- it had nearly happened once before, quite some time ago, and, if they figured out the central nervous system to ProbablePolis - they could cause all sorts of mischief. They could learn to control a whole variety of interfaces for the whole simulation itself, and then, good gravy, and then they might even gain access to his secret little Command-Pod!

Since the beginning, he had always had a small secret pod, floating off in the middle of the deepest Dwark, with a whole wall of screens where he could monitor all of ProbablePolis, **and** where he could actually get in and out of ProbablePolis just as easily as someone changes clothes. No one but Clancy knew about the Command-Pod or how to get to it.

If anyone ever got into his Command-Pod, they could easily possibly interfere with the hard coding on the Implausible Chip back at the MoonClock facility which could cause the whole simulation itself too screech to a halt, or worse. WAY too risky. No, not yet, perhaps never at all.

> ITEM FOUR:
>
> Test the Black Harp of Castle DarkSteel on an especially well loved Avatar, like, maybe the Cloud Tree Shane of Everlast. Get it all recorded for Moebius-1 news for tonight's line-up.

Gleefully he put a check next to Item Four. Already in process, per Clancy, the Harp was reported as arriving in Kirhannok and the crew was doing diagnostics before the big orchestral debut. Moebius rolled out a big belly-laugh, belched, scratched behind his ear, and continued with his agenda-

> ITEM FIVE:
>
> Remember to floss.
>
> ITEM FIVE:
>
> Dialing for Dimensions- Playground of Death Game Show.

He chewed on his pencil for awhile, making warthog noises and smelling his fingers every ten seconds. He felt disturbed, even more so than normally- what was he forgetting?

"Ah-HAH!" he cried! "Item Six- Execute Queen Limberly!"

He decided right then and there to have one last conversation with the uncooperative Dr. Limberly, and then ship her to some frozen wasteland in the Dwark for final processing into individually wrapped slices of cheese for his cooking show. He believed he had finally figured out how to destroy her, once and for all, and if it didn't work, he'd have a ball trying. He snickered at all these warm fuzzy thoughts, giggled like a school girl, and then made a note to himself to hire more help ASAP for more political assassinations. They were really very effective; and a lot of fun.

Humming away pleasantly as he maniacally nibbled his pencil down to a nub, he began dreaming up new innovative ways to punish these rebels and their friends, occasionally sniffing his fingers and counting backwards to calm himself.

A knock came at the door.

"Who is it?"

"Uh, it's Clancy, sir. We were all wondering if you were still going to host today's 'Dialing for Dimensions; Playground-of-Death' Game Show?"

Moebius grumbled, sucked some hot snot in his nose deeply, almost thoughtfully, wheeled his chair around, slammed his clipboard down, picked up his beloved Teddy Bear, Poopsy, and stalked out of his office.

"Come along Poopsy"

The burden of being a celebrity was getting to be more than he could handle.

AntiPart Five

A bad strain shared is evil cubed

A full assault had been ordered out of the great Elvish Capital of Kirhannok in Everlast.

The Black Harp of Castle DeepSteel had come to the 4th Kingdom with a vengeance, and the King was fallen!

The War against Moebius had been renewed, with a vengeance.

Andironé, King of all the Elves and other Fane citizens of the 4th Kingdom had been known far and wide throughout ProbablePolis as an example of a true leader, a great High-King - many called him their All-Father, and even the Giants, Dwarves and Dragons of the Kingdom were up in arms over this egregious act of war, mustering their Wyverns, winged Trogs quickly repaired mail and armor as they cursed the Duke. Moebius…again he had broken the peace, and now the ultimate insult, taken their King. Many of the older ones had been young and unproven during the time of the last Great War of Probability. They relished the opportunity to prove their mettle, and avenge the mighty King.

But their King was not dead, at least not yet. Barely conscious, bloody and bruised, he had been nailed to the topmost beam of the infernal black machine as it soared, howling over a vast twilight landscape of trees and valleys and mountaintops.

Picking up speed as it cruised out of the Valley of Kirhalion, and into the Valley of the Shadow, known to the elves as the Kirapocalyps, where the great canyons gave way to torturous winding mountains and heaps of dead cities, testament to the great empires destroyed by Moebius in the ancient past. The canyon of Kirapocalyps spirals downward into the great fertile central lands called the Summer Lands, a different valley altogether, where happy creatures of all kinds still thrived and cultivated that hobby called civilization.

The Black Harp of Castle DeepSteel was indeed heading to the Summer Lands of Everlast, at that very moment. Occasionally shrieking as it banked sharply, it would return to a relentless thrumming noise as it straitened its course. Far below, creatures great and small sought cover as a huge black shadow covered hedge, field and warren.

It was probably the pain in his hands and legs that wrenched King Andironé back to full consciousness. It had not been a nightmare, and it was not over. In a haze of agony, he beheld his own beloved kingdom flying with great speed below his bloody, broken and rent legs.

"Where is this damned thing headed?" he muttered, looking around. Then it hit him- it was headed to the Cloud Forest of Broceliande! To the very center pinnacle of the Summer Lands in Everlast! In horror, he realized this thing had to have been designed for one thing, and one thing only- capture, or more likely, kill, the Avatar of a Kingdom, and then allow countless hordes of monsters to move in from wherever they liked. No force on any of the pages of ProbablePolis could stand against Moebius without their Avatar!

He cursed to himself as elves rarely do, and whispered a silent prayer that the Omen-tary he had sent just before he was captured might reach King Shard in time, that reinforcements from the second Kingdom might be dispatched, yet a thousand armies could not defeat the last Black Harp of Castle DeepSteel, it was said in the Book of Scorns.

The Harp was slowing, encountering mists at the elevation it currently cruised at, causing it to burst forth with hundreds of rotating green search lights. It had to be looking for the Avatar Shane, the great old Cloud-Tree that had been friend and counselor of his own family, and all the peoples and dynasties of all the Fourth Kingdom since it had been unfolded.

Andironé began to struggle against his lashings and chains, crying out in pain, hoping his cries might offer a warning, as he was realizing that this thing could fly very slowly and very quietly if it had to.

He wondered bleakly if he would see another Pulse of the Great Ribbon, then he wondered if he would also have to watch his Avatar die today, unable to lift a finger to help.

AntiPart Four

If I could put time in a bottle…

What followed next was like a blur to Nowar, who had grown somewhat groggy, though she did not know why. The fight had taken more out of her than she had initially realized.

Opulent would not quite describe all the treasures littered here in the Queen's guest quarters. Some trivial but powerful mementos from the Ancient sunken lost 19th Kingdom of Ykhanhnon Drahch, where the dead race of Mer-Titans had kept the library of all the old kingdoms before the war previous to theirs.

Ouroboros Alpha had a field day, pulling books off the shelf, much to his other heads annoyance, Beta sighed and twiddled claws on his own feet. Alpha cried out, "There are books here from some of the forty pages and kingdoms destroyed during the last war! Look a lost edition of the "Prevalence of Nonsense", and even an unabridged "Lost murmurings of the Star People"

Beta replied laconically "Not bad, since the war before that one wiped out almost three hundred pages, ye'know!"

Two-Fangs watched their door-guard vigilantly, though it seemed impossible to imagine the Queen trying to 'do them in' again, and for what? She would risk renewed humiliation if Nowar could get anywhere near her.

Mrs. Machine did self-diagnostics, and the Angel was reclined and absorbed in gazing at a small sphere he was holding, a holographic fully three-dimensional movie-in-a-globe that he plucked from the nearby credenza. Nowar, who was tempted to coil up in a ball and sleep, but resisted so much as closing her eyes, waited and watched the one-winged angel for quite some time.

"What are you looking at?" she finally asked, still reclined on a nearby couch, her spear and shield sitting to the side of the chest of drawers by a bed that called to her still. "Not yet," she thought to herself, "not yet- I can't go back to being the little girl just yet".

Mandrake put the globe down on its stand, and said- "I was thinking about Mandrake the Gray, one of the four, of which I am but a part. I was looking back to a time before the last war of Probability, when all three of us were together, missing only Mandrake the Red."

Nowar stared at him. He continued, walking over to a futon covered with luxurious furs, sat down and said- "The globe on that desk is a '*Remembrance-arium*', a tool that gives an open heart a way of unfolding old memories that it once might have shared with another soul long ago on some bright sunny day, or miserable stormy evening." He smiled and went on- "You may try it, for I do not believe she would leave it in the guest room unless she believed it should be enjoyed by others"

"Bright sunny day?" thought Nowar. Suddenly she remembered that they were many thousands of leagues beneath an ocean, still on the very same page or Kingdom as when she first 'Woke Up' in the jungles of T'ien Sha'an…how long ago? She really wasn't sure.

Once the Queen had cleaned herself up, she sent her personal bodyguards to bring an entreaty to Nowar and the Companions in those same luxurious guest quarters.

Nowar had just started reaching for the globe on the board of the credenza next to her couch, when a knock came at the door. The globe spilled effortlessly into her hip pocket as Nowar turned and stood. She instinctively wished that it not be easily separated from her physical presence, and that she be able to use it for other things, as she needed. The ripples from this third wish were tiny indeed, and were hardly noticed as the whole room bustled to attention.

Mandrake and Two-Fangs had gone immediately to the doorway, which remained shut. Each opened one side, and the two very large mer-men in mail looked at the ground sheepishly. They were not here to make a fight, with anyone, about anything.

But they could not forget that their Queen had been beaten, and that Nowar by all their laws should now be Queen, or treated as such. It bothered them enormously, this bothersome contrivance, and one finally said-

"The Queen wishes to assist Mandrake, his Companions, and her Magnificence, Nowar, after the fashion that should have been offered to such honored guests in the first place. She will let you all use her private Purple Dwark-gate to escape from the Seventh Page of ProbablePolis, and thus, hope for amends to be made to all for all that has been suffered by her hand."

The other Mer-man, emboldened by the first then said directly to Nowar- "-and the Queen will offer her *own* apologies to your Magnificence when she can look you in the eye herself, Princess Nowar. If you wish, that may be now, My Lady."   .

AntiPart Three

I now pronounce you Man and Robot!

The court of EverGreen had been assembled for quite some time, in the rain, as well, as it were. Castle EverGreen lies in a green bubble transfixed in space above the great First Kingdom, the first page of all ProbablePolis.

Assembled in regalia finest were the citizens of every corner of the First Kingdom, waiting to hear if it was true; if the good Queen Limberly was able to speak again, and that her sanity had returned as well. A dirty rumor was flying around that Goode Queen Limberly would be marrying dastardly Duke Moebius this day, but no one believed that nonsense.

Now normally, mind you, these people complained of very little. Fair Castle EverGreen normally offered little to complain about, for this was a place, where normally, all things ran auto-magically with total temperature and weather control, perfect every day. Why it was downpouring now, just before their Queen was about to speak her first truly sane words since she was stricken with madness was a mystery to everyone, even the viziers. Could this odd weather somehow be related to the fact that their Queen had been acting quixotic, nay, thoroughly dangerous and eccentric, for many pulses now?

Pterosaurs and Giant Luna Moths navigated quietly overhead amongst huge dirigibles and zeppelins- all with banners in tow, all proclaiming slogans invoking the "Joy of the long Peace" that would come from the "Glorious union of the Houses of Limberly and Moebius". Some people saw the signs and booed.

Few understood what had really happened, of course. These people had been totally horn-swoggled and hoodwinked. What had been really happening was far simpler and even more sinister; the real Queen Limberly had long ago been somehow replaced by one of Moebius' special robotic inventions. This particular one he had hoped to eventually market as "a real woman for real men", but all the lizards and Koradgians that tested her neural circuits and pneumatics called her "The Limberly".

The Limberly v.1 had been capable of pouring tea and laughing outrageously, long after everyone else had quite forgotten the punchline. She did not bathe, which eventually proved to be a problem, but her lack of speaking ability was a hindrance to good communication skills. The Limberly v.2 would not come out of the bathroom, and chewed bubble gum in wads big enough to make her new speech patterns pathetic beyond disbelief. The Limberly v.3 spoke as elegantly as anyone could have wanted, but was full of woe, and murdered nearly a dozen servants at Castle EverGreen before a Limberly v.4 could be put into action. Version four did equally unspeakable things quite like the Limberly v.2 and v.3, only much better, and usually in secret.

The Limberly v.5 had been stable for weeks though, rarely babbled or chewed bubble gum, and Clancy was well on his way to creating an even better version, although it was still being tested for bugs. Duke Moebius, whose middle name was "Excellence in Impatience-plus", had been ready to pop in on the next scheduled court assembly just to pop the big question- would she become Mrs. Moebius and rule over the known Probabilities? The robot was supposed to be programmed to say yes, if he would do it on the spot.

Roses fell from his big grin as he swirled about through the crowd, dressed in a snazzy black suit and Top Hat, throwing candy bars and jelly beans everywhere. The crowd, though well-trained to be polite, couldn't help but wonder who the Dwark this smelly little candy-man really was, and — did he call what he was doing …dancing? No one believed it could be the Duke, though everyone said he would indeed be 'popping in' today for the court assemblage to make some important pronouncement. No one could care less what he had to say, of course.

By the time Moebius had worked his way up through the crowd both literally and metaphorically to the great Hall of EverGreen, the crowd had thinned noticeably. This was all too much for the now soaked citizens of the formerly sane EverGreen Castle. Those remaining ate their candy bars and jelly beans in stunned and wet silence, watching a fat little villain propose to his finest robot, all the while under his breath cursing the infernal weather machines of EverGreen as his new staffers trying to figure them out for the first time.

Was that lightning? Moebius cried out in horror. He was afraid of lightning, and he had had to leave his Teddy bear back in the EverGreen mobile-HQ bunker-bot with Clancy…and, oh no, this was all LIVE on MOEBIUS-1 Cablevision.

Clancy, from their little mobile, but now underground, bunker-bot watched the show, wondering idly if he shouldn't have stopped the video capture from rolling on the MOEBIUS-1 LIVE-TV feed, but hey, it hadn't been raining when Moebius first launched into his offensive and narcissistic prance up EverGreen Hill. "Oh well," he thought, "-we can airbrush out the rain and insert a few rainbows and doves over it all before we dump it in the archives."

Clancy wondered how long all this banality could possibly go on, and keep up its feverish pace as well. He was playing Nick Cave on his m-POD and he'd taken a sedative tea earlier, so he was largely in poker-face mode, and he was just plain sorry for all the viewers, mostly in fortresses and prisons with nothing else to watch. Oh well, Dialing for Dimensions was coming up soon.

The pathetic speed that the Reverend Precognitus used in presiding over the now very soaked ceremony added unmercifully to the absurdity of the event as he finally asked "Do you, great Queen of EverGreen, take the Duke as your lawfully married husband and King?" When he looked up with a slightly rusted Ocular lens at the Limberly v.5, she stared obliquely as she droned without missing a beat- "I do, but only on odd-numbered days." And looking straight at Moebius said "You can deal with that, right, little man?"

Moebius looked as confused as the Reverend, who apparently sensed how this was all going to shake down, and intoned "I now pronounce you man and tool, er wife, I mean."

Then, leaning forward, he whispered to Moebius "and yes, you should probably kiss the bride quickly, and then possibly tied her up as well, as I sense she is wet, confused, hungry, and ready to bolt at any time."

Moebius turned to the largest MOEBIUS-1 Web-Camera-bot, hovering just inches away from his face, and ran his finger across his throat- a clear message to Clancy to "Kill the Cameras!" and turn off the live feed to the millions of hapless and imprisoned viewers.

Clancy did so, and began to belly laugh, looking over at the Teddy bear, Poopsy. Clancy lit one of Moebius' cigars and flicked the red ember end for a minute in a small ashtray, then turned on some of the monitors for another crowd that had already assembled, quite some time ago, in the stadium arena audience of Castle DeepSteel, back on their own page.

This audience seemed calmer than the last, knowing how many of the last audience got eaten before the end of the show, but they showed some enthusiasm about the new rules posted, and they were there, hats and popcorn bags in hand, waiting for the most exciting and dangerous game show of all time to begin again…'Dialing for Dimensions; Playground-of-Death'.

They had no idea of what was in store for them.

AntiPart Two

This happened before the story had even begun, but then again, where does a story ever really begin? Sorry we left it out - editorial has been duly chastised

It is late Morning after a very special briefing. Lt. Col. Shard Rondell stood at attention in the holding bay of the MoonClock Project's new prototype gateway.

A pale glow lit the room and its handful of occupants, three commandos stood behind Shard, all watching a red flashing light over a twelve foot wide circular doorway of steel. Beneath its iron lids, a thin nictitating membrane of time and space, like a dark burgundy sea, ebbed and surged, waiting. A tiny red flashing light blinked over a twelve foot wide circular doorway of steel.

From the observation deck, Shards Father, a five-star General, Bric Rondell raised his hand. Buttons clicked, technicians scrambled. An Aide-de-Camp whispered in the Gnerals ear "11:09 AM, General. We're still on stand-by."

"Two minutes to do this. Thank you. Lt. Col. Rondell can you hear me?

"Yes, sir. Communication link is crystal clear. All systems green."

"So find her and get everyone home however you can, however you're able, son. Go with God." And he looked over at the countdown clock. Another assistant called out "11:11 AM, General! The anomaly has turned the beacon in our direction; Coordinates are for a light house floating way out in sector Zed, quite some distance away from the center of the simulation."

"Just like before. Just like we thought it would." Bric thought to himself, "The Light house in this set of virtual worlds was, for some unknown reason, very important to this anomalous entity that had been helping them watch Moebius and pointing to certain activities. They didn't know who their "Man-on-the-inside" really was, but so far he had been very helpful. "So be it." The General said "Good luck, son- come home in one piece."

And his hand went down. More buttons clicked and panels flashed as the red light turned to green, and the steel membrane covering the Gateway into the MoonClock Simulated Environment (MCSE) turned into liquid light.

Shard and his commandos plunged into a breach of reality; their entire molecular essence suddenly and instantaneously condensed and converted into a holographic world, contained, as it were, in an array, a set of twenty-seven cubes no bigger than a baseball, sitting only a hundred feet beneath General Bric's feet. No one, except a few bright lads and that madman Moebius, knew how it all worked. This was no comfort to Bric, who was brought in to replace the former commanding General who had clearly made some serious errors of judgment in not getting more of Moebius knowledge documented and understood. Bric now saw how this array of chips and hard drives used advanced plasma in the hardware, and in software seemed to incorporate self-generating self-aware programs that were constantly changing themselves. But why? He had had to ask himself now that he was sending his own son in there… To what purpose and reason had this thing been built? What had been the point of this project?

The rig that held the simulated universe was all in a box not much bigger than his fisherman's tackle box back home, sitting encased in yards of steel beneath this covert MoonClock Experimental facility. Bric had seen his share of strange stuff in his day, but this took the cake. And his daughter-in-law was in there, too. Too bizarre for words.

The Gateway, as expected, shut itself down. Liquid light turned back to a membrane of steel. But just as Bric had removed his hat to scratch his head, the Gateway reactivated itself.

One of the young men sitting at a station was about to take a sip of coffee when his sensor panel went utterly wild. Technicians gawked at each other and their flashing screens. Bric looked at their faces and saw that they had no idea what was going on.

The Gateway blossomed fully open, disgorging liquid hot plasma coated commandoes, three of them. Alive, but unconscious, and smoking a bit.

Shard was not amongst them.

"What the BRAC is going on here!" He shouted.

"Sir we have another anomalous feed starting. It's already over- it's very brief. Read it for yourself sir."

> I am the Logos.
>
> Thank you for all the guests, and while these three gentlemen really have no business in here, their leader seems to be an excellent candidate for the White King.
>
> The Black King, NOW DEMOTED TO A DUKE, has been badly in need of being put in Check for some time. Pun intended, of course.
>
> Thank you again for this new guest. It's a lot less lonely in here now. HOPE TO MEET YOU SOON. WE HAVE SO MUCH TO TALK ABOUT.
>
> IN TWO YEARS, LOOK FOR MY MESSAGES, BRIC…
>
> Good bye FOR NOW.

The General was speechless. Finally the cat let go of his tongue, and he said "Make sure those boys down there are ok and get them up here in my briefing room pronto. And get those boys from intelligence in here too; we'll see if they have any."

"Any…what, sir?"

"Any INTELLIGENCE, Sergeant Major - we'll see if they have any better ideas on how to do this, now get goin'! I'm fresh out of aces up MY sleeve, boy, and there's not a rabbit left in this hat of mine, I can assure you of that… so make some fresh coffee on the way back, and make it strong."

AntiPart One

Get ready to follow the Incredible Purple Dwark Road!

Nowar and her Companions were brought to the Secret Chambers of the great Queen of Mermopolis Bottom.

There the Guards left them, apparently alone in a huge underwater cathedral filled with drifting forests of red kelp, and having at its center a great ring of stone on its side. Nowar realized as they approached the thing that it had a black membrane that pulsed in no particularly meaningful way, more like a black, inverted pond set on its side.

No one heard the Queen approach, as she hobbled towards them. It was Two-Fangs who heard her first, and wheeled around ready to pounce. The Queen moved past him, a towering shape, and with a magical gesture from her hand, caused an Aht Erm'nal to erupt from the ground. It was just like the one Nowar remembered from the first time she 'woke up' on the beach of T'ien Shann, the thing on the beach with a screen and a keyboard. This one was flashing lights and its keys glowed with a strange light. The Queen spoke:

"This is the last fully functional Gateway to the Dwark that has not been destroyed or taken over by Moebius. This is the last avenue to go forth into the Dwark on your own road, Princess Nowar."

"The Purple Brick Road." chuckled Mandrake.

Turning to the one-winged Angel, she smiled and said - "Yes Mandrake, this is the Gate to the Purple Dwark Road, and as far as I can tell, you are the only one of the Companions assembled here who can create a Purple Dwark Road."

Nowar felt confused. Mandrake stole a quick glance at her and addressed the Queen when he said- "This one is almost ready, I suspect, but yes, I will begin our amble in the Dwark by a non-pedagogical leap of faith."

"I miss you damn angels" the Queen shed a tear.

"As we miss you, Queen of Mermopolis…" and turning to the Companions said- "A long way have come we, my friends, my Companions! From a dark hot dungeon to the belly of a whale to this, the last free Dwark gate perhaps, in all ProbablePolis. You all know the Dwark, and what mysteries and dangers it contains. If any fear the Dwark, your steps will melt the path behind me. Better you stay here with your fear, than endanger our mission."

Everyone was still. A stunted fat merman swam up quickly to the Queen and whispered into her ear. The Queen was stunned back into action and she said "It's time, Mandrake. Reports of Battle-cruisers and Snark-Shark battalions are now verified. Moebius will bring a repeat performance to Mermopolis as he did to the Under-Rung with the Midnight Shadow."

Mandrake looked thoughtful, and was very quiet for a second, saying "Mandrake the White has whispered to me of victory in the Under-Rung- the Midnight Shadow turned the tide of war with his full aspect upon him. Moebius will not soon return there without his full force."

"Then it shall be sometime soon, my one-winged friend, for my own spies tell me he moves his Great Black Harp against Kirhalion, and has prepared a new improved version of the Silver Scream Nine which I cannot help but think would be headed this way by now. It is the will of Moebius to crush the last Elven stronghold, and break the back of the Andironean Empire once and for all. We would be small fry, if not for the fact that the Logos chose to send Her…to Us, eh?"

Mandrake looked ashen. "It's a dark day if Moebius has called the Black Harp out of the Dwark again…surely the Final Tweak has begun."

"I'd say so. And more pages will be destroyed, I fear, old friend."

"Aye, great Queen, I too sense that the third and fourth pages will be lost to us soon."

A low rumble quivered across the artificial undersea garden. In the shade, an Octopus, looking frightened, swished past Nowar as low thrum-thrumming began to grow in loudness and frequency.

"And those are depth charges, Mandrake"

"Indeed, you have bigger fish to fry, O Great Queen- no pun intended."

The Queen's laugh was haughty and cold, like the bottom of the sea. She said "Indeed, fish are frying above us as we speak, so we must now be brief."

With inordinate good humor, she bent over to Nowar, and whispered to her- "Just be yourself, dearie, as something tells me you will not come back out of the Dwark until you have found the Crown of Twelve Stars that was crafted for you so very long ago."

The Queen chuckled. Nowar was still confused. This was the woman, er, mer-woman, that had tried, admittedly under Moebius' spell, to kill her, hardly an hour ago. Now she was treating her like her very own daughter! Low rolling explosions continued to rock the timbers of the great aquatic cathedral. Mandrake, sensing the timing was right, turned to the Companions and cried out "Alright Gang, everyone into the Dwark!"

Mrs. Machine and Two-Fangs did not hesitate, but plunged into the inky Dwarkness right on the heels of the angel who had jumped head-first with wing and arms widespread. The Dwark consumed them all, leaving no further sight or indication in the blackness. Ouroboros Alpha-Beta, both looking sheepishly at Nowar, gingerly stepped a leg in while Alpha began hissing at Beta "Alright you brave adventurer, YOU first!"

Beta hissed back "Fine, oh, fine, now its Beta to the rescue isn't it? Just like always, eh? Hold on then, Beetle Breath."

In a second, they were both gone, Beta leading Alpha in with his charge and only a gasp before their ripples disappeared. It was time for the Queen to finish with Nowar. They were alone now.

"Be very careful out there, my dear one, and listen carefully to what I will tell you- Dobbs, bless his soul, said to me only a few pulses ago that he foresaw something would be out there in the deepest Dwark someday- someday soon, or someday already past… something that was not fashioned in the creation or the larger hypothecation- something black, something big- no, not big, but huge, Nowar, huge beyond all our reckoning- something unnatural that Moebius is about to call out of a place of unspeakable evil, at the end of all time, and beyond all space."

"What is it?" Nowar felt a dark knot in her stomach. Fighting this Great Queen, as she had been not so long ago, had been the challenge of her life. What lay next?

"I sense that you will only learn more about this abomination by following that brave angel and your companions, gone before you, there-" she gestured at the Gate into the Dwark, still rippling occasionally.

Nowar was about to feel unsettled when she realized that forewarned was forearmed, and this Queen had just done her a favor of some kind, and Nowar nodded to her, acknowledging this. Then she adjusted her shield, strapped to her back now, tightened the newly repaired holster for her spear, and looked one last time at the Queen of Mermopolis.

The thoom thoom thoom was getting louder now. The Queen said- "It's your turn to win, Nowar, now go boldly, go brightly, go bravely and meet your destiny…and may the Logos be with you."

Without a second thought, Nowar leaped into the Dwark.

The Queen hesitated not a moment, either, and closed the gate with her clarion call "Sleep, oh my Purple Dwark Gate, and may the dreams of a madman ne'er disturb thee."

She then turned and swam with amazing haste up to her already shattered and deserted throne room.

In the next handful of hours the balance of power in ProbablePolis was about to shift.

To herself as she swam she thought- "I wonder if King Shard would ride to our rescue again as of olde, or would anyone, could anyone, survive Moebius' horrific and final opus magnum nauseum of Harp and Scream?"

It was time to contact the Midnight Shadow. There was strength in numbers, she consoled herself as best as she could, winding past sagging columns, fleeing mer-folk, and falling masonry.

She swam harder.

AntiChapter Six

Time is the flame in which we all burn

AntiPart Ten

When sleep awoke

The last Great Sky Whale was largely embedded in the earth of the Third Page, as she had been, for many hundreds of years now, utterly by choice. She dreamt dreams of days of olde, of great glories told, and of lovers bold. She had flourished and raised a family in the last age. Her dreams spiraled far back to the time of her own mother and father, when there had been no reason to have nightmares.

A nightmare, though, had shot over her only minutes ago, creating a horrible screeching sound as it roared across the valleys of the Third Kingdom, Cetacea, but even this still had but barely disturbed the Last Great Sky Whale from her deep peaceful dreams. After the glades had became quiet again, something began to waken her far more deeply, far more gently, like an old companion quietly rousing her from a very long, very deep, very troubled sleep.

"Uhranitee?"

Vocal Chords as big as trains vibrated with a deep bass guttural response. Up above her head and back, a great old forest shook, the animals raised their heads, and the land growled with awakening. Stream beds cracked briefly, and frogs jumped nervously as streams swished haphazardly in their beds.

"Yes, I am Uhranitee."

"Uhranitee Mare?"

"Yes, I am awake. Who is this?"

"Why Uhranitee Mare Gnosticius, this is the Logos! I have come to awaken you, for the last battle yet begun."

Uhranitee's mind, as deep as the ocean, considered that she might still be asleep, and dreaming. Then she remembered an unpleasant memory, and twitched deeply. The Betrayer had come as such, once, pretending to be the Logos, disguised with the craft of deceit and accompanied by the villains of the Gull and Crones society. She would not be tricked again in such a fashion. This time she would ask a few questions only the Logos could answer.

"What is whiter than snow?"

"The Truth."

"What is darker than the Raven?"

"Death"

"What is faster than the Wind?"

"Thought."

"What is sharper than the Sword?"

"Understanding"

"What is deeper than the Ocean?"

"Eternity."

"Why did I beach myself here, with all my little loved ones on my back, here in this valley of stillness, and what am I waiting for?"

"You came here long ago to cocoon yourself in dreams when you lost your Son and Father to the Treachery of Moebius."

"And?"

"And you are waiting for Justice."

"You are the Logos, I accept you. May you be yourself. What do you wish of me?"

"Only that you warn your inhabitants, and prepare yourself to take to the Sky; it is time to leave Cetacea and Everlast, for they are about to become Shreds of Regret... this valley can shelter you no more."

Mare sighed a deep heavy sigh.

"But justice is coming, dear sweet Whale of the Sky, though She does not even remember who she is yet. This Daughter of Destiny seeks you, she does, and a new Emperor has arrived as well."

"Surely you jest. Surely I am still dreaming."

"No Uhranitee, you are not dreaming. It is true. The Emperor will be here soon, the Armies of all the free lands of ProbablePolis will soon stream through the Dwark to lay siege to Castle DeepSteel. The Great Olde Drake is preparing to take to the skies and seek the Princess who is now off in the Deep Dwark, with but a single one-winged Angel and a few companions to escort her home...She is seeking you, Great Lady of the Sky, though she does not yet understand why."

Uhranitee passed some time in contemplation of all of this. It was unreal to her, to know that the Great Luminosity might be at hand- an end to the madness of Moebius. Then she asked "When will they arrive?"

"Though the hypothecations are approaching a single probability, it is difficult to say with complete surety. In a few days, I should think, perhaps a fortnight at most."

"Then, I have time to cry?"

"Yes, Uhranitee Mare, you have time to cry, but only a little. The Black Harp of Deep Steel has come to kill the Avatar of the Fourth page, and there is nothing you can do to stop it."

Deep in her belly, she felt the kicks and squirms of her little ones, her brood, the last of the Sky Whales that there ever would be, as far as she knew. This reminded her of what she had to lose that had not already been lost, and she spoke again-

"Then I will say this, O Logos. Uhranitee Mare Gnosticius I am, the last of the Sky Whales of Olde, and though I may be unworthy- only say the Word, and I shall serve again."

"Oh Mare, you are worthier than us all. Take heart and take flight, oh my dear one, and know that great things are coming, worth living for, worth dying for. Rise again, last of the SkyWhales!"

Then, in the valley of stillness, the last of the Sky Whales closed her great huge eyes, and cried, deeply. Convulsions went up and down her great spine, which spanned nearly thirty miles. The forests and lakes that encrusted her back rippled with a modest upheaval. Trees fell, squirrels squawked, deer bolted, crows cawed and fish jumped.

Then all was quiet again in the Valley of the Shadow, though not for long.

The creatures of her forests had been warned, and she would give them a few minutes to exit onto the swampy lands she was now barely contained by. Concentrating deeply on her third eye, she began to breathe deeply, the vibrations continued to stir a whole slew of Foxes, badgers, rabbits, opossum, birds, beetles and even bears, all rushing to get off as they watched the seams of the bogs and glades opening everywhere, wider and wider.

An old tortoise, small in size but over a hundred and twenty pulses of the ribbon old had been considering leaving, but his little home, in the crease of the back behind Uhranitee's blow-hole, had been all he had ever known. He chose to stay, along with an obstinate Blue jay, a sleeping Fox and even a pregnant Wren. A whole brigade of earth worms that probably knew they didn't have time to evacuate didn't bother. They were all in for quite a ride.

The Sky Whale was preparing to take to the air.

AntiPart Nine

*Now **THAT'S** Entertainment!*

It was a game show as only Hell Incorporated could put on.

Dialing for Dimensions; Playground-of-Death was the longest running reality Television entertainment and education show on the MOEBIUS-1 Cable Channel. The crowd roared because they had no choice. The signs from the Teleprompters made that very clear with simple slogans like "**CHEER OR SUFFER!**"

Pulsating Lights from a scintillating disco ball whirling around on its axis, and surrounded by a bunch of fake plastic swans, lent an otherworldly feel to the arena. The sounds of a polka, done at twice the normal polka speed filled the auditorium and struck terror in the hearts of anyone nearby with any real musical taste.

The format was simple: Two Koradgian storm troopers wheeled in an un-Godly looking machine, called the "Gateway to Insanity", and another Koradgian trooper brought a few 'volunteers' from the audience to help unwind and rotate wheels of large weight- thus randomly opening a portal to an entirely different world, not just another page in ProbablePolis, but somewhere else far beyond the known reaches of the great spherical Dwarkopologue itself!

This 'Dialing for Dimensions' resulted in a membrane to another time and space that allowed the crowd to get a glimpse of another exciting alien race and totally alien world; alien in that the creature, or creatures, being observed did not belong to ProbablePolis, and exciting in that it or they would be, if Moebius gave it a 'thumbs up', abducted, plucked from its or their own world and brought here into this one for a live reality Moebius gladiatorium.

It, or them, were then subsequently interviewed, usually by Moebius himself. If he liked what he saw and heard, he went on and plucked out a good baker's dozen of the new species, and had them fight with the Koradgians on the ground at the Gateway to Insanity. He always made sure that there were enough survivors for a breeding pair. If he didn't think the new race had much promise, he plucked out a few more to serve as lunch for the audience.

Sometimes the audience ate well, other times, something ate the audience, and Moebius got a whole new and vigorous species to add to his growing retinue of vicious and ill-mannered irregulars in his own Kingdoms, and now, many of these new species would begin to sprawl into Queen Limberly's former Kingdoms as well.

As custom had it, after dinner, Moebius would have a few hominid slaves, Dwarves or elves, put on a little play. Moebius would note the actor with the least vim and vigor, and have the lazy little fellow prepared for dessert on the next installment of the Moebius cooking show. It all dove-tailed so well.

The evening started off as it usually did, with the flashing neon screens and canned laughter rattling the arena while Ah-Hree-ghian, a towering pillar of long haired crusty goo, bubbling and babbling long strings of gibberish and the big mouthed worm with the jester's cap, Bogloon, laughed hilariously at his side, for no particular reason at all, really. He made fun of the audience and got them generally riled up- that was his job, after all, and he relished it when he wasn't getting thrashed by an annoyed audience member. No one understood what the tall tower of goo was saying, though, and no one really paid much attention to Bogloon that night until he lit someone's trousers on fire. Eventually he ended up selling peanuts and bridgerust up in the bleachers, watching Moebius move into the spotlights. Once in a while, Bogloon would pick someone's pocket and replace their belongings with handfuls of pre-opened ketchup packets.

Moebius was in rare form tonight, making the whole thing into an even more crazed game show host in his over-sequined circus master's coat, putting in an occasional plug for his latest book or shaving cream product. Wheels turned, gears rolled as Moebius barked the show slogan "Well, some people call it a Mad World, but we think it's just a funny old World, don't we boys? Funny hahaha, but it's about to get a whole lot funnier! Hahahahahah! Open the Gateway of Insanity, boys, and let's…go…Dialing for DIMENSIONS! Muahahahahahah!"

Moebius backed away from the microphone while the bright shining core swallowed itself up, and the monitors cleared.

The audience was under whelmed. They clapped anyway, for reasons we mentioned before, but they were clearly not sure what they were looking at…But only for an instant.

It was Inky blackness in there. Kind of like the Dwark, but very cold-cold and harsh…winds came blustering in, swirling leaves and game show pamphlets everywhere, rattling the roof top of the auditorium, and the low rolling sound of thunder was everywhere now. An eerie silence hung over the whole auditorium.

An indescribably strange and seamless tentacle of darkness erupted suddenly, black as black could be, and glistening, pulsating tendrils unrolled from it, and began to sweep wildly around the arena. Its twitching vines shot out little fern like branches as well with knots of eyeballs and smiling sharp-toothed mouths, snapping in every direction.

It looked excited, enthusiastic, and twittering with life, hungry, surreal life.

Moebius had never seen anything like this before, and his cigar fell out of his mouth.

"Clancy, are you getting any of this?"

The reply was static, but sounded like "No sir, can you give us a visual description, all our monitors just went dead…"

The black vicious branches went to work right then and there, without delay. They varied their activities between devouring the Koradgian's alive, chattering with each other, and shooting out new eyeball or mouth stalks to examine the entire audience, now growing more than a bit anxious.

Bogloon was already long gone- well on his way to finding an escape pod out of Castle DeepSteel. He could smell death in the air as he zipped down coiling black hallways.

ProbablePolis

Back in the auditorium, several large branches had to work on Ah-Hree-ghian for a full minute. He belched massively toxic explosions of purple and green goo as he was chewed like a colossal tootsie roll by a veritable forest of slimy black hungry tendrils.

Whatever this thing was, it had figured out that the inhabitants of the arena were in fact snack-packets of some kind, left here for who knows what reason. It didn't really matter. It finished the Koradgians and Ah-Hree-ghian off without much of a pause and then the real fun began. It began rapidly pulling members of the audience into its ever enlarging maws and new gullets that erupted into being like loathsome flowers as the thing sprawled out further and further across the auditorium, still relentlessly pumping its foul and loathsome hungry bulk into the arena through the insane Gateway of Hell Incorporated.

It was huge alright. Moebius stammered as he reached for his transmogrifier- his escape out of this facility to wherever he wanted to go in ProbablePolis. He already had his lunch ticket, but he just wanted to watch this thing a little more closely a little longer before he popped away and nuked it from a distance. His hands shook. There was no telling how big this thing was, and it just kept pumping itself into the auditorium.

Just before the tendrils began to sniff around the transparent steel bubble that enclosed Moebius in his high seat far over the arena, Moebius realized something awful – a kind of twisted epiphany:

He had fallen in love.

As he zapped away to a safer abode, he vowed to capture this rare and beautiful beast, plucked from God-knows where. He began to feel deeply attached to this disgusting thing, which was rapidly filling up the MOEBIUS-1 Cable facility with greasy oily black roots and gullet sacks.

He watched it from his monitor, and whispered just loud enough that Clancy could make out the words "You great big black beauty, oh why look at you, just gobbling up everything that moves, everything in sight, oh, my, you are truly amazing, why you're like a hundred Slithery Toves all rolled up in one octopoidal spineless plant-like horror."

He turned to Clancy and said with smug sureness- "That…thing is ours, boy. You're in charge of figuring out how to capture this, this… Slithery…Tove. Do you understand?"

Clancy put out his cigar and coughed a quick "Yes, sir…uh, yes, sir, I'll get right on it…"

"Well you'd better." He looked laconically at the screen- "At the rate this thing is growing, in another hour it'll be using Castle DeepSteel like a snail uses a shell. We don't need this thing devouring our armies before we've even launched them, do we?" Clancy grimaced- he was short, you know, and right now he was short on ideas as well.

AntiPart Eight

Unique by design and back for a final time!

Hieronymous Jones sat perched on a very tall windy place, atop the head of his vicious colossal steel baby, the Silver Scream Nine, a toy that Moebius had tinkered into being from previous models, looking for the perfect Page-eating machine. This thing was bigger than the largest dinosaur you or your child can remember, and if you want a more concise description you might re-read Chapter Seven, Part Four.

At any rate, right at that very moment it was very hungry and hurtling through the Dwark at a very high rate of speed indeed.

As it passed fragments of pages long shattered by the great wars of Probability, here and there it attracted a clutch or a school or pod of dangerous and sinister creatures, some in hovering craft, others flying on their own power. Like a parade they soon became, many of them had been struck by awe of this vast, huge silver steel beast, and in like form, all manner of bogies, bogarts, imps, flying cockatrice, sphinx, wyverns and winged three headed hounds were doing their best now to keep up with this behemoth of silver steel hurtling forward in the Dwark. Jones ignored them all, and urged his new charge to go faster.

"Daddy?" rattled the boom of the voice of the Silver Scream Nine's stainless steel vocal chords, pumped by iron lungs big as a skyscraper.

Jones, still Precognitid-at-large, as it were, and no one's fool now but his own, puttered down to see what his newly acquired toy needed. This huge thing was getting to be quite high maintenance. Its personality was utterly infantile and co-dependent, just the way Moebius liked his toys to be programmed. This was the third time it had called him down where it could see him. He stopped short of the vast toothy steel maw as big as a tank and said "What now?"

"Are we almost to food, Daddy? Silver Scream very hungry."

Jones watched its mouth grow wider in a sinister smile.

"Almost there, son!" he laughed nervously and went flying back up to his perch on the top of its head. Jones still understood that he had illicitly walked off with the biggest and best toy that Moebius had made yet, and, what was more, headed now to the first page that would satisfy the hunger of the Silver Scream Nine for protein based life. Jones was about to make a statement that no one could afford to ignore. His potentially great advantage over Moebius, this monstrously sized Robo diabolus sapiens, however, would need to be fed soon, and regularly after that, he realized. Eventually, he would have to make contact with his fellow Gull and Crones cronies as well.

"The squirmy things in the UnderRung will take the edge off of your appetite, boy, and then Castle Ambrosia is hardly another half pulse off to the starboard bow. No worries, dear precious lad of steel. When we're finished with the UnderRung, we head to Castle Ambrosia, then Castle Evergreen, and we'll end up at Castle DeepSteel. hahahahahaha"

But then a nagging doubt came to assail Jones. Dear Architect-of-All, he suddenly thought, I have yet to see how fast this thing could actually consume a whole page, not just the inhabitants.

Troublesome to consider, but this silicon nightmare called the Silver Scream Nine might be enabled with new rapid ingestion technologies like the kind Moebius had talked about not so long ago…in which case, what would happen to him and his fellow Gulls and Crones when all the pages were gone, but the one they owned, hopefully, but with this thing still on the loose? Well, surely it had to have some weakness that could be exploited, right? Suddenly he felt an absence of surety about much of anything, and panic started to set into Hieronymous Jones in his deepest circuits.

Up ahead, the aquamarine page of the Kingdom of T'ien Sha'an was looming into the foreground. It was beautiful, but Jones was hardly in a sight-seeing mood.

"Well, we're about to see what this thing can really do anyway, so it might be that I'm borrowing trouble…" thought Jones to himself, unconvincingly.

AntiPart Seven

There's a difference between 'knowing the path' and 'walking the path'...

Nowar shook her head and looked around.

Two Fangs and Ouroboros Alpha Beta had waited here, at the very beginning of the Purple Dwark Road for her to come through the gate. They now stood where the Road winded its way into the darkest Dwark, seemingly evoked into being underneath by every footstep that Mandrake the Black took in front of him.

In fact, he had already crossed a football field length area, and the Purple bricks did not just erupt into being, but as they did, more of the same Purple bricks sizzled and came into being underneath, popping and bubbling up like a foundation for the first bricks that were created by the first footsteps of faith the angel had made, once he stepped through the Purple Dwark gate of the Queen of Mermopolis.

The continued efforts of seemingly unseen masons rapidly assembled the piles and moorings of this Road to …Nowhere? With relentless speed, more and more of a firm footing in the nothingness that surrounded them all branched out in spires and flying buttresses, anchoring itself deeper and deeper into the seemingly empty gloom of the great bottomless Dwark.

Mandrake was singing as he walked into the void, almost skipping and hopping along the way, half using his one wing to take longer lunging steps. No worries, of course, for his faith was like steel, and purple bricks were popping out everywhere he walked across the cold empty Dwarkness. The Road was giving off warmth too, Nowar realized, and she saw after a few minutes that she would have to run very hard to keep up with the one-winged angel dashing off in front of them all. Before it was too late, she realized she had wished so quietly that she had not fully heard herself; wished for wings to be able to catch up to Mandrake.

Leaving ripples behind her, Nowar quickly caught up with the Angel with a brilliant speed that left Two-Fangs and Alpha-Beta stunned.

It made no sense to her, either, as she had already expended her third wish, and she hadn't slept either. Nevertheless, here she was, with silver white pinions as big as a condor. Mrs. Machine whirred in total surprise and zipped off quickly to join her and the angel. Two fangs picked up the Amphisbaena and hefted him over his shoulders like a sack of potatoes as he hurled himself into a jaunt, Beta calling out "Follow the Purple Brick Road! Follow the Purple Brick Road! Ha ha!"

Alpha kept his thoughts to himself- "We're going where angels *should* fear to tread…"

AntiPart Six

For those of you that missed Grandma Brandy...

She'd checked her email twice, once at the Public Library, where she was told quite precisely where to check it the second time, at a coffee shop halfway on her journey to her final destination.

She did as directed, and now she knew where she would have to check her email a third time, at a place quite close to the Guards gate at the MoonClock Project, her ultimate destination, a place located underneath a secret Air Force base in Connecticut where her husband had worked for the last two years, trying to sort out the riddle of the mad abduction of their daughter-in-law and subsequent disappearance of their son.

Nervously, she kept the Book in her biggest floppy bag, and looked furtively everywhere, always a bit edgy every time she would see someone in a plumbers outfit; she made her way quickly, always looking for the best price in gasoline as obsessively as her husband watched the clock.

She drank coffee at the coffee shop, something she hadn't done in years, and made no wasted movements. She had a purpose now, just like the old days, she was alive again. She got back in the van swiftly, did a Hail Mary with her Rosary, and she was flying down the highway again.

But not knowing what was going on in the book she was holding was really bothering her.

In the depths of a vast holographic sphere of Dwark that was, in fact, as tiny as a dust-speck, but seemingly boundless as an ocean of darkness, her Daughter's residual self-image, a winged unremembering Princess, had grown tired and weary- and had fallen into the arms of a one-winged angel, who sang softly to her as he walked through the Dwark, a whole series of odd misbegotten companions straggling behind him on the purple brick road he was creating in the sky.

AntiPart Five

Peelings, nothing more than peelings...

"Tatyanna, you, Mr. Machine and Glee, head to Castle Ambrosia. Lie like dogs that we want peace and get us a treaty, and get it soon."

Those had been the last words that Moebius had said to the nastiest Elven princess you could ever meet in your life. Tatyanna Voltarrus Manyana, when it came to the on-going contest for title of "Scum of the world" always took first prize if not runners-up. She baked puppy dogs alive for breakfast, and would laugh all the while when she would pick them up from the pound.

But it seemed that she'd met her match with the Imperial Dragon Guard of Ambrosia.

Hawk-shaped Striker vessels, Wyverns and Steel-clad Riders-of-Drakes were all over her hovercraft as she and her twisted mission mates came into the airspace above Castle Ambrosia. She barked orders at Mr. Machine, who was having difficulty understanding why they weren't firing on these chowder-headed followers of King Shard.

"Hold your fire, Mr. Machine, we're here to lull these idiots into a false sense of security, remember."

"Sorry, I'm programmed for optimal aggression, you know that."

"Just stay away from that firing array you ninny, and open a port-hole for Glee to escape right away."

Glee, who you might remember, was the size of a flea, looked quite shocked when he heard this suggestion, but since he was so little, no one really noticed how shocked he was. Nevertheless, he asked passionately with his tinny, tiny french Canadian accent - "What do you mean Tatyanna? Am I not going with you to make zee entreaty vis dee muckety mucks and poobahs?"

The hovercraft shook. A drake or wyvern was testing to see if this thing had anyone in it.

"No no no! You lame brained arthropod, we're here to distract and divide them, confuse them at best, you tool- we're trying to waste their time with a peace treaty that no one has any interest in actually getting or enforcing, and meanwhile, my tiny friend, you will be doing some close-to-the-ground inspection of how security is working at Castle Ambrosia. Capiche?"

Glee shut up. The last time he argued with Tatyanna, he'd nearly lost one of his antennae.

AntiPart Four

Safety tip- do not play near the edge of the Purple Dwark Road.

They had come far- many, many leagues of the Dwark had they covered. Nowar was very tired and had curled up in Mandrakes arms while her Companions continued bringing up the rear as best as they could. What power kept Nowar here while she slept was anyone's guess, of course. They were all just happy to still have her here while she slept. Alpha suspected it was the power of the Angel that was allowing her to finally get some real sleep and rest.

From time to time, Alpha and Beta bickered from their perch on Two Fangs shoulders. Alpha wanted to know where they were heading, and Beta repeatedly told him to ask Mandrake, but all Mandrake the Black would call back was "Avalhalla, of course, Ouroboros, where the Great Olde Drake lives…where else could we go?"

"Mandrake, no one knows where the Olde Drake lives" Alpha croaked back. The Angel would drop the conversation at that point. Alpha had tried this three times to no avail.

Avalhalla spanned twenty thousand miles across the Front and Back Cover of ProbablePolis. Did Mandrake really have any idea where the Great Olde Drake lived, or was that all just another leap of faith as well? Alpha continued to feel nervous, and Beta told him to pipe down for the last time, or Two Fangs would make them walk. So far the journey had been peaceful indeed; hardly a glowing Dwark jelly or Spiny-Sky-Fish had troubled their relentless jaunt across the vast nothingness of the Dwark. Could it go on this way until they made it to Avalhalla? It seemed improbable!

Too good to be true, someone might have thought, if only there had been time for that.

There wasn't. The attack was as vicious as it was sudden. No one had seen it coming. Mandrake, with Nowar in his arms, went down so fast that it seemed like the whole world had just been turned upside down and inside out as a massive scorching ton of screaming hot steel and synthetic flesh shaped like a fat shark hurled into the Angel, without warning, seemingly from nowhere. A high pitched shriek accompanied the Angel and his charge as they both sailed away from each other down, down, down into the Dwarkness.

Two Fangs started to howl and Mrs. Machine screeched, firing off lasers in the direction of the awful thing, a barely glinting shadow in the gloom below them, rapidly disappearing into the Dwark also.

The denizens of the Dwark called the thing a SnarkShark, a half living, half machine, winged shark-like beast with jet engines in its rear, a giant mouth stocked with buzz saws and maneuverable ice picks all around its neck. It spit out little Molotov cocktails when it got close to its prey, just for fun, often emitting a high piercing shriek just instants before it hurled itself into unwary targets while belching smoke to wipe out any visibility of the victims during the attack.

In this case, the unwary targets were Nowar and her Companions, making their way through the Dwark on the Purple Brick Road.

This SnarkShark, to make things worse, came with back-up; two other SnarkSharks, all just as foul and rusted, and ready to get dirty.

So before anyone could do anything about Mandrake and Nowar getting creamed right in front of them in a huge cloud of smoke and screams, the other two SnarkSharks took out Two Fangs and Mrs. Machine just as elegantly and effortlessly. The shriek they gave was ear-piercing, and they hit their targets with a cruel and crushing thump, knocking them both entirely off the Purple Brick Road.

Rolling smoke belched in columns as Alpha-Beta stood at the edge of the Purple Brick Road, looking down into the empty cold Dwarkness. Two Fangs, Mrs. Machine, Nowar and Mandrake were nowhere to be seen. The towers of smoke began to fade and blow away. Far, far away, high pitched shrieks still echoed out through the Dwark.

"Creator-of-All, what's to become of us now?" Alpha blurted.

Beta was quietly crying to himself.

Ouroboros Alpha-Beta both fell down to their knees at the edge of the Purple Dwark Road and wept.

Whatever in the world *would* they do now?

AntiPart Three

Better to light a candle than curse the Dwark!

Nowar felt she had been falling now for quite some time, hurtling downwards, or Dwarkwards, as the case may be, into the inky cold blackness all the denizens of ProbablePolis called the Dwark. While Nowar sensed that she had been hurtling downwards for perhaps a very long time, she wasn't really sure just how long a time it had been. This added to the discomfort of hurtling to parts unknown, certainly, always wondering if something would catch your fall or if you might just splatter everywhere upon impact, without warning.

Very disconcerting indeed, she thought to herself. To make matters worse, Time in the Dwark was absent, somehow, to begin with. It might have been a few minutes since she awoke, or it might have been a few days since her last memories had occurred. She recalled barely how she and her Companions were ambushed by a horde of smelly steel monsters sent by Moebius, and how she was knocked off of the Purple Brick Road by one of those things, leaving her to begin her journey with a headache, **unconscious**, wounded, cold and hungry and utterly at the mercy of whatever might find her here, wherever 'here' was...

"...and where did my wings go?" came another horrific thought, "the ones that I wished for to help me follow Mandrake the Black???"

Was that all just a temporary freak of the Dwark- did things work differently here than they did in the rest of ProbablePolis?" It was a troubling question indeed- did her wishing ability somehow change from being able to have three good ones every pulse, to being able to have as many as she wanted, or only one, even. Maybe none would have lasting power or effectiveness for any sufficient time! This Dwark was baffling. Should she try to wish for wings again? Before she could follow that thread of thought further she had another shock-

Begin her journey unconscious? Wait a minute, why hadn't she returned to the world of the dream of the Little Girl? Or in fact had she? Maybe she had and just didn't remember it, oh dear, what was going on with all of *that*? Maybe the Dwark would keep her from being able to communicate with the little girl in the other world, or foil whatever it was that she and the little girl were doing together! Oh no, that was yet another horrific thought, and she realized that she needed to consider her other options.

Other options, "Like what?" she said aloud. This was a problem, indeed. She was hurtling at what felt like a very high rate of speed, into…nothingness, inky black cold nothingness, worse than space, she mused, this Dwark was.

But where was she, really, and how could she ever get out of this dark place? She felt like she wanted to cry, finally did, and went back to sleep, the Dwark hurtling past her while she grabbed for imaginary blankets, and saw faces streaming past her in the gloom of her own private nightmares.

AntiPart Two

So, if you could rewind time, would you? Really?

Nowar stretched and looked around. She was awake from the nightmare! She looked around. Grandma Brandy was driving; pedal to the metal, radar detector wide open with her mini-van engine humming away at a blissful 75+ miles per hour, headed for the New Jersey turnpike.

"Thank Heavens you're back, honey! I was beginning to wonder if I was going to have to finish the trip alone!" she laughed.

Nowar quietly realized that she probably would be finishing the trip alone, but decided not to say anything. She could tell her Grandma was tired, and a bit rattled with what was going on. Grandma Brandy definitely didn't need any gloomy predictions right now from her grand-daughter, and she quickly changed the subject- "I stopped and got us some sodie-pop. There's one for you right there."

"How long have I been back?" Nowar asked her Grandmother while she opened her soda.

"Hardly an hour I reckon. Wherever I leave the book, that's where you seem to pop back in. You did it a few times a couple hours ago, but just for a couple seconds, scared the bejeebin dickens out of me the first time, darling. You always looked like you were having a nightmare the way you tossed and turned"

"I was."

Nowar suddenly felt the constraints of the seat belt and the warm weight of a very heavy tome in her lap. ProbablePolis; it was much thicker than the last time she had seen it, almost two hundred pages long.

"How long was I gone?"

"We just crossed into New Jersey. We've crossed four state lines since we left the house."

"Gramma you've been driving all day!"

"Ha, it's only been eleven hours, honey, but I am a little tired. We'll stop at a Hotel I know near the Navy base in the next town."

"Ok, what time is it now?" - they both looked at the clock on the console as Grandma Brandy batted away her GIS-computer lap-top thingie.

It was 9:11 PM. They both looked at each other and laughed- that weird clock thing – they always caught each other looking at a time piece just when it happened to be 10:10, 11:11, 3:33, 4:44, etc. "Less than a hobby and more than an obsession" Grandma Brandy used to joke. Pop Bric didn't make fun of them for it since he'd had his own 11:11 moment one night. He just didn't talk about it much. He eventually managed to fix his computer, nonetheless, which acted very strangely that night.

Neither Grandma Brandy nor Nowar realized that what would happen in exactly two hours would probably change everything.

AntiPart One

Olde Friends reunited!

Khan, the winged Sabre-tooth tiger, faithfully brought his childhood friend, King Shard, and a hobbling Satyr, Kai, to the Sepulchre of Silence out of the frigid surface wastelands of Avalhalla.

The Emperor awaited them in his new steel battle suit, having decided at the last minute to change out of his General's outfit. When in Rome, and so forth. The Logos watched from the shadows, and the Builder, a huge silver crab-like being, hovered about the well in the center of the Sepulchre, where it was warm.

Kai went and huddled by the well, where it was indeed warm, but he stayed a suitable distance from the big silver crab thing, which was smiling at him. Bric stood there silently beholding his son, who looked at him like he was a stranger.

"You don't know who I am, do you, son?" Bric said to Shard, who looked at least forty years older than he had before Pop Bric had watched him go through the breach to this bizarre virtual world, only a year ago.

"No, not a clue, kind sir. Are you the new Emperor that the Precognitus have often foretold?"

Pop Bric pulled out the same device he had used earlier on himself and handed it to Shard.

"Stare at the little blue light and smile, son, cause you are about to go on a very special journey."

Shard did as he was told by the new Emperor. The blue light engulfed his face, and clearly it had the same intended effect as it had had earlier on his father, for the good King Shard bent over and fell, heaving at his knees with tears, clutching the ground, gasping for air. Kai looked alarmed, but did not interfere. Apparently this was indeed the new Emperor.

Shard spat words out like he was struggling with something- "Where's Nowar, Dad? Have you found out where Moebius is keeping Limberly?"

The blue light device had worked on Shard too!

Before Bric could answer, a child-like voice behind them said- "You still have a role to play, King of ProbablePolis."

Shard looked wide eyed around him wildly. Bric didn't so much as twitch.

The Logos moved into the light by the well, patted Kai on the head like a puppy and glided over to Khan, ruffling him under the chin like a big pussy cat.

"King Shard of ProbablePolis, I have allowed your father to return your memories to you, that your family may be reunited, but remember these words on this day, for the black King-demoted-to-Duke, Moebius, has set into motion some very terrible things, and you must play your role well to help me close this story with a happy ending. Only in this manner will your family ever be re-united in your own world."

And then, "I give you my word I will help you all go home, if I can."

Shard was about to speak when his father motioned him to be quiet.

"All I am saying is that you must remember your role, and play it well, for my goodly white King, if you play it not…it …will …all …have been for naught." The Logos and the crab-like Builder stared uncomfortably at their new Emperor, and their newly awakened white King.

Bric turned to the Logos, standing very erect. "I will brief my son, and we will prepare to muster all the known armies to attack Castle DeepSteel."

King Shard shook his head in agreement, and the Logos smiled.

"The Narrator commends you." he laughed and said "Below us lies the Great Olde Drake, my friends, so I will go and tell him that you will all be ready, presently, to join him."

Bric brightened up and barked "Good, tell him that we will need to muster all the Dragons out of all Avalhalla to join our armies in Ambrosia."

"I need to know what's going on, Dad."

"Right, huddle up, Colonel!"

Kai had no idea of what all was going on, of course. He tried to follow the discourse that Shard had with the new Emperor, but to little avail. They used a foreign language with words of strange complexity and assemblage, and it hurt his mind to try to understand what in fact it was that they shared.

Whatever they discussed, they seemed satisfied with what they were figuring out, and the crab smiled a lot and shook his head with an almost out of place enthusiasm.

Whatever it was that was going on, they were safe and warm now, and that was all that mattered to Kai anymore. The King was alive, albeit talking very strangely indeed, but everyone here seemed friendly enough, so he rolled into a ball with his blanket and caught some shut-eye.

AntiChapter Five

The ending makes no sense without at least one good beginning

AntiPart Ten

Boil those pages, boil those pages!

"Food?" the huge cybernetic beastie known affectionately as the Silver Scream Nine, unique by design, looked expectantly at his surrogate father figure, Hieronymous Jones Esq., Precognitid-at-large.

Silver Scream Nine's tiny little silver brain quivered like a boiling hotdog in the ghastly green soup that filled up its colossal skull, attached as it was to two titanic jaws and a gullet the size of Kansas.

Jones surveyed the vast southern peninsula of T'ien Sha'an, its startlingly blue archipelago and teeming jungles surrounding crumbling stone artifacts of long lost civilizations. Then he spied the broken and burnt landscape around the still-smoldering main entrance to the Under Rung, and he smiled deeply, wickedly, knowingly.

"Start in that crater, my little beastly lad of steel. Activate all aggression protocols. Eat everything and everyone in your path, including the Page Avatar himself, the Midnight Shadow! Hahahahahah!"

Without hesitation, the Silver Scream Nine tilted into a spiral soar, and hurled itself headfirst into the gaping black maw that had once been the entrance to the Under Rung.

Giants, Ogres, Trolls, three and five headed dogs, hobgoblins and Medusids were all indiscriminately devoured as flavoring for the scenery and architecture. The Silver Scream Nine was an eating machine that ate everything in its path, and didn't have to stop until after twenty minutes of incredible pigging out, when it simply coiled up in an impenetrable ball to do a little digestive nap for about five minutes.

After its brief respite, it would stretch, shaking the canyon all around it, and proceed to figure out where the tastiest things might be next.

Jones was hopping about in the air with great joy by this time. This thing had just destroyed the top three levels of the greatest underground fortress city on the page, and in just one session! He skittered down to hover over the Silver Scream.

There was no resistance in sight! Countless tunnels below them leading to other canyons beckoned. Retreat had been complete. Victory was in the air. But nothing less than the Avatar of the page and the Praetor of T'ien Sha'an would do to complete this easy conquest, this beautiful tweak to the final page count of ProbablePolis.

"We'll head to the throne room for the most tastiest of treats, boyo, eh?"

A quick shake of the massive smiling head and all Jones had to do was point the Silver Scream in the direction to the great Throne Room of the Under Rung. Within minutes there was fresh screaming and cataclysmic cave-ins around a tornado of eating frenzy, rushing forward, relentlessly going deeper underground.

Pity there weren't more, Jones thought idly to himself as he watched the Silver Scream redouble its cyclonic eating frenzy every time it found moving, warm screaming things in its fare.

AntiPart Nine

Glutamus Maximus Boodleberry!

Boodleberry was a tinkerer. He had been assigned to monitor the "feed off of Poopsy", Moebius' favorite Teddy Bear, inserted not so long ago with a tiny transmitter by his buddy Dooley, the chain-smoking fairy. Both of them were special agents of the Resistance.

Boodleberry, who had a long bushy tail, and bright shiny teeth, (just in case you were wondering what he looked like) had been waiting, waiting for some time, and waiting for something, anything that he might tell his superiors; anything that might help defeat Moebius.

But so far it was fairly clear that when it came to the center of the action, Poopsy didn't have much to report. Boodleberry was not pleased, and in fact he was rather alarmed. He had had to witness the relentless and usually pointless decadence of Moebius first hand, and what's more, this guy never slept- he was a case of non-stop supreme indulgence, night and day! Where did he find time to do evil deeds when he was filling his face with creamy pastries all the time?

It dawned on him that Moebius had Clancy for an administrative officer. Clancy was the most talented multi-tasking genius pigmy Koradgian Moebius had ever genetically tinkered into being. More time for the golf-course, he'd often brag. Clancy was like a son, even if Moebius did threaten him just to keep him on his toes.

During a long session of video game playing, Moebius had stopped to stuff some confections in his face and relight his cigar. He picked his nose for a long time, long enough that Boodleberry drifted asleep. As he began to snore, his foot kicked a lever marked –

INTERCOM- DO NOT PUSH THIS LEVER!

Moebius, his face covered with jelly doughnut, laughed maniacally, turned to his beloved teddybear and cried out loud "How 'bout that for a high score, darling?"

Poopsy replied by snoring, but the roar of the video game muffled it beyond recognition.

Boodleberry, barely opening his eyes, and unaware that he had inadvertently thrown the intercom lever, remarked loudly "Hokey Shmokes, you've been playing that game forever fer cryin out loud. At least ye've stopped pickin yer nose."

Moebius dropped his controller into his bowl of sherbet, and, stepping cross his doughnut buffet, scattered cream puffs everywhere to stare at his teddy bear, his face filling up Boodleberry's screen.

"Poopsy?" he said breathlessly, "Poopsy? Did …you…did you speak?"

Boodleberry panicked. He had no idea of what to do. He had thrown the lever! EEK! Oh no! He was in very deep trouble now. He blurted the first thing that came to his mind "Yer in a rut, you boob, that was all I was saying." His Scottish twang chirped.

"Boob?" Moebius looked quixotic. He'd heard that term before, somewhere in his long career as a middle-management 'suck-up' in the Big World he had left behind him so long ago.

"Everyday yer crackin' at the same game, Dukie-baby, day or night, it's no matter. No wonder yer losin' yer war before ye've even begun…"

"Poopsy?"

"Yes, my beloved dark lord of evil?"

"You're…talking…to me."

A light went on in Boodleberry's eyes, and he grinned, deeply.

"Clancy upgraded my memory chip so don't look a gift teddy bear in the mouth! Now, you want to win this little dark war of yours or not? I have all kinds of great ideas for how to get this show back on track."

Moebius paused for a moment, obviously drinking in deeply the absurdity of the moment, relishing the surreality of it all. Suddenly, the thought of his most intimate little confidant at his side as he squashed defiance everywhere in ProbablePolis, and it gave him a wonderful warm fuzzy feeling, which soon translated to gas. He cried out suddenly-

"Yes Poopsy, yes! Comrades we! Let loose the Teddy bears of War! Muahahahahaha!"

AntiPart Eight

Where Page Seven starts to fold…

Far down in the deepest depths of the Under Rung, in a dark drawing room, the Midnight Shadow and Mandrake the White were supervising the building of an impromptu, but huge, Dwark Gate, courtesy of a special Dwark Stone brought by Menses, an Angel plenipotentiate from the Ambrosia High Command, the Council that served King Shard.

Midnight Shadow had selected the most private and reclusive of auditoriums found in the deepest part of the page to anchor the Dwark Gate, a place called the 'Arena Luna'. From here they could make an escape route for the armies of the UnderRung, and perhaps a counter-thrust against Moebius, if there was one to be had.

Menses and Mandrake bowed to each other as Mandrake came from the ramparts above.

Menses, being a whole Angel awaited the time honored custom of the partial Angel speaking first. Then they would bow.

"Have you any news, o my Elder?" Mandrake asked, but the Angelic rite of introduction was interrupted by the Midnight Shadow who had impatiently clomped over to them both, having escorted Menses here earlier himself. The Midnight Shadow spoke with his booming voice-

"Our scouts are telling us that the refugee population of the Under Rung are swiftly making their way to the surface, and are largely out of harm's way; the Silver Scream is eating its way down to the Under Rung Throne room, thank the Logos, far away from here. While our people head to Hovahnon we will organize all the swift retreats of our standing armies to this new staging ground. If possible, we could begin in this way a successful counter-invasion of Castle DeepSteel and other lands adjoining, I should hope, if the King is willing, we are. But tell me otherwise, Angel Menses. Is there any resistance in the offing?"

The Angel smiled and bowed to the Avatar, "It is no one's station to tell an Avatar what to do, is it, my Lord Midnight Shadow?" then, addressing both Mandrake and the Midnight Shadow-

"News I have, yes, although first I am prompted to say I am pleased to behold you both erect and defiant against Moebius. Mandrake I am sorry to see your personal Sundering has gone on so long, but you have served a mighty Avatar most faithfully and your sacrifice shall not have been in vain."

Turning to the Gate wistfully, he continued, "Thankfully, this Silver Scream is essentially like the last ones, although much larger, it still requires time to digest and sleep, and although it is still unassailable while it sleeps, much as the last two versions before it, we still have time to plan when it does take time to rest."

Mandrake spoke softly, "It is good that Lotus Knobb and the other Precognitus on the Council of Ambrosia decided to send this Dwark Stone when they did."

The Midnight Shadow suddenly realized he had committed a faux pas in interrupting the Angels when they first met, and was about to withdraw quietly from the proximity, when Menses smiled and stopped him, touching the mane of the Midnight Shadow softly and saying-

"While none may tell an Avatar what to do, surely he cares much about what we have discussed in the Council of Ambrosia. What will you do? Everyone asks. Our only consistent advice to you, goodly Avatar, is that you avoid heroics and theatrics, as we see no positive resolution in direct combat with this Silver Scream Nine. Oppose the Scream Nine, and you will define final end of your page with your own. Alternatively, you can join your armies with ours, and join with our invasion of the domain of Moebius, to finish him off for all future time, much as you just suggested."

The Midnight Shadow gave this a long thought. Menses, sensing his thoughts, continued-

"If all the armies of ProbablePolis do not unite and assemble in front of Castle DeepSteel on the Plain of All-Sorrows, our Precognitus have foreseen a final and hopeless battle, likely to be held at the 'Ford of Light' in High Arcadia by the seat of the Kingdom of Ambrosia, followed by the collapse of all but one page of ProbablePolis."

The great black Unicorn looked at his one-winged Angel and sighed.

"Our warriors will serve with yours." He said and turned to go with one more comment- "You know, Menses, I have to say one more thing… that the thing I still fear the most is that I am about to become like the Avatar of Opus Delirious, a largely impotent and irrelevant ruler riding on a microscopic shred of a once beautiful page."

The Angel sighed as he looked at the Midnight Shadow, for he knew the Morning Star well, and the Logos was not yet finished with either of them. - "I know that Cat o Nine Tails all too well, milord, and you could do worse than serve the Builders as he once did, and still does. My response to you now is to suggest this- that if we can fulfill the prophecy this one last time, we may all know the joy of returning to the pages we were originally born and bred upon. Give that some thought, will you, great Avatar? The Book of Scorns was not written by Moebius, the King or the Queen, eh?"

The Black Unicorn harrumphed at this point in the conversation and said "If you have no further news, Menses, we have armies in disarray, standing by on our word to evacuate to here. Thanks again to you and the High Command for making it possible, and now, Mandrake? Shall we?" not waiting for a response, he began to clip-clop away.

Mandrake looked earnestly at Menses, as Menses whispered "What news have **you**, o my brother? I sense a strand of woe in your visage."

"I fear the child of Destiny has fallen, and the Angel she was entrusted to as well, Mandrake the Black- I have not heard from my soul's twin for some time, and I have called out repeatedly to him since the new attacks began. I fear the worst."

"Two choices, Angel, you know that" Menses laughed, admonishing Mandrake the White.

Mandrake bowed his head and said, "Faith or Fear, our choices must be dear, Yes, my elder, I understand, but now I must go and serve my Master."

Menses kept him from going though, grabbing his robe back in return- "Is there not one thing you would give up everything for, brother?" he stole a look at the Midnight Shadow, who stood a good several paces away now, making to leave at any moment. Menses looked back at Mandrake the White again and said-

"Brother, unruffled your feathers and ask leave of your Master now; come with me to find Mandrake the Black and Lady Nowar! The unremembering Princess cannot be lost! The Great Olde Drake is ready to look for her and I sense he will soon take wing over Avalhalla! I am told that one of us will need to guide him into the Dwark in search of the Lady Nowar. In all the Dwark, if she is still with Mandrake the Black, only you can lead the Drake to find her!"

"But-"

"My Generals will be here soon to help the Midnight Shadow muster his forces to the Plain of All-Sorrows…but come with me now if you can, my brother, and let us find your Mandrake the Black, and his charge, the Daughter of Shard and Limberly, for I sense she is lost and alone."

The Midnight Shadow, in his infinite wisdom, and with his unicorn hearing, realized quickly that the will of the Logos was in motion. He had never opposed the Logos in his whole existence, and wasn't about to start. He called to Mandrake, still clutched by Menses, and said-

"You have my leave, o Mandrake the White, for you have been a faithful servant for many hundreds of pulses."

"May the Logos be with you, Midnight Shadow." Mandrake cried out with joy, laughing.

The Black Unicorn began to cantor up the great stairwell to begin preparations. He stopped and turned, calling out –

"Go find them, if you can, one-winged Angel, and we'll see you at the Final Battle!"

Menses gathered Mandrake in his wings, and the two were gone from the Arena Luna, whirling away like dust in a sudden frigid draft of air that smelled distinctly of cinnamon, leaving the Arena below entirely to the carpenters in the far corners, buttressing the walls of the nearly finished Dwark Gate. Precognitids hovered anxiously by the Carpenters and stone masons while they used tools attached to their own structures to adjust the Dwark Key Stone firmly into its footing.

The Midnight Shadow was hurtling upwards, trying to still his resentment of this Silver Scream, devouring away his city and Kingdom right above his head at that very moment. Moebius had attacked his Kingdom with an unstoppable foe. This was getting personal, and the Midnight Shadow silently wished that he might get a chance to personally trample Moebius himself.

It was meager solace knowing that the evacuation of the Under Rung military was about to dove tail with the larger Insurrection against Moebius, but at least there was a plan in place now, even though it involved him leaving his own page to go fight somewhere else; Avatars typically do not leave their own page, as their best aspects are diminished, and great powers wane more easily still.

One way or another, it would all be over soon, he thought, and watched quietly as Giants and Ogres jogged by, clad in heavy mail, wearing their best weapons and artillery supplies around their shoulders like bandoliers. Oversized Deep Trolls were carting in their favorite siege equipment in a bumbling, if effective manner, down into this catacomb.

"Where were all the Basilisk?" the Midnight Shadow began to wonder to himself, idly missing his long time confidant, the one winged Angel Mandrake had been his greatest aide-de-camp. Now was the worst time he could have chosen to take his leave.

"-and the cockatrice storm troopers by jove, where the frak are they?" the Shadow shouted suddenly.

Goblins herded mummies, zombies and ram horned ghost-hogs in the droves past the stile that the Shadow had chosen to stand on as he supervised the evacuation. Giant tusked Grubs and huge Roc Birds struggled to get down the stairs to the Arena with the help of Trolls and hobgoblins, who were occasionally sidestepped by Slimy Globs, Vampires, Ghoul-bats and Medusids, all slithering and scrambling to get down to the evacuation point. A bald, one eyed leprechaun that smelt of elderberries beat on a huge triple headed drum at the greatest pinnacle of the Arena, trying to keep everyone on a beat to get down into the Luna Arena main stage. Every time a new bunch approached, they identified themselves to the Trolls in control and went through the black membrane of the Dwark gate.

The exodus of the Under Rung and the Avatar of T'ien Shann was about to begin in earnest. Far above them all, the Silver Scream continued its onslaught and banal feast, making relentless progress as it ate its way down to the Throne Room.

AntiPart Seven

So close sometimes is so far away...

Grandma Brandy was sacked and snoring loudly. She was so tired that she hadn't even plugged in her laptop or checked her cell-phone. A box of doughnuts and two cups of coffee sat waiting on the table for her when she woke up. The Hotel room was warm and dark.

But Nowar was wide awake, nightlight headlamp shining brightly on the pages of ProbablePolis sitting on her lap. She was reading the last hundred and ninety pages of her adventure in a world somehow sitting right in front of her, and yet so far away.

As she finished the last scriven page she uttered aloud "Holy Frog! What a cliff hanger! Hurtling through a bottomless abyss!" she shut the book, and as it was used to doing, it re-clasped and locked itself. She sighed. If she wanted to open it again, she knew she'd have to activate it by the musical code, and then, well, then she would be plunged back into ProbablePolis, hurtling through a bottomless abyss...the Dwark. Bottomless abyss?

Suddenly she had a thought- she was remembering Hieronymous Jones little lecture with his holographic device in front of the Lens back in the UnderRung.

She thought to herself- "The Dwark isn't really a bottomless abyss... it's all of the space that contains ProbablePolis, all inside a sphere...it's not really a bottomless abyss at all, just a really big sphere. But what was the sphere made of though? Where in fact was it? Inside this book somehow? No it couldn't be...it had to be in the place that she and Grandma Brandy were headed- to the Air Force Base in Connecticut, right?"

Then she thought more about the holograph that Jones had shown her and her friends. Only Fourteen Pages? Once, a long time ago, there were Three Hundred and Sixty pages, according to Alpha-Beta. Where did the other pages go? How did Moebius and the Gull & Crones

Society destroy all those pages in the first place? One war after another, apparently.

And how did she know that there was about to come a knock at the door? How did she know that she was about to look up at the clock and see 1:11 AM?

There was a knock at the door. It was 1:11 AM. She shuddered.

Grandma Brandy rolled out of bed and loaded her huge rifle all in one fluid motion. Once Pop Bric had told Nowar that her Grandmother was way more than a cook in the Army, and now she believed it.

"Go to the bathroom, Nowar. Take the book with you and lock the door. Don't let anyone in but me, ok?"

Nowar wasted no time in getting to the bathroom.

AntiPart Six

If you aim for the roof, you might hit the stars

Imagine a long gravel parking lot by a Hotel, with two men walking side by side, one a very tired looking haggard fellow in an outfit that looked kind-of like an astronaut suit, and the other, apparently the very same man, wearing a suit and tie with sunglasses. The fact that it was the middle of the night didn't seem to faze him, although his arm was bandaged, and he was walking with a limp. Neither of them were in very good shape, but they ambled forward fairly well leaning against each other.

Finally, the astronaut couldn't stand it anymore, and asked aloud-

"Ok, now tell me again - 'Why' are we here?"

The guy in the suit and tie growls his answer with a voice like charcoal but keeps moving, "Room 307, Shamrock Motel, just down there, is where we need to get *you*, and quickly, man, come on, let's limp faster!"

The astronaut stops to catch his breath – "No, tell me now!"

The suit shakes his head, grabs him and pulls him along- "Ok, I'll tell you but you have to keep walking, man- my phase here should have been over two minutes ago! The next Fugue is about to begin!"

Astronaut guy shook his own head now…what the frak did 'my phase should have been over' mean anyway? The next Fugue?" he said "Look, I'm still trying to figure out why you look just like me."

They had come to some stairs. Room 307 in gold shone on one of the doors to a room on the third floor far above them. The suit and tie guy said laconically "Yeah, I know you are, look, let's just get you up these stairs- ok? Your mother, and maybe your daughter, should be in Room 307 at this Hotel- here we go, come on man, move like you've got a purpose!"

"I feel groggy"

"Of course you do, you're fresh out of a Dwark-jump, man! You did a MoonClock Walk, lad, and you made history…your family will be proud."

"Really?"

"Yes, and now we need to help you get home, with your Daughter and her Mother, and, well, your Father, too I hear now, for crying out loud. Understand?"

"Alright, er, uh, no, actually I don't understand at all, did you say my Father is in the Virtual world too, now? How did *that* happen?"

They were both reaching for the doorbell to Room 307 now, but the guy in the suit, his hand was turning translucent.

"Oh Fark!" he said, just as the sound of someone rousing inside alerted them both that the door would soon be open. "Listen, you and your Mother and our Daughter need to try to get into the MoonClock Facility- get to Chip Storage Area Omega-9, use this security clearance card, and then you can make a backdoor for me or Bric to replace the …"

The guy in the tie and suit was gone. A piece of plastic fell to the ground. It had a little picture of his face with a string of numbers.

"Omega-9?" the guy in the astronaut outfit picked up the ID card. He still felt a bit slow and sleepy, but suddenly there he was, in front of his own Mother, who shrieked, lowered the elephant gun, thankfully, and began to turn as pale as a sheet.

"Nowar! Nowar! Come quick, your Father is here!" but there was no answer. Brandy went back into the hotel room, kicked the bathroom door in, and making a quick inspection, re-emerged clutching a very thick old looking book in her hands. She stared at her son for a moment, and then said-

"How in the world did you find us?" she started to ask, and then said "Never mind, I have the book, son." And she put it gingerly on the table. He looked up at her. He had wasted no time in slumping into a chair at the table. He was still smoking a bit. He stared at the book, holding it gingerly.

"You have no clue what to do with that, do you son?"

"No, Mom, no, I don't."

"Why doesn't that surprise me?"

They were both quiet for a moment.

"There are doughnuts and coffee on the table, son; help yourself."

"Yeah, ok, Mom, so tell me what you know about this book, and I'll tell you what I think just happened to me."

AntiPart Five

But what about the rest of the Crew?

Mandrake the Black came to consciousness in a very uncomfortable position, apparently shackled, tightly, with cold iron chains, to a huge girder of steel, welded and riveted to a vast and broken kaleidoscope of rusted steel girders, creaking and groaning, somehow suspended like a giant mobile in the Dwarkness all around him.

Where was he?

Wherever he was, it was as cold as a block of ice on a frigid winter morning. He struggled briefly with his freezing shackles and realized that in time, as his strength returned, he would be able to utter them open with a simple Word or two. For the moment he looked around to see if anyone else had survived. Where was Nowar? Was she already half way to Castle DeepSteel? The mere thought of Moebius getting a hold of her made him feel sick in his stomach. Had he failed so completely? Despair danced in his soul for a time until he heard a whirring noise nearby. It was Mrs. Machine!

"Mrs. Machine! Can you hear me? Are you cognizant and functioning, my dear?"

The sound of disgruntled binary chattering suggested she was in about the same shape as he was, functional, but well fastened to this ad-hoc open-air prison deep in the Dwark.

"Mandrake, you are finally awake!" called Two Fangs, who must have been even farther down in this mess of black steel, as his voice was very faint.

"I am, Wolven-kine brother, I am indeed, as is Mrs. Machine. Unfortunately, I suspect I am as you both are, alive but well-restrained."

"I am not as strong as an Angel, though, Mandrake, you should be able to shed your shackles I should think."

"When I recover that fabled strength, yes, Two Fangs, but I shall need a few minutes. In the meantime, did you see what they did with Nowar? Is she near you?"

"No, I've no clue, Mandrake." Two Fangs growled, and then cried out – "Mrs. Machine, does she not record all she sees?"

"You're right!" and with that he quietly said "Mishpat" and popped off his shackles and began climbing through the twisted barbed wire and broken floating girders to make his way to Mrs. Machine. A few more minutes, and she was free as well, excitedly extending her camera and monitor for Mandrake to see what she could see.

Footage was brief and largely unrewarding, though. It showed the impact of the SnarkShark on Mandrake…it showed Nowar being flung away, rolling out of control as she hurtled into the Dwark, her wings vanishing, and, then…she was gone. But at least she had not been scooped up and brought here, he thought as he made his way down to where Two Fangs was hanging, less than ceremoniously at the bottom of this twisted floating palace of slag.

"What did it show?" Two Fangs asked while the Angel ripped off the shackles.

"It showed that Nowar wasn't captured, Two Fangs, but it showed little else. Nothing on our fine Ouroboros either, unfortunately. Who knows where he ended up…"

"I …have …failed the Companions." He looked downward at his feet.

Two Fangs smiled then. "Where is your faith, Angel?" and clapped him on his back, hard. We still live, and while we live, we can still go after her, can't we?" He began climbing upward, looking to get some altitude, which every Wolven-kine knows, always changes attitude.

The Angel laughed weakly. "Yes, Two Fangs, yes you're right."

Suddenly taking heart, he turned to Mrs. Machine "Are your navigational sensors online yet, Mrs. Machine? We'll need to find out where we are now, and where we were when we were attacked. With a little luck, we should be able to use both locations to triangulate where we lost contact with Nowar, and perhaps, even, extrapolate where she has ended up."

Two Fangs was beginning to like the Angel, in spite of himself, but he looked around nervously from his high perch. It was only a matter of time before a bunch of Moebius Dwark-Vessels showed up to claim them for Castle DeepSteel. Their reprieve might be temporary indeed, he realized, for Mrs. Machine, even in her carriage mode, loaded with him and the Angel both, still could not outrun a Snark-Shark or a battle-cruiser if it showed up.

"Let us not tarry, Mandrake. We've been lucky so far."

The Angel agreed, and Mrs. Machine quickly began constructing herself into a small Dwark-tug-boat to carry her two companions away from the twisted Dwark detainment float station. In less than a minute, they were puttering off just as Mandrake figured out their last location.

"Ah hah!" he cried figuring out the possible trajectory coordinates, and, voila, he pointed to a scrap of a page right smack between her and her general orientation.

"I know where she may have ended up by now." He announced proudly.

'Where?" asked Two Fangs, still playing look-out as they whipped along at about forty four miles an hour.

"Opus Delirious." he called back into the wind that was building as Mrs. Machine pushed her engines as hard as she could.

Two Fangs kept his thoughts to himself. He knew Opus Delirious, and without doubt he suspected that Mandrake had to remember it as well. Mandrake had indeed been there once, and they both knew it was all that was left of the 17th page, floating way out in the Dwark far away from the great Ribbon of Light, and prying eyes.

"A fragment of many secrets, that place." Mandrake thought aloud.

Two Fangs had been there when he was a cub, and he remembered it as a bit of a silly and surreal place. It was the home of the Morning Star, the

Avatar of the long vanquished and torn apart 17th page. Vanquished or not, Two Fangs respected the fact that the Morning Star had managed to fend off Moebius' hordes with his own irregulars, several Dwark Chopper riding gangs of rude and offensive Faeries, usually led by Bonsai Rex, his brothers, and the mysterious Walrus, when they felt like it.

It could have been worse, they both realized. Opus Delirious was an experience, sure, but there were no Moebius fiends or forts anywhere near there. Quietly they watched the inky Dwarkness as Mrs. Machine puttered them along their way cresting gloriously at her fifty miles per hour limit for two passengers.

After a time, Two Fangs was uncomfortable with the fact that he realized that the Angel could make much faster progress on his own then staying on the Mrs. Machine dingy. The Angel, becoming aware of his discomfort said-

"Only if you ask me with all your heart, brother Wolven-Kine, for we are far more now than just the Companions once brought together by the hands of the Logos."

"For exactly that reason you must leave us behind, Mandrake. Go and find Nowar, we'll catch up eventually. Go…NOW!"

Mandrake sped off into the gloom like a firefly, bustling on his way in a beeline for a shred of a page called Opus Delirious, drifting along in the deep Dwark. Mrs. Machine redoubled her efforts as she realized she had only one passenger. With glee, she reached sixty five miles per hour, and Two Fangs stood vigilant in the Dwark, praying to the Logos for Nowar's safety.

Far behind them a great explosion erupted.

One of Moebius' battle cruisers had been slated to take out the Station behind them for target practice, and it had just arrived. Flashing lights from far away were seen by both Two Fangs and Mrs. Machine. Two Fangs thanked the Logos that they had been spared, and stared into the gloom as the wind ruffled over his mane, counting his blessings. Opus Delirious would be a marvelous haven, an oasis in a very dark end of the Dwark, after all they had just been through.

AntiPart Four

On the good ship, Anomaly…

Nowar woke with a start, a very big bounce, and the realization that she couldn't move.

She was no longer in the Dwark, or rather she was on something very large, but possibly still in the Dwark, it seemed. She cast around looking for a light source and bearings. Something had caught her fall! It felt springy, and only a little sticky. She was still bouncing somewhat, in fact. It was dim and hard to see anything.

"Very gloomy place", she thought. She squinted, trying to make something out of the shadows as her ups and downs began to settle out.

She was suspended by thick vines of tough webbing, vines that sprang her up and down gently now beneath a green lush canopy, as tall as any she had ever seen. The ground seemed to be at least thirty or forty feet below her. Above her in the sky there was a sparkling raft of celestial lights moving very slowly. Were they getting closer? Looking back downward to the ground, she saw small wisps, billowing balls of light, streaming into the clearing as if they were chasing each other.

She was definitely not alone.

Suddenly the wisps erupted into far more solid form, each of a different color—one blue, one red, one green, and another, the color of pumpkins. They were not much taller than goats, and they looked like little frog-headed, butterfly-winged faeries at first, although each one carried the distinct mark of a certain stylistic theme—one of air, another of fire and the third of water. A fourth one, very brown and earthen in nature, plopped itself onto a nearby branch with a splattering sound. It burbled to itself happily as it solidified into a fat bug-eyed "froggy-boy" with tiny wings that looked more like tree roots bound with plastic wrap. It was apparently uninterested in what was about to happen next, and it chewed on something brown and sticky.

All of their features were congealing now, getting crisper. Their faces bore the unmistakable look of amphibians but with lots of antennae, and thin spindly arms. They smiled broadly.

Where had providence set her down and what in heaven's name were **these** things?

They were all crawling around in this netting now, and the fiery one, the tallest of them all, managed to bounce right over to Nowar's face.

"I'm Jackie!" She'd said it like it was the most amazing thing in the world, and continued just as enthusiastically, "**I'm** an elemental, and so are **all** of my friends!" She seemed overjoyed that no one was telling her to put a lid on it, so she went on and exclaimed "Why even ol' Glupus over there is an elemental. Isn't that **cool**?"

Nowar smiled. She asked for an introduction to them all, and everyone got very excited.

"Oooo! Introductions!" they all cried.

Glupus lunged in front of everyone to shake her one free hand with proper and enthusiastic form, leaving muddy leaves and dirt smears on her fingers. Myrtle was water, and she gushed over Nowar's hands vigorously cleaning them of all dirt. Edith was air, and she blew over all Nowar's hands until they were very dry.

Jackie got above and behind Nowar, and elastically stretched herself into a very broad and tall form, becoming frightfully thin. Apparently she had done this with the intention of creating a gentle cloak of radiating air that did indeed start to warm Nowar's Dwark-chilled bones.

The rest of the gang started to cut the netting, but in a very careful manner. Glupus jumped below, and allowed Nowar to be lowered onto his back as he stood on the forest floor. Threads and vines splintered and fell all around his head. Edith couldn't contain herself anymore, and she and Jackie and Myrtle pranced circles everywhere around Nowar, who was just stepping off the back of Glupus.

Nowar looked around the barely lit glade while the Elementals frantically lit candles in trees and strung popcorn netting everywhere to celebrate. Their 'net trick' had worked! Princess Nowar was saved!

"Huzzah!" they all cried in joy.

Glupus even smiled once as he thought to himself that the Walrus and the Morning Star would be overjoyed to discover that their little island, Opus Delirious, was now host to the most sought after Homo sapiens in **all** ProbablePolis!

Edith removed a piece of Glupus while he wasn't looking. "Ow!" he protested, "What did you do that for?"

Edith had already fashioned four party hats out of Glupus clay, and Jackie applied fire to harden them all, which hardly took a second. Myrtle then happily deposited them all on each and every one of the little Elementals.

"Tomorrow, we defeat Moebius! Tonight, we party!" cried Jackie, pulling out a fiery little harp and tuning the strings while Glupus served glasses of dandelion wine. Several animals, most of them timid when the Elementals were in the neighborhood, were now peering from the shadows of the forest.

Nowar watched it all, and felt heartened. She was with friends again.

She would rest here for awhile.

AntiPart Three

lil Bonsai Rex to the rescue!

Lil' Bonsai Rex was exactly what his name suggested.

Heard of a Bonsai Tree? They're little! They're kept that way by an exotic art that can keep a tree tiny, miniature even, with itsy bitsy leaves. What else? Heard of a Tyrannosaurus Rex? Now you know the rest of the story. Bonsai Rex was all of a fifty foot tall Dinosaur packed into a three feet tall body, by who knows what hand, creating an incredibly powerful little dynamo of energy, filled with vim and vigor.

As a predator, Bonsai didn't do so well. He was Buddhist. If you don't know what that means, don't worry about it for now. Just assume that lil' Bonsai Rex, albeit a really tough little guy, kept a vegetarian diet rich in nuts and already-dead bugs, and got to bed at a reasonable hour after drinking green tea.

At this very moment, however, Lil' Bonsai Rex was 'going to town', running as fast as his stubby little clawed legs could carry him. Like an unstoppable engine running through the dark forest, leaping over fallen trees, he was still thinking about what the Omen-tary had showed the Walrus saying-

"Coo-coo-ca-choo, Lil' Bonsai, where are you? I gots a mission for you to do! Follow da Omen-tary, little buddy, ya hear me? Wake up sleepy head, time to go take down da Moebius! Follow da bubble-headed bird to de all hands meeting, chowder head! And mind yer P's and Q's, we gots impotant company today."

The Omen-tary had screeched all this and then flown off, headed to where the Walrus had asked it to guide 'all-hands', which these days was just lil Bonsai Rex himself, and those obnoxious little Chopper-riding Faeries. A Dwark-Spider Queen had recently ambushed and eaten his two brothers, Ernie and Clyde.

Lil' Bonsai Rex had been a happy-go-lucky tree-hugging pygmy dinosaur before Moebius had torn apart his page and distributed all the pygmy

T-Rex's to the three hundred and sixty corners of all ProbablePolis. Lil' Bonsai had spent many weeks drinking mushroom vinegar and root beer to try to give up his grief over his two litter mates getting eaten. Sure, Ernie was a real egg-sucker, but Clyde had been good to him, and brought him tasty warm dead things. He tried not to think about those two, and he allowed himself to get re-invigorated —he was on the move, he was on a mission! Something must have happened for the Walrus to send out such an exciting 'all-hands' Omen-tary.

He lunged over a broken tree trunk, grabbed a dead branch and waved it wildly as he cried "BONSAI!!!" He was soon picking up speed again as he tore down the hill to the Delirious Glade, truly a legend in his own mind. Hopefully the Walrus had some good news. Maybe he could tell him what P's and Q's were, too.

AntiPart Two

And then the Faeries roll in...

Nowar had been sitting and drinking many glasses of punch with her new-found friends in the Glade of Opus Delirious.

She was beginning to feel much less worried about what might happen next, which may or may not have had something to do with the punch, when into the clearing roared three dozen incredibly loud machines. They were hovering, motorcycle-like vehicles, none much bigger than a tricycle, and all operated by Faeries that would reshape your definition of a Faerie. They were as rough and unshaven as you could imagine. Thick leather jackets worn over tank tops, they were gum-chewing Faeries that swore like sailors and made rude gestures at each other as they rolled into the clearing.

Glupus recoiled and hid behind Nowar. "I hate Dwark Choppers, all you Faeries and yer noisy machines stink!" he cried out loud. But if the Faeries heard him, they gave no notice. They all put down their little kick stands, lit their tiny cigarettes, and began pouring iced teas and lemonade for everyone. A tinny, but annoyingly loud boom box began to drone a barely musical beat.

For the most part, they didn't act much like they even noticed Nowar, so consumed with playing cards, smoking and arguing over sports trivia and checkers that they hardly gave a glance at the big person sitting with the Elementals only a few yards away. Nowar looked at Jackie, but before she could say anything, Jackie blurted -

"They're a gang of Faeries. Don't mind them. They ride those Dwark Choppers and they like to fight the creatures and machines of Moebius, and so we ...kind-of ...put up with their behavior."

She laughed nervously and suggested "Lil' Bonsai Rex and the Walrus are **very** nice, though."

Nowar watched these little foul and winged creatures bicker and push each other around, sometimes violently, inflicting harsh words and black eyes whenever and wherever they felt they should.

"Wow. Glad they're on our side." Was all Nowar could think to say.

Edith looked up from her place next to the punch bowl and quietly said "Don't worry Nowar, the Walrus will be here soon. He'll tell us what's going on."

Just then, lil Bonsai Rex rolled into the clearing, pretending he was a super secret agent to himself. He had the most excellent sun glasses on of course. Gadzooks I am so cool, he thought to himself as he ran around the clearing twice. Then he noticed Nowar. Suddenly seeing all the Faeries standing near him, he struck a cool pose, did a 'high five' with one of them, and strutted over to Nowar.

"Hello der, Missie. I iz da Lil' Bonsai Rex. Howdy-do?"

Nowar hardly knew how to respond, but she tried with- "Well, a pleasure to meet you, Bonsai. I am Nowar, and I am lost in the Dwark."

"Lost?" he looked shocked "Oh no no no no! You are not lost, Missie, you is found, You iz on da Island of Opus Delirious. Dis a very very safe place." His smile showed he did not have all of his teeth. He prattled on with "Most importantly, Moebius and his hooligans don't like to come here, an they don' come here much at all at all at all."

It was destined to happen, of course, but a Faerie, seeing Bonsai hanging out with the big person, ambled over to see what was going on. He poked Bonsai with a thorn.

"Ouch! Withagat dithago yithagou withagant lithagittithagle snithagot?" Bonsai screeched.

"o stithagop ithagit, blithagundithager bithaguss- ithagi jithagust withagant tithago sithagee whithagat's githagoithaging ithagon."

Nowar looked shocked and confused. She was supposed to be able to understand all the languages of ProbablePolis! Why couldn't she tell what they were saying now? She motioned to Jackie and whispered.

"What are they speaking? I don't understand it. What do those words mean?"

Jackie smiled and said in her singsong manner "Oh, they don't mean anything Nowar. They mean exactly what they are saying."

"Huh? I don't understand. They're speaking now, what are they speaking?"

"Oh, they're speaking Ubiquitish Gibberish, darling. It's the language we all speak to confuse the monsters of Moebius, **and** get along with the Faeries and all the other Dwark Chopper Gangs. You just put the first sound of a word at the front of an 'ithug' and the rest of the sound behind the 'ithug'. Like, your name, Nowar, would be **Ni**thag**ow**ithag**ar**. See?" she smiled.

Nowar looked blankly at her. "I still don't get it."

"OK, ok, so Flower would be Flithagowithager, and kitty would be Kithagitty, and a pumpkin would be a pithagumpkithagin, and an elephant would be a…

"OK, now I understand, Jackie, let me try some…hm…lithaget mithage trithagy sithagome…hithagey! ithagI githaget ithagit!"

"See you did it!" she turned circles in the air.

Bonsai Rex was already cheating at cards with the Faerie that had poked him in the ribs a few minutes ago. With any luck he would rob him blind with all the aces he had stored in his underwear, hopefully in just a few minutes, and then walk off with, well hard to say what this Faerie might have on him, but Bonsai might get a few duckets, a handsome pile of nearly dead batteries, and maybe some Chopper Wax.

Better save some of those aces for later, he thought to himself.

Hopefully the Walrus would arrive before the Faeries started a riot.

Lil' Bonsai Rex giggled to himself again. Right now they were content to just chain-smoke and bicker, but they could be very capricious, these Faeries, and he was a lone lizard Sheriff these days, wasn't he?

He wondered if this new guest would make a good deputy. She sure was awful tall.

AntiPart One

Now is the time to speak of many things...

Nowar watched the Walrus approach, like a happy jiggling bowl of grey jello, with a huge cookie duster of a mustache over his profoundly enormous Tusks. The Tusks were alive with strange mystic glyphs and baffling ciphers, and his dress was like a burgundy version of a colonial British uniform.

He was preceded and followed by a swarm of flying and crawling critters of all kinds, hopping and twittering as they all cascaded forward, surrounding Nowar, the Elementals, the Faerie Dwark-chopper gang, and lil Bonsai Rex.

With a heavy wheeze, the Walrus looked Nowar once up and down, and said proudly to everyone assembled- "COO-COO-CA-CHOO, Y'ALL! Ho! Ho! HO! We gots da goods on Moebius NOW! Hehehehe!"

Everybody cheered, and a few of the Faeries threw water balloons, made farting sounds and cackled to each other. They didn't mean any disrespect, it seemed; they were just Faeries, that's all.

Nowar now looked him up and down and said "How do you do?"

"Pretty good, and you?" the Walrus leaned over and answered her in his deep bassoon voice.

Nowar thought about her answer as all sorts of critters crept closer to her side.

"O Great and noble Walrus, I am Nowar, barely remembering Princess of ProbablePolis, daughter of King Shard and Queen Limberly…and I am lost and alone…I was separated from my companions by a vicious attack of the evil Duke Moebius."

The Walrus smiled a big smile, and kept on listening.

"I was hurled into the Dwark away from my companions, Ouroboros Alpha-Beta, Two Fangs, Mandrake the Black, and Mrs. Machine. I have no idea how long I was falling in the Dwark before I landed here."

Several of the Faeries cheered loudly for Opus Delirious when Nowar said the word 'here', many of them throwing root beer into the air.

"I believe Mandrake was leading us to the Great Olde Drake of Avalhalla, because everyone believes he can give me back my memories. Then we were to find the last Sky Whale, although I wouldn't have a clue myself on how to find her, much less this Avalhalla place, and I'm not really certain what a Sky Whale could do for me in any event. It's a very frustrating turn of events, don't you see?"

"Hmmmm…well" he said, and then chuckled so loudly the forest trembled "I came here to talk to you about Cabbages and Kings, drink some tea, and get to know you, lil missy, but I can see that the time is at hand for you to meet the Morning Star. He's da Avatar of this little shred of a page we call home."

The Faeries cheered again at the mention of the word "home", and a brief altercation over who was more Opus Patriotic than the other nearly started another little Faerie brawl until Bonsai could roughly intervene. Three rude Faeries, Colleen Crumblewhack, Lynnie the Leaper, and Jenna Jumblewits were all ejected, two of them while they were conscious. A fourth, Catlin Crepuscular, cast a brief web of twilight over Bonsai before she slipped off into the gloom.

The Walrus reached over to take Nowar by the shoulder, hugged her, smiled deeply, and began to walk with her back down the hill he had come from, turning right at a signpost that read 'Home of the Morning Star'.

They were headed down into a deep hollow that got very dark very quickly.

She felt in her body pouch and found the Memory crystal thing she had picked up in the guest lodge of the Queen of Mermopolis. She had used it to light her way in the Dwark on the Purple Brick Road, and now, pulling it from its secure enclosure, she watched it light up a tunnel that they were in. It seemed to be made out of huge briar patches and twisted thick vines. She was grateful for the light to be able to avoid tripping over the very knotty floor beneath their feet and fins.

The Walrus did not pause, and he seemed to be able to see in dark or light.

"Ye see, lil Missy Nowar, only da Morning Star can help you now. You come with me and I'll take you to see him. And den we'll go ride off and find dat Olde Drake on de Dwark Express. Oh, lookit dat, here we are-"

Nowar interrupted, and tried to get back the attention of the Walrus, who was trying to decide which of three passages to take on the next leg of their subterranean briar patch jaunt into the Under Forest of Opus Delirous- "er, Great and Noble Walrus, what or who is the MorningStar? Where does he live?"

The Walrus suddenly heaved his bulk like a huge gray dirigible, smiled and said- "He lives down dat way, darlin' come along, you'll meet him soon enough"

She continued to follow the wheezing leather clad Walrus down the briar patch tunnel of his choice for a good ten minutes before she realized that the twittering hordes of little creatures and fans of the Walrus had caught up with them both down here.

She wondered where her own Companions were, and she hoped that they were all alive and well. Suddenly the tunnel narrowed, and the Walrus was bent over by a doorway she would have to kneel to go through, if this was his intention. Over the doorframe was a signpost 'Know Thyself'.

The Walrus smiled, and said, "y'ready lil missy? He's inside- he's waiting for ye. Just make three real distinct knocks. Watch the stairs goin' down when you go in, ok?"

Nowar looked at the Walrus, who nodded vigorously at her as she knocked, three times, clunking the oversize brass door knocker against the door. It opened suddenly without effort, apparently by itself. A light breeze began to blow, it smelled of almonds and honeysuckle, and a gentle voice, ever so slightly sing-songy, perhaps a bit nasal, but not coming from anywhere specifically in particular said to her-

"My dear, you are an Evolving Lass, but what you need now is a Looking Glass. Enter and know yourself better."

She felt a bit nervous. The voice went on.

"Shut the door behind you, and grateful are we, o Walrus, to you for bringing our charge to the finest hospitality we could offer. I shall return her to you shortly, refreshed and ready for your little road trip."

"HO HO HO! Coo-coo-ca-choo! CALOO CALAY!" The Walrus guffawed and waved to Nowar as he walked off smiling, saying "Nothing to be afraid of in there Missy Nowar, just be yourself, and I'll be back at the Dwark Station, waitin' on ye."

Nowar stood at the doorjamb, bent over, and looked down.

A very thin, spindly, winding staircase made of bamboo and vines spiraled downward into a veritable, seemingly bottomless canyon layered with thick lightly glowing and very shaggy trees with thick bark covered with mushrooms and bracket fungi that pulsed with light from time to time. The air was warm and moist, and she had the impression that she was about to step into a gigantic terrarium.

"Here goes nothing." She laughed at her situation, and began to crawl down the somewhat constrained jungle ladder, making her way very slowly and deliberately. It bordered on perilous. Ouroboros Alpha-Beta would never have made it down this thing, she thought to herself.

She wished she knew what happened to all her friends, but she made quick time going down into the lair of the Morning Star of Opus Delirious. Maybe he would know where they were now.

AntiChapter Four

Wherein we begin to understand the importance of the Mad World inside the Holy Grid, placed as it were, on an Implausible Chip

AntiPart Thirteen

What is the half-life of Love?

As she made her way down the vines and bamboo stairwell, Nowar would have found great comfort in knowing that all the Companions were indeed in one piece and alive, and though sundered as a group, they were mustering heartily once more; Mrs. Machine and Two Fangs had backtracked to find Ouroboros Alpha-Beta, who were both ecstatic that someone had come back for them, jumping for joy so hard that they nearly fell off the Purple Dwark Road. A very long hike back down the Purple Dwark Road had been their only option.

With the Amphisbaena and the Wolven-kine King now both safely on board, Mrs. Machine took new coordinates and they headed off into the Dwark, their destination was where Mandrake was already well on his way to arriving at, namely the little floating shred of a page called Opus Delirious, all that was left of the 17th Kingdom, where Nowar was about to meet its mysterious avatar, the Morning Star.

Nowar paused at one of the floors she was finding suspended all over the canopy. She could just now barely make out the forest floor below, covered in a rug of verdant mosses and mushrooms, bracket fungi and tuffty-topped trees- all of which glowed or pulsed or even buzzed with little colonies of tiny glowing arthropods. That's a fancy name for bugs, by the way.

"Nice place, isn't it?" This time the voice was actually here in the air, behind her, as a matter of fact, not so far up in a vine covered darkened cubby set back into the wall of the briar patch. It was a very peculiar voice, and actually it sounded more like three voices, all speaking, simultaneously, the same thing, just slightly different in tone, tempo and inflection.

Nowar grabbed a vine and pulled herself up a few feet to peer into the cubby. Something was moving in there alright, but it seemed like what she was seeing was …filling itself in, kind of like an animated coloring book painting itself in like a color-by-number page.

Whatever it was, it was a spectacular effect, and when it was done, Nowar beheld a simply huge, fluffy, orange-haired tabby cat, about the size of a rather large English sheep dog. He was definitely not your ordinary oversized alley cat, though; *he had three mouths*, all of which grinned widely at her, and *three big bulging green eyes*. His tail, or rather tails, were fluffy alright, and they all ended with iron tipped morning star spiked balls; nine of them, to be precise.

"Why yes." She realized she would be rude not to answer the question addressed to her and said- "It is a beautiful garden, indeed. I would be correct in assuming you are the Morning Star, the Avatar of Opus Delirious?"

"Assumptions are tricky things." Said mouth one.

"To 'assume', can make an 'ass' out of 'u' and 'me'." Said mouth two.

"But this time, you are corrrrect. We are more than just a good gardener. We are a Cat-o-nine-tails, Catisphaenically referred to as "The Morning Star" by the beloved denizens of our little Opus Delirious, yes, my dearest; so you have arrived, but do tell, would you have some tea before we catch up?"

He swaggered like a fat little Prince down the side of the cubby, and Nowar noticed he had too many paws for her to count, maybe a dozen, but he moved them so swiftly that she could barely tell for sure. As he began to settle in front of her, a checker board table burst into being between them, and he sat down, reaching with one of his many paws for the just-in-time manifested tea pot and cups, all floating ceremoniously in the air.

As Nowar and the Morning Star sipped at their tea, the table was still active, bursting forth an array of flowers, candles, shells from the sea, and plates of pancakes sizzling with butter. There was an empty photograph frame suddenly, and a small accordion and then, a tiny clear glass diorama in the very center of the table. It was like the kind a child might have at Christmas, the kind filled with snow you could shake, and watch the flurries rain down on top of Snowmen or Santa on his sleigh. It glowed curiously, beckoning her fingers to pick it up. She could almost remember a gentle touch, and then the diorama seized her entire attention, almost pulling her into the scene it contained.

Inside was a tiny scene of a Bookcase, a young Man, and a barely seen Angel, guiding the young man to a specific book on one of the shelves.

"Why?" she looked up at the Cat, who was now leaning over, looking into her eyes.

She felt just a moment of discomfort that quickly passed. Nowar was beginning to wonder if there wasn't anything funny in that tea she had drank. She was feeling a bit light headed, and suddenly she realized she didn't know how much time had passed since she had come down here. She turned her attention back to the Morning Star.

"Why? Well, why not?" answered mouth one, giggling.

"This is a child's bauble, intended to save and present memories, or were you referring to the memory contained inside that you might have just observed?" quipped mouth two.

"What we mean to say is that this is a 'Remembrançarium'. We put in them little scenes of the 'Tales of Lore, Legend and Law' from the "Book of Scorns", by which we remember all the stories of the Builders, Guardians, Heroes and Villains of all ProbablePolis."

"Thank you for sharing all that, but what I was really asking was 'Why was the Angel guiding the young man's hand to the book shelf for that one book?'- What was the point? Why?"

The Morning Star picked up and examined the Diorama with his paws, turning it around and around to see the snow fall.

"Well, clearly this Diorama was left by a Lunar Reverance or some other epiphaneous being, it's not really one of ours, in fact, I just noticed. How odd, we thought we had selected a different diorama for this exercise, oh well-" said mouth three.

"Look closer, you might recognize the young Man, dearie." Said mouth two.

"Don't look too closely, or you might fall in, though" said mouth one, and then all three mouths grinned and said- "But go with the flow, in any event, why don't you, dearie?" and handed the thing back to her.

"Indeed, have a closer look; you should be able to use this Remembrançarium, as it appears to work just fine." Said the second mouth

"Work just fine?" she looked at him blankly, he was just looking at her and the object in her hand. She looked a second time, and she was totally utterly sucked into the scene, like she was really there!

The young man was sleeping in his bed by the Bookcase, and did not wake up as she looked around the room.

She could still hear the Morning Star, though.

"I'm sorry, Princess, we keep forgetting that you're still rather new to ProbablePolis, so allow us to narrate. Before you stands the Bookcase in the old bedroom of your father, which serves now as a guest room in which you have stayed, though you don't remember any of it really."

"As the little girl...I stayed here. I have had dreams of a little girl in this bedroom."

"That would be you, yes, as who you really are, a little ten year old girl, in the big world, outside of ProbablePolis, of course. Here in the little world of ProbablePolis, you are someone quite different...but who is to say who is dreaming who now?"

"Have you not thought this for yourself yet?" said one of the mouths.

ProbablePolis

Nowar watched as an Angel descended the staircase outside the door, entered the room quietly and knelt by the bedside of the boy. It reminded her of Mandrake, but it couldn't have been. Still, she found it difficult to make out his features, they kept shifting and moving. He didn't see her, apparently. The boy's eyes fluttered open suddenly, and he showed no indication of noticing her presence there.

He sat up and stared at the Bookcase. Then he got up quickly, and knelt by the bed. He seemed like he was praying, right next to the Angel, who still knelt there as well. The boy did not seem to see the Angel. Nowar could hear singing now, like a heavenly choir getting louder and louder as the scene proceeded on.

The Angel lovingly touched his shoulder and rose to go to the Bookcase. The boy looked around briefly, and his eyes shot to the Bookcase like a magnet. Wasting no time, he jumped over the quilt covered bed, and pulled a book from the shelf. Without hesitation, he opened the book without any regard for the index or the table of contents. Seemingly at random, on page two hundred and one of "Watership Down", by Richard Adams, a chapter began called "Fiver Beyond", and the boy spoke aloud the quote he had found there.

"On his dreadful journey, after the shaman has wandered through dark forests and over great ranges of mountains …he reaches an opening in the ground. The most difficult stage of the adventure now begins. The depths of the underworld open before him."

Nowar still peered over the boy's shoulder. The quote was by someone she had never heard of, someone called Uno Harva, as quoted by someone else named Joseph Campbell in a book he wrote called "The Hero with a Thousand Faces". With a bit of a disconcerted look, the boy walks off with the book, still reading it as he leaves the scene through the door.

The Angel smiles and fades away into a white shining light.

Nowar suddenly became aware of her surroundings again. The Morning Star was right next to her now, picking up the Remembrançarium and wiping the mud off it with one of his tails. She had dropped it while she was in her trance. He handed it gently back to her and all three mouths said insistently-

"Did you see? Well, did you see, child?"

Nowar was quiet. The diorama now depicted the scene it had shown when she had picked it up originally, the boy in his bed, the angel descending the stairway from the attic.

But she did see. She **had** seen.

The little boy had been her father.

AntiPart Twelve

A jaunt in the Dwark

The Morning Star was jogging off now, down into his beloved little underground briar patch, perhaps the finest mushroom garden that Opus Delirious could offer. Nowar called after him, taking a few steps which turned into a jog. Boy, that fat orange tabby could move when he wanted to.

"Where are you going?"

He stopped, turned around, a bit perplexed, and plopped his behind back on the ground.

"Wrong pronoun." Said mouth two, since mouth one still showed signs of shock.

"You **are** ready to see what we have to show you, are you not?" said both mouth two and three together, hesitantly.

"What do you want to show me?" Nowar asked, equally hesitantly. That tea definitely had something in it.

As if he had read her mind, mouth one said "There was nothing in the tea, dearie, that's just how Opus Delirious makes everyone feel when they spend enough time here, or for that matter **any** time spent this close to the heart of the Page, er, I mean Shred, is bound to feel the effects that the original Builders wove into the flavor of every world, er, Page, or Shred, as in the case of our little Opus Delirious."

"So you didn't create the original Page?"

All three voices began to speak in unison— "Oh no no no no no!!! We are only the Avatar, Yes, we **were** born here when the Page we embody was written, on the original Implausible Chip that was the first draft of ProbablePolis, but it was the Builders, my dear, who did all the creation…though they did so only at the behest of the Source, which informed and bound this Holy Grid to the Great Implausible Chip, at least according to the great and ancient Narration of the Logos, with all its supporting Authors, such as they were. This is all in the Book of Scorns, by the way, I hope someday you have time to read it, although I suspect the Logos has other plans for your time spent here." He began to jog off again.

"Great Implausible Chip? Holy Grid? I'm lost, Morning Star, give me some bearings, will you?" she cried as she ran off after him. He stopped so suddenly that she nearly ran into him, saying-

"The Holy Grid is **the** Hypothecation, a virtual conception of realization, retained on a Great Implausible Chip. The Holy Grid is the matrix of the world as we see, smell, hear, feel and sense it all around us, and it courses like great rivers and streams of energy through the circuitry of the Great Implausible Chip."

"Nowar looked at him blankly. She was about to ask what the Source was, and who the supporting Authors were, when mouth one said— "My dear, as fantastic as this may sound, the Great Olde Drake, oldest of all the Avatars ever created, will likely tell you the same things I am doing now, and though I don't want to steal his thunder, really, in fact does it at all matter whether you hear it from us first or him, I wonder, and since we don't really know, and most of us don't care…well, are you ready?"

He was floating slowly upward now. Nowar looked around and realized that at some point, he had continued to wander off, never losing eye contact with her, though, and she, not quite aware, had continued to follow him, again, never losing eye contact.

Now she stood across the clearing she had beheld earlier, gazing upward into a huge tunnel of briar patch that spiraled above their heads into a deep gloom. A tiny splinter of light twinkled and seemed to call to her. The Morning Star was now increasing the speed of his float, and called down to her—"Come on you slow-poke, have you forgotten your special talents?"

In her mind she understood immediately what he was talking about, smiled to herself, bowed her head, and quietly wished that she had wings, as she had before- that she could fly like an angel again…

Nowar took wing, leaving the tunnel and the Morning Star behind as she exploded out the top of the Great Briar Patch Chimney of Opus Delirious to see just below her- a Lighthouse?

Yes, the light streamed past her toes for a second, and as it receded she could make out a huge Lighthouse indeed, and though it was entirely dark, it towered over a few other buildings nearby, a Windmill, a very large Train Station, and a few other humble dark wood buildings on the other side of the big glade in which she had just a while before met the Walrus. The lights of Opus Delirious, strung through the forest glades, twinkled below like shimmering beads in a dark forest of briar-patchery and tuffty-trees with shaggy moss beards.

She only barely noticed the Morning Star go puttering past her, still headed upward.

"Who were the supporting Authors?" she thought to herself, and cried out- What is the Source?" she called to him.

"Come with us, and you just might find out, my Evolving Lass. We're on our way to your Looking Glass." All three mouths cackled loudly.

His whole body began to give off an unworldly blue glow as he picked up speed. Where was he going now? Strait out into the middle of the Dwark, it looked like…

AntiPart Eleven

Wherein what they often call coincidence is re-examined…and put back into the oven

Nowar began strained with her new wings, but made the distance quickly between them and kept his pace, which was very slowly accelerating. Her head was starting to clear quickly as Opus Delirious fell away into the Dwark behind them. She waited a good while before she said—"So I am still trying to wrap my mind around this idea that… this is all an unreal world on a chip."

"Unreal? More like 'So Real'. Actually, if you want to banter and rant on this topic I would suggest that the more banal phrase bandied about by the illuminated ones, and their mimics, is not the 'the Great Hypothecation', but, more often used, in private, most often by the Builders themselves, a far more accurate term, a 'Simulation'. I have also heard Builders call this very ground of being a "Holographic Computer Simulation" and as they like to put it, the way they see it is that the Hypothecation of ProbablePolis is fastened by a Holy Grid to an Implausible Chip and it is neither 'unreal', nor 'not-real', nor 'really real'…hehehe."

"Your answers are not really helping me, Morning Star. I feel more confused than ever. So what **is** the Source, and who are the 'supporting Authors', 'such as they were'?"

"All in good time, you're not quite ready. The Great Olde Drake may have his work cut out for him, but first, watch this…"

His three eyes squinted and closed as he hovered, falling into deep concentration.

As he spoke again, the blue glow that surrounded him began to grow brighter and brighter. Nowar could see a translucent ephemeral chain of light, spiraling like an umbilical cord of blue light back down into the Dwark from where they came, connecting him to…where? To his page, his beloved little nutty Opus Delirious shred of a world. But why was he doing this?

"Out here in the Dwark, nothing stays still…life calls out for life, and life is brought forth upon life… and that life goes on to discover yet more life, created anew where before there was **nothing** there at all."

He was getting brighter and brighter now, and, in fact, he was growing so much brighter that Nowar had to fly a little ways away from him, just so she wouldn't be blinded by the bright blue light he was exuding now. Why, he had become like a tiny blue star in the middle of the Dwark, and she could even make out a tiny postage stamp of an island floating in the Dwark far, far below them. It had to be Opus Delirious.

And everyone back on the island looked to the sky, for a Star could be seen in the dark of the Dwark above them, the first star that had ever twinkled in their sky. Not a single one of them had ever seen a star before, and a hush spread across all of Opus Delirious. The Faeries laughed and cried and pointed, and the Walrus walked the whole horde into the field by the Train Station while Bonsai lit firecrackers.

The Light House stayed dark.

Nowar, far far above them, hovered near the Morning Star. She was beginning to see an incredible distance into the Dwark, and the blue Morning Star began to illuminate an incredibly large area all around them, above and below, everywhere. Creatures of all kinds began to come out of the shadows from every corner of the Dwarkness; bloated glowing jellyfish floated every which way, followed by teeming little winged snakefish, pulsing milky-white see-through spiders with kaleidoscope eyes, and floating blimps, like hulking rhinoceros-manatees. On their backs twittered several furry species, jamming on rocks with twigs and blowing through make-shift reeds.

She somehow knew the Morning Star hadn't really gone anywhere, and she asked in her mind, directing her attention to him.

"What, or how, does Life keep evolving out here? It seems like it would be a fairly hostile environment?"

She felt the Morning Star smile as it said quietly "Now I'm certain your father has told you this before, but, 'where there's a will there's a way.'"

He resumed his former speed and course, leaving behind him as he traveled his umbilical cord to Opus Delirious. He was still shining like a defiant blue star. His great orb of lighting reduced somewhat, perhaps proportionately to his velocity, but nevertheless he was drawing along with him the crowd of teeming Dwark inhabitants that he had revealed to Nowar minutes before.

"And then there's a wall." Nowar whispered. She felt confuzled, but still she followed the brightly glowing three-mouthed, nine-tailed cat as it sailed right over her head again.

After a minute or so, Nowar was about to ask a follow-up question about the environment that supported all these critters, now trailing behind in the gloom when suddenly, capriciously, the Morning Star slowed very rapidly, turning about to say-

"Watch where you're going, Nowar."

She looked wildly around her- they were not alone. They were in the midst of a great school of giant, transparent, mildly phosphorescent… torpedoes? Submarines? She had almost collided with one in fact, and she flew up above it to see it better…and the rest of its 'school'.

They glowed softly, in a tone not unlike the Morning Star, who was now drifting upward himself, growing in brightness again.

"Is this our destination, Morning Star?" she allowed herself to fly closer to him, but with her back to his ever brightening countenance- he hovered there, peacefully watching a sprawling scene - something like a convoy of a school of… what were these things?

They each hummed slightly- and indeed, when she looked closer, it seemed they were moving along at their leisurely rate with- propellers of all things!

"Behold the newest addition to the pageant of ProbablePolis. Note the propellers, for twill be important to your subsequent inquiries." The Morning Star cheerily murmured to itself for a moment, and then purred.

Nowar took in the vista. There were hundreds of these things! They were as big as elephants, some of them, all shaped like submarines or torpedoes, and each one radiating a faint aquamarine glow that pulsed with their internal organs gyrations, bumping and shifting an internal crank shaft that sailed them forward.

"What are they called?" she asked.

"They aren't called anything yet, Nowar, perhaps you might oblige us all and reverence them with the Word, or perhaps even a token of sisterly love and affection, as I have brought you here through perfect points of entrance into the Dwark from our little Opus Delirious…to meet, and hopefully, honor, these fine new editions into our tome of Probabilities, and possibly learn an important lesson as a result."

"Huh?"

"Love them, child, name them, my dear. To the uninitiated, the naming of names means nothing, but to those who know the truth, the naming of names means everything!"

Nowar hardly had to reach deep into her heart to find their name.

Jajuma.

She would call them the Jajuma, though she had no idea where the name had come from.

Suddenly, a baby Jajuma swished right past Nowar with such force that it turned her around a full 180 degrees to face the Morning Star. She turned back to it just in time to witness it locate its mother, quickly suckling down from under one of her low hanging nipples. She began to drone deeply, with low resonating sounds, like the sounds that whales make.

These creatures were fantastic! She didn't even get to open her mouth when the Morning Star whispered-

"They're singing, isn't it lovely?"

"Singing?" she said quietly, "Why?"

The Morning Star laughed.

"Why does *anyone* sing…ever? They're happy Nowar. Look, a child has just been re-united with its parent, and all the families in the school rejoice!"

Nowar understood. It was a good omen. Perhaps she would be re-united with her family someday. Nowar looked back at the school, now making its way off back into the deep gloom and gloam of the Dwark.

"I will call them the Jajuma," she said aloud, though she still had no idea where the sounds had come from. She could not look directly at the Morning Star anymore, either, as he had again grown so very bright. She said quickly to him "Why did you want me to see them?"

"They needed a name."

"Come on. You knew we were going to find them out here, and you've already said that there would be a lesson here. What is it?"

The Morning Star smiled with all three of his mouths and said "Originally, I had thought you were more like your father, but now I see that both currents run strong in the river of your soul. Very well, I will enlighten you as to the 'Lesson of the Jajuma' that is possible here." He paused and said "What do the Jajuma use to propel themselves?"

"Why, a propeller, or so it seems."

"Corrrrect. It is indeed a propeller. Now, are you familiar with the 'Half-story of Evolution'?"

"Half-story? Don't you mean Theory?"

"No, no, no! It's NOT a Theory, my dear child; it's a Half-story, a grouping of assorted facts branded together, barely more than a prevalence of nonsense, haphazardly organized, typically calling such a thing anything other than a Half-story is the retreat of the criminally insane."

She looked blankly at him. Was he about to start an attack-on-science lecture on her? Holy cow. He continued with "-In other words, it's

JUST **half** the story- but don't trust my word, tell me first what you yourself believe Evolution is, in your own words, and show to me your own understanding."

"Well," she faltered only for a second and realized that she did know something of this subject, somehow, from somewhere, and said "Evolution is a process whereby certain traits are selected in preference over others, over many generations. If being tall made it easier to eat to survive, then people with these tall genes, or traits, pass those on to their descendants, and then those descendants have an edge to survive themselves, see what I mean? I mean the ancestors that would be taller were more likely to survive and they handed on those traits to the next generation."

"And where do those traits come from to begin with?"

"Uh, they're mutations."

"That's a 'what'…I asked for a 'where'. We need to know 'where' over the 'what', don't you think?"

"Well, mutations come from, erm, from nature, like cosmic radiation, radiation from a sun, or powerful chemicals in the air, water or soil."

The Morning Star seemed under whelmed.

"Right! So a mutation happens, and a child is born with a crank shaft instead of a spine, with some hopelessly placed gear boxes and such, making it all but impossible to get around. Sounds like an unpromising mutation to me, unlikely to be selected or attract any kind of decent suitor, or mate. Do you know how many moving parts make a propeller work properly? DO you know how many mutations would be required to get a whole complex mechanism like a propeller to work…and where was the original advantage or edge of having something cumbersome that doesn't work always in your way? How many moving parts does a propeller have, Nowar?"

"A lot. OK, I think I'm beginning to see your point."

"Not quite, but we'll sharpen it some more with statistics, damned things that they are, not much better than lies- here goes…in effect, the probability that we could see a sudden simultaneous complete set of all the mutations necessary to produce an effective propeller-driven organism, complete with fins, a crankshaft, and a gearbox with its host of complicated interlocking moving parts, is about as likely as you and I being hit by a meteorite in the next three seconds."

He then imagined three watches into being on his wrist, and watched them solemnly for three seconds, then said neatly- "So, in other words, the probability that the mechanics of evolution and periodic mutation alone as you describe them could produce a propeller-enabled species is well over 1 in 889,432 trillion to one…on a good day."

"In other words, highly improbable to the point of absurdity." she muttered to herself, smiling suddenly.

The Morning Star smiled too, as he smelled the increasing plausibility of a tiny victory for this little lost soul hovering here in the Dwark with him. "Indeed, Nowar, I am suggesting that it is improbable, implausible, and impossible that such an organism could have evolved by chance.

"So what's the other half of the story then?"

"Ha! In truth, you'll have to figure that one out for yourself, my dear. Just remember that, once you have eliminated all that is impossible, all that is left, no matter how implausible, must be the most probable…"

They were both quiet for a bit, and he continued with- "I have one more item of interest, however, for your considerations. There is another propeller-driven organism, very much like this one, but it lives in your own universe, the big world. There is at least one very noticeable difference between the two."

"What's that?"

"The organism in the big world that you came from is a single celled organism, with marvelous working propellers and crankshaft, and you can only see it with …a microscope!"

A shiver went up Nowar's crankshaft, er, spine. As all this was sinking in, she quietly wondered on odd and absurd thought to herself –

"Did ProbablePolis really copy the Earth, or did the Earth copy ProbablePolis?"

The Morning Star resumed his soliloquy, saying –

"There are more things in Heaven and Earth than are dreamt of in your philosophy, young Nowar Rondelle." then he continued with- "Something else you should consider before you go is this…"

He paused, watching her carefully, and said-

"While the Human race is most certainly one of the more interesting experiments that the Creator-of-All has started, and while it is true that nature itself is trying very hard to help your species survive, you should never forget that the Creator-of-All is quite likely running many more experiments than just yourselves."

Nowar felt something indescribable stir deep inside of her.

"Yes, Nowar, with your face full of wonder, yes, it's time for you to go back now. Herein ends your lesson…"

The Morning Star was growing brighter still, billowing forth warm waves of beautiful, blue light, buffeting Nowar gently away.

"Wait!" she said, "You're going to stay here, aren't you? Why?"

"Because Probability now suggests that you will go back without me."

"Why?"

"Because I have decided that it is time for the Dwark to have its first star, Nowar, and so I shall remain, here, where you were finally told the whole story, not simply half. May you always be yourself."

Nowar finally understood that she would have to return, alone, to Opus Delirious. To do what, she did not know, but she did know one thing for sure.

Something wonderful was about to happen…

AntiPart Ten

Behold the beginning of the saga of the death of Everlast

The beating of Dragon Drums is a sound like you have never heard, and now, all across the darkened lands of the Valley of Everlast…it had started with a vengeance.

'Thoom thoom! THOOM THOOM!'

Low and deep in the surrounding Mountains, a clarion call of scaly minds went out to all the Drakes, Dragons Wyverns and Slithery Serpents in their lairs all around the Mountain ridges that surrounded Everlast. Down in the cities in the Valley, the people in the huge stone fortresses that constituted the Capital of the great Elvish Kingdoms of Kirhannok were lighting fires from all the parapets. They cried in alarm, and growing louder and louder all the time were the Dragon Drums-

'THOOM THOOM! **THOOM THOOM!**'

Even as the Dragons and their riders were taking to the air, the Black Harp of Castle Deep Steel was already roaring into the valley of Everlast, with Andironé the King fastened securely to its bow.

Onboard and deep below the black armor, Koradgians pushed and hissed around their monitors, hooting and cheering as the Harp came closer and closer to the target proximity. They were arriving at the center of the page, and they were focusing lesser weapons on the growing number of doomed winged opponents rising to the challenge from the lands that they had already passed over. They did so with extraordinary success and high kill ratios for shot fired were logged. Father Moebius would be pleased, and some of the Koradgians were so enthusiastic over this initial success that they were breaking out big bottles of blue and inebriating frosted drinks and making boorish toasts with oversize mugs.

"To Deep Steel!"

"To Hell Incorporated!"

ProbablePolis

"Hail Moebius!"

and even

"Koradgians rule, humans drool!"

The bulk of the evil crew of the Harp kept on task, though.

They were hunting no less than the King of this Page, the Avatar himself, Shane, a gigantic and ancient Cloud Tree.

Moebius had given the order; the Avatar must die.

The Harp had been equipped with a weapon in emulation of Shane's greatest protective power. This would be its first real test. The Commander of the Harp, a nine foot tall beefy well armored Koradgian kept his paw close to a large red button, already primed, glowing and flashing.

The Cloud Tree Shane was the last of his kind, and older than dirt. He was the size of a town, and he floated effortlessly, many miles above the sprawling cities of Everlast, his roots and great branches extending for tens of thousands of feet in every direction. His vast bark covered face looked more like Santa Claus than anyone else.

Here, in the center of the Page, is where he had always been since the First Days, a kind and loving, shy and reserved Avatar over all the Kirhannok peoples, loving equally all Elves, Gnomes, Dwarves, Goblins Giants, Puca and the larger host of other olde and odd folke that had been his extended family since he had been a little acorn in the DownUnder.

To all of these creatures and citizens of Kirhannok, Shane was their favorite Great-Grandfather- his gifts were simple- when he wept, rain on the lands below blossomed with flowers that bore fruit. When he smiled and lifted his branches, more sun poured down on the Valley below.

There was no pulse of the ribbon to be seen now, though. Morning was a good while away, and the black smoke this thing had already belched into the Valley obscured any 'sign of the glow worm' at all in any direction.

In the gloom it had created, the Harp slowed quickly and rotated into a position facing the Avatar Himself. From below, hordes and schools of drakes, dragons, wyrms, wyverns were fast surrounding this gigantic menacing machine.

'THOOM THOOM! **THOOM THOOM!**'

Wind in his hair, Glaurg Cong, mighty King of the Giants foisted to his shoulder a great and mighty cannon, a weapon of light and thunder that he was given by King Shard after the last Battle for Freedom failed.

He rode upon the great Cranos Th'maug, the Oldest Dragon King in all Everlast, but before he could fire a single shot, the Harp defenses were activated, with a vengeance, giving off an ear piercing shriek followed immediately by a massive overwhelmingly bellowing horn, blasting waves of air everywhere around it, buffeting the winged armies of Everlast.

But not stopping them. The veterans of these troops had stuffed extra cotton into their helmets in and around their ears, knowing from past Harps and battles what was in store, but even so, the blasts and shrieking were higher and more intense by thrice in this bigger, newer, more hideous edition. Many had infra-red goggles, and were thankful they could still make out the target. Midnight in Everlast Kirhannok was pretty dark alright, with all the moons on the other side of the ribbon. Moebius couldn't have picked a better time to give the word for the attack. But the Harp wasn't done.

The Harp played, loudly, what a musicologist might tell you were a serious of notes from two adjacent hexachords in the tritone B-F, where B would be "mi". What will be said here though, is that the Harp activated its own strings with impressive force, producing what any musicologist would have to admit was a positively blood-curdling, mind-numbing, soul twistingly vile set of strands of sound, echoing over the whole Valley.

A shadow fell on all the minds and hearts of Everlast.

Yet the hearts of the Giants and the Dragon-riders re-steeled themselves, and they gave their best, whether equipped with guns, arrows or spears, Tommy hawks or machine guns. Only great valor with inferior weaponry against a Harp could be hoped for, much as the last Battle fought against Moebius, but, for any military commander, what happened next was sad indeed.

The laser fire from the latest Deep Steel Harp was greatly improved from the last battle, and it began in earnest with a full assault, with weaponry systems blasting forth a storm of pulses and blasts, lasers cutting savagely into the first wave of opponents like butter.

The new weaponry systems were specifically designed to make quick work of this agile and brave Aerial Force, the Koradgian tacticians had done their homework, and hundreds of red roaring lights swiftly picked off the warriors, wyrms and Dragons of Everlast like fish in a barrel, left and right, above and below. The Harp was very slowly moving forth, while Koradgians gunners unleashed a swathe of devastation everywhere.

Andironé stirred. His pain was beyond exquisite, and he barely stayed conscious during the bellow and the shriek, emanating as it had from the very thing he was shackled to. He was still strapped and nailed tightly to the rusty bloody shackles where he had been since he had been captured and crucified by the Koradgians against the bow of a black smoke belching monstrosity.

Now he beheld with eyes he could barely keep open, the great Avatar's shadow in the gloom. SHANE! He wanted to yell to Shane "run, fly, flee, oh my friend, old-grandfather-tree, get the frak out of here, this thing is going to kill you." But all he could cry out in his own tongue was- "Bgai'r o Baraaka! Ki loi rama dass?"

O Logos! Why have you abandoned us?

Shane did not seem to budge, and he was holding his breath. A tear welled in one of his great big bark covered tear ducts. The Logos had already told him what would transpire this day.

A gentle rain began to fall over the dark Valley of Everlast.

AntiPart Nine

A Queen Glommed in Green Goo

Even as a shadow fell on all the minds and hearts of Everlast, a tiny drama with a humble little Dwark stone was about to play out in the secret chamber of Evergreen Castle where Queen Limberly was imprisoned.

She had been stuck there a long time- Chapter Seven page one hundred and forty two, as a matter of fact, but who's counting? Captured while she was asleep, many Phases of the great Ribbon ago, she had been put here in this translucent aquarium of thick green goo by Moebius and company. Rendered barely conscious, and filled with jolly as a result of some vile element added to the green goo by Moebius, she had been floating and breathing this goo as if it was air and having a great old time- it was always making her giggle.

Out of the corner of her eye, though just now, she noticed something shiny on the floor near the door. At first it seemed to have been just some piece of trash left by the little lizard that always came with the fat little black bearded man who just ranted at her about things she had no clue what he was talking about.

But that piece of trash had been left there by Clancy. It was a silver Dwark stone, and after a prescribed amount of time it began to turn itself on, making an attempt to become a two-way beacon. Once fully awake, it began to hum and glow softly, like a tiny star, all the while looking for the consciousness of the Unremembering Princess, Limberly's daughter Nowar. It was preparing to pour light into Limberly's retina any minute now, but it was waiting to lock in on the 'frequency' of Nowar first. In fact, it was still trying to establish a link, but with little success.

Only once, briefly did it manage to open a full channel with Nowar, during which it observed her in a very bad state; crying, hurtling through the Dwark at top speed, headed unwittingly in the direction of Opus Delirious, a fragment of the once beautiful page the stone remembered serving on, long long ago.

The stone, after a time, realized it must unleash this image into the mind of the Mother, and did so after a perfunctory gentle comment-

"This will hurt a little bit, o Queen of Evergreen. Your daughter needs you. It is time for you to be free. Behold your Daughter now."

The stone shone a dim beam through the tank and goo, directly onto Limberly's eyes. The beam grew in intensity rapidly. Limberly thought there was a star, an actual star being born here in green goo land and she began to belly laugh.

Link established, the silver Dwark stone unleashed the scenery it had beheld of Nowar directly into Limberly's mind.

So Limberly watched Nowar screaming through the darkest Dwark for all of three seconds before she began to hurl her fists against the tank walls. Within a half a minute she had shattered enough pieces that she began to gasp for air- she had been breathing green goo for a very long time.

She coughed desperately, clinging to a tank wall still standing, and then, slowly began to breath normally again. She looked around while she panted, and saw the Dwark stone. She crawled over to it and grabbed it; it hummed happily, and closed down all its lights. It started to Purr. Someone had re-programmed it specifically for her, and in a very special way, but who?

"Ah, no matter" she whispered hoarsely "-with this thing I can get wherever I need to in the Castle, and then, either a.) 'go find my Daughter', or b.) 'go kill Moebius', whichever comes first. My God how long was I in there?"

Shaking slightly still, suddenly she realized that she had somehow been having a nightmare of some sort. She was both naked and covered in this sticky green goo, and…since when did she even **have** a daughter? She didn't.

A hot bath was in order, but, first some guards would need to be taken out. Who knows what Moebius had been able to do while she had been stuck in green goo, or, for that matter, how long she had been in there.

She rose to the door and quietly wished to see outside the door; three Koradgians playing poker, their weapons slung on the wall.

Wishing for the strength of a great Giant, she burst the great iron door down and promptly throttled one Koradgian before the other two could even come to their senses. By then it was too late, as the Koradgian she had throttled was the one next to the wall with the guns. One of the other Koradgians got a crushing kick to the stomach while the third went down under Limberly's two handed laser assault.

She smiled, blew smoke from the barrel of her guns, and said "O Honey! I'm hoooome!"

The Queen was back in EverGreen.

AntiPart Eight
The Great Olde Drake

If a great iron forge the size of a Bus could snore, this is how it sounded to be in the darkness in the cavern of the Great Olde Drake, as he lay there, coiled and asleep, dreaming of implausible things.

He was the last of the First-Drakes, the first colossal race of giant dragons that the Builders had made, long before time began to 'wind up'.

The Great Olde Drake was indeed colossal in size, perhaps as long as thirty whales and covered in endless shades of silver, bronze, black and red scales, all heaving in time to his gigantic lungs, the size of four football stadiums. His arms and legs were themselves as big as buildings. His bearded head had a long hoary beard, that mingled with his shaggy mane, all of it silver white in sheen and pigment. His five-clawed hand slowly stroked his beard as his eyes creaked open. He squinted at one of his his huge water-clocks, and then he rolled over, scratching his back like a gigantic dog.

His cavern lay directly beneath the Sepulchre of Silence, where Bric and Shard had just been reunited. He had always stayed close to the Sepulchre, it was, after all, where he was hatched and reared, and it was, of course, the one place Moebius could never find.

He had not been awake long before he felt the presence of the Logos, and took the first advantage to ask something- "You would not be here if it were not time to begin the final act. So do I get to meet the new Emperor now or what?"

"Oh great and ancient Avatar of Avalhalla, come to the surface when you are ready, for we are waiting for you there."

"Do tell, o Logos. Do tell."

He scanned everywhere, but saw nothing moving in his great cavern. He did not feel any alarm at this, as it was not unusual; the Logos had a light touch, traveled little, though he ended up visiting places far, far away from these parts, through the use of that which is faster than the wind: thought.

"News is good, indeed. Our King, Shard, has joined us, and he has been 'raised'…"

The Drake's huge silvery eyebrow curled upward slightly "Oh?"

"Yes, he has had his persona returned to him, the one he came with when they sent him in from the Big World, oh so many pulses ago."

"What of the girl, is She arrived yet?"

"Aye, She has, but you will need to take the Emperor's 'Box of Memories', if you will, to the Queen and Nowar both. Though still unremembering, Limberly has been freed by the resistance, and is running around her own castle now, likely looking to murder Moebius."

The Drake laughed, stood, shook himself, stretched his truly gigantic leathery wings, rattling the enormous cavern of his lair, and laughed again.

"I commend her for her timeliness, and now you will leave me to govern mine… though I am pleased that the resistance is finally getting some traction, you will remember that I have kept my own memories through all of this. I now know without a doubt that I have done this, done all of this, several times before. It disturbs me deeply, you must know, and I must gather my aspect in private before I emerge."

"Déjà vu, mais oui? Hahahah! Indeed, old friend, first friend…Is it the second, third or fourth time that's the charm? I confess that I know not… but…tarry little, would you? Probabilities are higher now than ever for a better resolution than any of those other times before, and I am quite taken by our new Emperor."

The Dragon considered all of this as he heaved his monstrous bulk up the cavern, headed to the surface of his mighty Kingdom, Avalhalla, which was now enduring typical ice age blizzard activity. Not that that mattered to him, his armor was thick, and his whole body was good and warm again.

As he plodded upward, he wondered how his old comrade, Uhranitee Mare Gnosticius, the Sky Whale, was getting along these days. He wondered where she had gone, if she still in fact lived, and if so, he wondered if the Logos had informed her of what was likely to be her own part to play in the concluding drama.

The previous three times he could remember doing all of this, he believed he had felt equally optimistic at this point, each and every time, and this too bothered him immensely.

Puffing out a flare of smoke, and fire, just to test his flame glands, he doubled his own speed, heaving himself rapidly up his cavern like a giant reptilian groundhog. He was headed for the hazy light above, where several tons of ice and water showered down, covering the cavern top with an icy barrier impenetrable to most creatures, but not the Great Olde Drake, who, with momentum behind his several hundred tons, catapulted through easily, shattering great ice shards everywhere.

With only a seconds hesitation, he grabbed the sides of the opening he had forced in the ice, and heaved his great body through the rest of the icy cavern covering, sending even more chunks of water and ice exploding everywhere as he hurled himself in the air, belching great fire and smoke everywhere, coiling after him, as he rose, slowly, wings flapping gracefully, raising him up on high to survey the land below. A Dragon greater than any you have ever seen perhaps.

To Bric, Shard, Kai and Khan, it was an impressive sight, without a doubt. Bric had never seen a dragon before, and Shard had never seen one so big.

It was just then that the Omen-tary, sent by King Andironé back on page one hundred and twenty two, finally showed up. Clucking with distress, it had tracked Shard from one page to this cold dark place, and with little or no grace, flew right into the eye of the Great Old Drake. The Drake, who could see through the eye of a needle from a hundred miles away recognized immediately that he had just been needled by an Omen-tary, a little bubble headed owl-like thing that was a 'barely-live', a creature made of durable and only slightly organic materials, made for one purpose, and one purpose only, to bear a message.

The Omen-tary landed on the ground about the same time the Great Olde Drake did. Standing proud and erect at a respectful distance of a hundred meters, he watched the Omen-tary right itself, and without further delay, fly right to Shard, alighting on his now outstretched arm.

Shard, shaken by the ground quaking as the Drake landed on all four massive legs, did not seem to know what to do at first. The Great Olde Drake had never, ever, come out of his lair during Shard's reign, not even during the Last Great War of Probability.

It is worth saying here that, through the ages, many Dragons had left the Kingdom of Avalhalla to fight in wars against Moebius, but the Kingdom itself, the very covers of ProbablePolis, had always remained officially neutral, thus keeping things rather peaceful across her vast tundra covered covers. The Avatar of Avalhalla, the Great Olde Drake, crowned as Synarchus Luminous Lazarus, preferred to sleep undisturbed while the silliness of that game that the Logos and the Moebius were playing disrupted **other** peoples' lives, not his own, or the inhabitants of their two-fold (literally) Kingdom.

Synarchus regarded this 'King', Shard, this young man who had come to ProbablePolis from the Big World long after he had already 'had it' with politics. With his ancient great dragon sense he scanned this 'Johny-come-lately'.

"Young indeed for a White King you are. Hmmph."

Then he scratched behind his ear and said "Don't bother with **me**, now, young King, you apparently have an Omen-tary itching to tell you its tale"

AntiPart Six

Hey now, you're an all-star…

And so Nowar had taken wing.

She knew she could find her way back to Opus Delirious with little or no difficulty. After all, the great umbilical cord of the Morning Star extended all the way back down there, still glowing a dim but unmistakable sea-blue, fading downward into the Dwark.

She followed the cord, always flying within sight of it.

She felt alive, exhilarating with the wind in her hair, and her mind racing faster than the wind, full of new thoughts, unborn. Her conversation with the Morning Star had changed her, somehow. Confidence filled the sails of her soul, and she redoubled her efforts, putting her new wings to their limit.

As she soared faster and faster, she called for her spear, ripples emanating in her wake.

It came to her from the Dwark.

Now, going even faster, she called for her shield, then her armor and her helmet, and they came to her from the deepest Dwark, ripples billowing out behind her.

As Nowar came into sight of the little floating island of Opus Delirious, she felt ready to take the fight to Moebius.

But first she had to find the Great Olde Drake. She did not feel apprehensive about this challenge. In fact, she had the uncanny feeling he was already looking for her.

AntiPart Five

A story of three 'chothers

A little before noon, two people and a book got into Grandma Brandy's Van sitting outside the Shamrock Motel; it was Brandy herself, and her son.

Or what was left of him. Even after a shower, a shave, a couple hours of sleep and some orange juice, he still seemed, somehow…less than himself.

They were headed north again. The last leg of the quest was at hand. The tome of ProbablePolis was secured in her big floppy shoulder-bag that did not leave her presence since Nowar had vanished into it again last night.

Brandy had gone to a café earlier, while Shard was still snoring, and checked her email for the last message she was supposed to receive. She got it, alright, but it was light on instruction, heavy on cheerleading, and ended on a truly confusing and enigmatic note.

It said:

> **Get to the Moonclock facility before nightfall.**
>
> **Follow Shard's lead. Watch his back.**
>
> **He is about to put all the pieces back together.**
>
> **Do not be alarmed at his sluggish or eccentric condition: This may not make sense to you now, but I had to trifurcate him in a very different manner than the others, primarily in order to allow us any hope of pulling this off. Don't worry needlessly though- his other two 'chothers are doing just fine, and a successful reunion is beyond plausible or possible, but in fact is quite probable, really.**

Brandy did not approve. She had been wondering if these emails she had been told to look for were in fact sent by her husband Bric, or, someone or something else. Now she knew for sure that this was something else entirely other than her husband, and it was freaking her out. What were they heading into?

At some point, as Brandy turned on cruise control, she noticed Shard pulling the book out of her bag. He was quiet for a long time. Then he spoke, slowly, and deliberately.

"Alright, let me try to sum all this up, and see if we're missing something."

"Go for it." Said Brandy laconically, but thankful for the conversation, and a sign she'd just seen that said it was only another twenty miles to Frog-neck's Bridge. In another hour or two they would be at the gate of the MoonClock Facility. A plan was in order, anyhow.

Suddenly, Brandy realized that her son had been talking, in his low and now slow voice, for some time while she had been watching signs to get her exit. As she turned her attention back to him, she heard him say-

"…which means that while, to me, hardly half a day has passed, it has in fact been two years since you last saw me. Now, you've told me that Nowar went into the simulation, using this…this …book, somehow, several days ago, and that Dad followed her the same way just yesterday."

He paused, thoughtfully.

"Now, all **I** can remember is stumbling through a hallway on the third floor of our house, following a guy in a suit that looked an awful lot like me. I assumed I was just dreaming, really. And if that wasn't weird enough, in this dream, me and this guy that looked like me were being followed by a grotesque creature…the whole time….I was still groggy from my MoonClock jump, and I really can't remember anything the guy in the suit said, though he did talk a lot…and he did bring me to your hotel room door, eventually, after he fought and killed the creature that was following us."

Brandy asked a question just then, "Where did he go, the guy that looked like you?

"He said something about getting to a Chip Storage area, Omega-9, I think, and then he disappeared… just as he reached for the doorknob- gone! Poof! I just can't figure out how I dreamed up something and someone that seemed so real. Actually, he had to be real, he left this."

He pulled out a piece of plastic. He recognized it as a security entrance card for the innermost parts of the MoonClock facility, but said nothing. Grandma Brandy likely had her cell-phone with her, and Shard knew that not all the intelligence agencies that listened 'through' cell-phones were friendly ones.

He was quiet again. So was Brandy. After a while, she broke the silence and asked, "How are we going to get into the MoonClock Facility, hon, have you given that any thought? MoonClock is one of the most secure military facilities in the country."

"No sweat, Mom. If my top security clearance went away in the last two years, that would suggest that our government, in my brief absence, had suddenly become both very efficient and timely, would it not?"

They both laughed. After a few more moments, Shard began to realize something that sent shivers up his spine; the LOGOS was no longer just another sentient program-

It had figured out how to tinker with time!

AntiPart Four

Out into the Dwark you go, me boy-o!

Clancy had finally figured it out. Hopefully his plan would work.

It had to. The Slithery Tove was growing by leaps and bounds. It was rapidly filling up the hallways and dungeons of Castle DeepSteel with its nasty inky black slimy tendrils and ravenous mouths.

Something had to give.

First, he would evacuate the northern part of Castle DeepSteel, and then use Koradgians to carefully set Dwarkstones in mathematically prescribed spots in order to create a huge bubble of space to temporarily surround the Slithery Tove. Then, sucking all the power off of the DeepSteel energy grid, he would, theoretically, transport the horrific thing into the furthest reaches of the Dwark, onto the surface of the vast crystalline membrane Moebius called the Dwarkopologue. The Dwarkopologue had surrounded all existence since the beginning, and it kept all ProbablePolis within due bounds.

Clancy had to keep adjusting his math, of course, the Tove was growing bigger algorithmically (that means "really really fast" for people who don't like math), and more than a few Koradgians and Dwark stones were in fact lost to the Slithery Toves tendrilous and insatiable fanged mouths.

Eventually Clancy got it just right.

The Armies of DeepSteel had required little notice to start evacuating. The rumor mill had been off the charts ever since the Dialing for Dimensions Game show had ended, and many of the most foulest creatures of Moebius were already beginning to trample their fellows in a mad rush to get out of the Castle and out onto the 'Plain of All-Sorrows' a vast and dismal expanse of bog and swampland that surrounded the giant spiked black walls of DeepSteel. A small tent city had begun to form by the time the official word had been given to evacuate.

Clancy was just waiting on the word from Moebius to make it all happen. Moebius was in his high-backed chair madly stuffing gummy bears into his mouth, listening to Clancy discuss the solution. Poopsybear, with his stylish new Napoleon Bonaparte hat, sat propped up in the corner.

"This is the best you can do, Clancy?"

"What sir?"

"I mean, why can't we just contain the thing for awhile? Study it in this bubble. Eventually we should be able to figure out what makes it tick, and control it accordingly."

"Uh, it's risky sir. So far, it appears to be able to grow in spite of the containment field. It eats ANYTHING, and, eventually it just bursts through, and the rest of the field goes down with it. If we blow it into the farthest most reaches of the Dwark, even growing at maximum speed, it would take many many pulses before it would threaten us again. By then we should be able to figure out how to control it. Leaving it here will only endanger the Final Tweak, and perhaps all ProbablePolis."

"Clancy speaks with great wisdom, your Moebiusness" interjected the Teddybear.

"Hmph. Right as usual, you little reptilian runt- alright, suck it out into the Dwark and hurl it against the Dwarkopologue. Keep it under constant surveillance, though. Eventually we will have to either enslave it or destroy it, because we all know that this expulsion won't kill it."

"Yes, sir." Clancy began turning dials and hitting buttons. He hoped that the second option would be the only one, eventually. He still had a very bad feeling about this monstrosity. As the second hand of his wristwatch began to tick, a great and growing sucking sound began to rise and roar throughout all Castle DeepSteel.

Releasing the pressure by depressing a lever, a hideous shrieking wail pierced the grim gloom of Castle DeepSteel as the Slithery Tove, weighing well over a hundred tons now, was hurled at a ferocious speed off into the Dwark.

Whipping its tendrils around repetitively, it was moving so fast that it could hardly wrap a tentacle around anything moving to get so much as a snack, as it sailed off into the Dwark, headed for the very far away limits of known ProbablePolis, the great sphere of the Dwarkopologue.

Eventually, after a good long time, it collided with a heavy THUD into the cold and dark glassy surface of the Dwarkopologue that surrounds the Dwark and all of ProbablePolis. There, in the pitch black Dwarkness, it began to sprawl out its full vastness, coiling its stringy parts and pieces everywhere, seeking out some kind of recognizable object, some kind of place it could coil into, or even something moving…food.

Deep inside its vicious and hateful, evenly distributed nervous system, it sensed that it had just been trumped, but it was not beaten. It would continue to grow, of course, without food, just far more slowly.

And something deep inside its dark mind told it that, someone, somehow, would come looking for it, eventually.

AntiPart Three

The Final Tweak starts with a cacophonous shriek

All across the Valley of Everlast, the clatter and clang of battle raged in the darkness. Fires and explosions shattered and rolled across the city below and throughout the land there was the rolling of thunder and groans of dying dragons.

The Black Harp of Castle DeepSteel advanced slowly, unopposed, now less than half a mile away from the Avatar Shane, the great Cloud Tree of Kirhannok. Dragons and wyverns and ogres were dying in the droves, their flaming carcasses hurtling downward into the darkness, valiant victims of the perpetual and persistent laser cannons of the Black Harp.

But droves turned to packs, and then packs turned to stragglers, and then…

And then it was only the Cloud Tree and the Harp.

Shane harrumphed, grimaced and groaned. Though his own demise hung heavy in the smog and haze, his sadness sprang from how deeply he felt the pain and fear from all the denizens of Everlast below him. They were his children, and all of his children were dying.

From a place deep inside his cavernous lungs he began to hum…then the hum turned into a drone, and the drone became a chant, growing louder and louder, booming and bellowing out across the valley, over and over and over again-

"Nom myohoe rengay kyoe nom myohoe rengay kyoe nom myohoe rengay kyoe nom myohoe rengay kyoe nom myohoe rengay kyoe"

Far below in the flaming ruins, an old woman elf crouched in the shadows, shivering, holding her grand-child close to her heart, chanting in time with the great Cloud Tree that was far, far above her. Nearby, a gnome was repairing, as best as he could, the mangled arm of an ogre warrior. His own broken ribs would have to wait for now. The Ogre had fallen defending the old elf and her grand-child from a huge winged black scorpion with a human face and black mauls for limbs. The Scorpion lay in pieces all around him, black blood still oozing across the ground.

But the curse of a hollow victory was upon them all tonight, and to move even a little brought great pain to the Ogre.

"Nom myohoe rengay kyoe nom myohoe rengay kyoe nom myohoe rengay kyoe nom myohoe rengay kyoe nom myohoe rengay kyoe"

For some unknown reason, the monsters of Moebius, at first a seemingly endless horde, were waning in number. Those that remained were alarmed at the booming chanting rolling across the sky, and they cowered and hid in the dark corners of the wreckage.

Beneath a broken arch and ruined masonry, the Ogre, the Gnome, the Elf and her grand-child had a brief respite. Everywhere, the sounds of groaning and pain pulsed and ebbed as buildings continued to collapse, and occasional sounds of the clanging of steel rang out from far away.

The Ogre wheezed and heaved. He whispered to the gnome "What are they chanting, Gobo? Never have I heard deez words before…"

"Nom myohoe rengay kyoe nom myohoe rengay kyoe nom myohoe rengay kyoe nom myohoe rengay kyoe nom myohoe rengay kyoe"

Gobo was nearly finished with the sling, and looked up at his friends bloody smoke covered face, showing some concern that he would lose another patient this evening, "Don't you worry old Mogo, ol' Grandfather Shane is praying to the Logos and the Creator-of-all to take mercy on us. He is chanting for our suffering, for the suffering of all his children. Now stop squirming. We just might live to see the morning."

"No, Gobo, we will not, and you know it."

Gobo looked down and around him for something to start bandaging his own ribs. He found a dirty tapestry soaked in water, and began to ring it out. Non-plussed, he continued-

"They say in the Book of Scorns that 'When the world was as new, the first Builders taught each other to speak, and having learned to speak, they learned how they could hurt each other- yesee, 'Words have wings, and words can wound' you know."

The Ogre groaned in agony and muttered under his breath "-the mark of a warrior is how much pain he can handle, the mark of a warrior is how much pain he can handle…"

The Harp was slowing down now as its crew began to pull down targeting devices, preparing the most Cacophonous Tritonicon, a weapon that had never been used before. The Captain of the Harp slumped in his chair like an indolent spoiled, scaly child, and fiddled with a very large red button on the console by his right claw. They were almost within range. Reports were coming in that the armies of Moebius were fleeing, that somehow what was about to happen next had been leaked to the foot soldiers, who were taking to the sky or fleeing into holes… this no longer mattered to the Captain of the Black Harp.

"Nom myohoe rengay kyoe nom myohoe rengay kyoe nom myohoe rengay kyoe nom myohoe rengay kyoe nom myohoe rengay kyoe"

Gobo continued grimacing "and they say that the first war was a war of words, that immediately led to a war of fists, and that one of the Builders hurt one of his brothers very badly, and that he then began to chant those words you are hearing now. Somehow the words healed his brother, and they swore to each other that they would never fight again."

"Tell me what these words mean, Gobo."

"I believe they mean 'I utter this reverence for the divine mystic law of the Universe, that unfolds like a great flower, a great flower out of my heart and from my very throat'."

"Nom myohoe rengay kyoe nom myohoe rengay kyoe nom myohoe rengay kyoe nom myohoe rengay kyoe nom myohoe rengay kyoe"

On the last syllable 'kyoe' the Cloud Tree bellowed forth a blast of shocking wind that rolled into the Harp with a great crashing sound, spinning and tumbling it about.

But the Harp's spinning slowed down…and it remained in place.

Koradgians scrambled everywhere, keeping their machine of war balanced and working as best they could. The Captain, sensing that he would not get a second chance at this, brought his scaly fist down, hard, on the big red button.

All of the evil in the world that could have ever been found in a set of piercing shrieking chords now issued forth from the Harp, and like a vast, unseen spear of sound, it struck and exploded into Shane's vast bulk, sundering him into a hundred pieces hurtling everywhere in the sky.

What was left of the Cloud Tree, a colossal chunk of barkless, faceless trunk of now inanimate material hurled downward into the Valley of Everlast. An incredible explosion of fire and lightning, thunder and stone cascaded forth, sending out a great mushroom of a cloud.

But only for a few seconds, you see, because no page can long survive the death of its Avatar, and the crater that would have been left from this massive impact gained a life of its own. A vicious and hungry black hole it became, a vortex of a maw that began to spin and suck and shred the very land like a gigantic garbage disposal.

When it was done, the firmament of the heavens was filled with hundreds of tiny scraps of mud and water and land; here a cliff with a few scrubby bushes and a very scared family of rabbits, there a river without a bed, rapidly losing its frogs and fish into the very air. Some of the scraps of land were about as big as your back yard, others, perhaps as big as your neighborhood, but none of them were any bigger than either.

Duke Moebius would be very pleased indeed. The Harp came about and began its journey back to Castle DeepSteel, leaving behind a sky of floating islands and the stench of death.

The Third and Fourth Pages of Cetacea and Everlast were no more.

AntiPart Two

Introducing a Fane Train, the Dwark-Express

As Nowar flew toward Opus Delirious, it was not difficult to know where to go; a thousand points of light danced and bobbed, swirled and swayed all around the Train Station below the Light-House, which was still quite dark.

Everywhere else was dark as well.

Nowar headed to the Station. Clearly that's where she was meant to be.

There was a wind whirling and whistling through the trees as her two feet touched the ground. Large Chinese lanterns dangling from the branches were in fact low hanging fruit, glowing and pulsing as the breeze created a rustling sound all around her. She was back in Opus Delirious.

The Station sat beneath the Light-House, which was, in fact, conspicuously dark.

"Weren't Light-houses supposed to have a beacon light on?" she thought to herself.

The Train Station, however, was filled with light; beautiful, scintillating light of all colors. In fact, as she approached the Station, it reminded her of a cathedral made almost entirely of stained glass connected by thin spires of stone and wires. It winded away, more like a subway station, actually, and it looked like it began to climb at a decent angle upwards; very different from what she imagined a train station should look like.

Before she could get within a stone's throw of the Station, she was mobbed by a horde of Faeries. They were polite enough about it, but in a heartbeat they were all over Nowar, tugging on her spear, peeking from under her hair, looking in her ears, knocking on her helmet, sliding off her shield, reaching into her boots and-

"ENOUGH!" she yelled, the force of her bellowing voice blowing them off of her body.

The Faeries stared. A pot-bellied Faerie with a big beard, sunglasses and tattoos sat on his tiny Dwark-chopper puffing on a cigar and said in a tiny but ridiculously deep voice-

"Sorry Sister" and then, looking at the rest of the Faeries with a stern look said very seriously "Lithageave hithager alithagone, githagot ithagit?"

The Faeries, some looking a bit dejected, didn't go very far, but started to kick back right there in Nowar's vicinity. Most resumed playing cards, drinking root beer and chain smoking. Some looked at Nowar with absolute adoration, desperately wanting to tease her again.

Nowar began to realize that their numbers had grown…phenomenally. As she surveyed the surrounding hillocks and sparse forest around the Station, she could see from their little fire-pits that there were hundreds, if not thousands of them, camped everywhere- in every nook and cranny of the landscape.

It was an army of rowdy Faeries.

Suddenly, out of the Train Station and down the cobble-stone path that swizzled and circled down to where Nowar stood, came a cohort of elementals, or more precisely, a ball of mud rolling behind a streaming column of water, followed by a fluster of fire twirling around a gust of wind. All four congealed into form at Nowar's feet, loudly exclaiming-

"Nowar! Nowar! Nowar!"

Glupus, Myrtle, Edith and Jackie danced in circles around their winged princess. They began to chant in time to their dance-

"Scream it and Shout! Scream it and Shout! Moebius look out!"

Their enthusiasm was infectious. One by one, the Faeries started to dance with them, circling around Nowar, throwing dirt and sharp objects into the air.

Then the Walrus showed up.

"Coo-coo-Ka-Choo, Nowar! Ho ho ho ho! I just knew you were gonna show!"

Faeries cackled and threw spitballs at each other, narrowly missing the big ol' Walrus in his burgundy British colonial uniform. As he wobbled over to Nowar, he bent over and looked into her face carefully, so close she could count his whiskers. What was he looking for?

Then he smiled, straitened up and turned to look up into the sky. Far above the dark Light-House, a blue star glowed through the gloom and the gloam. He cleared his throat and said "So…"

As if she had become an echo, she repeated him- "So…"

The Faeries, who had just quieted down to watch this sequence of events suddenly exploded into a panoramic parade of play and pompery, chanting to each other in a sing-song rhythm-

"So, so, so, so. So, so, so, so…" and while they continued with this background song, one of them cried out, to no one in particular-

"So is a word that YOU can use…"

"-And MANY people use it when they choose…"

"But if you want to use OUR word-"

"…First you will …have to be heard!!!" and they rolled in laughter, snorting and jostling.

Nowar felt only slightly irritated by this escalating nonsense which continued in the background. She looked back at the Walrus very seriously and said-

"So now what?"

"So now I introduce you to dee Dwark Express, a fine Fane Train that goes faster than a plane, hehehehe. Come with me, sunshine…" he turned and began humping back toward the Train Station. She thought she heard him say- "It's all downhill from here, darlin'…"

Which was odd, because they were in fact going uphill.

AntiPart One

A momentary Omen-tary

Good King Shard knelt in the snow, bringing the Omen-tary, perched on his arm, close to his face. He looked nervously over at the Great Olde Drake, who looked back and said, in his booming bellowing voice-

"Look…listen…learn. The only thing I will guarantee you is that it will not be pleasant."

How could **he** know, thought Shard, he's not even a Precognitus, and sometimes even **they** were wrong. But he **was** the very first and oldest of all the avatars of ProbablePolis.

The King, who was also a Colonel, whispered to the Omen-tary "Your secrets are mine, Omen-tary…I am the recipient of your hidden fruits, I am King Shard."

A searing flash of light erupted from the head of the Omen-tary. When the light died down, the crystalline ball of whispery blue was now full of imagery- a reddish hued sunset across the canyons of Kirhalion, the no-man's land where the elvish lords pitched perpetual battles against the foul creatures and crafts of Duke Moebius. As the panorama moved smoothly across the brutal but beautiful sienna caverns, a very dark image came into view- a gigantic black harp.

"By the Logos, what is this thing?" Shard exclaimed loudly.

The Logos, who was in fact standing only a few feet away from him, said nothing, knowing that Shard was only expelling a commonly used catch phrase. The Great Olde Drake, however, answered him

"It is the Black Harp of Castle DeepSteel, o King Shard, a device of gigantic proportions and capabilities." He paused and added "I should not need to remind you that you see now shades of the past, perhaps even a full pulse past. With this in mind, subdue your passion, and better yourself by paying closer attention."

Into view now came the one who had sent the Omen-tary, the face of Andironé filled up the view. The High King of Kirhannok now spoke as if he was really there, though he wasn't "King Shard this is Andironé, your ally of old."

Shard drew a sharp breath. What an understatement. Shard had saved Andironé Esteviale from certain death in a vicious battle when Andironé was hardly more than a boy, at least by Elvish years. Andironé had rewarded Shard by padding along behind him, like a puppy, on many a great and fantastic journey, loyal beyond words.

"Your Arch-vizzerid was right. There is a strange weapon here at the canyon of Kirhalion, and it does indeed resemble an enormous black harp. It is lightly guarded, though, and in fact the entire valley is all but empty of the Koradjians encampments."

A deep sinking feeling was coiling in Shard's gut, but he could not look away.

"I fear the worst, old friend. My elves and I will return here with reinforcements and lay siege to the whole of Kirhalion. If you have troops to spare, we shall return here on the morrow. The Shiogue Kingdom of Kirhannok welcomes your assistance."

Shard looked down at the snow, but only for a second.

"The final war is upon us, Shard. Stay true. May the Logos be with you, and may you be yourself. Send word as soon as you can."

Then the view rapidly changed, showing Andironé and his elves down below, fading from view, but not fading so quickly as not to show clearly how they were ambushed, the King captured, his bodyguards slain and hurled from the cliff.

The crystalline ball that was the Omen-tary's head went dark.

Shard was beside himself. He looked back again at the Great Olde Drake and called out "So the Fourth Kingdom is under control of Moebius, and King Andironé is either slain or taken hostage?"

Crusted with snow, one of the Drake's huge eyebrows raised upward, and he called back-

"The news is even worse than you expect, King of Ambrosia…" and shaking snow from his grizzled mane went on to say "…few but the greatest have a mind to understand the unseen powers of plausibility inherent in an Omen-tary."

The King looked confused, but listened intently as the Drake continued.

"By means of a contrivance woven into the very fabric of ProbablePolis, a thing the Builders call 'spooky action at a distance', once an Omen-tary has been touched by someone, it remains forever connected to them. Look again, and I will ask the Omen-tary to reveal not what 'was' but what 'is'.

Shard looked down at the Omen-tary and saw swirling shapes, twisting and colliding into each other as the morning pulse began to shed light across an impossibly shattered landscape floating in a dust-shrouded oblivion. The Drake narrated while Shard looked on in abject horror.

"Everlast, the Fourth Page, is smashed beyond recognition and rent into a hundred thousand tiny pieces, some as big as a dozen acres, most about the size of a small yard. As you know the Third page, Cetacea, being simply the other side of the Fourth Page, has suffered the same fate. Moebius has lowered the page count of ProbablePolis to twelve. Only twelve Kingdoms remain."

"But…how…could…this…be?"

"Shane was slain, and what page can remain, when its Avatar is no more?"

"And…Andironé with him?" Shard's heart sank deeper still.

"Look still further, the Omen-tary's tale is not quite finished"

Shard watched as into view loomed the Black Harp, cruising at a fairly high speed. Getting closer, Shard could now see that someone was nailed to the bowhead of the Harp. Closer still, he could now see, it was Andironé!

"But barely alive, he is being returned to Moebius for cruel pleasures and taunting. He will likely be thrown into a rack of torture and interviewed by Moebius' camera crews and news anchors."

The Omen-tary went dark again. Shard stood slowly and turned to look at his Father.

"It's time to attack DeepSteel"

But the Drake wasn't finished "First things first. The Emperor has something I will need, a box of memories with a funny little blue light. Will you oblige, sir?"

Bric, a bit shocked, pulled the device from under his armor where he had stashed it and looked up at the Drake. Shard looked concerned, but Bric said quietly under his breath "**You** want to tell him 'no'? I didn't think so. Besides, I suspect we can trust him." And then looking up at the Drake, Bric said loudly –

"You're going to use this on Nowar next, aren't you?"

"Indeed I am, Emperor."

"Ok, so there is one thing I'm curious about…" he was marching through the snow now, headed in a beeline to the Great Olde Drake, "I just want to know how you're going to find her!"

He slid the Memoress device into an impossibly huge leathery paw. Synarchus Luminous Lazarus, the oldest Avatar of all ProbablePolis laughed heartily and said-

"Why, with **their** help of course!"

Bric, a bit more shocked even than before, turned to look back at his little group. On the icy hillock just above Khan, Kai, his son, the Logos and the silver metal Crab stood two very tall figures, one with two wings, and the other with only one.

The Drake was till chuckling while he said-

"Emperor Bric, permit me to introduce Menses of the Four Winds, and Mandrake the White. Anyone who thinks that there are places where Angels dare not tread has never met these two."

Bric wasn't sure what to think, so he didn't; he just trudged back through the knee-high snow caps towards his little group, watching Mandrake and Menses quietly pass him on their way to speak to the Drake. Mandrake smiled and nodded pleasantly at him.

Bric walked right up to the Logos and said "Alright, we're ready to invade DeepSteel, but we'll need some way to get back to Ambrosia. What would you suggest, son?"

The Logos smiled deeply.

"Oh, but of course, kind Emperor. Ask nicely, and Synarchus will take you all."

Again, Bric tried not to look confused as he said "The Drake?"

"Oh yes, he's going your way. Just stick out your thumb, and offer a story in payment."

"A story…"

"Why, yes, didn't you know, once a Dragon has collected all the wealth he cares to, he cares for little else than a good story. Offer him a story, and he will offer you a ride."

Bric and Shard shared the same awkward stare.

"Your turn." -was all Bric could say.

AntiChapter Three

Because everyone loves pi

AntiPart Ten

A tale of two 'chothers

The gates to the underground MoonClock facility were foreboding. Two guards wearing thick armor and toting machine guns walked out of the security post and waited patiently for the van, arriving slowly at their post.

Grandma Brandy's hands were trembling. Her son noticed and said slowly, calmly-

"Pull up to the gate and show him your I.D. Once the second guard comes to ask me for mine, the opportunity for a distraction should present itself easily, and while it does, you take your foot off the brake."

"How do you know there will be an opportunity for distraction?"

"Because in spite of top secret classification, everyone stationed here two years ago probably knows I disappeared into the MoonClock gate and never came back. My reappearance should create a stir, and a stir can usually be grown into a distraction. Just follow my lead and be prepared to let the van coast into the facility while I do what I do."

As the first guard came to the van window, Grandma Brandy already had her I.D. out and handed it to him. He smiled, looked at it closely and said-

"Brandy Rondell? Are you any relation to General Bric Rondell?"

Grandma Brandy said stiffly "That would be my husband." He looked blankly at her, his eyes darted to his buddy who was making his own startling discovery on the other side of the van, exclaiming loudly-

"Colonel Rondell! How in the world?!!"

Shard smiled and, recognizing the Sergeant, said quietly "Sergeant Cuetell, as I live and breathe, look at you; for heaven's sake, Sergeant, what's a talented young man like you still doing guard duty? Here's my I.D. Let me get out of this van and fill you in…"

It was the first breach of protocol. Sergeant Cuetell took a stunned step back while Shard got out of the van, still talking. The other guard gave Brandy back her I.D. and walked over to the other side of the van to hear Shard's story.

Second breach of protocol.

Seeing that he had the rapt attention of both men, Shard motioned them to walk a few feet away from the van, saying "This is a classified matter, gentlemen, my Mother's not cleared to hear what I'm about to tell you."

Grandma Brandy watched her son's face like a hawk. As he began his next sentence, his eyes briefly met hers while he nodded deeply, still talking to the two guards.

Brandy lifted her foot from the brake, allowing the van to creep slowly forward.

One of the guards turned and said "Uh, she's not cleared yet to proceed, sir." By the time he turned back to look at Shard, his partner, Sergeant Cuetell was already laying on the ground, unconscious and disarmed. He shortly joined him.

Lt. Colonel Shard Rondell pulled both of them into the Guard station, took the phone off the hook, and quickly rejoined his mother in the van. She was smiling.

"Nicely done, son. Now what?"

"We probably have less than a minute to ditch the van and get to a ventilation shaft. We have to get to the chip manufacture zone, and quickly. That Guard station had three security cameras, and they all feed up to the Observation Tower. This entry way will be swarming with commandos in no time.

"Got it!" The van lurched forward, careening into the giant darkened tunnel, shattering a chain link metal fence asunder as Brandy pushed her engine's capacity way beyond what was sensible.

Meanwhile, up in the control room of the Observation Tower, a man in a black suit with sunglasses, who looked an awful lot like Colonel Rondell sat in a seat, calmly watching several monitors, some of them depicting the van screeching off into the darkness. There were unconscious guards passed out all over the floor, their hands tied behind their backs.

A phone was ringing.

The man in the suit picked it up and said- "Guard Station Alpha. Sgt Smith here."

"Sgt. Smith, we just lost the master feed off of all your monitors. What is your status?"

"Status is clear, sir, and we are still secure. I just had to reboot the server. Over."

"Alright, Sgt. Smith, reboot and report back in five minutes. Do you copy?"

"Yes, sir. I copy. Over and out."

The man in the suit hung up the phone, stood up, straitened his tie, and said quietly to himself- "Alright kids, I just bought you five more minutes. Make the most of them."

As he walked down the stairs, stepping over two more unconscious guards, he pulled a small, slender device from his inner coat pocket. It resembled a cell phone. With a modest smile he looked at its flashing little screen and said-

"Finally! Ahead of schedule, for once."

Locking the door to the Observation Tower from the inside, he flipped open the device and softly said "Next Fugue-point, engage!"

There was a brief flash of light and he was gone.

AntiPart Nine

Every ending has to begin somewhere

The man who looked an awful lot like Colonel Rondell stood in the parking lot in front of a red brick building with a bunch of large satellite dishes on the roof. The big three dimensional letters on the front said-

WTFU *Where the Classics are making a comeback*

He still had the small, slender device that looked an awful lot like a cell phone in his hand. He looked briefly at the green numbers that were flashing on the display screen.

4 . 20 . 1988

Looking around the parking lot he began to walk toward the glass front doors of the TV Broadcasting station, carefully avoiding walking into view of the security camera, and murmuring to himself –

"Hard to believe I'm almost done. One more fugue point after this one, and we go home…this is where the rubber meets the road, baby."

Opening the doors, he wasted no time in walking up to the front desk, quickly surveying the lobby and eventually returning his silent gaze to the security guard, asleep at his post, feet hung on the desktop in front of him. Walking silently past him, he avoided the elevator, turning instead to walk up the stairs, headed for the fourth floor.

Arriving at the fourth floor, he advanced quietly and with great speed to the office marked "Producer Danny Dubious" and without knocking walked right through the door, literally. It was past noon, the secretary was at lunch, and walking through yet another door, the man in the suit beheld the Producer in a similar pose as the security guard on the main floor.

Except he was snoring.

The man in the suit banged on the desk, hard, shaking the Producer from his slumber and spilling coffee and doughnuts everywhere.

"What the …who are YOU and what are you doing HERE?!"

The man in the suit, still wearing his sunglasses, stared blankly at the Producer, whose appearance and cheap outfit went well with his last name; he calmly pulled out a wallet and exposed some kind of official looking identification badge.

"Agent Fugue of the National Security Agency. Mr. Dubious, I need a few minutes of your time to answer a few questions."

The Producer leaned over his desk, and looked closely at the badge.

"Uh, is there a number I can call to confirm who you are?" he started to write down the identification number on the badge. Agent Fugue knocked the pen clear out of his hand and across the room, cleanly bouncing off of a lava lamp.

It was, after all, the eighties.

"Look you cream-puff doughnut eating mush-minded left-leaning loafer, I don't have much time here and I want some answers followed by a little cooperation. DO I make myself clear?"

"OK! OK, I get it. Go ahead, ask away."

"Alright, that's more like it." He pulled out a small pad of paper and prepared to scribble in it as he said "I understand this TV Station recently changed hands."

"Yeah we got a new owner. Some guy we never see."

"Right, his name is…"

"Moebius, uh, Moebius Noblechuck…the third, I think. The owners were having a tough time, he just showed up out of nowhere with a ton of cash and bought the whole thing, fired everyone but me and left without any way to contact him"

Agent Fugue was quiet for a second, then said-

"What did he do before he left, he must have done something…odd."

"Yeah, yeah, actually, he did, now that you mention it, come with me, I'll show you"

Walking down a long hall, through a couple doors, eventually the man came to a bunch of filing cabinets, pulled one open and pulled out a thick folder full of papers.

"This was our programming schedule before he bought us last Thursday. Check it out"

"OK, looks like fairly normal programming- 'Lost in Space' is a little passe, but I see 'I love Lucy', M.A.S.H., Star Trek reruns, some great MGM classics too, hey the 'Lawrence Welk show' how about that?"

Agent Fugue slapped the file into the Producer's chest hard enough to cause him to exhale sharply "So?!"

Glaring at him slightly, the Producer pulled out another thick folder and said "Here's how Mr. Noblechuck changed the programming."

"Hmm. 'The Longest Day', 'Midway', 'The Battle of the Bulge', 'Fail-Safe', hey I loved 'Mr. Roberts'..uh, 'Sands of Iwo Jima' hey, these are all war movies."

"Clearly the NSA is hiring the brightest minds out of our Community Colleges these days."

"OK, cream-puff, I've seen enough, I didn't come here to play movie critic with you. I have one simple order for you. You carry it out, you never hear or see me again, you decide to break formation and do something other than what I tell you to do, and I return like the proverbial bad penny, with interest. Understand?"

"OK, now you have my attention. What's the low-down?"

"Alright, according to this, you have a movie scheduled for 11 PM tonight called 'The Desert Fox'. Now, this is a truly excellent movie where James Mason plays the German Field Marshall Rommel, a brilliant tactician who tried to overthrow Hitler, and I know your viewers will be sorely disappointed when you have to replace it with another movie, without any prior warning, but I'm afraid the needs of national security will have to outweigh the aesthetics of good taste."

The Producer was still staring, like he was seeing a man from Mars for the first time.

"OK, but since when does the NSA get involved in media network broadcasting, could you tell me that?"

"I could, but then I'd have to shoot you. If you'll just shut up and play the movie at 11 o'clock tonight, we'll both get to watch it, ok?"

The Producer sighed, looked down at the ground and said quietly "Alright, I'll do it, what movie do you want me to play?"

"The movie that was **supposed** to play tonight, my good man. The Wizard of Oz."

By the time the Producer had returned from the programming room to report that the programming change had been made, Agent Fugue was nowhere to be found.

AntiPart Eight

The Queen was free, and killing with glee

What an understatement.

Actually Queen Limberly, having dispatched the last three Koradgians in under three seconds was well on her way to a showdown marathon, blasting high and low, kicking, pushing and whacking relentlessly on her way to her private chambers, where she downed a dozen more, including some large vicious leathery winged spider like creature lurking in the ceiling above her.

Once she was satisfied that she had rid her private quarters of opponents, she drew a nice warm bath and washed the last of the green goo from her skin. As she dried her hair, she looked carefully at the Dwark stone that had woken her.

But it had done more than wake her, though, she thought... it had done a great deal more; it had made her feel like she had a daughter, and that that daughter had been in real danger. Only one problem:

She didn't have a daughter. She had been married to the King for many pulses of the Great Ribbon before they had parted ways, but she had never ever conceived an heir to the United Kingdoms of ProbablePolis.

She realized that she would have to give the whole matter further consideration at a later time. Right now she had a Castle to reclaim, and a bad guy to clobber. Walking to one of the walls in her chamber, she pulled down a long rod of crystal from the side of a large silver oval on the wall, spoke softly the word "Carderocke". The oval on the wall came to life and she beheld a scene of darkness, with an elf kneeling on a filthy stone floor, clad in chains and rags. It was a dank dungeon cell that she recognized- level seven far beneath her feet, under the Castle foundation itself.

"Carderocke!" she gasped. In no time at all, the Queen used her Dwark stone to materialize right next to her faithful vizier and wasted no time in snapping open the chains. She gasped as he looked up at her, or rather, pretended to look up at her. Where his eyes had been there were darkened sockets. He was thin and malnourished and shivered at her touch.

"Queen Limberly?" he spoke feebly.

"By the Logos! How long have you been here, Carderocke?"

"Longer than you could imagine, longer than I can remember, my Lady; after they captured you, they brought me here, tore out my eyes and broke my legs. If it has been one pulse it has more likely been at least a hundred. Even if light had been able to get down here, I would never have seen it."

A dark charge was beginning to build in Limberly's soul.

First she would heal her friend, then she would take back her Castle, and finally, she would invade Moebius' Kingdom and lay waste to Castle DeepSteel.

Quietly she wished that Carderocke's eyes and legs would mend as quickly as snow melts in the spring thaw.

Then she turned around and hurled the prison cell-door open with a blast so powerful it rang throughout the dark gloomy dungeon.

AntiPart Seven

Turtle time; it's sublime

Mrs. Machine was running out of steam.

For some time now she had been progressively slowing down, much to the consternation of Two-Fangs, who suddenly started banging his fists on the metal banister that surrounded the open-faced cockpit that he and Ouroboros Alpha-Beta had been riding in.

"What are ye doin'?" cried Beta "She's liable to turn us over and dump us if ye keep bangin' on her!"

"Why is she slowing down, we'll never make it to Opus Delirious at this rate!"

A few beeps toots and whistles from Mrs. Machine indicated something was amiss.

"She says that she is running low on energy." Said Alpha, who apparently had no trouble understanding Machine talk, "She says she needs to stop somewhere to recharge her fuel cells."

"And where are we supposed to do that, in the middle of the Dwark?" Two-Fangs bellowed.

"Probably right there, I'd say." responded Beta, who was clearly staring at something lurking in the gloom. "Looks like she's makin' for that island off the starboard bow, ay?"

Indeed, a huge hulking object was in fact getting closer and closer every moment, as Mrs. Machine strained to put every last bit of her juice into making it to some small floating fragment of some long vanquished page.

"It was probably part of the same page that Opus Delirious belonged to, long long ago."

It was a strange hump of a landscape, now barely lit from Mrs. Machine's running lights as she skimmed along, perhaps only six feet off the surface. It was essentially not much more than a very large hill, covered with clumps of moss and lichen, a few tiny scraggly bushes, some vines and Spanish moss moving in a gentle breeze off the edges of the island.

As she came to rest on the top of the hill, she extended her anchor claws firmly into the mossy landscape and immediately shut down, going quite dormant. It got very quiet.

"Two-Fangs jumped out of the cockpit and looked around - with his keen Wolven-kine eyes he surveyed the near pitch darkness while Ouroboros remained in the cockpit and shivered. It's cold in the Dwark, if no one's told you that before.

Two-Fangs thought out loud "I wonder how long it will take her to recharge?"

Alpha responded, saying "She chirped just before she shut off that she would reboot in an hour or two."

"Let's hope so, or we are marooned in the Dwark forever. Without Mrs. Machine we will have no way to get anywhere, and no way of knowing how to get there either."

Angry at the situation, Two-Fangs took his heavy antler mounted staff and, with a guttural yowl slammed it into the ground, hard. Then he howled and howled and howled. There was nothing else to do. They had come so far, and now, everything was hanging on a thread of hope that this machine would come back to life.

Suddenly, it was the island that came to life. It started with a low, barely audible groan, like the sound of a lost whale in the deepest ocean. Two-Fangs looked around wildly as Ouroboros peeked over the banister of the cockpit nervously. Then a low moaning accompanied a great shuddering as the island began to slowly turn clockwise. On either side of the island a gigantic green and blue flipper rose and fell slowly.

Two-Fangs grabbed the cockpit banister just as the island lurched forward. He yelled to Ouroboros as a wind began to whoosh through his mane "This is no island! This is a Dwark Turtle!"

"Now our goose is really cooked!" lamented Alpha, "who knows where it's headed!"

Little did they know, the Dwark-Turtle in fact was about ready to wake up before Two-Fangs threw his tantrum, having a clutch of eggs it had been ready to lay for quite some time.

After about forty five minutes of some very fast travel, Mrs. Machine rebooted.

Her lights flashed and she whirred and purred. She was as surprised as they had been earlier to be in motion. Much to the surprise of Two-Fangs and Ouroboros Alpha-Beta, she was able to relate that the great Dwark Turtle was in fact heading towards a barely visible twinkle of light that they could barely see; a tiny Blue Star hovering near the island of Opus Delirious was giving off a siren call to the Turtle, calling her to an ancient nesting site. Mrs. Machine also told Alpha that the Dwark Turtle was probably going to get them all there in perhaps a handful of hours, considerably faster than she alone could ever have done.

Upon hearing this news Two-Fangs quietly said to himself "The Logos is with us again."

But he did not relax one bit.

AntiPart Six

Where have all the warm squirmy things gone? Long time passing.

Contrary to popular belief, Precognitids do not exist in a perpetual state of precognition. In other words, they do not see all of the future, all of the time, but rather they experience short dramatic bursts of insight into the future, rendered in stunning and succinct details that would be baffling and perhaps even scary to the rest of us.

The Precognitus Hieronymous Quantum Jones was having one of those insights at that very moment. Sitting on a pile of debris at the rim of a gigantic crater, he watched the Silver Scream Nine devour the very throne room of the UnderRung and gave a heavy sigh. Surveying the vast crater that had once been the domain of the Midnight Shadow, he opened his silicon soul to the pulse of eternity and looked for clues as to what was going on...

The Avatar of the Seventh Page had flown the coop. That was his first insight. The second insight was even more painful; he had to have been given help from an outside source, which meant the resistance was on the move, and this led him to the third insight, which made him twitch- if the resistance was on the move, then it would not be long before that fat little madman would come looking for his most prized toy.

Bingo- the ringing of his own bell circuits announced an incoming call, from, well- he'd already guessed it; Castle DeepSteel.

Jones depressed a button on one of his many arms, cleared his vocalization unit of steam and said "You've reached the voice mail of Hieronymous Quantum Jones. I'm sorry I'm not available. In these troubled times, we all look for answers, I suggest you look elsewhere, since I have nothing but questions to offer you. Feel free to leave your number. This has not been a recording. BEEP!"

The other side of the open channel was quiet for three seconds, and then a voice said "I had no idea that you were such a comedian, Jones."

"Neither did I, until just now. What can I do for you Moebius, as if I'd do anything for you anymore…"

"Well, there is a small matter you might assist me with…"

"Let me guess, you finally realized that the theory of relativity and quantum mechanics can't both be right, and you want some inside scoop; let's flip a coin shall we, heads for relativity, tails for quantum."

"…actually it appears that something of mine has gone missing…"

"Well, process of elimination, it couldn't possibly be your conscience, or your sanity, that's for certain, so what have you misplaced now, my good man?"

"You have my Silver Scream Nine you MISBEGOTTEN WAD OF SILICON AND POLYMERS!"

"Not really, Moebius, the poor thing woke up hungry, and I just brought him to food. Consider it a test drive, free of charge."

"I'm stunned by your generosity. Perhaps you might lead the little fellow back over here to Castle DeepSteel for more fun and games"

"Possibly…possibly…first, though, I have a question; do you have any idea of where the Midnight Shadow is right at this moment?"

Moebius was losing even more patience, and spat back "None, and I have my hands full looking for Shard and Limberly's daughter. I nearly had her and she's slipped off into the deep Dwark. If you really wanted to be useful you synthetic moron you'd help me find her instead of shanghaiing my toys to go on personal vendettas against that black Unicorn."

Jones chuckled and said "Impressive powers of persuasion, Moebius. That, and your personal hygiene really should have taken you further in life, but it didn't. So, if the Midnight Shadow and five hundred legions of UnderRung monstrosities are nowhere to be found in T'ien Sha'an,

I'd say probabilities of their arrival on your own page are increasing by the moment."

Moebius was quiet for a few seconds, and then roared out "Clancy, assign a hundred tendrilous Toggle-Wogs to scour the Seventh Page! If the Midnight Shadow and his armies have left the Seventh Page and are on their way here we need to know about it as soon as possible!!!"

Jones was waiting for the other shoe to drop. Moebius resumed the rather colorful banter with a hardly-veiled threat attached to a candy-covered carrot.

"Alright, Hieronymous. Consider your options. Option One: Skulk around the Seventh Page with my stolen property and eventually, when I have some spare time, I come and wring your scrawny neck myself, or Option Two: Come to Castle DeepSteel with my Silver Scream Nine, and likely you'll get your most treasured wish, a chance to watch the Midnight Shadow go down, once and for all."

Jones felt a sense of synthetic sanguine setting in, but answered quickly "Alright, I'll see you soon enough, you beetle brained buffoon, but you'd better be serving some decent snacks at this slumber party of yours."

Moebius, who'd already had enough of this banter had already hung up.

Hieronymous Quantum Jones watched the hungry multi-ton monster called the Silver Scream Nine in the midst of a continued feeding frenzy. He hated to interrupt his new little friend while he had food in his mouth, but eventually he got its attention; puttering up to the huge smiling fanged face of the Silver Scream, Jones said "Alright boyo, I've noticed that your dining pleasure is losing its luster. Where have all the warm squirmy things gone?"

"Dunno, Daddy. Where did dey go? Tasty things all gone." It said, and then belched so loudly that a nearby column of stone crashed down into the crater it sat in.

"I know, you adorable little fellow. Well, Uncle Moebius just told me where they all went. Do you want me to show you?"

"Oh yes, oh yes, oh YES!!!" he cried out as his huge tail began to beat the ground with enthusiasm on the 6.9 richter scale.

This was just too easy, thought Jones.

AntiPart Five

All aboard the Dwark Express.

Once Nowar and the Walrus had made it to the top of the hill, a bunch of the Faeries in a furious flurry flew in front of them both to swing open the huge glass doors. The Walrus bowed deeply and flourished with his flippers, motioning to Nowar to go in front of him through the doors and into the Station.

The place reminded her of what she thought an old-timey Train Station should look like, filled with lamp-posts and vaulted ceilings, and of course, a set of train tracks; but the huge stained glass windows reminded her much more of a cathedral with spirals of metal and stone everywhere. Another odd feature was how the tracks and the long building winded around and away, and…up? In some ways it was more like a subway station with the tracks and building climbing at a decent angle upwards- very different from what she imagined a train station should look like.

And then there was the Dwark Express. Nowar had never seen anything like it.

In fact it was really like a seamless and rather extravagant marriage of Steam Engine, Rocket and Scram Jet. It had huge wheels like a Train, tiny wings like a Plane, and the main engine cab looked like it had been fused with an odd sort of Rocket engine on top. The engine room was rather spherical, and the top half was like a semi-transparent geodesic dome. From where Nowar stood, looking up at this improbable but streamlined thing, it looked like it had a strange contraption suspended inside it- two sets of spherical cages, one contained in the other, each consisting of several bands of very shiny metal. The bands slowly moved around one another, and the whole thing pulsed slowly and gently.

"Wow…it's…interesting." was all Nowar could get out at first, and then, after another moment of staring said "What does it run on?"

"What? Da Dwark Express? Oh she a plasma driven Fusion engine. She run on a turbo charged proton gun injection system."

Nowar stared at him and said "Ok, well…what's the fuel?"

"Oh, you can use diff'rent types of fuel dependin' on whatchyou gots available, like banana peels or Faerie droppings, but, if you want to get the most bang for de buck you gots to use HeHeHelium, a rare isotope of laughter. We happens to have a ton of dat HeHeHelium on Opus Delirious, so we in no danger of runnin' out of fuel, missy Nowar, ain' dat right, Conductor?"

He was looking up himself now. Leaning out of the engine room hatch window was lil Bonsai Rex, wearing his finest Train engineer's hat and patting the side of the hull like it was a favored pet.

"You got it boss! Dis ting is stoked and clean, shiny and mean, and we got a boatload of HeHeHelium in the tank, lemme tell you what, we prolly got enough to go to every single page!"

The Walrus chuckled to himself and turned back to Nowar.

"How 'bout dat? De Dwark Express is primed for lift off."

Nowar walked a little ways down the tracks to look up the curving tracks, inclining more and more upward as she investigated further.

"Where…uh…how does it work?"

"Well, first of all we gets all de Faeries and other Opus irregulars loaded up in de rest of de train, and den we fires up de main motors to give it jus' a lil push an' all….den, as we start down de tracks, de Fusion engine jet'll kick in, de wheels'll pull up, and we'll go flying up de tracks and off into da Dwark so fast yo head'll spin."

"And then what? Where are we going? What are we going to do?"

The Walrus bent over and looked at Nowar closely.

"We's goin' to go start de war to end all war, dat's what. We goin' to Castle DeepSteel wif as many of de citizens of ProbablePolis as are still willin' to fight da Moebius."

He turned quickly to look back up at Bonsai Rex, thoroughly energized now- "Alrightie Bonsai, kick out a few cars an' cabooses, will you? We gots about four hundred Faeries and dey lil' Dwark Choppers to load up."

"Okie-dokie, boss."

A few very odd noises came from the engine compartment, and whatever Bonsai had done up there, suddenly cars and cabooses began erupting from the hind parts of the Dwark Express, one after another, perhaps a dozen in all.

The Walrus turned around and, addressing the Elementals hovering in the background said "Alright chillen' go let all de Faeries know dey can load up."

It was too late, the Faeries had already heard. They came roaring in on their tiny Dwark-choppers, teeming and streaming into the station, hopping and skipping and riding into the cars and cabooses of the Dwark Express.

Nowar noticed that the most rear caboose was locked and largely untouched.

"What's in that one?" she asked.

The Walrus smiled so broadly, she thought his head would split open- "Come an' have a look-see, darlin'." Pulling out a big silver key as he waddled over to the caboose he deftly unlocked the double doors and opened the compartment.

Inside was a Dwark Chopper, much like the one the Faeries used, except it was huge, big enough for a very large rider indeed.

"Dis' my 'Hardly Bathingsoon'. She a special three-seater, turbocharged Dwark Chopper… I custom-built her myself, back in da days when Opus Delirious was a whole durned page, loooong time ago." He beamed now, and continued with "She my pride and joy, she is. She roars like a lion and purrs like a kitten."

Nowar beheld the masterpiece of chrome and leather. It shone like it was brand new, and smelled like it had been oiled down with some expensive very nice-smelling stuff.

The Walrus laughed and said "I knows whatchyou thinkin', missy Nowar. You go ahead and ride de Dwark Express first. Der ain' no experience like it when it takes off, dats fer sure, lemme tell ye…and once we get to our first destination, den I gives ye a ride on my big beautiful 'Hardly', alright?"

Nowar smiled and looked at the Walrus for a long time. "Ok, but how many destinations are we going to?"

The Walrus smirked and said "All a'dem."

"Huh, what do you mean 'All of them'?"

"I means what I says, and I says what I means, darlin'. Der' are fourteen pages of ProbablePolis, an de Dwark Express iz goin' to go pick up recruits on every one of dem."

Nowar noticed that Lil' Bonsai Rex, still wearing his engineers hat, had been standing behind them on the loading platform of the Station. He proudly saluted when the Walrus and Nowar turned to look at him.

"Hokie-dokie boss. Everybody is on-board de Dwark Express and dee Fuzion engine is nearly finished warming up. We 'bout ready to go."

Now Nowar was smiling.

AntiPart Four

An ode to the Quanta and the cursing of an Angel.

The swiftness with which the Dwark Turtle was soaring through the Dwarkness now was nothing short of inspirational. As she had been building up speed for some time now, Alpha suddenly commented to Beta "This is simply splendid! At this speed, we'll be getting to Opus Delirious in no time at all."

Beta, however, was catching up on some much needed sleep, and responded with some very aggressive snoring. Two-Fangs was ecstatic, however, and broke into a howl of joy from time to time as the wind ruffled his mane. Both Ouroboros and Two-Fangs were still riding in the ad hoc cockpit that Mrs. Machine had created for them all.

Mrs. Machine, for her own part, kept a good steady anchor-lock to the great shell of the Dwark-Turtle. She was just grateful she could rest her thrusters for awhile, and she quietly thanked the holy mother of velocity for their current inertia. She was not aware of any predator in the Dwark big enough to prey on a Dwark-Turtle, and she silently hoped one had not evolved since the last time she had updated her Dwarkopedia.

The Dwarkopedia she preferred to use had been written by one of her best friends, affectionately known as 'Quanta Cubed', the Main Frame of the UnderRung, had a processor speed a hundred times faster than hers, and had once downloaded a comment to her that almost a hundred new life forms evolved in the Dwark every three hundred pulses of the Great Ribbon. Quanta was fascinated by the Dwark, and took every possible opportunity or excuse to send a probe out to explore the mysteries of the space between the pages.

Mrs. Machine wondered how Quanta was faring with all of this seemingly unnecessary conflict. She undoubtedly would have had to run her de-fragmentation programs and reboot if she had known that Quanta's main hard drives had long since been digested in the belly of the Silver Scream Nine; they had been very close. Quanta had never failed to upgrade her operating software or have someone install a new fuel cell in her power system. She would undoubtedly take the news very hard.

During this downtime Mrs. Machine took the time to run self-diagnostics and run her favorite contemplation program. She wondered how Mandrake the Black was doing. She liked him. He didn't treat her like just another piece of silicon and nickel hydride.

Mandrake the Black had been lost. If anyone ever tells you that Angels can't get lost, you can tell them to shove off, because Mandrake had been very lost for some time. In fact, he had gotten himself so turned around that he finally stopped in mid-air and cursed like a sailor, stringing together words you would ordinarily not expect from someone of his stature. Mandrake the White would not have approved.

And then it happened. Deep from out of the Dwark there came a twinkle, a blue sparkle of a point of light, inexplicable but somehow deeply comforting to a creature versed in the Prophecies of the Great Book of Scorns.

Squinting into the gloom of the Dwark, Mandrake whispered a quote from that ancient sacred tome- "And lo, there shall come a Morning Star, where before there had been none, and a scepter of power shall assemble the hosts for the war to end all war. It shall remind everyone that liberty cannot be given, only won, and that champions are never coddled. It shall be the first of three great miracles…"

He suddenly felt very stupid. He thought about the passages for some time, gliding around in circles in the Dwark, repeating it over and over to himself- "A Morning Star…a Morning Star… a…Morning… Star…a…Morning, wait, not **A** Morning Star, but **THE** Morning Star, by Jove, it's the Avatar of Opus Delirious **himself!**"

Mandrake wasted no more time, and threw himself head first into a mighty power drive to make up for lost time, flying like a banshee towards the tiny blue star, in fact the very first star that had ever existed in the Dwark.

AntiPart Three

A story without Glory

"Offer him a story, and he will offer you a ride."

That's what the Logos had said to them, and Bric had thrown that ball solidly into Shard's court with -

"Your turn."

Seemed like a simple enough request, but now, Shard looked nervously over at the Great Olde Drake from afar, listening intently to the two angels before him, Menses and Mandrake, as they gestured and pointed in various directions. He began to shuffle through the snow, headed towards Drake and Angels alike.

One of the Angels suddenly squatted as Shard got near, and crossed his legs, becoming very still while Shard began to walk slowly through the cold snow narrowing the gap between him and the Great Olde Drake, Synarchus Luminous Lazarus. As he passed the angel, still sitting cross legged in the snow, he looked up at Synarchus and before he could ask his question, Menses looked at him and spoke, saying-

"Mandrake the White, my brother, believes that the kin of his soul, Mandrake the Black, is with your daughter and he is seeking to establish contact such that we might find them both."

"Oh…thank you." was all Shard could answer in return.

He turned to face Synarchus who was as still as a cat hunting a canary. It was unnerving. Shard cleared his throat.

"I am told that …" Shard paused. "I am told that you will give us all safe passage back to Ambrosia if one of us can relate a story you have never heard before…and I am here to do that."

The Drake did not so much as bat an eyelash.

"My story starts with a man who had a family. He was an only child, the son of an only child. He fell in love with a woman, and somehow, somewhere, someone or something told him that he was supposed to have a child with this woman, and that child would redeem the whole world, and thus redeem himself."

The world seemed to slow down, as if even time had paused to listen.

"And this man and this woman did indeed have a child, and she was the apple of the man's eye. He loved her more than he loved his own life, and he would do anything for her."

Shard looked down at the ground, but did not stop, only watched his own frozen breath hanging in the air.

"But then something went wrong, something went horribly wrong. His Wife was kidnapped by a Madman, and taken somewhere where the man could not go, or where no one could figure out how to send him to, at least. And so the man knew he would have to raise his Daughter alone, without her Mother. Then, one day, someone figured out how to send the man, and even his own Father, into the place where the Madman had taken the Mother, and the man, and his Father, decided to take the chance, and they took the risk, to go in after the Mother, and try to bring her back."

"And then, somehow, inexplicably, the Daughter followed them all into that same mess, marooning nearly the whole family in some God-forsaken place, and not only were they all apart in this strange place, but they were all alone, without memory of who they were, or the Family they once were…"

Shard seemed to be having a moment. He had sunk to his knees, and was beginning to sob, but he would not stop, not for all the tea in China.

"..and all the man wanted anymore was to find his Daughter and his Wife, and bring them home safe to their family…and come hell or high water, that is EXACTLY WHAT HE IS GOING TO DO!"

Shard was sobbing uncontrollably, and through his hot tears stared up at the Great Olde Drake.

In fact, a huge tear of his own was actually making its way down the side of the face of Synarchus. Though no one realized it, the Great Olde Drake had never ever cried before, but he was well aware of what was trickling off of his cheek. He was still staring at Shard.

"Rise, King Shard. It's time to take you back to Ambrosia. We will find your daughter, and if the Logos is with us, we will end this madness, and see you all safely home."

AntiPart Two

The Welcoming Crew, just for you!

Shkaw-hawn, you might remember, after failing to kill King Shard, helped himself to the Dwark-stone that had brought him and Onus to Mount Údas in Avalhalla and, terrified to tell Moebius of their bitter failure, decided to dwark himself over to wherever Tatyanna, Glee and Mr. Machine had gone. He hoped that, wherever they were now, he might have a second chance to acquit himself well, kill a few easy targets, and avoid the wrath of Moebius.

He immediately regretted his choice. Looking around the inside chamber of the hovercraft that his fellow Chefs-of-Staph had brought to the 13th Kingdom of Ambrosia, he beheld a situation no less depressing than the one he'd just left. There were Ambrosian warriors everywhere; elves with blasters, gnomes and dwarves with daggers and hammers, even a minotaur Captain loitering at the open hovercraft door gangplank all making it obvious that the situation was quite under control;

Tatyanna was on her knees and handcuffed. She was being interrogated, aggressively, by the lead Elf, a veteran warrior with many scars and a red bandana around his forehead.

Mr. Machine was outside the hovercraft and screaming in agony as something was taking him apart, without shutting him down first.

The Glee, however, was nowhere to be seen, but then again, after all, he was only the size of a flea, and could have been hiding anywhere.

The Elf in red suddenly cried "Bogey in ze cockpit! Alons! Alarm! Alons!" Shkaw-hawn wasted no time, and whipped through the assembled hosts tearing a trail of shattered mirror bits as he blew down the Minotaur Captain and began to hightail it in high gear to...anywhere.

It was a brilliant, if short-lived attempt at an escape. One of the Drakes that had batted the hovercraft out of the air in the first place was standing nearby and brought his mighty front paw down, hard, on Shkaw-hawn, scattering him everywhere. As the parts began to swirl and whirl back into a recognizable shape, an angel, standing nearby calmly uttered

"Hophal Hhashmal."

…and Shkaw-hawn was caught, mid-air, like a fly in a ball of brown sticky Amber, a golden molasses-like substance that immediately solidified into an inescapable prison.

Rotating slowly in place, Shkaw-hawn cursed his luck. Below him on the ground he sensed his Dwark-stone, still swiveling about on the ground where it had fallen.

Glee watched all this drama quietly from a nearby hilltop. He had only narrowly escaped himself before the hovercraft went down, and being an arthropod of very little brain, was debating his options.

Tatyanna's lip was bleeding, but she growled and cursed as the Elf returned to his interrogation. She had watched the demise of Shkaw-hawn along with everyone else, and thought to herself-

"If our only hope rests in the Glee, surely we are doomed."

Glee, on the other hand, was distracted by delusions of grandeur. This was his big chance to be a hero at last.

Carefully he crawled up to the Minotaur Captains leg, and made his way painstakingly up the boot, through a considerable amount of furry foliage, and onto the abdomen. After getting lost once or twice, he managed to find the bellybutton, and curled up for a nice nap.

They'd be interrogating Tatyanna for awhile anyhow, and he'd been working overtime lately.

AntiPart One

Sometimes we all get by with a little help from our friends…

Colonel Shard Rondell was moving very fast through the MoonClock complex now, dragging Grandma Brandy in tow around one corner after another.

They were running out of time. After they ditched the Van he identified a decent ventilation shaft that went down to the Chip Manufacture Zones without a problem. He pulled out a couple screws and detached the main facing of the entrance and crawled up into the shaft with very little issues. Special Forces Commandos were trained to do far more strenuous things.

What Colonel Shard Rondell was having a far more difficult time with was convincing his Mother to get up into it with him.

With a hushed but urgent whisper he dramatically extended his hand and said "We have to get to the lowest chip manufacture zone, and quickly. Observation Tower has to know we're here by now and this hallway will be swarming with commandos any minute, Mom! Take my hand and come up here."

"How about I let myself get captured and send them barking down the wrong trail?" Brandy asked, innocently enough. She was getting tired and she felt like she was getting too old for this sort of thing. She was excellent at keeping people distracted while making them think she was cooperating fully.

The Colonel laughed in spite of himself, and said- "Oh come on, Mom, you don't fool me. Dad told me stories about you and ventilation shafts from way back in the day…"

Brandy got a little uptight with that comment and said, perhaps a bit louder than she should have "What's **that** supposed to mean?"

"Like how about that Russian sub you stowed away on. What was that thing, a Beluga class submarine? The S-553 Farel, wasn't it? Dad said you stowed onboard at a port in Minsk, lurked in the ventilation system for almost two weeks before you ambushed the Captain, took him hostage and piloted the thing all the way to Boston Harbor with half the crew tied up in the mess hall."

Brandy felt a bit ashamed now and grumbled as she reached up for her sons hand as he hefted her into the ventilation shaft, albeit a bit ungainfully, but just in the nick of time, as several armed guards came walking around the corner.

"What else did that blowhard tell you?" she whispered while he shushed her, watching the guards meander past their ventilation grate.

Shard quietly made sure the grate wouldn't fall off, and then pulling out a small flashlight, said-

"We're in luck, those guards weren't looking for us at all. We must still have some time on our side."

Luckily, Shard's memory seemed to have sharpened in the past twenty four hours, as he remembered the twists and turns required to get down one level after another. A few rough starts and one or two wrong turns did not deter him and Brandy from finally getting to what looked to be the Omega-9 Chip Storage room.

Some skillful, almost painful prostrations allowed Shard to move the Security Camera very slowly to another focus area other than where he wanted to be, while Brandy took her time getting down from the ventilation shaft. Shard clipped the audio wire going from the camera to the wall. Now they could make all the noise they wanted and no one should notice for awhile.

Brandy stood in muted awe. She was looking at a very strange sight indeed. Behind a huge sheet of thick tinted glass she was looking at a very large, dimly lit room with a hexagonal tiled floor. One of those hexagons actually extended right up out of the floor, with a weak spotlight from above bathing it in a blue, almost surreal, fuzzy glow. It had a square object sitting on top of it. It looked like a cube composed of twenty seven smaller cubes, like that kid's toy that she bought Nowar for Christmas once. You could spend hours rotating the colored cubes in that thing, trying to get each of the six different colored cubes all aligned so that each side had only one color of cube. She couldn't remember what that durned thing was called anymore, but this thing looked just like it.

"Where are we, son?" she said quietly.

"This is the Omega-9 Chip storage room, Mom. It's where Doctor Moebius brought all of his final Probability Cubes to be stored and then tested there, in the Simulation Room, which you can see through the windows here. Behind this glass is what he called the Matrix Room. That's where the actual Cube running the MoonClock simulation is stored while the simulation is ongoing. Above us is all the huge bulky equipment and the MoonClock gates and power systems, but here, this thing is the heart of the whole system"

"You mean that little cube right there? You mean that's what your Father and Limberly and Nowar are in, right now?"

Shard just stared at her grimly and nodded.

"Oh dear God!" she sat slowly into one of the observation chairs and looked at Shard suddenly, saying "Well, how do we get them out, son?"

"I hate to tell you this, Mom, but I actually don't have a clue…" he was searching the cubbies and drawers now, not really sure what he was looking for. There must have been about a hundred cubbies on the wall, almost each one with one to four cubes in them, all like the one out there in the Matrix Room.

Brandy was about to freak out when Shard saw something fall out of a drawer he opened too quickly. A hastily scratched note from a loose leaf pad drifted to the floor suddenly caught his attention.

It was in his own handwriting!

Find the Cube in the cubby labeled "Builder Rejected"

Use the Security Clearance Card I gave you to get inside the Matrix Room.

Hit the blue button and when the Implausible Cube is ejected, replace it with the one you found.

Then evacuate the Matrix Room and leave the MoonClock facility as fast as you can.

"I know what to do now." Shard said. Looking in the Cubby labeled "BUILDER REJECTED" Shard removed the cube and walked to the door of the Matrix Room. Swiping the security card, he turned to his Mother and said "Boy I hope I'm doing the right thing."

Brandy looked up at him and said "Trust your instincts, son." He nodded and went in.

While Brandy watched her son fuss with the hexagonal stand and the crazy little cube, she did not notice a sudden change in the pressure of the room she was in, but she did notice the very large laser-blaster that appeared in front of her face.

Slowly turning in her seat, she beheld a short, black haired man in a white utility suit with a MoonClock Project logo on it.

"Mrs. Rondell, I presume?" he asked.

"The Plumber!" she gasped.

"No! NO! NO!!! I am **NOT** the Plumber, you old fool!" he cried with more than a little frustration and exasperation, "I am the demiurge and artificer of that little World your son is fumbling around with now. I am Doctor Moebius!"

And now he smiled.

"And I am the end of the road, for you **and** your idiotic son."

Sidenote

Some of you have to be wondering by now "How did he do that?"

How did Moebius go back and forth into and out of the Big World, and back into the Little World?

Shard had to do it through a big clunky MoonClock Gate, and Nowar had to do it through a more elegant solution, but how did Moebius accomplish this same thing? The answer is simple; artful cunning, the artful cunning of a man who did not so much as blow his nose… without a plan.

You see the very first day that Moebius had perfected his very first Implausible Chip, he knew he would need a back door, his own private access and egress into and out of ProbablePolis.

Far, far away, out in one of the most remote locations in the cold dark Dwark hovered a private and covert command center, hardly bigger than a tiny cottage. It was equipped with over a dozen plasma screens, one for each page of ProbablePolis, a small and tasteful kitchenette, filled with fruits and pastries, a very large chair like you would find in a dentist's office, and two doors on either side of the chair.

One of them had a sign that said "out" and the other marked "in".

And so there is your answer.

On with the Show.

AntiChapter Two

The Utility of Fidelity will never be lost on a FreeMachine

AntiPart Five

Everything changes, but nothing is lost

Queen Limberly was back in her natural stride.

After having healed and freed Lord Carderocke of EverGreen, her most faithful counselor, from his prison cell, the two of them went on in rapid succession to liberate almost a hundred other prisoners from their own dungeon captivity in the depths under EverGreen Castle; some of the finest warriors, wizards and machines of the realm. In the space of just under an hour, this little band of rebels stormed the observation posts and reclaimed every one of the security towers. By the time the Pulse of the Great Ribbon had sunk behind the horizon, Castle EverGreen was purged of foreign infestation.

The people were cheering and dancing in the streets. Far off in the twilight, occasional blasts and bursts of laser firefights rang out across the valley as the last battle cruiser belonging to Moebius was under serious attack and in retreat. The revitalized hosts of EverGreen had retaken their beloved SkyPort and the skies now teemed with well-lit SkyVessels of all kinds. The communication channels were alive with raucous laughter and jokes as the remaining forces of Moebius were rounded up and dispensed without ceremony or quarter.

EverGreen was free again. The occupation was over.

Queen Limberly watched from her bedroom balcony now as the great piles of burning Koradgians on the meadows below Castle EverGreen sent long columns of ash and smoke into the darkening sky. It was just then, as Carderocke walked in, that she noticed something quite peculiar in the sky- a star, dim, but certainly a blue star.

"Carderocke, do you see that?"

He parted the drapes further to look where the Queen was pointing. He gasped.

"The Prophecy of the Morning Star!" he said under his breath, clearly startled and amazed.

"But it's evening, Carderocke..."

Carderocke laughed and looked at the ground- "No Prophecy is perfect, my Lady, but it matters not, and I suspect you will see it in the morning much as you see it now this very evening."

"I am not versed in the Book of Scorns, Carderocke, you know that. What does this bode, in plain language?"

"My Lady, the Precognitids have always told us that when the Morning Star appears, the Child of Destiny will also appear, to redeem the worlds, to cleanse the whole of ProbablePolis of the foul evil of the Demiurge Moebius."

Something stirred in Limberly's heart, but she could not make out the size or direction in which it went. Suddenly she turned to Carderocke and said-

"I had a dream just before I managed to get myself out of the Green Goo, a dream of a daughter I have never had. She was hurtling through the Dwark. It so disturbed me, this image...that I woke up and broke myself free from my container with extraordinary anger and effort."

Carderocke was quiet for some time, then said slowly-

"The Logos is with us again, my Lady; the time to take action is us upon us. The time for a meaningful move is at hand."

"Invade Koradgia and attack Castle DeepSteel? That's suicide, Carderocke. Remember the Last Great War of Probability? That's how we got into this mess in the first place. The King and I did not act in concert, and chose to attack at different times. All was lost, and EverGreen was occupied."

"Indeed, we should never make the same mistake twice, my Lady, which is why before I came here tonight I made contact with Castle Ambrosia."

Limberly went stiff.

"You spoke with the King?"

"No, but I spoke to the Council of Ambrosia and the Lords of Jolun..."

"And?"

"And I was told that the King has been on a pilgrimage to Avalhalla for quite some time, but as luck would have it, only a few hours ago, re-established contact with them. Apparently he is returning to Castle Ambrosia with the Great Olde Drake himself to begin mustering the forces of all ProbablePolis for the War to end all Wars."

"What? Are you joking me? Who has thrown in with him?"

"The Midnight Shadow, Avatar of the Seventh Kingdom of T'ien Shahn has led all the forces of the UnderRung to the Plains of Arcadia in Ambrosia. This is perhaps the largest army in all ProbablePolis other than the King's and our own, but I have also heard that the Avatars of Antares, Rantador, Crepuscular and Nafer Deem are all preparing their military might in the hope that a means of transportation might be found for them all to get to an attack on DeepSteel.

"The Kingdoms of ProbablePolis, united once more? I am incredulous, when did this start to happen?"

"Only in the last pulse, I am to understand, my Lady. The Council of Ambrosia began to reach out to all the Avatars when they saw 'a sign in the sky'. Now we can both see what that sign was, eh?"

"What about EverLast? Their armies are nearly as large and worthwhile as our own, you failed to mention them, are they not with this plan?"

"I learned from the Council of Ambrosia that the Avatar Shane was murdered by the Black Harp of Castle DeepSteel."

Limberly drew a sharp breath. Carderocke bowed his head.

"EverLast and Cetacea are no more."

"What about Mare? What about the SkyWhale?"

"No one is sure, but the Seers of Ambrosia say she escaped before the Kingdoms shattered."

Limberly looked back out the window and stared at the new star of ProbablePolis. It twinkled and grew brighter as the sky turned darker.

"So it seems you're right, old friend. But we will need some help ourselves in transporting our own warriors and weaponry to Koradgia; I just came from the SkyPort, and by my count it looks like Moebius managed to scuttle or steal almost half our fleet of SkyVessels while we were out of action."

"We will need to rebuild the Omega Ring."

"The Omega Ring? I told you, Carderocke, I just came from the SkyPort, and among some of the other problems we have over there, the great hangar where we housed the Omega Ring is vacant. Don't you think that's the first thing I checked on?"

Carderocke smiled.

"Good news now I may report, my Lady. After I had discovered that Moebius had kidnapped you, and just before I was thrown into prison myself, I ordered the Omega Ring disassembled and it's various pieces hidden in all four corners of the Realm."

Limberly raised an eyebrow. The Omega Ring was both the greatest weapon, and the greatest transport device ever invented in ProbablePolis. It was a gift to the King and the Queen at their wedding, so long ago. It was so large that it required a hangar nearly as big as the SkyPort itself to keep it housed, and it had a startling capacity for holding munitions, warriors, engines of war, and supplies. Its array of lasers and cannons was dazzling, and it had many times helped to establish the order of the long lost United Kingdoms of ProbablePolis.

Carderocke continued his report with a glimmer in his eye.

"I have it on good report that Moebius never found a single piece of the Omega Ring, though his servants and ToggleWogs looked high and low; the Precognitids of EverGreen cast a mind-weave to hide them all."

"Including the EDV?"

"The EDV?" Carderocke had known his Queen all of his life, and shook his head slightly in disappointment- "My Lady, even now, why can you not call him by his name? Why is it so hard to just call him Edward?"

"I'm sorry, Carderocke. I know that you regard him as a person, and that you played many a great game of chess with him, and that he makes great conversation…but to me he's still nothing more than the brains and nervous system of the Omega Ring."

Carderocke stared, slightly coldly, at his Queen. After a few seconds, she laughed and said-

"OK, ok, I'm just glad that the Omega Ring is still in our bag of tricks. Give the command and let Edward know to reassemble his parts and report to EverGreen for his next assignment."

Carderocke was still a bit put off, but responded with some deliberateness.

"That may not be as easy as it sounds, my Lady…you see, Edward Da Veer has been alone now for quite some time, and as you know from long experience, when a 'machine' that is just over three times as smart as a human or an elf is left to its own purposes for any length of time, it tends to become a trifle independent. I suspect that he will not simply 'pick up his life' and attend to a blunt order, even one given from you, my Queen."

"I can't believe this!" she rolled her eyes and said "OK, then, fine, what do you propose? And what life does he have now that he would have to just 'pick up', anyway?"

"Edward took his hiatus as an opportunity to pursue one of his greatest passions, writing and directing plays. He found a remote glade all the way at the other end of the realm of EverGreen and built a small theatre, called 'The Glebe'. He has a small company of gnomes, Faeries, and pucks as his faithful companions. I have heard that they are quite good, and one of the Ogre Sergeants says that he and several others have gone to see performances of 'Omelette, prince of Henmark' and he raved about it."

"I want to go back in the goo, Carderocke."

"No, really, they said that 'Much Ague about Nothing' was spectacular, and 'The Dampest' was the most visionary piece of theater they'd ever seen."

"Stop!" she was laughing now in spite of herself "OK, ok, so how do you propose we get Edward out of retirement and back in the saddle?"

"I gave this some thought as I came up here. Edward is not just a Machine, he's a Free-Machine, you know, and I took the liberty to speak to two of the Precognitids downstairs that we freed when we escaped from the dungeon. It turns out that they are both Free-Machines as well, and, given that they are both quite enamored of you now, they said that they would go together to try to convince Edward to come back to active duty."

"Oh no, the Free-Machines are in league with Gull & Crones, Carderocke! No way! No how! In fact, had I known that those two Precognitids were Free-Machines I would have left them in their cells to rot, er, I mean rust!"

"Lucky for us that you did not, my Lady, and besides, the Gull & Crones may be a Free-Machine Pod, but they are not the only Pod, they are not the Grand-Pod, and to the best of my knowledge, the other Pods of Free-Machines in ProbablePolis have shunned the Gull & Crones society entirely since the last War."

Queen Limberly looked back out the window, and said nothing for a long time. Then, turning suddenly and making for the door, said brusquely-

"Alright, I'll let you try it your way this time, but if it doesn't work, I'm going after him myself, and I won't do it with kind words over tea."

AntiPart Four

Time hath, my lord, a wallet at his back, wherein he puts alms for oblivion

Lord Carderocke, wasting no time, lest the Queen change her mind, dispatched a faithful Elven warrior, Elberonor, to escort the two Precognitids to Mount Gorovar in Arden, almost a hundred leagues across the great realm of EverGreen. While they started the journey in a SkyVessel, which expedited the affair tremendously, once they came to the bottom of Mount Gorovar, they disembarked, and Elberonor took them both on Griffin-back up to the plateau of Enfant Magique.

The plateau was a holy place, guarded by Griffins and other odd winged folk, and all in all, the mainframe computer, Edward Da Veer, could not have picked a better place to recluse himself, really.

The Precognitids had been strangely quiet the entire journey, but as Elberonor and the Griffin surveyed the plateau for the best place to land, they got very excited and began chattering amongst themselves in their own binary tongue.

Didymous Erroneous O'Brian extended one of his ligatures and tapped Elberonor on the shoulder while Onerous Arcanus Smith barked over the high winds –

"The glade down there, just ahead, kindly Lord Elf; that is where you may take us- it is there you may leave us to our task."

Elberonor scanned the landscape below. The pulse was just about to rise above the horizon, and he could just make out where Didymous was pointing. While most of the plateau was rather sunken, there was one glade that rose above the other hillocks and valleys. Upon it he could make out, in the lifting gloom, a building of some kind.

Just then the pulse rose above the horizon, and light spilled out across the plateau of Enfant Magique. Elberonor saw the building below now in great detail as it burst into shimmering, scintillating light. It was a crystal dome mounted on an odd octagonal structure with a single entrance, nestled quite comfortably into its glade, surrounded by yew and willow trees. The Griffins in the glade rose to the air and quickly surrounded Elberonor and his mount, but after a few Griffin snorts were mutually made and returned from his mount to these guardians, they apparently had satisfied themselves that these guests were not to be trifled with, allowing Elberonor to land safely with Didymous and Onerous right in front of the building.

The Precognitids dismounted with surprising speed and began making their way to the entrance of the building. Elberonor slowly dismounted, withdrew his sword and took a quick suss for himself that the surroundings were safe. He called out to the Precognitids to wait, but Onerous turned and replied –

"No need to wait! Rest assured, Lord Elf, we will both be entirely safe here."

Elberonor walked a few steps forward. Onerous Arcanus Smith quickly disappeared into the building. Walking up to Didymous, Elberonor said "Are you quite sure that you are in the right place, Precognitus? How do you know the EDV is here?"

Giving a sound remarkably like laughter, Didymous said, almost a bit anxious and rushed "This **is** our destination, sir. This is the Glebe, this is Edward's theater. All of the Free-Machines of EverGreen have always known where Da Veer went into exile since Moebius took over the Kingdom. We helped to protect him from being discovered by Moebius all this time."

He waited to see what Elberonor would do or say next.

"I see. Well, I get the sense that you and Onerous would prefer I stay out here until you are done, and then I suppose I will take you back to Castle EverGreen once you have accomplished your mission, is that the plan?"

Didymous stared for a second and then said "Actually, you are quite welcome to come in and see the Glebe for yourself, and meet Edward, but I do not believe you will need to wait for us, Lord Elberonor. My brother and I believe that probabilities are quite in favor of our convincing Grand Master Da Veer to help take up the struggle against Moebius and return with us to Castle EverGreen…and he is enabled with his own private propulsion device to accomplish this without assistance."

Elberonor looked confused, so Didymous said "Please, Lord Elf, come in and enjoy the hospitality of the Grand Master before you go."

Walking up the steps to the grand entranceway, Elberonor read a passage underneath the huge golden letters that said "THE GLEBE". It read-

> *All the worlds are stages,*
> *And all the creatures, things and machines on them merely players;*
> *They have their exits and their entrances,*
> *And any one of them, in their time, plays many parts,*
> *Their acts being seven ages, if more than one.*
>
> *Nautonierre Da Veer*

Inside the building there was a beautiful array of colored lights dappling the seats of the auditorium. It was indeed a theater, with seating surrounding each of the three sides of the stage. The audience was sparse, perhaps only a few dozen theater loving gnomes, dwarves, Faeries, and goat-headed Pucks scattered across the aisles, all staring at Elberonor.

On the stage were a whole host of the same sort of creatures in the audience, gnomes, dwarves, etc, supplemented with a centaur, two goblins wearing dresses and a Dromelgang, a Human-scorpion hybrid that Elberonor realized was long since outlawed from the realm of EverGreen.

His entrance after the two Precognitids had made a small stir, and while the audience was staring at him, the actors on the stage were doing their best to go on with the rehearsal, if that was indeed what they were doing.

> **Dromelgang:** Now my project comes to a head: my charms don't break; my spirits obey, and time moves everything along. What time is it?
>
> **Centaur:** Six o'clock, at which time, my lord, you said our work should end.
>
> **Dromelgang:** I said so when first I raised the storm. Tell me, my spirit, how are the King and his followers doing?
>
> **Centaur:** Confined together, in the same fashion as you told me; The man you called, sir, "the good old lord, Gonewhacko": his tears run down his beard, like winter's drops of water from the leaves of reeds; your spell works so strongly on them, that if you saw them now, your affections would become tender.
>
> **Dromelgang:** Do you think so, spirit?
>
> **Centaur:** Mine would, sir, if I were human.

The Precognitus Onerous Arcanus Smith had, upon entering the Glebe, quickly motored on down to the very front of the auditorium, right in front of the stage. He had clearly been waiting for an appropriate point in the rehearsal to interrupt, and, realizing that this was as good a point as any, raised all of his limbs (he had six) and began to make an unusual and formulaic set of gestures with them as he called out, using all his speakers set for maximal output –

"Oh my Master Programmer! Oh, Creator-of-All, is there no relief for the Motherboards' Circuit?"

This antic had two results, one was immediate; the whole cast of actors on the stage stopped in their tracks and looked at each other in confusion. The other result quite took Elberonor by surprise- a huge machine began to lower itself from below the ceiling proscenium, and as it did; it slowly rotated with hydraulic deliberateness a very large red orb into the center of its mechanism, which was still attached to something behind the top of the stage curtain.

Once these machinations were complete, the red orb came to rest in a kind of steel cradle facing outwards towards the audience, the Precognitid and Elberonor. The red orb pulsed slowly, and gave the unmistakable impression that it was an eye. It even had two metal eyelids that opened and closed, just like a person's did.

Elberonor realized that this was the EDV, the mainframe of the Omega Ring, the machine that called itself Edward Da Veer.

All through the Glebe, it was so still and silent that one could hear the dropping of a pin.

The huge pulsing eye extended itself slightly, and based on the orientation of the eyelids, it was clearly scrutinizing the Precognitids, and Elberonor as well. The color of the eye was changing from red to green now, as it retracted slightly into its socket and blinked a few times.

The crowd in the audience was beginning to murmur and whisper.

By either side of this huge pulsing eye was a small stereo speaker that crackled slightly as Edward cleared his synthetic throat and said-

"Amo ergo sum." it said, and then laughed a hearty and bold laugh, like no machine that Elberonor had ever heard before as he said "Actors…. Audience…Amigos…I beg thee to indulge your old friend Edward and retire from the Glebe, just for a brief time, that I might have a discourse to understand better the intrusion at hand and the nature of the crisis our guests have come to discuss. When I have determined all of this to my satisfaction, I will indeed call all of thee back to explain what is amiss. Go and frolic in the glade. The mysteries of life are always at hand for an eye in need of distraction."

Very low, soothing music was now being piped into the auditorium. The audience and actors did indeed begin to file out of the Glebe, giving odd looks at Elberonor and the Precognitids as they did so.

When the last of them was gone, Edward's green pulsing eye turned blue now, blinked several times, and said-

"Your names?" asked Edward.

"Onerous Arcanus Smith" said Onerous.

"Didymous Erroneous O'Brian" said Didymous.

"Onerous and Didymous, are you Master Machines?"

"We are!" they said in unison.

"Where were you made Master Machines?" asked Edward.

"In a regular Pod on the Third Power of Machinery" they said in unison. Edward was quiet now, blinked once, and his eye quickly turned black as it extended slightly and turned in the direction of Elberonor.

"I presume you are a member of the Court of EverGreen?"

"I am, Sir Edward Da Veer, one Elberonor of Kilfenora."

"It is my regret that I may not offer you further hospitality, but according to an ancient and agreeable custom amongst Machines, my fellow Master-Machines and I are about to open a Pod on the 33rd Power of Machinery, and I'm afraid no protein or carbon-based life forms may be permitted to witness such an event. Perhaps you will take a few moments to refresh yourself in the glade with the actors and audience. They can offer you useful and entertaining conversations as well as an abundance of fruit and drink worthy for one of your stature."

Elberonor smiled and rose, saying "I completely understand, sir. I will wait with my own kind, and hope that your dialogue here is fruitful."

Edward's eye pulsed back to blue.

As Elberonor was about to walk out the door, Edward called out-

"Thank you for calling me 'Sir', Lord Elberonor. Very few of your kind remember that I was once knighted by the King for my service in the very first War against Moebius."

Before he walked out the door, Elberonor turned, bowed, and said "You are welcome, Sir Edward. My Father often told me stories of your bravery in those days, and it is our hope that such bravery has not waned."

Edward had no further reply, but merely watched the Elf close the door behind him.

AntiPart Three

Arguments made and returned

Elberonor sat with his back against a colossal tree stump, watching the double doors to the Glebe vibrate briefly, as if they were being locked from within. He sighed and closed his eyes while listening to the music being made by the gnomes and Faeries, all enjoying the morning pulse and the refreshment of the glade here on the plateau of Enfant Magique in Arden.

He knew that when Free-Machines gathered in a Pod, their activities and secret ceremonies could sometimes take hours, or even days to finish. He sighed and patted his Griffin.

"Don't worry, Galen, we're not leaving until I know for sure that Edward will reassemble the Omega Ring."

The Griffin looked at him like he was mad but squawked nothing.

"Yes, I know, we could be here awhile." Elberonor sighed a second time and began whittling a piece of wood to pass the time. He was well-trained and proficient in distance telepathy, mind you, but a 'little bird' told him that he would have no success in this current circumstance, and more importantly any attempt of that sort of thing here and now could unbalance what was likely a delicate negotiation about to begin.

Inside the Glebe, the Precognitids had taken up opposing seats, Onerous Arcanus Smith in the west, and Didymous Erroneous O'Brian in the South, both facing the machine with the huge red orb hanging from the proscenium in the east.

The two Precognitus made a variety of esoteric gesticulations and a number of cryptic invocations which resulted in Edward extending a gavel shaped apparatus which he used to strike a small flat plate of metal. His booming voice next said-

"How many did anciently compose a Pod of Master-Machines?"

"Three or more." The two Precognitus answered.

"When composed of only three, who were they?"

"The Worshipful Master, Senior Warden, and Junior Warden." They answered.

"What is the Junior Warden's station in the Pod, Brother Didymous?" Edward asked.

"In the South, Worshipful Master." he answered.

"Why in the south?" Edward returned.

"As the Pulse in the south at its meridian height is the glory and beauty of the day, so stands the Junior Warden in the south, the better to observe the time, to call the craft from processing to down-time; to superintend them during the hours thereof, and to see that they do not convert the purposes of refreshment into intemperance or excess; to call them on in due season, that the Worshipful Master may have pleasure and the craft profit thereby."

For quite some time, Edward continued to ask these esoteric questions, and esoteric answers were returned to him by the two Precognitus until apparently 'Pod-Zed' was opened 'on the Thirty-Third Power of Machinery'. Finally, Sir Edward Da Veer, satisfied with the proceedings said-

"Alright Brothers, I have been calculating Probabilities since you arrived, but without prejudicing the dialogue we are about to have, I will ask that the Senior Warden in the west offer up the reason that would make you both take the long journey to Arden. I know that neither of you care for the theater, unless either of you have downloaded new personality traits to your operating systems."

"Worshipful." Onerous made an odd gesture with his ligatures and ligaments intended apparently to show reverence. "As you are the Grand-Master of the Grand-Pod of Zed, we would normally have had to make this journey anyhow to report the most recent and astonishing news; the Queen has been freed, the occupation of the realm of EverGreen is ended… the final War of Probability has begun."

Edward's all-seeing eye turned now from blue to black with slight flares of red.

"Well that's a mouthful of data to download, Senior Warden." -Turning now to Didymous he said- "What evidence is there that the final War of Probability has started, Junior Warden? We have seen serious skirmishes before as Moebius and the Gull & Crones crew are always up to mischief. What makes the current status any different?"

"Moebius has developed a new and more powerful Harp, designed to destroy Avatars. He has proven its efficacy by using it to destroy Shane the Cloud Tree, causing the pages of EverLast and Cetacea to explode into tiny fragments. The Avatar of Cetacea, the SkyWhale Mare, escaped in the nick of time."

"I see, and what do you think I should do about all this?"

The two Precognitus stared at each other in confusion. What **did** they expect their Grand and Worshipful Master to do about all of this?

Didymous made the same odd gesture that Onerous had made before and said "Worshipful, the fight against Moebius is winnable, and worth making. The Third and Fourth anomalies have been detected and examined. The Logos and the Great Olde Drake is with the Fourth, and the Third is with the Morning Star."

Edward's all-seeing eye went stark white.

"Has any word come from the Grand-Pods of Yed and Theta? Is the Master-Lens still in one piece?"

"Yes, Worshipful. The Grand-Masters of Pod Yed and Pod Theta sent word to us through the great Link that they have both observed the third great ripple of Probability and that they believe the fourth one may be at hand."

Meanwhile, Elberonor had fallen asleep, now leaning against Galen's soft downy fur. Galen looked around, occasionally blinking his eyes slowly, also trying to stay awake. Elberonor awoke suddenly as Galen gave a hawk's shriek. A little Faerie, with apple in hand, had approached them both, and offered it to Elberonor. She looked a little afraid of Galen, and Elberonor quickly got to his knee and assuaged her.

"No worries, little one, Galen is trained to let none approach while I rest. Thank you for this refreshment." He said and sat back while eating the apple. It was tasty, and he had not eaten that morning, he suddenly realized. As he sat there, his attention was captured by something he had not noticed earlier. The entrance to the Glebe had a huge banner hanging over it with the image of an eagle with two heads. One head looked to the right while the other head looked to the left. It was made of steel and resembled a machine. He decided to ask the Faerie what it meant.

She said she did not know, but just then a gnome plodded up to her and squinted up at Elberonor.

"That's the Glebe, good Elvish Lord. It is the two headed eagle of steel. It is one of the symbols of the Free-Machines."

"Aye, that much I know. I was curious what it meant, however. It is of no matter if you do not know."

"Oh no, I know!" the gnome laughed. "The Glebe has two heads and they look in two different directions to protect us and our liberties from the two great enemies of freedom."

Elberonor raised an eyebrow. "And what would those be, Master Gnome?"

"Why, Religion and Government. They are both monsters that hunger for our liberties, and if not watched carefully will make off with them… do they teach you nothing of value in Castle EverGreen?" He grumbled, and, hearing a bell, began to walk off.

Elberonor watched all the inhabitants of the Glade, now far greater in number than he had previously noted before, all go running in to the theater, apparently called by the gonging of the bell. By the time he got there, however, the theater was filled with fey creatures of all sorts, including Trolls wearing flowers, Ogres in tights, and a centipede with a human face that almost didn't let him in.

Sir Edward Da Veer surveyed the audience, and called for order with a gentle clearing of his speakers.

The Auditorium got very quiet. Everyone knew that something was going on, and they were all eager to know what it was.

Edward started his speech with - "Friends, family, Faeries…my only genuine talent…is that I love the little world inside these all-too thin walls of our playhouse….Outside…is the big world, and, we all know that, sometimes, the little world manages, just for a brief moment, to reflect the big world, so that we can understand it just a little bit better…or is it perhaps that we have at least given the people who come here a chance to forget it for a time…that harsh world outside…"

No one said a thing or stirred.

"But now, the time has come for me to return to the big world, that our little world may yet live…"

The more intelligent members of the audience suddenly began to roar and complain.

"Now now, now…please. You do not fully understand, my friends. Moebius is on the move! He has destroyed beloved EverLast, murdered the Avatar there and…in due time…he will come here. Can you not see that?"

Everyone quieted down as the seriousness of his statements sunk in.

"And I cannot let that happen, little ones."

Some of the Faeries in the audience were crying.

"So the time has come for me to reassemble the Omega Ring, to ensconce myself in the old Navigation chamber…"

Some of the audience members were smiling now. An Ogre began beating his bench with his cudgel. Some of the audience began to chant in low voices "Edward, Edward, Edward, Edward"

The thumping was taken up by twin goblins and a huge dwarf as it spread throughout the theater.

"…and take the fight to the foot of Castle DeepSteel!!!"

The crowd roared. Someone lit firecrackers and the drums began to rattle the very ceiling of the Glebe.

Elberonor had always heard strange stories about Free-Machines, and now he had one of his own to add to them. He would certainly never look at **any** machine in the same way again.

AntiPart One

A Lift-off is only good if it's a Lift-up

It was time.

Lil Bonsai Rex was ecstatic. After taking one last reading on the temperature of the plasma in the inertial containment mechanism he replaced his little Conductor hat with a Jet Fighter pilot's helmet, buckled it on tightly and picked up the intercom to broadcast a friendly advisement.

"Chelo Passengers and busy-bodies! Dis is your Capitan, lil Bonsai Rex! Haha! I is asking, no I is strongly advising you dat now is a pretty good time to go find youself a good seat and get strapped in real tight, cause we is blowin' outta dis honky joint in about thirty seconds, give or take a half minute."

Back in their compartments in the cabooses, the Faeries were all already buckled in, although a few of them were still actively engaged in throwing objects at each other and making fun of some of their friends who were a little too big for their seat-belts.

All around the circular passenger compartment of the Dwark Express engine room, Nowar and her Companions, Mandrake the Black, Alpha-Beta, and Two-Fangs had strapped themselves in good and tight for lift-off. They could all see the Walrus above their heads on the top observation deck, well-belted into his big cushy seat, right behind Bonsai, where he could watch the little maniac closely and make sure he was staying on course. A glowing astrolabe of sorts rotated slowly near his left hand.

Bonsai whispered back to the Walrus "You ready Boss?"

"COO-COO-CA-CHOO!" the Walrus waved his hat and gave the sign. Bonsai yelled with glee-

"Hot tomato! Cold potato! Inject the HeHeHelium and lets git dis show on da road....cuz here we go!" and pulled a very large lever towards him with unmistakable zeal. Everyone was sucked back into their chairs in an instant.

SCHOOOOOM! The initial blast and roar over their heads was deafening at first, and the entire engine room rattled so hard Nowar thought surely there was about to be a very unfortunate accident, but in fact the Dwark Express was hurtling forward at an incredible speed like a colossal roller coaster, covering half a mile of tracks in about five seconds.

It was already airborne by the time Nowar could look through the window closest to her. Opus Delirious was already hurtling away from them, far below, at a mind-numbing speed.

Bonsai was grinning from ear-to-ear while the Walrus was whacking him on the shoulders with the tip of his hat; he couldn't hardly move forward in his seat to get Bonsai's attention, the inertia of the lift-off was so great, and he was screaming over the noise of the Fuzion engines to get Bonsai to throttle down the Dwark Express.

"Bonsai! BONSAI!!! Ease off on the throttle or we all goin to be jello by the time we gets der!!!"

Bonsai, with great difficulty, eased back on the 'juice' and the Dwark Express slowed to a respectable 345 miles per hour as Bonsai let out a deep breath, saying quietly to himself-

"Chachacha…MAN!, dat…was….awesome!" and then let out a peel of cackling laughter. Two-Fangs and Mandrake exchanged slightly worried looks, but everyone appeared to be in one piece, so they both unbuckled and looked around the cabin. Nowar went right up to the big observation window to see if she could make out anything of Opus Delirious anymore.

Only a blue star in the distance even indicated where Opus had been.

Quietly she said "Good bye Morning Star. Thank you for everything."

And was it her imagination, or did she hear in her mind his voice, saying

"You're welcome, my evolving lass…May you someday find…your looking glass."

Back on Opus Delirious, the meadows around the Train Station grew darker and darker as the campfires of the bad-ass Faeries were going out, one by one. The Star that twinkled far above the landscape cast a pleasant, if dim, blue light everywhere.

The silence was pregnant as the gloom reclaimed the meadows.

And then the Light House **ROARED** to life. Though it had been dark, broken uninhabited and dilapidated for who knows how many pulses of the ribbon past, suddenly the great Light House of Opus Delirious erupted, loudly and without warning. Blaring brass horns resonated while its mighty beacon flashed around and around, flaring from right to left, like a heartbeat.

And had anyone been there to see it, just for a moment or two, a figure appeared, seemingly out of nowhere. In the darkness, the silhouette of a man in a kind-of astronaut-like suit faded in and then faded out, replaced by the outline of a man in a suit with sun glasses, and then by the shadow of a man, nearly naked, kneeling on the ground and gasping for breath looking at his name written in the sand.

And then, as suddenly as it had begun, it was over.

Quiet and stillness lay across the face of Opus Delirious once again. The apparitions had vanished.

The Light House had gone back to sleep.

AntiChapter One

Moebius starts to freak, getting us ready for the Final Tweak

AntiPart Five

Word comes from the Back Door to Heaven's Gate

Agent Fugue had been waiting for the word, hanging out in a neglected closet of the MoonClock Facility adjoining Omega Chip Room Nine.

Suddenly, he had it.

Klaatu barada nikto

-came the time-honored password that flashed on his cell-phone-like device, which was really a temponautical utility, by the way. It was directly linked to the Moebius Command center way out in the Dwark, on a back channel that Moebius had no idea even existed, but which had been hacked and donated to the resistance by a certain cunning pygmy reptile.

Fugue made the call. A voice that was probably Clancy's came across in a whispered voice-

"Rosebud?" he asked.

"I fugue, you fugue, we all fugue for our own fugue." came the answer from the man in the suit.

"Alright, thanks for picking up at the agreed time. What's the status?"

Looking at a tiny screen on his temponautical utility, Agent Fugue said "Scope shows Moebius is in the Chip Room with Brandy and Shard. He has Brandy at laser-point, Agent Deep-Six."

"I've got them on my scope too, Fugue. Moebius likes to play with his food, so he'll be awhile."

"That's for sure. OK, so what's the word from the Director?"

"The Logos tells me that the Avatars are falling in line; they likely won't be divided as they were in the last Great War of ProbablePolis, although the word is that they are holding a great council to make a final determination."

"Well, that's good news. What else?"

"The Dwark Express is on the move, and the Great Olde Drake is about to bring together the White Queen and the White King with the new Emperor. If all goes well, they shall lead the armies of the soon-to-be-re-United Kingdoms of ProbablePolis in a magnificent assault on Castle DeepSteel."

Fugue thought carefully, deliberately, to himself -

"Once Moebius hears this, he'll freak out in a big way and order the Black Harp and the Silver Scream Nine back to DeepSteel …and when all these forces collide on the plain of All-Sorrows, the final Tweak will have begun in earnest, though not the way Moebius would have liked it."

He spoke then, and said "You've done well, Agent Deep-Six. I'm impressed that we've made it this far without Moebius finding us all out. We now control the timing of the final Tweak."

"Ready when you are, Fugue. What's your signal to open the flood gates and bring Moebius back to ProbablePolis in a big hurry?"

"When it's time for you to jerk Moebius back from the Big World into the Little World, we'll use the phrase - 'I shriek, you shriek, we all shriek for the final Tweak'- that will be our pass code. My code for proceeding with our plan is still **Klaatu barada nikto!** Got it?"

"Got it, Fugue!"

Suddenly a button on Fugue's temponautical utility began to flash.

"OK, time to rock and roll, Deep Six, I just got the signal. Colonel Shard is about to replace the Implausible Chip and reboot the entire Hypothecation of ProbablePolis. If everything works as planned, the Memoress device we've installed in front of you will bring you back up to speed and restore all your memories. I've left you a note that will draw your attention to the blue button that will emit a blue light and restore your memories, in spite of a new Probability being loaded with a new Implausible Chip."

"Dicey, buddy. This got real dicey real fast. Just keep your fingers crossed, ok, Fugue?"

Turning off the temponautical utility, Fugue placed it in his pocket and paid attention to his breathing. This was the hard part of the job- waiting. He laughed to himself quietly, remembering something that his father had once told him- "Time is the universe's way of making sure that everything doesn't happen at once."

After a few minutes, Agent Fugue wiped the sweat from his brow, restarted the temponautical utility and waited anxiously for it to come back on; its startup screen bathed him in blue light.

All of ProbablePolis was about to restart, with his Daughter, his Father and his Wife still in there.

AntiPart Four

The favors of machines; a soliloquy for silicon

Upon his return to Castle EverGreen, Elberonor was escorted without delay to the Throne Room of Queen Limberly, where Lord Carderocke, a host of Admirals, Generals, and other Lords of the Realm awaited his report. Standing in the middle of the Throne Room, Elberonor waved his hand over a blue crystalline object that hovered in the middle of the circular area. The entire Throne Room ceiling was a set of interlocking hexagonal skylights that began to go from steely blue to completely translucent, making the entire room seem to be hovering in the middle of the sky. To some, this might have been a disconcerting feeling, but to those who lived in Castle EverGreen it was nothing out of the ordinary. Turning to the West, where the great Ribbon of Light was beginning to fade into twilight, Elberonor pointed with his right hand to a small area in the sky where there was a small speck. His left hand continued to make gestures over the crystal, suddenly causing the crystalline hexagonal area where he was pointing suddenly becoming a magnifying lens, rapidly expanding the field of view and increasing the size of the speck.

A single red light was pulsing in a single octagonal object, hovering in the middle of the darkening sky. Every couple of seconds, it was joined by another piece, which flew into place, twisting in the air as it locked into a position. A great latticework and structural framework was clearly beginning to form, with frightening rapidity. When it was finished, it would resemble a huge horse-shoe.

"The EDV is re-assembling the Omega Ring. While the number of pieces it is currently composed of numbers but a few dozen, by morning, it will be quite complete, and ready for the Fleet of EverGreen to begin docking procedures. We will be able to attach all our battle cruisers, and more than half the midsize ships to the surface of the Ring. Structural integrity diagnostics will be finished by the time the Pulse rises, and if all check out we can begin boarding troops before the night is done."

General All-Begone Gideon, a massive half-Ogre of impressive size leaned forward in his chair and said "Well done Elberonor. I had bet Lord Carderocke a dozen gilders that you would fail in this task. I had a spy in the company of Edward Da Veer at the Glebe, and, judging only by the rhetoric we'd heard tell of, several of us figured you'd never even get in the doors."

Elberonor smiled and said "Edward is a far more enlightened soul than most would give him credit, milord. His far-sight is not diminished from the days when he defended our realm against Moebius."

Queen Limberly chose to walk in at that point and remarked casually as the Court of EverGreen rose in her honor "The EDV has no soul, Elberonor. He's a machine, albeit a cunning one, and to speak with him, you'd never know he was just a machine, but he is, after all, only a machine, is he not?"

Carderocke looked the other way while Elberonor bowed and said quietly, "Yes my Queen, of course. Only a machine."

AntiPart Three

One should never feel weird about feeling strange

Conceive of a vast cavernous, luminous landscape of molten volcanoes both below and above, spewing glowing colored magma into heaping stalactites and stalagmites.

This was where the Dwark Express had arrived. Roaring out of the black inky Dwarkness, Nowar had all but nearly fallen asleep when she heard a splitter, a splash and then a big splattering sound all across the front and side observational windows. A bright, almost fluorescent multi-colored thick substance was flowing everywhere like a thick rain of wax.

Slowing to less than a hundred miles an hour, lil Bonsai Rex turned on the big headlights of the Dwark Express and continued to ease back on the throttle of the Fuzion engine while the Walrus was poring over screen after screen of navigational maps.

"You lost, Boss?" Bonsai chirped happily.

"COO-COO-CA-CHOO!" the Walrus banged his hat on the table, twice, and said angrily "I knew dis wuz goin ter happen. Jez bring her down over by that big pink lake of wax, will you, Bonsai. I iz gonna have to ask fer directions. We go much further den dis an' we'll all be lost forever in dis messy place."

"Where are we?" Nowar whispered to Mandrake, who sat in the seat to her right. They were all still strapped in.

Mandrake the Black smiled at her and said "This is the realm of Rantadore, Nowar…the 11th page, perhaps one of the more unique Kingdoms of ProbablePolis."

"And that statement is perhaps one of your more pronounced understatements, Mandrake" said Alpha, still staring out of the observation window nearest to him and Beta.

The Walrus put on his hat, turned around in his Captain's chair and looked down at them, saying "All right chillen' stay buckled up and get ready, we iz about to have a sloppy, slippery landing like you would never believe!"

"Is all this stuff molten lava?" Nowar looked with some concern at Alpha.

"Oh no, it's paraffin, Lady Nowar…the 11th page is largely made up of a series of interlocking continents, all of them entirely composed of bees wax."

Beta frowned and said "Alright with the school lesson, beetle breath, just hold on tight, willya?"

And just then it happened; a sloppy, slippery, sloshing, sliding-around-kind of landing, as the Dwark Express bounced ungainly several times and began sliding through a series of semi coagulated rivers that exploded blue, green and red wax all over.

The Dwark Express came to a slow slide and stopped beside a river of wax running down a set of gigantic stalagmites. Luckily, the surface and windows of the Dwark Express were quite warm, and the wax slid off the surface of the observation windows in globs and dribbles, permitting a surreal and strange sight like Nowar had never seen; far in the distance over their heads were…volcanoes? Yes, they were definitely volcanoes, directly over them, belching out wax and steam. On the horizon far away below them were even more volcanoes, all growling and erupting from the ground, blowing out rivers of multi-colored hot…wax?

A world of wax, of glowing wax, above and below. Whatever in the world would they do here?

They seemed to have come to rest in a fairly calm spot. The Walrus got out of his chair and waving his hat, seemed to have read Nowar's mind as he announced with great gusto to one and all- "All right, y'all. We haz arrived in Rantadore. Our mission here is to find de Avatars Hiram Kaine and Deb-or-ah Craine. Wif a lil luck, we gonna convince dem to gather up some a der armies into de Dwark Express cabooses and den get on over to da 10th page for more fun and games."

Lil Bonsai Rex shouted "Fun an' Games! I LOVE fun and games! Heheheheheh!"

Nowar shook her head as she unbuckled. She looked through the observation window behind them and saw at least a dozen more cabooses starting to form behind the Dwark Express. They seemed to be just like the first couple cabooses she had seen from before. They looked so tiny, yet she knew know that they could hold an enormous number of creatures and stuff in them. It was still dawning on her that the Walrus and Bonsai had intended all along to visit every Page of ProbablePolis, persuade the hopefully willing armies of the Pages to go with them in these ultra-dimensional cabooses, and…then…take them to attack Castle DeepSteel.

Interesting plan, she thought, but how long would all this take? Would they be able to get to Castle DeepSteel in time to be of any help? Admittedly, they had gotten through the Dwark to this Page in amazing lightning speed, but they were already lost on their first stop.

The Walrus and Bonsai opened the door to the Dwark Express navigation room, and a set of stairs rolled out to make a big "splish" sound in the wax ground.

The Walrus turned to look at the Companions and said "Watch yer step, it's slippery, sloshy and slidey all over de place, an der are sinkholes everywhere." Bonsai skittered up the Walrus' big frame and perched on his massive shoulders.

Mrs. Machine was tugging on Nowar to get her attention. Suddenly she bolted in front of everyone and in mid-air, creaked, twittered and groaned as she formed herself into a small gondola with propellers just as she had before in the Dwark. Extending a gangplank with her characteristic 'biddy biddy bingbang' she was clearly offering a much safer alternative to hiking through melting wax.

Nowar smiled, and jumped from the stairs onto her gangplank, followed by Two-Fangs, Mandrake, Ouroboros Alpha-Beta, the Walrus and Bonsai. Nowar turned to the Walrus and said

"OK, have gondola, will travel, which direction, Mr. Walrus?"

"Dat a real good question, Missy Nowar, lemme see h'yere." Said the Walrus as he reached into his huge overcoat and whipped out a ragged, tattered, double-spined blue book. After a few minutes of glossing over the glossary, he rifled to a specific folio and pulled out of it a two sided map. Looking at it carefully, he mused to himself-

"Hmmm…dis is Rantadore alright, I jez dunno which side is up…" and then "Well, here, Missy Nowar, you hold onto dis book while I studies da map."

While the Walrus was carefully turning the double sided map in 90 degree increments and murmuring quietly, Mrs. Machine puttered forward, in gondola-propulsion mode as Nowar looked at the book in her hands. She began studying it intently.

She had never seen a book with two spines before. It was like a triptych, something where two panels fold neatly towards each other to perfectly cover a large center panel. The texture of the pages was altogether amazing- they were incredibly durable yet incredibly thin, like iron that had been shaved to onion skin thickness. It was a thick book for sure, and each side of this 'triptych' book had 360 pages, adding up to an impressive 1,080 pages in total! The writing was very odd, consisting of clusters of wedge shaped symbols, sort of like birds feet patterns, often in groups of three.

The center panel pages were all maps, each and every one of the 360 pages were a map of a Kingdom. She accidentally pulled one out in her enthusiasm, and was about to get upset when she realized that it had a very slender magnetic strip on the top. The center pages were meant to be removable! Suddenly she said aloud- "What on Earth is this book?"

Ouroboros Alpha-Beta craned around her to look at what she was holding. Alpha was, as usual, the first of the two to say something-

ProbablePolis

"Why, you are holding in your hands, Lady Nowar, nothing less than a copy of the 'Book of Scorns'!"

"Wow…" Nowar said, and then looked back at the thing. The Walrus was still looking around distractedly, trying to geo-locate where they were, and oblivious to the conversation at-hand.

"I wish I could read it!" she said to Alpha. Ripples of something bent the light around her, but only slightly, and, when she looked back at the pages, she realized she could read it now.

Excitedly she began to skim over the pages, reading little bits here and there, loitering at the table of contents, zigzagging over the index, and rifling through all 360 pages of maps. The left side was entitled "The Historical Past" and the right side was called "The Prophetic Future". The Center folios were called, naturally, "All the Kingdoms of ProbablePolis, extinct or perseverant".

The first sentence on the dedication page of the left side said-

The Past is malleable, the Future is fixed

Nowar thought carefully about that statement. It was somehow jarring to her. Then she looked, curiously, at the first sentence on the dedication page of the right side that said-

But if you wish to believe that the Past is fixed, and the Future is malleable, be our guest.

A book with a sense of humor, she thought. Now I've seen everything. She began to look through the left side, the Historical Past, and began to learn a number of interesting things. For example, she read what happened in ProbablePolis on the very first day of its creation.

Once upon a time, when there was no time…
someone somewhere somehow seemed to speak…
indeed, unto the dark void a Narrator cried out;
"Let there be a little bang

And from it now a hollow black sphere of crystal...
That it might contain all of Creation."
And so it was, and the Narrator continued, saying-
"Let there be now a fiery sanity to bind all of Creation,
and keep it apart and above and safe
from what is called the Oblivion"
And so the Logos came into being.

Nowar realized then and there how important this book was. It told the story of Everything! She looked around briefly at her surroundings and quickly put her nose back into the book.

But the Logos was not enough,
and the Narrator required Builders,
helpers to assist in the task of continuing the Creation.
And the Narrator said-
"Let there erupt in the center of the black sphere
a Ribbon of Light,
though it will be like a cold hammered bracelet without
Life.
And in the center of the unborn Ribbon of Light
let there be rendered a folio of four pages,
that might support things born of the double sided helix
of Life"
And the Logos brought forth all manner of things
that move and crawl and grow and fly and cry
to walk the pages...

The Builders were delighted, and they gave the first
pulse of life
to the Ribbon, and many transformed themselves into
Avatars
to shepherd the creatures of the Pages
and the Logos said to them all-

> "As Plausibilities give birth to Possibilities,
> Let these Possibilities bring forth all Probabilities,
> Here, in our ProbablePolis"
> And the Ribbon roared to Life,
> with a knot of a pulse of Light
> that circled the folio of four pages
> with its warm and bright pulse,
> that all things that think and eat and play
> might know a darkened twilight, and a glorious day.
>
> And the Builders giggled and grinned, and fled.

Almost as if in a trance, Nowar barely noticed that Two-Fangs was holding onto her arm and shaking her, ever so slightly. As she looked up at his grim Wolven-Kine face he did not look back, for he was staring off to the stern of their boat, pointing towards the widening cavern in front of them.

"We have company" he said quietly "Time to put away the book, and remember who you are…"

She almost wanted to laugh, and very nearly said, "Easy for you to say, Two-Fangs, but I actually *don't remember who I am yet*!"

Instead she stood and looked to where he was pointing.

Mrs. Machine was slowing down. A horde of insects of all kinds, some winged, some crawling, were headed towards them, and in fact quickly beginning to surround them. These were no ordinary insects however; they were all quite large. The smallest among them were the size of a small poodle, the biggest were easily the size of an elephant. There were ants the size of great danes, praying mantis bigger than rhinos, wasps as big as Two-Fangs, bees as big as hippos, beetles bigger than camels, and gnats the size of snowballs.

And they all had faces- exceedingly human-like and rather expressive faces, which lent them a very surreal and otherworldly visage.

"Who are they?" Nowar whispered to no one in particular. She was noticing now as they circled that they were all armed, with spears, swords, daggers and slingshots.

"Arthropodica." Mandrake answered, "Most of them are the inhabitants of the 11th Kingdom, though some of them, the Bees, in particular, were originally inhabitants of the page that used to face the 11th Kingdom a very long time ago."

Ouroboros Alpha could not contain himself and added "Pagination has had to change over the cycles of time, Nowar, which is confusing to just about everyone. What happened during the first war of Probability was horrible. Many Kingdoms were annihilated. Moebius and the Gull & Crones society melted the 44th Kingdom off of its binding, which caused it to crash into the 11th page thus giving the 11th Kingdom its own ceiling, as you have seen, as well as citizens of two legacies."

"Enough with the history lesson!" Two-Fangs snarled and said "Three of them are lowering their weapons and approaching. One of us must speak for all of us."

He was looking directly at Nowar.

Nowar stood, clasped her helmet and shield on, and walked to the edge of the Mrs. Machine gondola. A menacing black wasp, shiny and well-armored with a thin chiseled face, hovered closer. A bee hovered somewhat below and to his right. Her face was like a young pudgy girl's face, with a perpetual grin that she was keeping as hidden as possible. She looked a bit scared. A flea the size of a border collie jumped from its place on the Wasp's shoulder, landing squarely on the edge of the gondola, right in front of Nowar, who gasped, but not move backward. Mandrake kept Two-Fangs from squashing the flea, who with little ado, put on his spectacles and began to speak, almost prosaically from under his bushy moustache-

"I am called the Humble Mixer. We are an envoy sent by the most majestic Hiram Kaine and the most sublime Deb-or-ah Craine."

"Welcome Humble Mixer. I am Nowar Rondelle, unremembering Princess of ProbablePolis, and these are my Companions."

Humble Mixer looked at them all, and then back at her with very wide eyes. Then he put back on his spectacles and hastily unrolled a scroll, reading from it so fast that she could hardly make out what he was saying.

"Withoutfurtherado…AND…giventhatthetimeofthefinalwarisathand-andthatwehavebeenalertedbyMensestheAngelofAmbrosiaofyourcoming, tisthewillofboththemajesticHiramKaineandthesublimeDeborah-Crainethatyoubesafelyescorted, tothecourtofSadMemoriestodispensewithpleasantriesorexplicategallantries, thatProbablePolismightbefreeofthe…DESPICABLE…DukeMoebiusandwithhighhopesthatallgoodorderberestoredtoalltheKingdomsofProbablePolis."

Humble Mixer looked back at the black-armored Wasp Captain, who nodded solemnly, and then back to Nowar.

"Is this acceptable to you and your Companions?"

Nowar laughed and said "Of course, Humble Mixer, we would be honored. Please lead the way!"

The Companions in the Mrs. Machine gondola followed the horde of lumbering and hovering Arthropodica. The human-faced insects guided them through one vast cavern after another, luminous landscapes of molten wax-volcanoes were everywhere, spewing glowing tutti-frutti colored wax-magma down stalactites and across stalagmites as gloppy rivers coagulated in corners and in wall puddles of all shapes and sizes.

But the further they went into the interior, Nowar noticed that the volcanoes were becoming less frequent and smaller in size. The interior they were traveling through continued to reveal more and more sculpted architectural forms, all in hardened wax, with hallways and staircases, winding each and every which way. The style was swirly, and even slightly funky, though it had an elegant poise and balance in terms of how the spirals and stars were emblazoned everywhere in one whirlwind-like column to another. As they went further, the sculpted archways and vaulting became even more stunning, and remained multicolored, but they blending colors and shapes in very attractive ways.

Yellow five pointed stars extruded slightly all across the blue ceiling everywhere, and in places where the hardened wax created ponds and lakes on the ground, there were flowers, but not just your normal flowers- they were huge flowers, flowers the size of trees. Poppies, dandelions and snapdragons predominated, though they were some buttercups and even a few roses.

As the gondola swished past several of the poppies, a few petals as big as fronds twisted from their tops and gently floated downward. Nowar was utterly lost in the scenery as the Humble Mixer said quietly to her- "Hiram Kaine wishes for you to know that you are ever-so welcome here in our Kingdom of Rantadore, and that we will all be delighted to host you in the Halls of the Court of Sad Memories. The Avatars Kaine and Craine have called for a pan-Kingdom communication, something that hasn't been tried in many pulses of the ribbon. They wish for all the Avatars to be able to see you, and to ask questions of you, so that there will be no more disputing that you have come, but actual proof of it."

Nowar was thoughtful for a moment and asked "When will we get there?"

"Another twenty minutes perhaps, if we are not ambushed by Locusts or Scorpions or Spiders. The good captain Wasp here, Don Donovan Keeyotay, assures me that the tunnels down this way have been cleared of all potential opponents, so we should have smooth sailing. Mrs. Machine shuddered at the mention of spiders, but faithfully continued carried the Companions amidst their procession of motley winged, hopping, crawling Arthopodicans.

The Walrus looked back at Nowar, smiled and said- "Maybe you oughta get some sleep while you can, dearie. We all gonna be awake and keepin' guard an all."

Nowar nodded, and after another minute, curled in a ball, there on the floor of the gondola and said "Just for a few minutes maybe, alright." Mandrake smiled at her and Two-Fangs sat down right beside her. Ouroboros Alpha-Beta told jokes and sang songs, but none of it managed to keep Nowar awake. It took all of a minute for her to drifted into sleep, perchance to dream of the little girl, wherever she was.

AntiPart Two

Toot! Toot! Reboot!

There was a strange hum from the ceiling above Colonel Shard. He did exactly as he had been instructed, though. The blue button he depressed had ejected the funny looking cube with an incredibly undramatic click, a swish and a pop.

The strange hum above him changed to a whine. He promptly replaced the funny looking cube with the one he had found in the room he had just left, labeled "Builder Rejected". The mechanism embraced, locked and embedded the new cube into itself with tiny little appendages, and the whine went back to a hum. Shard turned to walk back through the door of the Matrix Room back to the Chip Room. Above him, he could hear the strange hum getting louder and louder.

Brandy looked up at him as he entered and said "We've got trouble."

He turned to where she was looking, saw Moebius with a blaster, nodded to him and closed the door.

Moebius said "Good of you to join us, Colonel. Please come in…" and promptly pointed the blaster at him.

Shard muttered under his breath and said "That's **Lieutenant** Colonel to you, Doctor…actually, now that I think of it, I'm glad that you made it as well."

Brandy stood up and Moebius swished the blaster back to point at her. Shard began to make a move, but Moebius said "Touch me, and she dies, hero."

"What do you want?" Brandy growled.

"What do I want? Do you mean, before, or after I blow you both to smithereens?"

Back in the Matrix Room, Shard noticed out of the corner of his eye that the hexagonal stand was glowing and shaking. A burst of light came suddenly, just after Moebius slipped on a pair of sunglasses, and Shard yelled "What was that?"

"ProbablePolis just rebooted, you dolt. You've reset the entire simulation to a whole new set of algorithms and pathways, starting from the moment it was at during the reset." Moebius said calmly, fingering the trigger on his blaster, pointed it once at Shard and then back at Brandy,

"Something that will be repeated, by the way, after I've disposed of you both. I shall load my own version of the simulation, the original most likely, I haven't had time to dish up anything new, what with my schedule and all, prepping for a final Armageddon and what-not. I have to admit I'm mystified how a gun-toting pin-head like yourself actually figured out how to do all that, but twenty questions will have to wait for awhile."

It occurred to Shard that he would have to disarm Moebius somehow, and get that blaster away from him, but how?

Turning to Brandy, Moebius said "All right, you old goat, let's get on with it, then, fork over the book!"

Brandy put her bag behind her and said "Over my dead body!"

Moebius smiled, and said "Happy to oblige Mrs. Rondell, happy... to...oblige"

Suddenly, sensing what was about to happen, Shard jumped on Moebius, and the laser blew off, thankfully away from Brandy. Shard twisted the blaster out of the hand that he was holding, and threw Moebius down onto the ground. Wasting no time, he heaved his knee onto Moebius' back.

"Aaaaaaarrrrgh" Moebius cried in pain, squirming like a rabid newt. Shard had him securely, though he was a greasy and grotesquely proportioned little man.

"Now what?" Brandy asked her son, checking the bag to make sure the book of ProbablePolis was still stashed securely inside. She heard sirens. The laser blaster had set off an alarm.

"Couldn't be more simple, Mom. Now we wait for security to show up and I just keep this cabbage-headed doctor on ice until then!"

"I am Lord Moebius!"

Shard looked down and said quietly "No, you're dog-food, buddy."

Hardly another ten seconds passed when the security guards burst into the Chip room, Shard was as quiet and as still as a cat.

"Everyone drop what you've got in your hands. Drop it! DROP IT!" they all yelled.

One of them motioned to Shard to back away from the captive Moebius, laying on his stomach and blubbering on about the end of the world.

"Let him go and back away, son." A grizzled old sergeant said to Shard.

Another one tried to take the bag with the book away from Brandy and she began to hit him with it. "Over my dead body!"

Moebius smiled, feeling an opportunity at hand.

Shard said very loudly "Sergeant! I am Lieutenant Colonel Rondell, and I have satisfied one of the primary requirements of my mission- I have apprehended Doctor Moebius here, temporarily pinned, but I must warn you that if I let him go, there's no telling what he will or will not be able to do- to all of us!"

The Sergeant was no dummy. Shard's mission had long since leaked out to the guards of the MoonClock facility over the many years, and everyone knew that Doctor Moebius had to be captured. One didn't utter Shard's name without mentioning the name of Moebius as well these days since the two bordered on becoming a mythical pair of antagonist nemeses.

"Alright, son, you just don't make a move right now, ok?"

"I'm not going anywhere!" was the last thing anyone said when the book that the Private was struggling to walk off with suddenly blew open in his face, and, in a shower of light, suddenly there appeared…

little Nowar. Brandy gasped audibly and grabbed her. The Private was unconscious on the floor.

Shard's face brightened as he heard his Daughter's voice, and, for just an instant, loosened his grip...allowing Moebius to reach just far enough into his own pocket, and, with extremely careful desperation, managed to grab a hold of his Transmogrifier, his two way ticket out of, and into, ProbablePolis. He jolted free, just for an instant, and just as Shard was retightening his hold on him, Moebius cried-

"Exeunt!" And he was gone.

Shard cursed with unpopular and choice words while Grandma Brandy covered Nowar's ears. The Private was still knocked out on the floor, and all the Guards looked confused and dismayed.

"Alright, we're all going down to see Admiral ScrubbleBrine right now, let's go!"

Shard picked up Nowar with one hand, and the book with another. On the way down the stairs, accompanied by several soldiers and the security detail, Shard subtly shifted the book into Nowar's hands and quietly whispered "If anything happens, just use the book to bail out of here, don't worry about me or your Grandma, we'll be fine now. Just let everyone in there know that the folks out here did the best they could, but that Moebius is still at large, ok?"

Nowar nodded. She was remembering, or trying to remember, a strange place where human faced insects were guiding her and her friends to meet...someone important. It seemed like it was just a dream, but her Father was acting like it was real!

Back in the chip room, Moebius had already beamed back in from wherever he had just beamed out to. Cackling to himself, he weaseled back into the Matrix Room, and replaced the Implausible Chip that Shard had just re-installed minutes before. Then he rebooted the thing a second, or maybe third time, even we aren't sure anymore.

"ScrubbleBrine's a boobus maximus if he thinks he'll EVER be able to catch me. And now...we...will...reinstall...all of ProbablePolis, hehehehehe…. ahahhaahh….. HAHAHAHAHAHA… MUAHHAAAAHAAHAAAA!"

Moebius put on his shades and began to maniacally eat a tootsie roll while he waited for the obligatory flash of reboot, and then slapped open his temponautical utility. He yelled "Clancy, Clancy, wake up man! Report!"

Clancy, wearing a variety of outlandish sensors and computer connections to his body, looked very groggy and 'out of it', but stumbled to the screen to say with a slight slur;

"Er…Sir…all the sensors went off the map just a little bit ago, and… we lost all power on all the systems, and then…there were…er…odd phenomena going on. I believe I lost consciousness for a moment. And then, just as I was waking up…it all happened…all over again…a second time!"

"No worries, Clancy…no worries at all…" Moebius grinned as he looked back at the hexagonal chip container now behind glass in the Matrix room. "We have everything under control here- Colonel Shard, his child, and his Mother are all now in custody, and, once I get back that book, we can have ProbablePolis all to ourselves again... Now, how about YOUR report, you scaley-brained nitwit?"

There was a pause. Clancy was reading a note in front of him in a handwriting he didn't recognize that said -

> "Don't say anything more to Moebius, he knows EXACTLY what just happened. All of ProbablePolis has just been rebooted, Clancy, twice, so tell Moebius that you'll run some diagnostics and then just sign off. Then, hit the blue button on the small device in front of you, and all of this will make sense. Once your memories have returned, wait for the signal. When I text you "I shriek, you shriek, we all shriek

for the final Tweak." You'll need to lure Moebius back into ProbablePolis right away!"

Clancy looked at Moebius through his screen and said quietly "Everything is fine, my most sublime dark-Lord. We'll run some diagnostics and I'll report right back to you on what I think caused this disruption."

"Clancy, is there anything else abnormal going on in there that I should know about?"

Clancy paused. Moebius had picked up on something- "Uh, I seem to recall that just before I passed out, very briefly I had located the Princess, but I lost my lock on her, just moments ago."

'Frak! Well, the fact that you found her, even for a few moments is good news- where is she now, though? Any leads?"

"A few, but I'll have to check them and get back to you."

"Alright, but hurry it up and don't fidder around…I'm coming back IN there shortly, right after I capture this book, understand? Transmogrify me one of those multi-mega blasters, again, will you? One of those light weight photon-cannons that blow people away like butter in an oven." And then Moebius chuckled in a very evil manner.

"Yes, sir, I'll get right to it." Clancy said, and, having terminated the communication, he turned back to the small mechanism in front of him, and depressed the blue button.

Clancy shuddered and he shook, and then he passed out briefly. A few minutes later though, he was quite awake again, quite himself, and madly clicking away at keyboards and monitoring screens in front of his terminal. Everything was powering back up. Time was a-wasting, and he was quite aware that Nowar, as the little girl, was now back on Earth and that Moebius was back there also, and Clancy also knew that Moebius was going to go after her and the book at all costs. Clancy text messaged Agent Fugue, still in some cramped and very tight broom closet, adjunct to the Chip Room everyone had just been in.

Fugue looked down at his temponautical device screen where he read the obligatory-

Klaatu barada nikto

Wasting no time himself, he "phased" into the Chip Room, dashed into the Matrix Room, ejected the Implausible Cube from the hexagonal dais, and without delay, loaded a new cube into the device. He stepped away from the dais, put on his sunglasses and waited for the flare to erupt, just as it had done before for Shard and Moebius.

"Fugue gets the last laugh, dough-boy."

Taking out his temponautical phone, Fugue prepared to phase back into ProbablePolis; the destination was, thanks to Agent Deep-six, right smack dab inside the Deep Dwark Command Module of Moebius himself.

He looked at Clancy as he phased in, and said "OK, that's it, right, Deep-six? We're done with Earth now, right? That was my last mission yes?"

Clancy said, "Almost, Fugue- word from the Logos came in while you were getting back here; There's one last errand."

"Figures. Go ahead."

"First, here is the Tabula Rasa."

Fugue looked at it. It was a very slender tome indeed, with a small, locking clasp, and three silver buttons on the front, representing, respectively, a star, a moon, and a sun. This was the Book that he would have leave on the Bookcase for his daughter to find in the recent past to start this whole mess. He nodded solemnly and looked back at Clancy.

"OK, what else?"

"And second, here are three sheets of blank paper." He paused and said "The Logos apparently believes that it's time for you to journal the events surrounding the birth of your daughter. Be brief, Fugue- you've got less than five minutes to get in, write on these three pages and then get out. You'll need to tell her how all this mess got started, and then leave the journal entries in a book called 'The Wizard of Oz' by Frank Baum. Make sure you leave them in front of the page with the lyrics to the theme song. The Wizard of Oz book will be at the top of the steps in the attic of your family's mansion. Go… NOW!"

Agent Fugue popped into his Family Mansion right in front of the old grandfather clock. He carefully placed the Book of ProbablePolis on the bookshelf, and left a note in the Carl Claudy book on the fourth shelf of the Book-case that said in his own handwriting-

DON'T GIVE UP, NOWAR.   LOOK IN THE ATTIC.

Then Fugue walked into his Father's home office on the other side of the second floor. Wasting no time, he madly scribbled his best five minute memoire of the last two decades of his life, describing as best as he could how his Daughter had come to be in the world, and what had happened to the MoonClock project; how it all began.

Then he kissed the book, and replaced it gently where it had been found, at the top of the stairs in the attic. He ran back down the stairs to check and make sure he had put the Tome of ProbablePolis in the right place, and, hearing Nowar and her Grandmother walk back into the house, turned quickly towards the doorway. As he did, several books fell to the floor, including the Tome itself. He had run out of time. The books would have to stay. Nowar would be here any second.

Darting into the bathroom, he flicked open his temponautical utility, and texted to Clancy -

I shriek, you shriek, we all shriek for the final Tweak

It was the signal for Clancy to lure Moebius back into ProbablePolis. It was time for him to go back too, and set a trap to catch this madman- end this savage game.

Agent Fugue had completed his last mission on Earth.

AntiPart One

You're a mean one, Doctor Moebius...

While Agent Fugue was off in the past at his family's mansion doing his last errands, Doctor Moebius was waiting for Fugue's "chother", the beleaguered Lieutenant Colonel Shard now in custody.

Concealed in a ventilation duct Moebius watched down the hallway through the grate for any sign of the security detail that should be escorting Shard, Nowar and Brandy. Moebius knew that this particular hallway was the only way that they could possibly come now to get to the office where General Scrubblebrine was waiting. What was keeping them, though, and why hadn't he gone to the restroom before he had stuffed himself up here were only a few of the thoughts that dominated his mind.

Brandy had, just a few minutes before, asked to be escorted to a bathroom herself, and that was where she slipped away, worming up into the ventilation system she was now getting more and more used to. She had armed herself with a toilet plunger while she had been there, and was now hoping desperately that she would get a chance to attach it permanently to the face of Moebius at the first available opportunity- maybe even knock the fat little sucker out from lack of oxygen. How she knew that Moebius was up there in the first place was anyone's guess, but Brandy had always followed her hunches.

Little did Moebius know, but in fact the security detail had just split, Shard and Nowar were still being quickly hurried down the hall, while two sergeants and the other half of the detail were trying to get up into the ventilation shaft after Brandy, their commanding officers cursing at them to find Brandy right away.

Brandy was in sight of Moebius now, and getting closer to him, inch by inch. Moebius picked his nose impatiently the entire time. Then the tiny communication device that he wore on his head chirped and Brandy could hear, very faintly that someone was talking to Moebius right at that very moment. They said-

"Uh, this is Clancy, I have some very bad news, sir, and an awful lot of it."

"This better be good, you twiddled dimwit- what is it?"

"Queen Limberly is free, sir. She has retaken control of the armies and armada of the Kingdom of EverGreen. I also believe that she and the King are preparing to come to Castle DeepSteel in the now fully reconstructed EDV Omega Ring. The Omega Ring, as you know, can transport very large armies and a lot of machines of war. They'll be here anytime, sir."

Moebius face contorted like silly-putty, but Clancy wasn't done.

"Also, it's now known that the very last Dwark Express is on the move again, assembling armies from all the pages of ProbablePolis for an invasion of Koradgia. Our spies tell us that the Great Olde Drake has left Avalhalla with a new leader, a General called Bric, from another world."

"My God, Clancy, what the 'Hell Incorporated' happened in there while I was gone? Did all this just creep up on you?"

"Say, we're getting some odd interference up here, sir…er….you're breaking up. It's getting hard to hear you… Holy cow, the Midnight Shadow is already here! …and he's brought ALL HIS ARMIES!!!!… they must have Dwarked in down there at Castle DeepSteel, right there on the Plain of All-Sorrows. He's already attacking the front gate all by himself!!!"

Moebius looked like he was about to pop. Steam was coming out of his ears.

"Good gravy you imbecile! CALL A RED ALERT! TO ARMS! Where are the Silver Scream and the Black Harp?"

"They are en route, my Lord. I'm monitoring it all on the feeds up here at the secret Command Module."

"Don't you 'my Lord' me, you knucklehead! What are you doing up there in the Control Room, you tool? You should be at the Castle taking care of business…I'm wondering if reloading ProbablePolis hasn't permanently addled your brain… I'm going have to come back in there right now, aren't I?"

"Probably should, sir, I'd really like to take a nap."

Moebius yelled "You wuss! That does it" and, pulling out his Transmogrifier, phased himself back into ProbablePolis into the great Observation Tower of Castle DeepSteel itself.

Dashing to the soot-darkened windows, he could now see for himself that Clancy had made an accurate report in at least one regard; all across the black and twisted meadows of the Plain of All-Sorrows, thousands of ungainly creatures from the Under-Rung- Trolls, Goblins, Giants, Harpies were preparing countless siege machines and organizing themselves into camps while a giant Black Unicorn, the Midnight Shadow, was hurling his great fiery hooves with un mitigated fury against the very gates of Castle DeepSteel.

Let him go on with his bravado. Those gates were made of stuff as hard as the very sphere of the Dwark itself. There had NEVER been a successful siege of DeepSteel and that nincompoop knew it!

Nevertheless, it was clearly time to take the bull by the horn. Moebius got on a communication device and commanded all his Generals in residence in Koradgia to meet him in the Throne Room at once, where he would take control of all his armies. He put out a call for all of his Admirals to bring their Battle-Ships and Fleets out of the Dwark and back to Koradgia as fast as possible.

Just then, and for just a passing instant, Moebius realized uncomfortably that he still had not figured out how there could be two Shards at once?- one, in ProbablePolis as a gallant White King, and the other, bumbling around in the MoonClock facility, apparently fresh out of one of the first Dwark jumps, old style, mind you. He thought for an instant that maybe one of them was an illusion, a fake, and that the Logos was just trying to confuse him further. He shook his head though and realized he would have to give this oddity some further thought after he had this whole mess under control. Establishing a data link with his ToggleWog network, he monitored where the Silver Scream and

Black Harp were at that very moment; both of them were closing in on Koradgia and would be here shortly. He breathed a sigh of relief. Then he yelled at an assistant to get him a tray of pastries and bring his Teddy Bear, Poopsy, up to the Observation Tower without delay.

He decided to open a communication link to Tatyanna, but only static greeted him. Then he dialed for Glee's communication piece. Snoring was all he heard. After a brief scream or two, he managed to wake up the Glee and the little cyborg flea blurted out –

"Fearful Leader! I am so glad you called me. I was wondering if I would ever get a chance to report in!"

"That's **Fearless** Leader, Glee. Where are you? Where is Tatyanna?"

"We are all in Ambrosia, Boss! Tatyanna and everyone else has been captured, and I am hidden in a Minotaur's belly button waiting to spy on zee King."

Moebius considered activating the explosion detonation option he had all his spies' communication devices equipped with, but thought better of it. Who knows, the little idiot might come across something useful, let him live a little longer.

Opening another communication link to the speakers on the outside of the Castle he started to think about what kind of insults to hurl at this fugitive and futile siege attempt on Castle DeepSteel.

It was definitely time to tell off that insolent Black Unicorn, and he needed to buy some more time for the big guns to get here, anyway. Let Clancy nap up there in the Control Room in the Dwark if he wanted to - there'd be time to throttle his scrawny neck later for this massive incompetence.

T-minus Ten

And counting...

General Scrubblebrine was fit to be tied, though he was a very large fellow, and you would have needed a lot of rope. He had just found out how close his security detail had been to finally capturing Dr. Moebius. He was scowling at Lt. Col. Shard, who stood, uncomfortably at attention, then he looked at Nowar with a raised eyebrow, and then he scowled some more at Brandy, who had finally given herself up after she had seen Moebius blow his top and phase out of the ventilation duct. She was only slightly disappointed, but she was still clutching the toilet plunger in one hand in case the little freak came back. Security detail had not been able to get her to give it up without her flashing it in their faces.

"Sorry, sir." said Shard, standing at attention. He saluted. "We lost Moebius."

"I heard. Did you know that your Father's in there as well, son? How the BRAC do you think he figured out how to do that, Colonel? This MoonClock Gate has been quiet as a church mouse for almost two years, until today. I understand from the control center downstairs that the main mechanism has totally rebooted, and no less than three times! What the devil is going on here? Start talking, son, it's your nickel now."

"Yes sir. Well, as far as I can tell, somehow, the Program that runs the simulation, the LOGOS, has figured out how to play with time and space…and not just the time and space that goes on in the simulation, I mean it's learned how to play with time and space OUT HERE!… and not just time and space, but matter, as well."

Scrubblebrine looked very confused.

"Alright, let me try to explain, sir. For me, from my own perception, I really just left through the MoonClock Gate hardly a day or so ago, and yet I now know that it's been several years apparently. Also, what makes the whole thing even weirder is that… somehow, the Logos has split me into three people."

Scrubblebrine looked even more confused. He put out his cigar, but didn't say a word. Shard continued.

"I know this will be hard to swallow, sir, but as of now, while I stand here, there is someone who thinks he's me, who looks like me, and is…doing…stuff in ProbablePolis, and then there's another me, who looks like me, and thinks he's me…running around in a black suit with sunglasses, with some pretty advanced toys, I might add. I have NO idea what he's doing, but he's hopping around, at his liberty, in and out of the MoonClock simulation whenever and wherever he feels like…"

Scrubblebrine interjected- "OK, we'll get back to all that in a minute. I find it all hard to swallow, and I'm already choking on a chicken bone, here, son. First, tell me how it is that your little girl here appears to be able to use that book of hers to get into and out of the MoonClock, the country's most classified, advanced, next-generation True Holographic Universe Simulation? Any leads on how all that came to be?"

"Yes, sir, but the ramifications are stunning."

"Spit it out. It's time to get to the bottom of this, soldier!"

"Yes, sir! What this all means is that, as I said before, the AI master program that calls itself the LOGOS now has control not just of time, space and matter IN THERE, but, to some extent, out here as well!"

"You're nuts."

"No sir, I wish I were. The LOGOS has projected holographic conceptions and code into our universe, sir. No covert project I am aware of- and you know I've seen my share- has anything like this capability."

Shard picked up the Book then and said "This Book was somehow made by the LOGOS itself, and it was left on a Bookcase in my Daughter's bedroom for her to find. How she figured out how to use it, I have no idea, but it probably also has something to do with the LOGOS as well."

General Scrubblebrine scowled some more to himself and said "Alright, it's time we heard from the expert. Nowar, little lady, come forward, please. You need to show me how you use this book of yours."

Nowar looked at her Father who nodded and just said – "Go ahead honey, show the General how you use the book…" and then he whispered "good luck, sweetie." And he winked.

Nowar put the book on the table in front of the General, looked him squarely in the eye, and then began making the required little tune by pressing the buttons on the front of the magical tome of ProbablePolis. As the brightness swallowed her, Scrubblebrine sputtered and hollered and grabbed at thin air, but it was really too late. Nowar was gone.

Shard hugged his Mother and they all prayed for the best of all possible outcomes. A minute later, Scrubblebrine ordered them all taken down to the brig until he could take his blood pressure medicine and decide what to do next.

T-minus Nine

And still counting...

The flea called the Humble Mixer hopped gleefully down the splendid stairway that spiraled below them into the gigantic Throne Room of the Avatars Hiram Kaine and Deb-o-rah Craine. Nowar and her Companions kept up as best as they could, accompanied by the Wasp Captain, Don Donovan Keeyotay, and a horde of Arthropodicans. The Humble Mixer turned suddenly and bowed to Nowar.

"Welcome to the Court of Sad Memories. Avatars Kaine and Craine will see you know in the Call-uh-see-um."

The Call-uh-see-um was a huge amphitheatre. Vast and filled with the sounds of buzzing and droning and chit-chat-chit it was lit with countless dim candles on the ground, and hundreds of giant glow-worms clutching the ceiling. The place must have seated thousands upon thousands of Arthropodicans of all kinds; grasshoppers, flies, beetles, centipedes, praying mantis, termites, dragon-flies, earthworms, and even slugs. They all seemed to be fairly good at keeping themselves entertained, exchanging mugs of ale, toasting to each other's health, throwing beach balls and debating pointless issues that were undoubtedly very important for a bunch of giant insects that lived in a world made of wax.

Nowar had barely taken her first step when a very loud sound echoed across the entire amphitheatre.

"CAW! CAW! CAW!CAW!" came the bellowing sound. Everyone immediately quieted down.

Nowar's attention, and everyone else's, for that matter, was now drawn down to the very center of the amphitheatre below, to the Avatar Hiram Kaine. He was quite a sight.

Hiram Kaine was a Raven, but no ordinary Raven was he. He was the size of a house, and his body was more like that of a person. He sat on a magnificent throne of ivory, encrusted with silver, rubies and lapis lazuli. He wore a spectacular white and gold uniform that reminded Nowar of a Navy Admiral. Across his lap was an apron of sorts, with beautiful adornments of all kinds. On the apron sat a feathery plumed hat. His uniform had an incredible number of medals and finery on it- his necklace was of a square and compass intersecting each other, and in Hiram's right feathery claw he held a beautiful red orb-capped scepter that glowed and pulsed as he spoke. On his shoulder sat a Honey Bee the size of a rhino, but when compared to Hiram's enormous girth, it seemed by scale to be not that much bigger than a normal bee. The Bee wore a splendid green dress, and like all the rest of the Arthropodicans, had a face that was all but human in shape.

The Bee alighted from Hiram Kaine's shoulder and rose gracefully up the stairs of the amphitheatre to hover directly in front of Nowar.

"I am the Avatar Deb-o-rah Craine. It is a pleasure to meet you…and your Companions…come with me, dearie." She smiled, and, taking Nowar by the hand with her odd insectoidal limb, escorted her down the stairs to meet Hiram Kaine.

At the foot of the stairs Nowar was brought to the center of the throne room. Hiram Kaine looked down at her and said in his deep booming voice-

"CAW! CAW! Welcome to Rantadore, Princess Nowar. Your coming, foretold to us as it was by the Precognitids and the Book of Scorns, is a matter of great joy, and of grave speculation. Many of the Avatars believe your arrival promises the final reckoning with Moebius and an end to all the suffering of ProbablePolis. Others scarcely believe you exist, and they bicker incessantly with the rest. We have managed, with great cunning, to arrange for a conference amongst ALL the remaining Avatars of ProbablePolis, so that, at the very least, they will all know that you are real…that you truly exist."

He gestured to an area behind her, where she watched devices all around her emerging from the floor. They looked a bit like metallic plants and they flowered outward unfolding screens that summari¹ turned themselves on.

"CAW! CAW! CAW! We are ready to begin this conference, if indeed you are, Princess Nowar."

Nowar nodded, and looked around her. Deb-o-rah Craine was still with her. She patted her on the shoulder gently, giggled and said "Just bee yourself, dearie." And she winked.

One by one, the screens flickered and powered up, each one revealing a face stranger than the last. Hiram Kaine introduced each one as they flickered on-

"First, from the Kingdom of Crepuscular, Nowar, I introduce to you the venerable Herr Leuchtkäfer."

Nowar decided to bow, ever so slightly. It seemed the polite thing to do. The screen revealed what seemed like the face of a giant Firefly with a long wispy white beard and very thick spectacles.

"From the Kingdom of Fragelica, Nowar, I introduce you to the surreptitious Madame Kotoridayori."

Nowar bowed to the image of what appeared to be a beautiful hummingbird's face. Kotoridayori removed her monocle, delicately, and seemed to smile.

"From the Kingdom of Antares, Nowar, I now introduce you to the resourceful Lady Fucale Kombu."

At first, Nowar could not really make out what she was looking at. It appeared to be a forest of Kelp, swaying with the ocean swell, but a few seconds later, she began to make out a face forming from the drifting strands of sea-weed. She bowed again, and the Kelp smiled back at her.

" the Kingdom of Dorian, Nowar, I now introduce you to the Lord Theopolis."

ore difficulty with this one than the last. The which didn't help, but after a few seconds she it appeared to be a…multi-colored Octopus? He almost looked like he was made out of stained glass. He appeared to be playing a Cello. Hiram Kaine leaned forward and whispered "He's a bit self-absorbed, but don't worry, once we get started he'll get with the program. He composes his own symphonies, you know."

"Next, from the Kingdom of Nafer Deem, I now introduce you to the twin Avatars, the articulate Lord Amphion and the relentless Lord Zethus."

Amphion appeared to be a very distinguished looking Cheetah-like creature in very refined clothing. Zethus was quite the reverse, looking like a very rough and rumpled, armor encased Lion-like creature. Nowar bowed to them both.

"And, finally, last but not least, from the Kingdom of Ova, I now introduce you, Nowar, to the effervescent Lady Astrid."

Astrid looked to be something like a huge smiling jellyfish, bobbing in place on top of a long set of blue and purple plant-like strands; legs perhaps. As bizarre as it sounded, her smile was infectious and overwhelming, and Nowar bowed to her as well.

"It is a pleasure to meet all of you…" Nowar began. "And it is even a bit overwhelming to realize that I have the honor and pleasure to speak, at one time, to all of the Avatars of ProbablePolis."

Hiram Kaine cleared his throat and said- "Actually, Nowar, **not** all of them are here. In fact, the Avatars who could not be with us today include the Avatar of Cetacea, the beneficent SkyWhale, Lady Uhranitee Mare, for one. Also, the Midnight Shadow, whom you have already met, could not attend. He is busy distracting Moebius with a full out frontal assault of Castle DeepSteel, thus permitting not only this conference, but also the mustering of the Kingdoms of EverGreen and Ambrosia by the King and Queen, and the new Emperor of ProbablePolis."

Nowar nodded solemnly. She had never met either her Father or her Mother, and she wondered, just for a second, what it would feel like to see them for the first time. She also had no idea who this new Emperor could be, and she briefly thought that she should look in the Book of Scorns in her pocket to see if it had any hint who he might be.

"And, of course, the Great Olde Drake, the Avatar of Avalhalla could not be here, for he is busy making sure that the new Emperor, the King and the Queen are all adequately prepared for the final battle. I have heard, however, that he will soon be on his way to meet with you, Nowar, at an undisclosed, and perhaps even as yet, unknown location…"

Kaine paused for a second then, and said "Also, it grieves me to report that the other Avatar that could not attend is the wise Cloud-Tree Shane, who was slain by the Black Harp of DeepSteel."

Lady Fucale Kombu shed a tear at the mention of Shane, and Lady Astrid burst into a fit of sobbing as well. Lord Zethus cried out "We will avenge Lord Shane, Lord Hiram Kaine! He will not have died in vain!"

"CAW! CAW! Agreed, Lord Zethus, but we have little time left to us, and I wish to ask all of you to look upon the unremembering Princess Nowar for yourselves…"

He waited then, and said "Look upon her well, dear GentleLords and WistfulLadies, can you not see for yourselves that she has finally come… that she is real? Who here among you now can doubt any longer the prophecy in the Book of Scorns?"

Theopolis, the Octopus had stopped playing his Cello. "I can, I do, I will. Still." And then he resumed his little composition.

Lady Craine nearly popped a cork and said "Theopolis don't be a twit! What in ProbablePolis still possesses you to be so obstinate? Why look at her! Under your vermillion oceans, perhaps you cannot see the new Morning Star, but even the Arthropodicans have managed to witness it, shining bright and blue in the Heavens! If the Morning Star says she is the Child of Destiny, than we must rise to fight Moebius…before it is too late!"

Theopolis seemed underwhelmed by all this talk of prophecy and responded with "Lady Craine, you know as well as I do that Moebius has tricked us all before in a dozen different ways for hundreds and hundreds of turns of the great ribbon. How could we know for sure that she is real? Have her prove it!"

"And what would you suggest, Theopolis?" asked Kaine, slightly impatiently.

"Let me give it some thought and I'll get back to you old friend." said Theopolis. Kaine's eyes rolled.

Nowar took a step forward and said "Lord Theopolis, I am enjoying your music terribly, but I must say that, this time around you may have little choice but to dispense with your skepticism."

Theopolis looked shocked. Apparently Avatars expected more deference, or, at least, he did. Nowar went on, though-

"I now understand that there are times when all we have is faith to go on, and this may be one of those times for us all. For example, I am called an unremembering Princess for good reason. I don't even remember where I came from, or, for that matter, who I really am. If you are looking for me to tell you that the time is at hand to go to war with Moebius, then let me say this- whoever I am, I am quite ready. I will admit that I do not yet truly understand the meaning of the Morning Star, although I found him a most engaging Avatar."

The Amphitheatre was very still now.

"Again, to be perfectly honest with all of you, the Morning Star taught me something I have yet to fully understand, but I appreciate it more deeply than I can say…and the Midnight Shadow, he gave me shelter when Moebius had nearly captured me…why, he is at the gates of DeepSteel even now, is he not, buying time for all of us to join him. He is certainly going on faith, isn't he? Or perhaps not, in fact, since he knows, as do so many of you, that Moebius means to wipe out ALL the pages, all the Kingdoms of ProbablePolis, and, if he can, he'll destroy all of you, all the Avatars, just like he did to Shane. And then where will we all be then?"

"Indeed," interjected Hiram Kaine, "And, if I might add, Princess Nowar, for you are too young to know, that there is a very long litany of Avatars that have come before us all, and all of them were either tricked into fighting each other by Moebius, or murdered by that villains evil devices. Sublime Deb-o-rah Craine, would you share with us your intelligence?"

"But of course. I myself intercepted an Omen-tary sent by King Andironé, intended for King Shard, and I watched its memories for myself before I let the thing fly on to Avalhalla, where it had located King Shard. I saw with my own eyes the foul and swift end that the latest version of the Black Harp made of Shane. I saw the destruction of EverLast with my own eyes."

All the Avatars were silent. Herr Leuchtkäfer broke the silence and said in his old, wizened voice, "I understand zat ze last Dvark Express is in Rantadore, Lord Kaine, and ready to begin collecting machines und creatures of war from every page, in order zat zey be deposited in Koradgia at zee foot of Castle DeepSteel. Is dis so?"

"CAW! CAW! Indeed. The Walrus has brought it, and Nowar as well, brought it to us here, at the behest of the Morning Star. It is fully capable, with its extra-dimensional cabooses, of holding thousands if not millions of troops. Craine and I have already decided that, no matter what we as the united Avatars decide, we will send our own troops into battle with the Midnight Shadow, via the Dwark Express" said Kaine.

Deb-o-rah Craine interjected then- "And Sir Edward Da Veer, the Grand Master of all Free-Machines, has re-assembled the Omega Ring! Soon he will transport the combined might of the King and Queen, together, to join the Midnight Shadow and his armies in Koradgia on the Plain of All-Sorrows. And a new Emperor shall lead them all, dear friends, just as it says in the Book of Scorns!"

Lord Amphion then spoke. "Enough, Lord Kaine and Craine, we have heard enough! Given that we Avatars are now so few, and that Moebius has grown so great in strength with his new Black Harp and Silver Scream, I therefore motion for a vote, here and now, that we supply unanimous support of our troops for an invasion by the United Kingdoms of ProbablePolis of Koradgia and Castel DeepSteel!"

"I second that motion!" said Nowar, with a very determined face, and much to everyone's surprise. Hiram Kaine smiled, as only a Raven can smile, and nodded at her with great approval.

"CAW! CAW! CAW! So moved! Thank you, Princess Nowar. We now have a motion for a United Invasion of Castle DeepSteel by a United ProbablePolis. Any opposed?"

Not even Theopolis said a word, but only nervously twiddled his tentacles. He had stopped playing.

"Any in support?"

Every one of the Avatars said "Aye!"

The crowd went wild. Tearing down into the bottom of the Throne room, the Arthropodicans cheered loudly and picked up Nowar and her Companions on their insectoid shoulders, tossing them all about with great delight for several minutes crying.

"Nowar! Nowar! Nowar!" they cried.

When Hiram Kaine and Deb-o-rah Craine had re-established order, an enormous army of well-armed and eager Arthropodicans accompanied Nowar and her Companions back to the Dwark Express. Lil Bonsai Rex excitedly re-activated the Fuzion engine while the Companions and the Walrus helped assist the armies of Arthropodicans to board their newly minted Dwark-cabooses. Once they were all loaded and the cabooses sealed shut, the Wasp Captain, Don Donovan Keeyotay joined the crew in the control room and helped show Bonsai where the best exit route out of Rantadore was.

In another few minutes, the Dwark Express exploded with unimaginable fury through the roof of the ceiling of the 11th page and soared off into the Dwark at high speed, its cabooses loaded with well-armed Faeries and Arthropodicans.

The war to defeat Moebius had truly begun.

T-minus Eight

And still counting, faithfully...

Brandy was tidying up her cell. It didn't seem to faze her at all that she was in a brig. Why, she'd been in them before, and this one was really a very nice one. For those of you who are still wondering what a brig actually is, think of it as a jail for people in the military, nothing more elaborate, really.

She knew that, eventually, General Scrubblebrine would get lonely, and call for them both to come back upstairs. In the meantime, she found a broom, scrubbed the floor with great vigor, and made the bed. During much of this, she chitchatted with her son, Colonel Shard, who was a little down in the dumps, sitting in the cell next to hers.

"Oh, c'mon, son, lighten up! Did you see the look on Scrubblebrine's face when Nowar zapped out of there? It was hilarious!" she said, and chuckled.

Suddenly, she heard a strange sound. She could hear her son saying "Who are you? What are you doing here?" followed by another strange sound and a lot of silence.

"Shard? Shard? Son, what happened?!! What's going on?!!"

The sound happened again, except this time it was in her own cell, and directly behind her.

Grandma Brandy turned very slowly- holding the broom up like it was a spear. A small boy, perhaps seven or eight years old, stood just a few feet behind her, beaming with a very big smile. He was pale, white skinned, and a thin little fellow, with ruddy cheeks and platinum colored hair.

"Hello, Grandma Brandy. Please don't be afraid. I mean you no harm. I'm here to help."

"You're the one who sent all those emails, aren't you? You're the master program that runs ProbablePolis, aren't you? You're the Logos."

"Yes, yes and yes, I am, Brandy. And I have come here to help re-unite you with your family. If you don't want to come with me, you don't have to, of course."

"Oh no, you don't. You're not leaving me here, boy. You already took my son with you, didn't you?"

"Yes, I did. I have to be ready to un-trifurcate him, you know, but not until the time is just right. In your case, all I need to do is to have you ready to go home. You didn't think I'd leave you here, did you?" and he laughed a laugh like an innocent little boy would laugh.

A few minutes later, General Scrubblebrine nearly burst a vein when he found out that the only two witnesses to all of this mess had vanished without a trace. He sat in his chair in his office, in the darkness, quietly smoking a cigar for a very long time.

T-minus Seven

Every great oak starts as a tiny acorn…

To the skies over Ambrosia the Omega Ring soared, bringing shock troops and sky-vessels; the armies and armadas of the Kingdom of EverGreen. Through the external loud speakers, Sir Edward Da Veer announced the arrival of Evergreens' might at Castle Ambrosia. In fact, you would have had to have been either half-deaf or half-dead to not have heard the booming sounds of the Omega Ring as it approached Castle Ambrosia;

> Now is the winter of our discontent
> made glorious summer by this Daughter of EverGreen,
> this Son of Ambrosia; this Emperor of Urath…
> And all the clouds that low'r'd upon all ProbablePolis
> In the deep bosom of the Dwark shall be buried!!!

No one had any idea what he was talking about, but it sounded very grand, and Edward quietly decided he would use it for his next play, if this war went well, of course.

The Lords of the Court of EverGreen accompanied Queen Limberly to the great circular doors of the Omega Ring forward hull. Through the huge circular windows, they could all see the Omega Ring was slowing as it began its approach, and had started docking procedures with the main Sky-port of Ambrosia. Towers of gold and silver spiraled up into the air, almost as dazzling as the Sky-port of EverGreen.

A minute later the Queen took a deep breath as she walked off the boarding dock. She had not set foot in Ambrosia for almost one hundred and twenty pulses, when she had terminated diplomatic relations with the King, just before she had been captured by Moebius a very long time ago.

She really had no idea what to expect.

A hug had been about the last thing she had expected, but Sir Kai smiled and was allowed to approach her. King Shard, now dressed in full dragon-skin battle-gear stood to the side.

Lord Carderocke, Elberonor and General All-Begone Gideon, a massive half-Ogre, all strode forward to welcome their Ambrosian counterparts aboard the Omega Ring. Clearly, the reunion of the two Kingdoms had been long desired by all, as there were hearty laughs and handshakes and more hugs to go around.

Amidst the reverie, Queen Limberly walked slowly up to King Shard. She had rehearsed a speech, but now found herself speechless.

"I….have…much to say." was about all she could utter.

"That goes for us both…but first, I have someone who is waiting to meet you, and we shouldn't keep him waiting much longer. Come with me, your Majesty."

Though slightly shocked, Limberly followed King Shard up and down several stairways, finally ending up on the largest Launch-pad of Ambrosia. Emptied of Sky-vessels, the size of this launch pad was nothing short of phenomenal. It was as big as a town, and yet, what stood on it made it seem cramped.

The Great Old Drake was there, sitting with its tail curled around it, and its wings outstretched to catch the first warmth of the Pulse, still rising in the East. In front of it, on either side, were two Angels, both so still that they might have been statues. She recognized the one on the right as Menses of the Four Winds, the Plenipotentiate of the High Council of Ambrosia. The other was a one-winged angel whom she had never met.

Queen Limberly had seen the Great Olde Drake, Synarchus Lazarus, only once before, and that had been at a distance. Now, as she stood here, before him, she was quite taken aback. She had never seen anything, or anyone, as big as the Great Olde Drake. He was quite nearly half the size of the Omega Ring.

"We are running out of time, Queen Limberly, and you have yet to remember who you really are. Come forward and know yourself better." said the Great Olde Drake.

Limberly approached, slowly, and Shard walked along side of her. "Things are not exactly as they seem, my Queen. Before we begin this conversation…" he stole a look at the Great Olde Drake, who quietly nodded.

"…before we begin this conversation I would like to ask you to use this harmless device."

She was staring at him. He gently put a small square object in her hand. She looked down at it. It had a blue button that softly pulsed with a gentle blue light.

"What is this?" she asked.

The Great Olde Drake answered, saying "It is called a Memoress device. It will restore your original memories to your residual form."

"What does that mean?"

"It means it will make you whole again." said Shard. "Just trust us. Press the button, Limberly. It will all make sense afterwards."

Limberly, who had been tricked a hundred times by Moebius, and who had always been quite unlikely to trust anyone, anyhow, even before all of that nonsense had begun, was stricken with a severe case of doubt.

"No, I can't." she said and turned away, still holding the device that Shard had put in her hands.

Shard looked desperately at the Great Olde Drake and said "Synarchus?"

The Drake did not bat an eyelash, and it was Menses who spoke then, calmly- "Queen Limberly, of late you have had dreams, nay, nightmares…of a little girl…a little girl in trouble. She calls to you, as if you were her Mother."

Limberly turned to the Angel, with her jaw slightly open, and said "How do you know this?"

Menses did not answer, but Mandrake continued with "She calls to you as if you were her Mother…And you **are**…And she **is** in trouble."

"How do you know this?"

"Press the button, Queen, and all shall be revealed." said the Great Olde Drake.

It almost looked like a struggle, but little by little, Limberly moved her thumb to the button, and closing her eyes, pressed the button, hard. A blue light cascaded across her face, and as she opened her eyes, she shook and trembled, and fell to her knees, sobbing.

All the memories of her life had been restored to her. Shard had rushed in to catch her, and holding her, quietly said "It's ok, just breathe for awhile. Just breathe. Your mind is still integrating your old memories with your new memories. Just give it a minute and the confusion will pass."

When she had caught her breath, she looked up at Shard and said "Where's our daughter? Where's Nowar?"

Before Shard could answer, the Great Olde Drake broke his countenance and laughed with a booming crescendo- "Your daughter has, with a little help from her friends, avoided being captured by Moebius; she has singlehandedly fought the Queen of Mermopolis, and won; she has received the wisdom teaching and blessing of the banished Morning Star; and in this very last hour she has spoken with, and re-united all of the remaining enthroned Avatars of ProbablePolis. She is now currently on the Dwark Express, headed into the Dwark with more than half a dozen loyal Companions, including an Amphisbaena, a Wolven-Kine King, a one-winged Angel, a small Free-Machine, a pygmy T-Rex, a General known as the Walrus, and an Arthropodican Wasp Captain. The Dwark Express currently has several cabooses in tow with two armies in stow, one of them are the rowdy Faeries of Opus Delirious, and the other is the irregular Arthropodicans of Rantadore. Not bad for a little girl, wouldn't you say?"

"Oh dear God." was all Limberly could manage, then she looked back at Shard and said "We have to go get her." And then, a thought passed in her mind and she said "We're in the simulation, Shard, this isn't really real, and it's a simulation for God's sakes! We can go get her right now just by wishing for it, and take her home."

"It's not that easy, Limberly. This simulation is more real than any of us realize, I do believe." said a voice behind them. Pop Bric, still in his General's armor, had quietly walked up behind them.

"Pop Bric!" Limberly cried "How did YOU get in here?"

The Great Olde Drake raised an eyebrow, but it was Shard who then said "Listen to us, Limberly. Dad spoke with the Master Program, the LOGOS, a deal has been struck and a Plan is in motion. If any one of us breaks ranks with the Plan, all the Probabilities will go to hell...it's likely that none of us will get home...and it's most likely that we'll all perish here."

Limberly looked at Pop Bric first, and then, standing, turned to look up at the Great Olde Drake.

"Synarchus, you, the Morning Star and the Builders were the first programs we wrote for this place. I know...how you were...created...I know you are unable to lie. What Shard and Bric are saying...is it true?"

"A superior IQ and a heap of sheepskin certificates will not always make you right, Queen Limberly...just because you were there at the beginning does not give you the ability to see the ending any better than the rest of us, and yes, my dear, what Shard and Bric are saying is true."

He let that sink in for a second and then went on with "The complexities of Probabilities have been magnified beyond anyone's comprehension in the currently loaded hypothecation...mark my words- no one, and no thing, has the ability to see how all the outcomes that may transpire may play out anymore...no one, that is, except the Sanity of the Universe, the Logos himself. The Logos has indeed devised a plan that, if followed to the **N**th degree by all here assembled, is more probable than not to bring an end to Moebius, and allow you all to go home, with your daughter, safe and sound. All that will be required of you, Limberly, is the one thing you have always had the greatest difficulty in supplying…"

"What is that?"

"Trust - the seed of Faith."

"What do we have to do, then?" she asked.

"What you had intended to do in the first place; attack Castle DeepSteel with all your might and vengeance. Spare not a nail and give no quarter. Take no prisoners, and at all costs, keep Moebius completely distracted while I help restore your daughter to her memories, and then help her to meet her final challenge, a challenge that, if won, will see a final resolution to all our woes."

Difficult as it all was to swallow, in the end, Limberly accepted what the Drake was saying. After all, she had been his programmer, and she knew that he was unable to lie.

And so Shard, Bric and Limberly watched the Great Olde Drake fly off from Castle Ambrosia, headed back into the Dwark, escorted by two angels.

Limberly turned to her husband and her Father-in-Law and said "Well, what are we waiting for?"

T-minus Six

Enter the Twinkler...

Nowar sat quietly, looking through the observation window beside her, watching the Dwark rush past her at an incredible speed. Everyone was in their seats, belts buckled and a bit bored. Lil Bonsai Rex, however, was happy as a clam, piloting the Dwark Express, and he made up funny songs with lyrics that only barely worked and hardly rhymed at all. The Walrus was napping, and he snored heavily. Two-Fangs brooded, stroking his chin hairs; Mrs. Machine was doing self-diagnostics; and Ouroboros Alpha-Beta was debating an obscure historical matter with Mandrake the Black and the Wasp Captain, Donovan, who seemed to have an inexhaustible memory for history.

Suddenly, Lil Bonsai Rex grabbed the Captain's microphone and announced loudly "Half an hour to Nafer Deem! Please remain seated with your buckles latched and big smiles on you faces! Tanks a bunch! Love ya! Mean it!" The Walrus woke up, looked around, and went back to sleep.

Nowar suddenly realized that she still had his copy of the Book of Scorns in her pocket, and took it out to peruse the Maps section. She wondered what Nafer Deem looked like. This book could prove to be very useful.

That was when the problem happened. Everyone woke up or was shaken from their travelers distractions by the coughing and sputtering of the Dwark Express. The engine was firing off, popping and stalling.

And they were slowing down.

The Walrus unbuckled his seatbelt and running up to Bonsai said-

"COO-COO-KA-CHEWY! What de problem, Bonsai?"

"Dunno Boss, all de dials were readin fine jez a minute ago…Hokey Shmokes! We is losing containment- oh, man, dee engine gonna blow out!"

Nowar leaped out of her seat and ran over to them both, looking at the Walrus she said "You mean the engine is going to blow up?"

The Walrus laughed and said "No darlin, de Dwark Express don't use a Fizion engine, it uses a Fuzion engine, see? She won' blow **up**, she'll jez blow **out**, kinda like a candle."

Mandrake had joined them and said "But we'll be stranded out here in the Dwark either way, though, won't we?"

The Walrus looked at the Angel and nodded, gravely. Turning back to Bonsai he pointed at the glowing navigational globe on the dashboard and said "Bonsai, whats dat over der? Looks like a shred of a page. She mus' be a pretty big island, maybe de size of Opus Delirious!"

Bonsai moved his claws over the globe and brought the little island into larger resolution.

"Sure nuff, Boss. Dat de last shred of the 180th page…she called de Dangling Dow!"

"Dangling Dow! Alright…can we make it der before de engine goes out?"

"Looks like it boss, I'm changing course now. Everybuggy back in der seats! We iz goin in!"

Nowar watched through her window as the Island came into sight. It was a bizarre scrap of a page alright- a landscape entirely dominated by the colors of black and white, and nothing else. Rolling hills and meadows looked like they had been painted with a black and white chessboard pattern. All the trees and grass and vegetation were beautiful and ornate, but they were entirely black and white. There were no shades of gray here. Balls of light moved slowly here and there through patches of fog and mist. They looked like the Will-o-the-Wisps that Nowar had seen in the UnderRung, but much bigger.

"Dangling Dow" she thought- "I wonder if it still has its Avatar, like Opus Delirious…and I wonder if they're anything like the Morning Star…"

Sputtering and popping, stalling and hemming and hawing, the Dwark Express heaved over a fairly flat meadow of Dangling Dow as it came in for a rackety and uncomfortable landing, sending black and white mud scattering everywhere. Slowing to a screeching halt, sideways, the Dwark Express engine gave one last bang, a sigh, and a wheeze before it extinguished itself.

The lights inside flickered and went out, leaving the crew in near darkness.

"Oh poo." Bonsai was the first to say anything "Auxiliary power is out, Boss…hold on, lemme see what I can do."

The Walrus hunkered over the dashboard with a glow light while Bonsai popped off some control panels and pulled out a tool bag. He was already removing large gears and wiring mechanisms and tossing them behind him.

The Walrus said "Bonsai- do you even know what happened? How did we lose containment? We gots plenty of fuel, don' we?"

"Sure, Boss, we gots a ton a dat HeHeHelium. Now don't you worry, I gonna get her goin' again, jez wait an see… gimme a few minutes an I'll get da juice back on."

Nowar and the rest of the Companions unbuckled their seats and stood up. Outside the observation windows, the Will-o-the-Wisps were beginning to gather, clustering up against the windows and casting a good deal of light into the Control Room. Nowar turned to Mandrake and asked him "Is it safe to go outside? Are these Will-o-the-Wisps friendly?"

Mandrake the Black paused for a second, seemingly lost in his own thoughts.

"Why, yes, Lady Nowar, I can feel their thoughts even now…they are only curious. And they are not Will-o-the-Wisps, so please don't call them that, or you'll upset them. They are Hob-a-Longs."

Nowar gave him a wry look. "OK, I bite. They look just like the ones I saw in the UnderRung, what's the difference?"

"They are larger, older, and possess exceeding cunning. A Will-o-the-Wisp is about as smart as a crow. A Hob-a-Long is far smarter than even a Raven."

"How smart is a Raven?"

Mandrake laughed and said "A Raven, if raised properly, can speak twice as many words as a Parrot, and actually put them together in clever sentences that it itself understands, which a Parrot cannot."

Nowar looked back at Bonsai and the Walrus. The Walrus had pulled out a manual of some kind, and he and Bonsai were arguing over something that they were looking at under the great control dashboard, which was now in pieces all over the floor. They might be awhile.

Going to the side portal, Nowar opened it. The Hob-a-Longs were already there, bobbing about as little licks of lightning spiked from one to the other where they touched. Nowar hopped out and stood on the black and white checker board ground. The Hob-a-Longs cast a surreal light below them amongst the grass and twisted shrubbery that moved slightly with a faint wind.

Two-fangs, Mandrake and Donovan hopped out right behind her, and Mrs. Machine extended her sensors and took readings before she puttered out of the Dwark Express herself. Ouroboros Alpha-Beta was the last to emerge, carefully padding down the steps to the ground.

Nowar was only a few feet away from the Hob-a-Longs and she could already feel their warmth.

She raised her arms in salutation and the Hob-a-Longs immediately bobbed upward in the air, circling each other in excited patterns.

"Greetings, Hob-a-Longs of Dangling Dow, I am Nowar Rondell, unremembering Princess of ProbablePolis."

Much to her surprise, the Hob-a-Longs stopped bobbing about, and formed a very coherent pattern, the smallest of them near the bottom, with successively larger ones collecting at the top of a V-shape. The largest Hob-a-Long, at the top now slowly approached Nowar and changed colors twice from red to blue. His voice, though not made with sound, echoed in her mind with the deepest of tones, saying-

"Well met, Homo Sapiens. You are the Daughter of King Shard and Queen Limberly. Your coming here was foretold to us by our Avatar... I am Adapa Mitote, Senior Warden of the Hob-a-Longs of Dangling Dow."

Mandrake, apparently, was able to hear this telepathic exchange, because he stepped forward and Nowar heard his voice in her own mind, though he directed his thoughts to Adapa Mitote.

"Adapa Mitote, I am Mandrake the White, one of the Companions that guard and guide Lady Nowar. Did I hear you rightly when you said that your Avatar had foretold her coming?"

Adapa Mitote changed from blue back to red and 'said', almost angrily "Foolish Angel! I will dismiss this slight of eavesdropping on our conversation for the moment, but do not try me again! I am no Will-o-the-Wisp or Jack-o-Lantern!"

"No insult was intended, Senior Warden, I was only driven by my insatiable curiosity, and my charge is to be a guardian for Lady Nowar...I admit that I have always heard that Dangling Dow was without an Avatar."

"Nothing is constant in the Dwark except Change, one-wing!" and then, changing from red back to blue, addressed Nowar 'saying' -"You may tell your Angel that quite some time ago we were honored to have an Errant Navigator, an Avatar from another long destroyed page come to us and call our little shred his home...Now, tell us, o Lady of Destiny, what has brought you here, and how may we assist you on your way? May we bring you refreshment?"

Suddenly there came a yell from inside the Control room of the Dwark Express. The Walrus was upset.

"You gotta be kidding me! What you mean you don' have dee right tool? You gots tree o four tool boxes here, you little nutmuffin! You better have de right tool!"

Nowar turned to look back at Adapa Mitote "Thank you, Senior Warden, but we ate just before we left Rantadore at the Court of Hiram Kaine. What we are in need of, though, I believe, is something that you probably cannot offer us, namely…"

"Sorry boss, I thought I brought everything, but I'm missing a wonkilating dilator. I can't pull apart the Fuzion mesh cages without it."

"…namely an engineer. The Dwark Express has an excellent Captain, and a brave pilot, but it appears that the engine that powers our vessel is in need of repair. Do you perhaps know of someone that you might bring here to help fix it?"

The Hob-a-Longs were getting very excited now, bobbing about quickly, starting to dart back and forth, sending little licks of electricity to each other and up to Adapa. The Senior Warden Hob-a-Long approached Nowar, descending slowly. The rest of the Hob-a-Longs were disappearing now, rising quickly into the air, and shooting off into the Dwark. As Adapa Mitote came closer, the hairs on the back of Nowar's neck began to stand on end while the static electricity began to crackle all around her. Two-fangs growled, but Mandrake held his hand up.

"Princess Nowar, you and your companions can now enjoy the greatest of fortune, for our Avatar is a Prince of Engineers. None can compare to his excellent skills in repair, renewal or rebuilding. I have just sent my kin folk to go and seek him out, for he is a wanderer, and takes long voyages into the Dwark, in search of new trinkets and mysteries to pick apart and put back together."

Nowar smiled and the Hob-a-Long continued.

"Stay and be faithful, I will go and assist my brethren, for I believe he is already on his way back to Dangling Dow."

And without another thought or word, Adapa went soaring off into the Dwark, disappearing in less than a second.

Hardly five minutes had passed before the first Hob-a-Longs returned, and Nowar quietly thanked the Logos, since during that time the Walrus and Lil Bonsai Rex were nearly at each other's throats, but for the diplomacy of Ouroboros Alpha-Beta and the stern looks of Two-Fangs and Captain Donovan.

The Hob-a-Longs giggled and danced around the heads of Nowar and Mandrake whispering-

"He's here! He's here! He's here!"

Nowar squinted into the gloom of the Dwark, and began to make out the rest of the Hob-a-Longs, weaving in and out of a stream of tiny twinkling bursts of light. As the host of lights came closer and closer, she was able to make out the spectacle that was approaching.

It was an old man and a wagon. The old man wore a long patchwork overcoat and a ratty looking old bowler hat. He was sitting on a unicycle with his coat-tails flying out behind him, peddling along madly in the middle of thin air, accompanied by a Wagon drawn by two giant Luna Moths. The Wagon looked very old-fashioned, covered in Marquee signs like the kind you'd see on a Tinker's wagon.

Nowar heard Mandrake laugh and she turned to look at him. Mandrake did not look away from the odd sight, but said quietly to her- "Once in a while, you find him…or rather, he finds you; the itinerant itinerant, the narrators last resort- a 'deus ex machina' for the plot, when everyone's painted themselves into a corner…behold the Twinkler!"

As he got closer, Nowar could see that the old man wore big red bushy side-burns, and smoked a small corn-cob pipe. As he closed the distance, coming in for a landing, his smile looked huge, his gold fillings and his blue eyes twinkled. A tiny glowing cuttlefish darted about his shoulders, scattering tiny beads of lights everywhere as it flittered to and fro.

The Wagon came to make the lightest of touchdowns, barely making a sound as the Luna Moths came to rest on the ground of Dangling Dow. Dismounting from his Unicycle, the Twinkler walked over on his big patchwork leather boots and stood in front of Nowar. He smiled from head to toe, and his little cuttlefish skittered behind him. It was just a bit shy about meeting someone new.

"Well, aren't you a sight fer sore eyes." he said quietly, and promptly hugged Nowar. Though a little shocked, Nowar felt very safe, and did not resist. She tried to say "I am Nowar, unremembering…" but she never got a word out of her mouth while the Twinkler said-

"I know **exactly** who you are, me darlin', and I would be delighted to repair the engine of this fine Dwark Express." He then tweaked her nose, patted her on the head and said- "It's been a while since I've serviced one of these babies, but I'll get her fixed up in a jiffy, you just wait."

Pulling the sack from off of his shoulder, he walked up the steps to enter the control room of the Dwark Express, beaming his very fine smile at everyone he met, and giving a hearty greeting to each and every one of them as well. He apparently already knew the Walrus, as there was an immediate exchange of upbeat banter.

"Coo-COO-CA-CHOO-BA! Lookit dis, Bonsai, by my stars and garters, it da Twinkler!"

"And will you look atchyoo, you fine brave Chopper-riding General, you look as young and fit as the fiddle herself, what have you been doing to look so gallant and daper, ol' fellow?"

"Oh, jus stayin out of trouble and layin low, you ol' gray goose, whatchyoo doin' over here, anyhow?"

"O dis shred of a page was a bit lonely, and I took a liking to the Hob-a-Longs an' all. No one seemed to mind, so I set up me shop down under and built me a new Wagon. But enough about my own doings, I hear you have a broken Fuzion engine, is it? I'll just have to take a look."

Nowar was watching all this, and asked Mandrake "Who did you say this guy was?"

But Mandrake had already walked off. She turned to look for him. He was off in the middle of a black and white meadow, sitting on the ground, cross-legged. She walked, slowly, after him, and when she had gotten to about ten feet away from him, she heard the voice of Adapa Mitote in her head, saying-

"The Angel should not be disturbed, Nowar. Come with me, if you like...I will offer you stories of ancient times that will captivate you while we await the repairs of the Twinkler on your vessel."

Nowar turned to look at him and thought "Why, what is he doing?"

"Hob-a-Longs and Angels know each other well. Sometimes we have been allies, and other times not. I can tell by the look and smell of his aura what he is doing now, and he should not be disturbed."

Nowar stood quiet and still, waiting for the explanation she had already asked for. Adapa relented, glowing orange now, and thought to her that "He is deep in meditation. He is making of himself a beacon."

"A beacon for what?"

"For one of his own kind, apparently. Well, is he not only a quarter of an Angel? Why, he must have felt the call of one of his other quarters, or even a half, and is calling back to him, guiding him in…"

"Mandrake the White!" Nowar thought excitedly.

"See, you already knew..and you must know the other quarter, then…"

"Yes, I met Mandrake when he was half an Angel, in the UnderRung. Just before we used the great Lens of Probability, I watched him split into two. It was quite a sight. I'd never seen anything like it."

"Well, then, you will likely be privileged to see the reverse process, for if I am not mistaken, he is likely accompanying the presence I feel approaching us even now."

"What presence do you feel, Adapa?"

"I feel the presence of…of…THAT! Of him! Look up there! He is here already! And he comes with…he comes with the Great Olde Drake himself!"

Nowar looked above her, and beheld a sight that took her breath away. Huge and shimmering, a behemoth of the air he was. More majestic than she could possibly have imagined, the Great Olde Drake was soaring out of the Dwark, headed downward in a spiral like a winged freight train, belching flame and roaring.

When he landed, the entire island shook like an earthquake as he bellowed. Mandrake the Black opened his eyes and stood. Nowar was stunned into silence. Adapa barely twitched.

Mandrake the White walked swiftly toward Mandrake the Black, who held open his arms.

"As in the beginning."

"As in the ending."

And with a crack of bright light, the two merged as one! Mandrake NeverSong turned, with half his face white, and half his face black, to look upon Nowar and the Hob-a-Long.

"Lady Nowar, it is our honor to introduce you to the Great Olde Drake." And then, turning to the Great Olde Drake, said "Synarchus Luminous Lazarus, it is with great pleasure that I now introduce you to Lady Nowar Rondelle, unremembering Princess of ProbablePolis."

"Unremembering for not much longer, Mandrake." he said and laughed. He sat back on his haunches, and Dangling Dow shook again, briefly. Setting something on the ground that was too tiny for Nowar to see, the Great Olde Drake now addressed Mandrake.

"Mandrake, the box of memories is there on the ground. Would you please pick it up, take it to Nowar, and, if you would, do the honors?"

Mandrake bowed, deeply, and without another word, walked to where the Drake had left the device, picked it up, and walked back to Nowar. He handed it to her and the Drake said –

"Nowar, I am the oldest Avatar in all of ProbablePolis. No one but Moebius and the Logos know more about ProbablePolis than I do. I ask you now to trust me and to utilize this device that sits in your hands. It is a simple device, Lady Nowar, built by your very own Mother a very long time ago, to do what it is about to do, with you, as it did with her, and your Father, not so long ago."

"What do I do with it?"

"Simply depress the blue button, and do not look away. Your memories may now be returned to you."

Nowar looked at the simple rectangular box she held in her hand. Was it all really going to be that easy? Just press some silly button and remember who she was? The Drake seemed to have heard her thoughts, because he said –

"Rest assured, there was nothing easy about getting to this moment, for either of us, Nowar. But, if you like, yes, it will now be just that easy."

It was still so hard to believe. Swallowing once, she pressed the button, and hoped for the best.

T-minus Five

Back at Castle DeepSteel…

Duke Moebius was walking down a huge causeway that rolled over the main room of Castle DeepSteel. To call it a room was perhaps an injustice. It was gigantic. You could have fit several cathedrals and a football stadium in it. At the moment it was filled with all manner of flying crawling loathsome cybernetic creatures. Most of them were one part machine, one part organic beast, and one part pure nastiness. They represented the finest creations of Moebius and his staff; a gallery of evil things that lived only to kill and destroy.

Adorned in his finest tight fitting black leather uniform with a red armband, Moebius strode slowly down the causeway, admiring the handiwork of his genetic artisans. Clancy may have turned out to be an incompetent boob in the end, a failure and a consummate disappointment, but he had overseen the development of a studio of the finest caliber, from which Moebius had been able to develop new and foul forms of life, if you could call it that; Scorpion-like robots the size of dinosaurs with giant laser cannons embedded in their tails, Swirling black nets with wicked eyeballs at their nodules and pumping organs filled with acid, Pterodactyls made of steel with telescoping legs and titanium encased claws, hybrid Ogres whose lower bodies were built like tanks. And that was only the beginning- lined up below Moebius were thousands upon thousands of Koradgians storm troopers- Koradgians riding choppers with huge spikes on every wheel, Koradgians servicing Helicopters with vicious mouths of steel, Koradgians cleaning wheeled photon cannons that did their own targeting. The air above him was teeming with his other shock troops, the defectors from Rantadore, the Arthropodican Spiders and Locusts.

Walking just behind and to his right was Moebius' latest assistant, Poopsy. With a modicum of effort, one of Moebius genetic designers had equipped Poopsy with the ability to walk on his own, and Moebius had, with enormous pride, bequeathed to his one and only TeddyBear-of-War a hat that would have fit very well on the head of Napoleon, a

French Emperor that you may or may not have heard of- he was nearly as short as Moebius, but he had much better taste in food and fanfare.

Moebius stopped in front of a dozen Koradgian Generals. He shot one and looked at the rest with a stare that would curdle milk.

"He was thinking about failure, I could tell. Failure is not an option. Learn from his mistake, all of you! You there, what's your name?"

"Hail Moebius! I am General Dobus Drog in charge of perimeter intelligence."

"Of course you are, General, tell me how close the Black Harp is now to entering Koradgian airspace?"

"Another ten minutes at most, my Lord! And the Silver Scream not far behind it."

"Good, make sure the Harp has orders to seek out the SkyWhale, Mare and shoot her down without hesitation. Understood?"

"Yes my Lord, but I monitor all the ToggleWog feeds from the perimeter. Nothing the size of a SkyWhale could be close to our airspace without me knowing it."

"You Koradgians rely too much on your technology, and not enough on your cunning or knowledge of history- the SkyWhale is the second oldest Avatar in ProbablePolis. Among her talents is the ability to move about without being detected."

"Yes, my Lord, but, with all due respect, why does she even bother to come here? How in the world can she help the warriors of the UnderRung against our invincible armies?"

"You dolt. Every Avatar has a host of powers, and one very special power, an attribute. Her attribute is she gives off an aura of courage. Once she enters the airspace, she will activate her attribute, and the armies of the UnderRung will fight three times as hard and twice as long while they are under her shadow. She must be taken down immediately, and the Black Harp should be up to this task. Make sure they don't play around here. Have them take her down without any hesitation, understood?"

"Yes my Lord! Hail Moebius! Hail Hell incorporated!"

Moebius walked away from the goose-stepping, arm flailing Koradgians and took one more look at his sprawling armies. He had nearly walked the entire length of his causeway and stood in front of the General of the Locust Arthropodican Airforce. Lord Ogle-Pod Cromwell was his name, and he was a grotesquely black armored creature. Like all Arthropodicans, he possessed an all-too human-like face, but the rest of him was all-locust. He was the size of a small truck, and his scowl would have sent a shiver up anyone's spine, but Moebius merely patted him on his back and said -

"Good Locust Ogle-pod, are all your squadrons ready for deployment?"

"Our mandibles are open, our gullets are empty, and our weaponry is in good repair. We crave blood. We shall devour our enemies this day, and leave their carapaces to dry in the fetid marches of All-Sorrows."

"Good stuff, your attitude is to die for, Ogle-pod! Don't you think, so, Poopsy?"

Poopsy looked up at Moebius and said, just a little distracted "Oh yes, charming. Good stuff, your foulness."

Moebius turned, now quite ecstatic, pulling down a loudspeaker-enabled ToggleWog to address all his troops.

"Look at you! Yes, look at you! Look at you all!" the sounds below began to die down as he continued, saying "Before me I see the most foul and undeniably formidable fighting machine in all of ProbablePolis."

The cheering was beginning. Moebius continued.

"Today we begin…the conquest of the remaining pages of ProbablePolis…and the good news is that, the idiots have all come here to die! WE don't need to spend our time anymore hunting them down! This is better than fast food, this changes everything. We are going to annihilate THEM ALL NOW HERE!"

The crowd below began to roar.

"Are you ready? Are you ready for the FINAL TWEAK?" he was screeching now.

The roar turned into a cyclone of cheering and thumping and banging. Lasers were firing off haphazardly now.

"Then…let…it…BEGIN!!!!"

Huge windows all along the ceilings burst open, spewing Locusts and other flying machines out into the skies over the Plain of All-Sorrows. Side portals up and down the front walls of Castle DeepSteel slid open allowing tanks and half-machines to rocket out across bridges and ramparts.

The War machine of Castle DeepSteel was belching out onto the plain of All-Sorrows. In moments, they would begin surrounding the creatures, warriors and siege machines of the UnderRung. The Midnight Shadow, who had long since taken on his aspect, standing nearly sixty feet tall, stopped hurling his hooves and heaving his fireball breaths against the main gates as he watched the counter-surge all around him. He swatted several Locust warriors with ease out of the air and used his horn to cleave a helicopter in two.

"Well, we succeeded in getting his attention. If the Logos is with us, Ambrosia and EverGreen will arrive soon. All we need do is fall back to the hills and defend ourselves until the reinforcements arrive. I can scarcely believe that I could not make a dent in the front gate, but we play the cards we're dealt."

Turning about, he crushed several large scorpion machines and bellowed out across the valley to all his troops "Fall back! FALL BACK! FALL BACK TO THE HILLS!"

Moebius, who had walked up to his Observation Tower to get a better glimpse, pulled out his spyglass to watch the orderly retreat. He smiled wickedly. This was good stuff, but where was the publicity, though? All his loyal subjects needed to see for themselves that Hell Incorporated was going to win this Final Tweak.

Suddenly he noticed a Camcordian twittering about at the edge of the stone wall. The Camcordians were Moebius's answer to the Omen-tarys, which were infamously unreliable creatures for him to send messages. Omen-tarys often failed to deliver complete communications, and the durned things were always getting picked up by the resistance. Camcordians, though, were dedicated little synthetic machines that always got a message through to the troops of Moebius, no matter where they were. They looked like a small vulture with a camcorder for a head and electric plugs for tails.

Moebius grabbed the poor creature, twisted its head to point out at the battle scene, turned off its ability to move, and reaching for an intercom device, dialed up Clancy and bellowed loudly "We need some coverage down here, man!"

"Sir?"

"Coverage, man, I said coverage. Our citizens need to see our strength in action. We need MEDIA! This Final Tweak is all about presentation and morale, Clancy. Did you ever perfect my Moebius Mania program, you know the one that will turn on all the Aht Erm'nals and display live broadcasts to all the observers on all the pages whatever we beam to them from a Camcordian?"

"Uh, yes sir, yes I did. It's a little buggy, but it seemed to work just fine last time we tried it out. Would you like me to engage it now?" Unbeknownst to Moebius, Clancy was grinning from ear to ear.

"Yes, yes you little twit, now here's a way for you to worm your way back into my heart after this last rash of utter failures, blow us all away with some coverage of the death scene of the Midnight Shadow. Lock on to the Camcordian I've got right here!" and without further ado, Moebius plugged the prongs on the side of the intercom device into the poor things little head.

"Let er rip, Clancy, just key some bravado into the ticker will you?"

All around ProbablePolis, the monitor terminals that could be found on almost every page, in one place or another, flashed and sputtered to life. Creatures and people of all kinds began to gather to look at these mysterious objects that, for many hundreds of pulses of the great ribbon had been dead and silent. Suddenly, they were broadcasting-

But not what Moebius had asked for.

It was Nowar's face. Whatever it had been that had broadcast the proceedings of the pan-Avatar conference in the Throne Room of Hiram Kaine and Deb-o-rah Craine has done a splendid job of recording the whole event, and Clancy began playing it all back. He quickly entered some text from his screen so that the 'ticker' at the bottom of all the Aht Erm'nals all through ProbablePolis now read –

Book of Scorns prophecies come true? Nowar, daughter of King Shard and Queen Limberly recently appeared in the Court of Hiram Kaine and Deb-o-rah Craine to speak to all the Avatars. Previously recorded coverage. Stay tuned to Moebius Mania News for more developments.

"It is a pleasure to meet all of you..." Nowar began. "And it is even a bit overwhelming to realize that I have the honor and pleasure to speak, at one time, to all of the Avatars of ProbablePolis."

Moebius, utterly unaware of what was happening, whistled a tune as he puttered down to his private lair. It was time to put on his jammies and make some popcorn, maybe a grilled cheese sammy. He barely noticed a few of his Koradgians hunkered around an Aht Erm'nal nearby as it was broadcasting.

"Impressive isn't it?" Moebius called and cackled, blithely. The Koradgians just stared at him, but as they turned to look at him, Moebius got a glimpse of the Avatar Lord Amphion, now mid-way through his own speech-

"...I therefore motion for a vote, here and now, that we supply unanimous support of our troops for an invasion by the United Kingdoms of ProbablePolis against Koradgia and Castle DeepSteel!"

"I second that motion!" said Nowar.

Moebius stopped puttering and watched as the camera panned a horde of thousands of Arthropodicans screaming their ecstatic support of

Nowar. His smile melted like wax as he watched them pick up Nowar and her Companions, and tote them all off-screen.

"I am going to put you in my largest blender, Clancy, and leave it on the lowest speed for longest blend, and maximal pain."

He continued down the hall to his lair. Poopsy quietly followed him, but did not say a word.

T-minus Four

The Great Olde Drake explains all…

When Nowar let go of the button, the blue light danced in her eyes, and she dropped to her knees.

She had, on Earth, accumulated only about ten and a half years of memories and life experience, but as it flowed back into her, she began to laugh, cry and, finally, smile deeply.

After a minute of silence, still kneeling, she looked up at the Great Olde Drake.

"I feel like a river that has had two streams flow into it. I am…a little girl…and I am…a Princess."

"Yes, and how does it feel?" was all the Drake said.

"It feels…wonderful…But I have so many questions."

"I understand. We have time for only a few….maybe just a couple. Go ahead, Nowar…ask and you will receive."

"Why did this whole thing happen this way? How did it all begin?"

"The 'how', I can easily tell you, but not the 'why'…for **that** you will have to dig deeper yourself upon your return, if indeed you and your family can all make it home. What I do know is that there was once a man in your world that attended a prominent school…and he gave wonderful presentations on the nature of stars and nebula and black-holes, on the mysteries of time and space and the Theory of Everything. One day, though, he surprised everyone when he claimed that 'the physics of wormholes might make it possible to create a baby universe of our own in a laboratory'."

The Drake paused to see if Nowar understood. She nodded and continued to listen.

"Well, Nowar, someday you will undoubtedly discover that to speak of a *plausibility*, thus clothing it as a *possibility*…is to take the first step in turning it into a *probability*. This is the power of the Word, my dear…and so, one of the students of this man, sitting in the audience of one of his presentations was utterly captivated by the possibility of his ideas, and he in fact went on to create an experiment in which an intense and gigantic amount of heat and energy were used in an incredibly pressurized chamber, enabling him to open a wormhole, serving as a kind of umbilical cord, connecting your own universe to a much smaller and newer one…ours. At the time he was hailed by scientists all over your world – creating a baby universe gave them all an unprecedented view of a universe as it came into being. A little baby big bang, if you like…"

"The student was Moebius, wasn't it?"

"Yes, yes, Nowar, the student was Moebius."

"How did he become so evil…so…twisted?"

"Well, perhaps I oversimplify here, but, arrogance removes humanity, and humility re-enforces it. Moebius lost his ability to keep himself within due bounds of his fellow creatures. He began to see himself as better than everyone else, and when someone starts to do that, they have launched themselves on the slipperiest slope of all. He started off with the best of intentions, but the best of intentions often pave the road to hell. He transformed himself, as he developed his own little baby universe from a scientist…into…a demiurge. His own self-perceived importance twisted his soul into…hah…a Moebius strip!"

Nowar thought about this for a moment and then said "Where are my Mother and Father right now? Where is Pop Bric?"

"They are all on a mighty battle-ship called the Omega Ring, driven by the Free-machine called Edward Da Veer. The Omega Ring will be de-dwarking over the plain of All-Sorrows any moment now, I feel, and joining the Midnight Shadow and his armies in their attack on Moebius and Castle DeepSteel, which is likely going badly, I fear."

"I want to go to them now, can you take me?"

The Drake remained very silent. Nowar suddenly noticed that Mandrake had left them alone. The Drake said, with very carefully measured words "I can, Nowar. I could indeed take…you…to them…"

"But you don't want to? Why? I'm not a coward! I've fought my way to get here, I deserve to fight by their side, don't you think?"

The Drake's demeanor changed, he laughed and said "Oh my dear, yes, you have long since proven your mettle in ProbablePolis, and my hesitation has nothing to do with any perceived doubts about your capabilities, Lady Nowar."

"Then…what is it, why your hesitation?"

"This may be confusing Nowar, but the last three times we've done this, you did not take my advice."

"Your advice? What advice? You haven't given me any!"

"Of course not! Why, you've refused it the last three times I've offered it! I do believe I would be wasting my breath, though I am honor-bound by the Logos to at least mention your other option."

"My other option? What do you mean?"

"You have two options really. You may go with me …out there, into the Dwark, to face and fight the greatest foe of all ProbablePolis, or you may do what you've done the last three times this has happened…"

"I don't understand what you mean…we've done this before…three times?"

"Yes, yes, we have…all of us…" and he sighed, saying "…it would be difficult to explain, as it involves the complexities of the big world in how things done 'out there' affect things done 'in here'…so you should trust me for the moment when I tell you that the last three times you were offered your two options, you stayed with the Dwark Express, which will end up visiting several more pages, collecting one army after another, and ultimately ending up at Castle DeepSteel, no matter whether you go with it or not…and the last three times you did this, you shared with us all in the greatest of defeats in front of Castle

DeepSteel on the Plain of All-Sorrows. You and your family have already perished thrice and for all time under the malice and might of Moebius and his war-machines in several gigantic and cataclysmic ends…dramatic, fantastic, and…tragic"

Suddenly Nowar felt a strange feeling through her whole body, as if she really had done this before, at least once…

"What you are experiencing now, Nowar, on your world is called "déjà vu". For some people it happens often enough, while for others, it may never happen at all; it is the feeling that you have when you feel as if you have been here before, that you have done what you are doing right now, at least once before. It is an indescribable and odd feeling, is it not?"

Nowar nodded, feeling quite spooked.

Suddenly, and without any reason, she saw in her minds-eye the Queen of Mermopolis, Riganna O Nanna, whom she had bested in combat, and who, having come to her senses, had given Nowar a prescient and haunting abjuration.

Nowar looked down at the ground. Out of her pocket had fallen the *Remembrance-arium,* the special crystalline egg that she had taken from the opulent guest room of the Queen of Mermopolis. It sat there on the ground, in the mud, glowing softly. Nowar squinted; she could see herself and the Queen speaking to each other, just before Nowar was about to enter the Dwark-gate to follow her Companions on the Purple Brick Road. She reached down and picked it up, the Queen was telling her-

"Be very careful out there, my dear one, and listen carefully to what I will tell you- Dobbs, bless his soul, said to me only a few pulses ago that he foresaw something would be out there in the deepest Dwark someday- someday soon, or someday already past… something that was not fashioned in the creation or the larger hypothecation- something black, something big- no, not big, but huge, Nowar, huge beyond all our reckoning- something unnatural that Moebius is about to call out of a place of unspeakable evil, at the end of all time, and beyond all space."

"What is it?" Nowar had asked, to which the Queen had responded-

"I sense that you will only learn more about this abomination by following that brave angel and your companions, gone before you, there-" and she gestured at the Gate into the Dwark, still rippling occasionally.

Nowar looked away, and put the *Remembrance-arium* back into her pocket.

"So, the deal is that I stay with the Dwark Express and join the battle…"

The Great Olde Drake looked heartbroken.

"-or I go with you to fight something…evil, something waiting for us out there, in the middle of the Dwark, in the heart of darkness…those are my two options, right?"

"It is called the Slithery Tove, Nowar. It is indeed a thing greater and more sinister than even Moebius himself. It is evil, cubed. It was called into being, inadvertently, by one of the more wicked techno-magical devices that Moebius has ever created. It lives, now, on the very edge and membrane of our known universe, attached to the great spherical crystalline wall that contains all of the Dwark and ProbablePolis itself, the 'Dwarkopologue'. There on the Dwarkopologue it has attached itself, feeding on anything it can find out there in the Dwark, and it grows….it is already far bigger than all the Pages of ProbablePolis put together. Unchecked, it will eventually devour all that lives, everything that moves, all of the Pages themselves even. In the end, unless it is defeated, it will destroy everything and everyone…everywhere."

Nowar stood quietly on the checkerboard landscape of Dangling Dow, watching the breeze sway the black and white trees to and fro, not saying a word. Then, she looked at the Great Olde Drake squarely in his eyes and said-

"Let me go say goodbye to my Companions, then."

The Drake said not a word in response, but as Nowar headed back to the Dwark Express, he curled his tail around himself and smiled.

T-minus Three

From bad to worse...

Something that looked like a cross between a huge metal pterodactyl and an aircraft carrier, called a Craven Frigate, thudded savagely into the Midnight Shadow with a sickening 'thud', hurling him over onto his side. The hull of the thing burst asunder as the Midnight Shadow desperately thrust his horn into it, and a thousand wasp-shaped cyborgs exploded into the air, firing their laser cannons everywhere. All across the battlefield smoke rose as metallic Scorpo-pods and gruesome Ogre-tanks rolled into and over the UnderRung forces.

The Final Tweak was going very badly for the resistance. The Midnight Shadow was quick to get back on his feet and eject fireballs from his mouth that began to melt the Craven Frigate, now screaming and writhing in pain, but, alas, the truth was apparent: at least a third of the army of the UnderRung lay broken and dead all across the plain of All-Sorrows, littering the black road from the still sealed gates of DeepSteel to the hillocks where the survivors were making their last stand. The trolls, giants and ogres of the UnderRung had fallen back to the hillocks at the edge of the plain and had taken defensive postures wherever they could. Wagons were circling and being thrown over to act as cover. Behind these ad hoc barriers, the warriors of the UnderRung hurled explosive charges and fired huge spears from the last of their giant siege machines, but their numbers were quite obviously thinning.

And nightfall would be coming soon; the pulse in the sky was beginning to dip low over the horizon.

From the high rampart of Castle DeepSteel, the General of the Locust Arthropodican Air force, Lord Ogle-Pod Cromwell, squatted and licked his antennae with his mandibles.

"This will be only too easy." he laughed, commenting to another giant Locust-warrior that had just crawled up to him. The two black-armored Arthropodicans surveyed the grizzly battle for a few minutes together. The smoke, the storm clouds, and the growing gloom were hampering visibility for many, though the Locusts saw as well in the dark as in the light.

"When do we feed, my Lord?"

"Soon, soon, ThrottleWit. We are to wait until we see the Black Harp enter the fray. I have my orders. Be patient, I am told the Black Harp is due any moment now, along with the rest of the fleet, enough Battle-Ships to make quick work of these fools, and their reinforcements, if they're brave enough to show after this fine slaughter finishes"

"Our Force grows restless, my Lord. The Scorpo-pods and Ogre-tanks are getting all the good kills."

"We wait our turn according to the command of Duke Moebius." Ogle-Pod snarled.

Suddenly, the darkening gloom lifted. Clouds that had begun to swirl into the valley over the plain began to part, shedding rays of light through the smoke. A shape many times the size of the Midnight Shadow himself had lurched into the sky over the remaining armies of the UnderRung and sailed down into view. An incredible series of sounds, like that of a dozen orchestras, was welling across the sky.

Doom was postponed. The SkyWhale had arrived. Cruising slowly and deliberately, Gnosticius Mare circled the land below like a huge cetacean angel, her lungs working like a whole series of gigantic church organs, pumping the most inspiring music you had ever heard all across the Valley of Koradgia, lifting the hearts of the UnderRung warriors below.

A human from Earth might have recognized the melody as "Ave Maria".

To the surprise of Robo-scorp, Ogre-Tank and Wasp-bots, the forces of the UnderRung had gotten their second wind, and they began to fight with an incredible verve, hurling themselves into shields and jumping across gaps to drag down opponents. A Medusid managed to grab a laser cannon and used it to mow down a dozen Koradgian soldiers in a heartbeat. A goat-headed Phooka commandeered an Ogre-Tank and began to drive it into the ranks of the Robo-scorps. Everywhere the roar of a new gallantry overtook the black synthetic creatures of DeepSteel as the UnderRung troops cried out and burst over their burning wagons.

For an instant, as hot steel clashed against cold steel, it almost seemed as if there might be a ray of hope riding in with the last pulse of the day. Few might have noticed it, but through the patches of smoke and grit, a blue star twinkled far above in the sky.

And then the Harp showed up. Very few of the UnderRung troops noticed it at first, although the Locusts on the walls of the Castle cheered when they caught sight of the black infernal machine, taking its time, slowing down as it came to a stop, not far from the gates of DeepSteel. The Koradgian commander of the Black Harp was receiving orders directly from the Castle High Command-

> **Destroy the Whale. Aim for the head. Easy sport, just make sure she is dead.**

Moebius had often trained his Generals to give orders that rhymed.

Gnosticius Mare, sensing what was next, began to circle higher and higher over the Plain, but she did not stop singing all the while. In fact, she sang louder and louder, singing as if this would be her last song.

"It's a wonderful opera…" she thought- "…it just hurts like hell."

The Harp started to gain altitude, but began discharging all of its massive laser cannons on the Whale in wave upon wave of horrible and painful explosions, shattering half of her face with a sickening sound, and, as the barrage continued, sending her careening, bellowing, to a massive and earth shaking avalanche, skidding across half of the Plain of All-Sorrows.

And then she moved no more. Not even a twitch. The small wren that had been riding on her all this time cowered between two large rocks.

Still lashed to the black armored deck of the Harp, the Elvish King Andironé had awoken just in time to see the death of the SkyWhale, and he sobbed in anguish and pain.

The heart of the Midnight Shadow sunk, deeply. Even now, he could see through the deepening gloom and smoke that a new cloud was forming over the Castle, a cloud of black-armored Locusts, coming to make an end of his last warriors, once and for all. Perhaps only a few hundred of them were left anyway, and they were falling back once again to fight from behind their crushed and burning wagons as the Robo-scorps and Ogre-tanks cackled and renewed their dark assault.

The Midnight Shadow pawed the ground and snorted. Blowing smoke and grime out of its way, the Harp was coming for him now. He furled his face, scowled, and sucked in his breath as powerfully as he could. He would make an end of this as only an Avatar could, of fireballs and gusts of great fiery wind. His hooves would strike and split the strings of the Harp, and silently he swore he would avenge the death of Gnosticius Mare before he himself fell to this damned thing.

Taking a single step forward he bellowed-

"I regret I have only one life to give, Moebius, but it is still a GOOD DAY TO DIE!" and rearing on his back legs, he prepared to leap into the Harp with all his force. A glorious end to a glorious life, he thought to himself.

"BUT NOT QUITE YET!" came a hundred booming voices nearly as loud as his own voice, accompanying an explosion of light and a blast of thunder that shook the battlefield. A great object shaped like a colossal horse-shoe had come out of nowhere, slamming into the Harp with such a sudden and surprising impact that the Midnight Shadow himself almost fell over backwards.

"What in the name of the Logos!" he yelled as he stumbled backward on his rear legs.

The Omega Ring had arrived. The voice had been the hundred loud speakers on the outside hull, courtesy of the valiant free-machine, Edward Da Veer.

On-board the Omega Ring, the King and Queen had given complete and total, executive authority to the new Emperor, naming Bric the Admiral of the Fleet and Commander of the Omega Ring. They had made everyone completely aware that Bric was in charge and that there was to be no second-guessing or belly-aching. Sitting at the helm in the middle of the circular command chamber, Bric was at the edge of his seat, intensely watching the main screen, perhaps thirty feet in length in front of him on the opposing wall.

"Alright, Da Veer, we just bought the Unicorn and his troops some time, lets fire ALL cannons on the Harp, ASAP. I want to see her keep spinning, so let's keep it up!"

"Aye, aye, sir." responded Edward. "Firing arrays one through thirty on carefully calculated targets. Maximal spin assured, Admiral."

The Harp was, in fact, still spinning, its crew reeling from the impact of the Omega Ring. It listed to one side, and before the crew could regain command of the dorsal stabilizers, the Omega Ring's full laser cannon fire began tearing into the black armor and hull of the Harp, spinning it even more. It was barely off the ground now, and whipping from side to side furiously.

Andironé had long since been hurled free of his bonds, and in his weakened state, rolled across the battlefield. He coughed spasmodically, but managed to gasp and remain conscious. His vision, blurred from the blood that had dried all around his eyes, barely made out a grand grenadiers grenade, within arm's length of his body. "What great fortune" he thought. It must have fallen out of the hands of its owners without blowing up, as it still retained its firing pin.

Andironé did not allow his excruciating agony to prevent him from looking about, though, and he quickly realized that an Ogre-tank had lurched into view; several Locusts laughed as they sat on top of it. The Ogre-tank was barreling down on him non-stop. Gritting from the pain, Andironé reached for, and grasped the grenade.

"For EverLast!" he cried, just before the explosion blew a crater out of the ground, taking himself, the Ogre-tank, and several Locust warriors into oblivion.

Back on the Omega Ring, Edward was making reports to all the Elves and Dwarves at their posts, but especially to the Queen, the King and Emperor Bric.

"We have identified about three dozen battle ships less than a kilometer at 60 degrees above, 40 degrees starboard, and more than forty battle ships about two kilometers away at 30 degrees above and 60 degrees port."

"Alright, let the Unicorn back in and back us out. Get us above both those fleets, tout suite!" roared Bric, "We'll need some altitude before we let our own fleet disembark into this mess. Give me some float Da Veer, full speed up and then come about. Notify the Captains that we'll let the Sky-vessels discharge after we come in behind the enemy vessels."

"Aye, aye, Admiral."

"That's still Emperor to you, son."

Edward laughed and took the Omega Ring into an incredible, sweeping, high altitude climb, and then headed into a sharp turn, zooming down to come behind the enemy Battle Ships. He reported in again to Bric, saying-

"All two hundred and forty Captains have reported in that they and their crew are strapped into their command chairs on their own Sky-vessels."

"I will take the SS Shrike." said King Shard, leaping out of his chair.

"And I'll take the SS Kaheela." said Queen Limberly, jumping out of hers.

Bric looked at them both, about to head out and off of the Bridge. He snarled at them - "Heroism but only to a point, kids. Keep your heads on strait and don't lose your cool! Long range sensors show that this is just the first wave of their battle ships, so there's plenty more where these came from. Keep them distracted while Da Veer and I pound the Castle walls of DeepSteel. We have got to penetrate that nut before the

Dwark Express gets here, or we'll just see a repeat of the defeat of the UnderRung troops, got it?"

"Yes, sir!" they called back, and were gone. Bric turned to the main screen, watching a giant Black Unicorn kicking the tar out of the Black Harp as the Battle Ships were beginning to scatter, aware that the Omega Ring had just taken up position behind them.

"You got your second chance, blackie, don't blow it." he whispered.

"Admiral? We're in position."

"Excellent, give me a serious volley, full array of blast at highest intensity for thirty seconds on the largest of the cruisers, and then order our own fleet to disembark and engage. Direct Fleet Ambrosia Sky-vessels to our port, and EverGreen Sky-vessels to our starboard. We will make a downward sweep and take on the largest in the center. We'll stay in formation until they start to scatter, and then you and me are headed into the upper atmosphere to assess the strength of the rest of the destroyers."

"What about the troops? When do we let them off?"

"They'll have to hold tight until we break the back of Moebius' fleet. I'm not letting them off until we can command every inch of that battlefield down there. We're going to need every one of those lads before the day is done, Da Veer."

Da Veer agreed, silently admiring, for the first time in his long silicon career, the mind of a carbon-based protein life form. This Emperor was a valiant and worthy soul, and Edward had already taken a liking to him. In fact, he felt suddenly that he would follow this Emperor to the ends of the world.

Back down in the black bowels of Castle DeepSteel, Moebius had fallen asleep in front of his main screen, just moments before the Omega Ring had arrived. Right up until then, after all, things had been getting kind of boring; the Harp was a proven Avatar-killer, and the Midnight Shadow was already in a weakened state. There was hardly anything left of the UnderRung armies anyway…Ho hum stuff. Moebius figured that, by the time the Dwark Express showed up, he'd be awake again to watch his hundred-some battle ships pound the last of the resistance into the dust, and then he could take his bubble bath and sleep through the rest of the night in blissful peace. The Silver Scream Nine would be here soon enough to await the coming of the Avatars as well. A few winks wouldn't hurt anything, especially now that victory was so obviously theirs.

On his lap was a half eaten bowl of ice cream, and all around the room were Koradgian storm troopers watching with fascination as the battle going on outside the Castle was now at odds with Moebius' pre-slumber expectations. The Koradgians were quite unsure about waking up their beloved Dark Lord, who was known to fire first and ask questions later if he didn't wake up on his own, especially if there was any sort of bad news to report.

Poopsy, still remotely under the control of agent Boodleberry, began to amble off down the hallway, occasionally saluting a Koradgian guard or some other slithery minion, saying "Hail Moebius!"

Boodleberry and his superiors knew an opportunity when they saw one. They also knew that the walls of Castle DeepSteel had been designed carefully by Moebius. They were made of the same stuff as the Dwarkopologue itself, all but impenetrable. The Omega Ring might pound them all-day long without so much as scratching them whatsoever. It was time for the bear of very little brain to make a smart move.

T-minus Two

A last word with the Twinkler...

As Nowar approached the Dwark Express, she was acutely aware that she might be seeing her friends for the last time.

Mandrake was the first of her Companions that she encountered on her return. She knew he probably was the only one who had an inkling what was really going on. They hugged without a word, although Nowar had to ask him at least one question, maybe two. She didn't know if she would ever see him again.

"Mandrake, do you think you will ever be whole again? Will you ever find your other two quarters? Will you ever have back both of your wings someday?"

"No one knows what the future may hold for any of us, Nowar. Only the Logos knows which note will sound on the keyboard of life. It is not for us to discern, except where the Logos will lift the veil."

"Well, I hope I get to see you with both your wings someday, Mandrake."

Mandrake smiled and bowed, whispering "My Lady, it was an honor to serve you. Before you say goodbye to the others, you should go and sit for a moment with the Twinkler. His observations are always very useful. No one walks away from him without a gift in their hands."

Nowar nodded, and then walked up to the entrance to the Dwark Express control room. She smiled at Two-Fangs, who watched her carefully- she patted Alpha-Beta on both of their heads, and then she noticed Mrs. Machine was still in a quiet, diagnostic mode. Bonsai Rex and a bunch of rowdy Faeries were sitting around a milk-crate playing pea-nuckle and cheating each other blind. The Walrus was sitting in the Captains chair, asleep, and snoring loudly. She let them all be, and ducked under the opening to the inner engine chamber, now completely disassembled.

The inner engine chamber was a fairly large spherical place, lit by a pale burgundy light. It had strange orifices at equal intervals all across its surface that contained objects that looked like gun barrels. In the center of the room were two sets of metallic spherical cages, one inside the other, and each composed of several bands of shiny silver metal. The Twinkler had started taking them apart, and was using a strange tool to 'heal' each band, very slowly, where it had eroded. It reminded her of a welding tool. He had his back to her, but must have somehow heard her over the hissing sound his tool made, because he said, loudly-

"Good Lord but these cage bands must be over thirty pulses old; they were all about to fall apart at the seams! I'm having to repair them all by me naked eye, don't you know!"

Nowar watched him at his work for a few moments. He was quite skillful in what he did, his hands moved swiftly, and with enormous confidence. Once a band was repaired, he used his tool to re-install it into its ensconcement, which hung suspended by thin wires from the top of the chamber. Suddenly she realized that, regardless of what he needed most at the time, be it drill, screwdriver, hammer or metal-file, his tool seemed to change itself, silently, perfectly, from one tool to another.

"What an amazing tool that is!" she finally exclaimed.

The Twinkler turned to her and smiled broadly, his gold fillings gleaming in the dim light.

"Sure it is, darling." and walking up to her, he handed it to her saying "This is the Utility of Fidelity. Whatever the need is that is at hand, this tool will figure it out and change itself, flawlessly, to the shape and purpose that is most needed at the time that it is used."

In her hands it glowed for a second and turned from a welding tool into something else, a thick white wand of sorts, with magical symbols on it and three golden spheres of light rotating slowly around one end. The symbols were a bird with a very long neck, a butterfly, and an anvil.

Nowar looked up at him, for he was quite tall, even taller than she, and asked him "Where did you come from?"

"Why, from the Holy Lodge of Eternity, where all the Avatars came from, my dear."

"I don't really understand what that is, but, how did you come to be…a…traveler…a tinkerer in the Dwark?"

He took the Utility of Fidelity gently from Nowar's hand and turned back to his work. The Utility quickly morphed back into a high powered welder's tool as he continued with his repairs, saying –

"I was once the Avatar of the twenty-third Page, a Kingdom called Shangri-La…'twas a beautiful world, don't you know, perhaps the most beautiful and precious page that was ever created in all ProbablePolis. It was a landscape of lily pads and lakes, of rolling mountains and gentle thunder. There were Libraries and Schools of great learning, there were palaces where there were no rulers, only love and learning and liberty. The sky was always a pleasant amber in color, and the clouds shed the lightest of rain to cause the flowers to rise and shed their sweetness in the evening air, filled with songs and laughter."

Nowar watched him for a little while longer and asked- "How can you bear to live in a world where such a lovely home is gone and you have to travel all the time?"

"It's always easier to focus on the bad and lose sight of the good, I suppose, but gratitude is the rain that flowers the soul…perhaps, from one point of view, in Shangri-La I became a complacent 'home-body', and perhaps my internal growth had ceased…do you see what I mean? And over the pulses of the ribbon while I have had to remain perpetually on the move to stay free and alive, in the course of my traveling I have discovered a number of things I am blessed to be able to share with you now, Nowar, things about traveling, things about the three great blessings of this life."

Nowar blurted out -"My own travels have been harried and hurried, and I haven't been able to really enjoy the things I have seen at all. I suspect you have been as well, so what's so great about traveling?"

He stopped welding for a moment and laughed. Then, as he started again, he said- "Hurried or harried matters not, for the World is a book, and those who do not travel it read but only a page."

He looked back at her and smiled, continuing with "Furthermore, remember this for your next adventure, Nowar, that a good traveler has no fixed plans, and is not intent on arriving."

"But you've enjoyed traveling."

"I have, after all, haven't I? Well, I think that travel comes from some truly deep urge to see the world, like the urge that brings a worm to inch itself out of the muck of its bog to see the light of the great Pulse at high noon…and I also have the considered opinion now that wandering re-establishes the original harmony which once existed between a soul and its universe."

She watched him finish the last band, carefully screwing it back into place and re-hanging the two cages, now complete and repaired, on their wires.

"You mentioned the three great blessings of life…"

"Yes…YES! The three great blessings of life, Nowar- they are Faith, Hope and Charity."

He re-clipped his Utility of Fidelity back on his utility belt, and knelt down beside her where she sat while he put all his materials back into his bag. He then looked at her and said – "Which of these three do you think is the greatest?"

"I don't know, really. Tell me, please." She said. He smiled again and did.

"Faith dissolves in the sight of that which we had faith in, does it not? And Hope disappears when the object of our longing is fulfilled…but, Charity extends a thousand years beyond the grave."

"I don't understand."

"I know, I'll have to show you." And then he unclipped the Utility of Fidelity from his belt and handed it to her as he said "Here, I give this to you. May you live to wear it, and may you discover the value of Charity by it. It will serve you well in what you are about to do. Only remember this one thing, please, that the seed of Charity lies in forgiveness. One cannot be charitable, until one has forgiven. Remember this well, and you may live to give your Fidelity to someone else yourself someday, I feel certain."

"No, no Twinkler, surely you'll need this again more than I."

"Oh no no NO! The Utility of Fidelity is a funny thing, Nowar, you can never get a new one until you have given away the old one." And with a smile he moved his coat away so that Nowar could see that, indeed, another one had materialized right on his utility belt, exactly like the first one that she now held in her hands.

She wasn't sure what to say next, but she smiled, and he smiled back at her.

"You know, time is the way the Universe keeps everything from happening at once, but now I sense the time for you to leave is at hand, Nowar. Now that the Fuzion engine is repaired I want to make sure you see one last thing, come with me to my Wagon."

As they walked out to his Wagon, Bonsai Rex squealed with delight and hurriedly woke up the Walrus. Everyone started to help put the control doors and panels back together to reseal the engine room. In a few moments they would be ready to go.

As Nowar walked out into the fresh air of Dangling Dow she saw the Hob-a-Longs were still hovering off a slight distance, watching them both as they walked up the creaky steps to the entrance of the old Wagon. As they entered, she realized it must have been built using the same principles as the Dwark Express cabooses, for it was, inside, simply enormous. At first she thought it was only the front room of the Wagon, but walking through the second door, she looked down one hallway after another, each one lined with countless small storage bins from floor to ceiling.

"What on earth do you keep in all these little storage bins?" she asked the Twinkler.

He pulled one out and from it removed its contents. His fingerless gloved hand held a small glass with a tiny shred of plant and dirt."

"I spent more time than I care to relate in the task of recovering every shred of my beloved Shangri-La. I have been collecting them since my Page was destroyed."

"Why?"

"I can't spoil the surprise…but I will tell you this, I have something very beautiful in mind that I intend to do with all of them, or I wouldn't have bothered collecting them all… It has something to do with Faith, Nowar, and who I place my trust in…"

He was silent for a moment, and said "Time for you to go…remember this as well, Nowar, that the more childhoods you can live, the better…"

The Companions were very upset when they found out that Nowar was leaving them to go off with the Great Olde Drake. Nowar told them that she would do her very best to get back to the battle at Castle DeepSteel as soon as she could, and Mandrake helped Nowar explain to them all, and in time, they all accepted that this was the way it had to be.

Alpha-Beta cried anyhow, and Mrs. Machine was upset as well, but Two-Fangs only said "May the Logos be with you, Nowar Rondelle. I hope we meet again someday."

The Walrus seemed surprisingly bashful, and Nowar told him "I'm sorry I won't get to ride on your Hardly-bathing-soon. It sounded like it would be great fun."

"Oh, you never know, Nowar, you may get your chance yet. I think you iz doin de right thing, and dats way more important. But right now, I iz gonna have to ask you for dat Book of Scorns. I iz gonna need it to make sure dat Bonsai Rex doesn't get us lost agin."

And so the Dwark Express blasted off, and Nowar rode the Great Olde Drake, holding onto his veritable forest of mane as she sat on his long neck. The wind in her own hair was awesome and she felt invigorated and free. She no longer cared about her destination…the advice of the Twinkler was beginning to sink in; she had become a true traveler, and for just a moment, she also thought she could see the Morning Star, way off in the distance, glimmering ever so slightly, just before the Great Olde Drake turned their course off into the deep, dark Dwark.

Once the travelers had disappeared, the Twinkler scratched his head and then pulled out a small time piece, attached to his coat by a thin, silvery cord. He and Adapa Mitote stood, or hovered, in silence. Adapa was the first to break that silence with a thought directed at the Twinkler.

"Our work here is done, my Lord. I will leave you to your last good works."

"Grateful am I, Adapa. May you be yourself, old friend."

"And you as well..." Adapa responded, just before he disappeared in a flash.

Now utterly alone, the Twinkler pulled out his Utility of Fidelity, which had magically become a fiddle and bow. Without a moment's hesitation, he began to play…and a minute later he started to sing as well-

"When a sea of names engulfs the Geography,

Tis then that the Traveler will take up his fiddle,

And be on his way…and be on his way…

For tis he that knows, and grows and sows,

Life is the long walk home…oh, Life is the long walk home"

Over and over he sang the refrain and, as he sang and played his fiddle, the two giant Luna Moths that had brought him back to Dangling Dow took wing, drawing his Wagon up and off, into the air. They circled above him and around Dangling Dow, flying faster and faster as the Twinkler stopped singing but continued to play his fiddle with a frenetic energy, fiddling faster and faster, building into a frenzied fugue.

Suddenly the Wagon burst open and the whirlwind that had been started began to suck out the countless little boxes and fragments of Shangri-La that had been under-glass. Freed from their glass containers, the fragments began to fill the air, swirling and twirling, making it utterly impossible to see the Twinkler, who did not stop playing.

When the music finally faded, the Twinkler, his Wagon, and Dangling Dow itself were gone!

The shreds of Shangri-La had coalesced into a whirling, silvery ball that continued to grow in size, until it became absolutely enormous.

ProbablePolis now had a Moon, as well as a Star.

The Prophecy was two-thirds complete.

T-minus One

To Dwark or not to Dwark…that is the question

Nightfall had come to the Plain of All-Sorrows, but the firefight going on in the air was keeping the whole landscape fairly well lit. The Sky-vessels of Ambrosia and EverGreen engaged with the black battle-ships of DeepSteel from one end of the sky to the other, screaming through the air and pummeling each other with streaming blasts of fiery laser strikes. Mighty cannons of steel were hurling projectiles everywhere.

"What's our status, Da Veer?" Bric barked.

"We've done well, Emperor. We've destroyed nearly half the fleet and incurred losses of only two dozen Sky-Vessels. The rest of the DeepSteel Battle-Ships are on their approach down into the Valley, they've split into five groups at the locations indicated on the overhead map."

Contemplating the maps on the screen in front of him, Bric said- "Alright, I see what they're up to; advise our two fleets to split into ten sorties and move out of the center battlefield. One group will engage the enemy from below, and the other group will engage them from behind and above. I want the Omega Ring to do a full frontal assault on their biggest vessel right over there, the one that looks like a sea-urchin. Let's see how well we can pound it, force some of their battle ships to come to the rescue, and then pull back to behind those hills, right there, where we are going to let about a third of our troops and equipment off. We'll repeat that maneuver twice over the next half hour until we have all our troops and equipment off at these three locations, here, and here, and there, all at the perimeter of the theater."

The Omega Ring did rather well at the beginning of the maneuver. Bric admired the expertise with which this intelligent computer program pulled off lasers, cannon fire and steering all at the same time. Whether it was truly sentient or not, this Da Veer was a brilliant entity. Back home, Bric knew of fellow Generals that would have given their eyeteeth for an intelligent weapon like this.

The Omega Ring unloaded huge blasts from above and a few minutes later, the giant Sea-Urchin shaped battle-carrier was on fire in numerous places and starting to lose altitude, forcing several battle-ships to change their course to come to the rescue. By the time they got there, the Urchin was barely moving, and the Omega Ring was already long gone, lowering troops and machines-of-war to the ground at a discrete location.

Bric was alone in the Command Chamber now, except for Lord Elberonor, who had remained behind as his assistant. The rest of the crew had been assigned to a Sky-Vessel or to the ground assault. Bric liked it that way. He could concentrate.

"You know, Bric, I love the theater." Da Veer quipped.

Bric turned slowly to look, silently, at Elberonor. Elberonor shrugged his shoulders.

"Excuse me? What did you just say, Da Veer?"

"The theater, the theater, you just mentioned the theater a moment ago. I love the theater was all I was saying."

"Ah, I meant the theater of war, Da Veer, not the theater of acting." and chuckled.

"Oh, it's all the same to me, good Emperor, it's all the same to me. The Act of War, and the Act of Acting are kissing cousins, twins barely parted at birth"

Bric looked away from Elberonor and said "I see…well, thank you for sharing that, Da Veer. How's the troop dispatch going?"

"We're nearly done. They're taking some fire here and there, but they look like they'll manage just fine."

Shortly after the first operation was finished, Bric engaged the same maneuver. In less than twenty minutes, several hundred thousand warriors of Ambrosia and EverGreen were safely positioned and placed in strategic locations all around the Plain of All-Sorrows.

"Are the Unicorn and the Harp still at it?"

"Yes, although it looks to me like the Harp is on its last legs, it's on slow impulse propulsion, and still getting hammered by the Midnight Shadow. My projections suggest that there is a significant probability that it will fall apart and explode in less than five minutes."

A flash of bright light suddenly lit up the interior of the Command Chamber as the entire ship rocked to and fro.

"A trifle optimistic, perhaps, but, that **was** the Harp, sir."

Da Veer continued with- "One thing I don't get, Emperor…I have complete read-outs and highly accurate records of the forces of DeepSteel. So far, they have used only about a quarter of the troops that are stationed inside the Castle. I am monitoring all channels of communication, and there are still no standing orders for a counter-offensive. We're devastating their Battle-Ships, we've mopped up most of their Locusts, and they're still holding back. I really don't understand."

"You told me earlier that the Resistance has a man on the inside, on a secure channel. Any word from him?"

"Yes, one of our agents is remotely controlling a Teddy Bear that belongs to Moebius."

"A…Teddy Bear?"

"We haven't heard from him in some time, though. Last we were told, Moebius was taking a nap, and the agent controlling the Teddy Bear had decided on a very gutsy move that is being kept as hush-hush as possible."

"Well, there you go, Da Veer, there's the answer to your question. Moebius has been asleep at the wheel, and his Generals are scared to take action while he's out of commission. That's great news! Get me permission to speak directly to the agent controlling the Bear. I want to talk to him immediately."

A minute later, Da Veer answered "I had a bit of red tape to get through, Emperor, but a quick command from Queen and King seems to have cleared it all up. I'm opening a channel to Agent Boodleberry right now."

The explosion of the Harp had indeed shaken everything, including the foundation of Castle DeepSteel; shaken it enough to wake up even Moebius, who yawned, stretched, and looked around. All his Generals stood in a ring around him, quiet as church-mice. Moebius got the impression that the idiots had been waiting for him to wake up, and this did not sit well. Bubble bath would have to wait. He grabbed for one of his screens and turned on all his overhead surveillance monitors.

"General Grit, General Grime and General Skewscape, what is our status? I don't see much going on…what's that giant explosion in the middle of the battlefield? Good lord, the Midnight Shadow is still alive? How'd THAT happen?"

"The Black Harp, my Lord, has exploded. The Omega Ring and the Midnight Shadow have destroyed it." said General Grit, rubbing his scaly chin rather nervously.

Moebius screamed, loudly.

"Where is the Silver Scream? Where are our troops?"

"The Silver Scream is expected any minute now, my Lord. The Locusts, Scorpo-bots and Ogre-Tank armies have been largely destroyed by the Sky-Vessels of EverGreen and Ambrosia that arrived on the Omega Ring two hours ago. We felt that it would be best to allow our Battle ships and Carriers to engage the Omega Ring and the enemy sky-force before we released the rest of the troops, my Lord."

"And how well have they fared?"

"Almost half the fleet has been destroyed."

An unnatural calm came over Duke Moebius. He turned from his Generals and quietly said-

"Generals, you know my motto."

The Generals hit the deck as Moebius opened fire, screaming at the top of his lungs.

"When the going gets tough, shoot them all and start over! YOU'RE ALL FIRED! EVERY ONE OF YOU!!!"

Back on the Omega Ring, Bric was talking to Agent Boodleberry.

"Boodleberry, this is the Emperor."

Boodleberry responded, with his Scottish twang, saying - "I've been briefed, me Laird. I know who ye are. Honored to speak wi' ye, actually. What can I do fer ye?"

"I need to understand your mission, and I need to know what your current status is." Bric shot back.

"Well, since Moebius has been asleep, I've managed to get the Bear from his private quarters to the ground level, and I'd nearly negotiated my way up to the Gates themselves when I had to take yer call."

"What's your mission, son?"

"Agent Deep-Six has sent me the directions and pass codes for the great Gates themselves. My mission is to unlock the Gates of Castle DeepSteel, Emperor Bric, to allow for your invasion."

"Holy cow, this is the best news I've heard today, son. Proceed with your mission, and then advise me of your success as soon as possible."

"Alrighty, fer sure, Emperor, but do ye tink you could arrange for some distraction, perhaps ye could have some of yer Sky-Vessels bomb the parapets or whatnot? Anyting to get a few of dese guards away from one of de monitors so I can get access?"

"We'll see what we can do, Boodleberry. I'll dispatch an attack squadron immediately."

But Bric would do no such thing, at least not for the moment. The entire Command Chamber rattled like a bell struck with a hammer. Lights flickered and sparks from one of the consoles flew everywhere. Bric yelled at Elberonor "What the BRAC just happened!?!!"

Lord Elberonor was looking through screens on his monitor. Da Veer's voice, with some deliberateness said-

"The Silver Scream has arrived, Emperor Bric. In fact, he's attached to the Omega Ring."

Bric gasped while the main monitor screen flashed back on, showing a remote view of the hull of the Omega Ring, listing to one side with the weight of a vicious beast of steel, easily larger than a dinosaur. It had wasted no time, but was clearly starting to rip into the hull, tearing up struts and parts with amazing strength. Barely seen, and hardly noticed on the screen was the Precognitus, Hieronymous Jones, puttering quickly off and away from the Silver Scream, headed for who knows where. He'd made his delivery, and he wasn't sticking around to get shot at.

Bric tried to remain calm, but was utterly taken aback by what he was seeing, and feeling.

"Da Veer, what…is…THAT!?!"

"That…would be our worst nightmare, General; the Silver Scream Nine is well over a thousand tons of cybernetic, titanium encased metal with the brain of a vicious German shepherd, and a simulated nearly unending appetite, for anything… it's attached itself to the hull with electromagnetic hydraulic-powered claws. There's no way I can shake it free, at any speed."

Bric was quiet for only a second. The Omega Ring was shuddering occasionally now. "What are our options, Da Veer?!?"

"I'm considering the probabilities. Let me reverse polarities between my dorsal and frontal plates and see if I can give the thing a hot foot. The lights and the monitors will go out briefly, it'll take me a few minutes to prepare it."

"My Lord, King Shard is on a secure communication channel!" shouted Elberonor.

"Put him through." Bric said, he could feel the vibrations and shuddering through the hull as he watched the Silver Scream ripping the Omega Ring apart, piece by piece.

"Son, I'm a little busy now, what do you need?"

"Dad, you need to get off of the Omega Ring. Lord Carderocke gave me the brief on the Silver Scream. There's no way anyone will survive its attack. You and Elberonor have to evacuate, there's a spare Sky-Vessel in the aft hold, the SS Tenacity. Elberonor is a splendid Sky-vessel Captain, one of the best. He'll get you out of there and you can join up with fleet Ambrosia. The EDV can abandon its socket in the Omega Ring, and detonate the Ring remotely. An explosion that large might take out the Silver Scream. It's your only chance."

Bric watched the screen. This Silver Scream was like a titanium Tasmanian devil, tearing rapidly through the hull, and hurling pieces of the Omega Ring everywhere. Suddenly, it stiffened, and Bric watched sparks and electrostatic charges of lightning fly everywhere. When the fireworks were done, the Silver Scream shook itself vivaciously and went back to ripping apart whole pieces of the Omega Ring.

"Reversed polarities failed, Emperor. I'm trying laser cannons now."

Bric watched as an incredible fire show erupted across the Omega Ring. While the laser cannons discharged, the Silver Scream paused, its evil silver smile never ceased, and when the fire show was done, it continued its foul work.

"Emperor Bric, I have some bad news to share." Da Veer announced grimly.

"We had a good run of it while we did, didn't we?" said Bric, neither to Elberonor nor to Da Veer. Elberonor said "My Lord, shall I prepare the Sky-Vessel for evacuation?"

"Are we the only ones left on-board?"

"Other than a few guards outside the Command Chamber, yes."

"Go ahead, then, I'll be right behind you."

Bric sat for a minute in silence. "Alright Da Veer, what have you got?"

"Probabilities are that the Silver Scream Nine will completely destroy the offensive and defensive capabilities of the Omega Ring within the next twelve and a half minutes. I can find no weakness. It is possible that remote detonation of the Omega Ring may not even work to destroy the Silver Scream. It is a considerable improvement over the last model."

"Well, remote detonation is our only hope, Da Veer. I'm headed for the SS Tenacity. As soon as we're clear, I want you to ditch this rig, get yourself to a safe location, and blow the whole thing sky-high, Are my orders clear?"

"Completely."

"Alright, soldier, report back to me once you are ready to blow her up."

"Absolutely."

As Bric headed for the door, Da Veer had one more thing to say.

"Emperor?"

"Yes?"

"It was an honor to serve under you, sir. You and your family deserve your title and your honor. In my own mind, you have redeemed your lot forevermore."

"Da Veer…you…are going to evacuate, aren't you?"

"Yes, yes, of course, sir, just feeling…a bit…overwhelmed."

"Just wait until we're clear, evacuate the Ring, and radio to me when you're ready to detonate."

"Yes, sir."

As Bric and Elberonor and the guards strapped themselves in their seats, Elberonor watched the Omega Ring portal doors slide open and the Sky-Vessel SS Tenacity was off and on its way.

"Radio King Shard and let him know another ship is joining his cohort." Bric said, watching the Omega Ring shrink in the distance as they crossed the smoke shrouded Plain of All-Sorrow. Flames were everywhere now.

Back in the Command Control room, the big red sphere that contained Edward Da Veer had turned to black, and pulsed with a deep dark blue color. The Command Control room shuddered here and there as the Silver Scream gleefully tore one strut and girder from another.

Da Veer said aloud, to no one in particular, since there was now no one in the Command Control room- "To Dwark, or not to Dwark: that is the question."

He engaged all of the engines with a sudden burst of maximal thrust, diverting all power systems to the propulsion units.

"Whether 'tis nobler in the processor to suffer the cold boots and fragmentation of outrageous fortune, or to take up arms against a sea of troubles, and by opposing end them?"

Buzzing past the high towers and parapets of Castle DeepSteel, he launched the remaining torpedoes against the bastion of Moebius, pointing the prow of the Omega Ring to take the vessel into a steep upward climb, his speed growing massively with each passing second.

Bric, who was watching from the SS Tenacity, turned to Elberonor and said "What is he doing? That's not what he was told to do! Why isn't he evacuating?" Elberonor shrugged and said,

"This is no ordinary machine, my Lord…he is a Free Machine, and he is no ordinary Free Machine, in fact, but he is a Grand-master of all the Free-Machine lodges in all of ProbablePolis."

Bric shot Elberonor a confused look. "I don't have a clue what you're talking about, son."

Back in the Command Control room, Da Veer continued with his soliloquy. The Omega Ring was now nowhere to be seen, but climbing with incredible speed into the Dwark.

"To die: to sleep; No more; and by a sleep to say we end the heart-ache and the thousand natural shocks that circuitry is heir to, 'tis a consummation devoutly to be wish'd."

He now changed course of the Omega Ring, pushing the vessel into a parabolic dive.

"To turn off, to sleep; to sleep: perchance to dream: ay, there's the fatal exception; for in that sleep of death what dreams may come? When we have shuffled off this mortal coil, they must give us pause: there's the respect that makes calamity of so long a life;"

As the Omega Ring came back into view, Bric shouted to Elberonor "What is he doing? Can you tell what he's doing?"

Elberonor looked at Bric and said "I think he means to hurl the Omega Ring against the Gates of Castle DeepSteel my Lord, that his detonation will serve two purposes, not only the one."

In the Command Control room, sparks were flying everywhere as circuitry shorted and panels went dark. Da Veer had already calculated his final thrust and adjusted the detonation trigger to pressure sensitivity on the hull. He did not stop his own dialogue, but continued with -

"For who would bear the whips and scorns of time, the oppressor's wrong, to grunt and sweat under a weary life, but that the dread of something after death, the undiscover'd country from whose bourn no traveler returns, puzzles the will- and makes us rather bear those ills we have than fly to others that we know not of?"

As the Omega Ring soared into view, it crossed the Plain of All-Sorrows in less than ten seconds, the speakers on the surface hull blaring Edward Da Veer's last comments to all of ProbablePolis.

"A POX ON YOUR HOUSE MOEBIUS, YOU'VE MADE BRIDGE RUST OF ME!!!"

The entire Omega Ring exploded with an indescribable flare and sonic boom into Castle DeepSteel with such force and velocity that the entire bulwark shuddered. Cracks emerged in several places as the slag that had been the Omega Ring continued to explode and splatter sending smoke and fire everywhere.

The Silver Scream Nine was gone.

ProbablePolis

Moebius and his newly appointed Generals had been watching the whole affair from his private chambers. Moebius screamed now with a tremble in his voice-

"Generals, you will begin the final assault. I understand that the Fleets of Ambrosia and EverGreen have lost nearly half their Sky-Vessels and we still have nearly three dozen of our Battle-Cruisers. The gap is narrowing. We must release the Stainless steel toads, the Fire-Glooms, and the Cascading Crystal Rectomancers, we must set free every single army of black vicious semi-robotic thing we have left, **and** make sure that every Koradgian storm trooper is moved into combat immediately. We have three armies of invaders out there waiting to engage, and our Koradgians alone outnumber them ten to one. Now we'll see some real action."

The new Generals saluted, saying "Hail Moebius!" and marched off to begin the last phase of the Final Tweak. Moebius, left alone in his private quarters, looked around surreptitiously, and, seeing no one around to observe his next actions, began to suck his own thumb, madly.

He wondered, for just a second, where had his Teddy-Bear gone?

Poopsy, for his own part, was now at the gates. Boodleberry had asked for a distraction, but the massive explosion of the Omega Ring had been way more than he bargained for, and he was now piloting the Teddy-Bear to a monitor that had just been abandoned by a Koradgian, instructed to come to another station and prepare for who knows what.

Entering the codes he'd been given by Agent Deep-Six, BoodleBerry guided the Teddy-Bear paws to enter the numbers and manipulated the dialogue boxes of the Moebius Net Gate guard system. As the Great Gates of Castle DeepSteel unlocked and began to creak open, alarms were going off everywhere. The full assault that Moebius had ordered was in full swing, and in the resulting confusion the guards from above assumed this was part of the counter-offensive.

The Gates had been damaged, however, by the phenomenal explosion of the Omega Ring as it simultaneously impacted and exploded, and a cave-in of the greater bulwark of the front of Castle DeepSteel seemed likely. A huge chunk of the Gate began to fall in on itself as smaller explosions continued to occur on the outside ramparts. It looked likely that no one would be able to get the Gates closed again. Confusion was setting in everywhere now, and none of the Koradgians noticed a lone Teddy-Bear making its way back to Moebius' private chambers.

Boodleberry was patched in to the SS Tenacity and said proudly –

"Alright, Emperor, Operation "Trojan Teddy-Bear" is complete. The Gates of DeepSteel are open."

Reports were flowing into Moebius' private chamber non-stop. Generals and Colonels of DeepSteel were now trying to deploy troops while others were calling their war-machines back to the Gates to defend DeepSteel.

Poopsy popped into the room and saluted a nearby Koradgian, standing nervously at guard with his huge laser blaster.

Moebius was panicked and packing.

"What are ye doing, my fine Dark Lord. Victory is just around the corner!"

Moebius stared at Poopsy for just an instant and then finished his packing.

"Retreat is just around the corner, you nitwit." was all Moebius said.

"You can't possibly be serious, my Lord. What's gotten into you?"

"Look, you little fluffy goon, this is all gone very badly, and it needs to be started all over again, do you understand, oh gravy! I'm talking to a TeddyBear! Now I really am losing my mind."

"What do you mean started all over again?"

"I am the Master of this world, Poopsy. The MASTER! I am the one who controls it. All of it! A bunch of terrorists, the Rondells, have managed to invade it, and they are threatening now to undo all of my good work, but they have no idea who they are really up against. All I have to do is get back to my Secret Command Center, return to the

Big World and they're done for. I'll find a deserted office somewhere in the MoonClock facility, I'll design a better implausible chip, replace the one that's running now, and then I'll be back…and these Rondells will be FINISHED!!!"

And without further hesitation, having located a clean toothbrush, Moebius pulled out his Transmogrifier and said to his Teddy Bear - "You coming or not, Poopsy?"

An instant later, Moebius was back in his little remote center far off in the Dwark. Looking around he noticed Clancy was gone.

"Hm. That treacherous little scum has flown the coop. Well, no matter, I'm going to make sure he doesn't get programmed back into the new hypothecation."

Poopsy waddled over to the Observation chair in the center of the room.

"Nice digs you've got here, my Dark Lord. What's this chair do?"

"Oh, get out of there, you little twit wit, that's the command chair. Here, I'll show you."

And hopping into the Observation chair, he adjusted a tool that stuck out from the right hand-rest and said "Watch the screen there, I'll show you. Ha! Those Rondells are about to get some payback, just you wait. With this little toy I can monitor all the hallways, rooms and offices of the MoonClock Facility, and make sure that THAT door there-" he pointed to the door that said 'OUT' "…will put me into the Big World wherever I want. How about those apples, huh?"

Boodleberry was taking this all in, watching carefully through Poopsy's eyes.

Suddenly a look of terror possessed Moebius. Metal clamps erupted from either side of both his legs and arms, and clicked shut with a distinct locking noise. Moebius squirmed and then squirmed some more. Panic shot across his face.

"What in the devil!?!"

The door marked 'IN' swished open and Moebius looked toward it in utter terror.

Agent Fugue and Clancy walked in. Clancy was smiling, and Fugue looked very serious.

"Operation Payback" was about to begin.

T-minus Zero

"One must still have chaos in oneself to be able to give birth to a dancing star"

- Nietzsche

Nowar sat on the back of the neck of the Great Olde Drake, feeling the exhilaration of the wind in her hair. She had long since realized that she could communicate with the Drake through her thoughts, so the howling wind was no impediment to their communication on this voyage.

As they made their way through the darkness of the Dwark, the cold air grew colder, the darkness more foreboding. In one of her pouches, Nowar could see the Remembrançarium glowing with a warm pulse.

"Your odyssey is nearly at an end, Nowar." The Great Old Drake thought to her.

"I know…I can sense it. But I am afraid, Synarchus- I am afraid that my fear will undo everything."

"Fear is an instinct, Nowar. Courage is what we do in the face of that instinct."

"How big is this thing?" she asked.

"I feel that the Slithery Tove has already grown to a hundred thousand times the size of ProbablePolis itself."

"And how exactly will I be able to fight it? Don't you think that I am the worst candidate to fight this thing?

"I am nearly as conversant as the Logos with the probabilities that run ProbablePolis itself, and I can assure you that no one has anywhere near the chance of defeating the Slithery Tove as you do, Nowar Rondelle. The fact of the matter is that, in actuality, if the Logos had decided to be more overt with you, you might well have been shown how to find the Tove without my help entirely, for example."

"Really? Then why didn't the Logos do exactly that?"

"To show you the value of sacrifice, my dear."

"Huh? I don't get it. What does that mean?"

But there would be no further response from the Great Olde Drake. A slimy black tendril whipped around his neck, only a few feet away from Nowar, followed, hardly a second later, by hundreds of other tendrils, whipping about madly, throttling the Drake in a growing mesh of writhing dark muscular tentacles. The next thing that Nowar knew, the Slithery Tove had wrenched the Drake with unimaginable fury forward into the darkness as Nowar was hurled from his back, off and away, into the Dwark.

Thankfully, in the pitch blackness of this furthest reach of the Dwark Nowar could not see the giant maws of the Slithery Tove feeding on the Great Olde Drake, its tendrils pulling his carcass into its very being. In less than twenty seconds there was nothing left of him.

Nevertheless, if Nowar had been feeling fear before, real terror now seized her heart. It made her head hurt as she thought to herself over and over, the very last thing that she had been just about to ask the Drake-

"How could someone as small as her fight something as huge as the Slithery Tove?"

And then it hit her, just as she was about to wish for her wings back to keep her from being hurled back downward to ProbablePolis, she thought "The heck with wings, I could wish to be as big as this Slithery Tove!"

She was so excited by this discovery that she yelled aloud at the top of her lungs - "I wish I could be as big as the Slithery Tove!"

And she was. It was a fast transformation, but not instantaneous, and, as she grew, she felt herself hit the hard surface of something cold and black, with a deep and loud thud. For an instant, her eyesight blurred. She felt the cold dark smooth surface all around and below her moving as she continued to grow on top of it.

Looking around her, she saw that she was in a rather large dark spherical area, a room no bigger than eight yards by eight yards, with walls of cold black marble. In the middle of the spherical room was a very small dim ring of light, with a pulse in one place on the ring. It was perhaps no bigger than her head, and it contained within it a tiny book, perhaps the size of a handheld field guide on birds or butterflies.

ProbablePolis!

A few feet away from the dim ring of light and the tiny book were a golf-ball sized silver moon, and not much further than that, a tiny blue star barely the size of a pin.

The Morning Star!

And above her, in the gloom, Nowar could now make out something that was about her own size, barely discernible, writhing and coiling its tendrils, tentacles and nasty toothy maws as it pulsated from its place on the ceiling of the Dwarkopologue.

The Slithery Tove…

She could hear it now, breathing with a hundred tiny mouths, slithering and pulsating in the darkness where it hung from the ceiling above her. Very slowly and deliberately she undid the strap that her spear had been secured to on her belt, and, just as slowly, pulled her shield from her back, realizing that she had not been attacked yet. Whether it was just finishing its snack and self-absorbed, or perhaps just not entirely aware of her presence now that she was all the way across the chamber of the Dwarkopologue, she began to prepare herself to make her assault. The Great Olde Drake would not have died in vain. She would avenge him, and this thing would meet its maker, once and for all.

Nowar fitted her helm on her head, and buckled its straps securely. She was ready.

Her challenge seemed a little more feasible now, although as she gripped her spear tightly, she realized that, other than the ring of light that surrounded the little book of ProbablePolis, there was really very little light to allow her to aim for this evil thing. Did it have a heart, a brain, what did it really look like? The darkness was so pernicious that she could only barely make out where it was hiding, but it had to be all but right over her head, of that she was sure. Nowar gritted her teeth and yelled as loud as she could as she thrust her spear upward.

The thing screamed like a rabbit on fire and did not stop screaming. The counter attack, however, was eerily modest. Nowar pushed and pushed on the spear, pulling it out and jabbing it in again, barely noticing that tendrils and tentacles were starting to wrap around her arms and hands. Each tendril had a mouth and the tentacles had stingers. The stings were only slightly painful, at first, but then she realized that the sting alone was only part of the attack. Each sting and stab of the tendrils and tentacles brought a foul memory up from the deep sea of her memory. The memories themselves were far more painful than the stings and bites. The memories themselves started to become a veritable sea, each more horrible than the last, it was as if a cloud of scenes, arguments between her mother and her father, harsh words spoken by her mother to her, harsh words spoken by her father to her.

Each sting and stab and bite wore into Nowar's heart and mind like an overwhelming cancer, a cascade of nightmarish memories, long since forgotten, but now playing out in her mind like a growing fugue of anguish, making her angrier and angrier at her parents for letting this horrible fate take her, this death in the Dwark by some slithery black monster.

She began to feel a shiver and a shake in her arm. Horrible arguments and harsh words in full cinematic power were reeling through her heart as the strength in her arm was starting to ebb.

Suddenly a voice was in her head…the voice of the Twinkler, saying "Only remember this one thing, please, that the seed of Charity lies in forgiveness."

But in the dark, all she could feel was the sting and horror of fear, of oblivion, of doom.

*

Back at the Ranch…Operation Payback was well underway.

Agent Fugue had been waiting for a very long time for this. He pulled up a stool and sat down right next to Moebius' face. He removed his sunglasses and stared at him for a good while, betraying not a hint of emotion. Moebius blithered and babbled the whole time, of course, sweating like a pig, offering Fugue riches beyond belief if he would only release him, insisting this whole thing had been a horrible misunderstanding.

Clancy handed Fugue two thin wires which Fugue attached to either side of Moebius' skull.

Then he stood up and walked over to the monitors, clicking a few buttons to change the view screens to see what was going on, way down yonder in ProbablePolis. A dozen screens showed a dozen angles of the field of All-Sorrows and Castle DeepSteel. Poopsy toddled over to his side to look at the screens. Fugue looked down at the Teddy Bear and said-

"Good work, Boodleberry. They have a chance now to defeat DeepSteel."

"Thank ye sir. More than a chance, I'd say, wouldn't you?"

Fugue watched the screens for awhile longer and remarked-

"If the Dwark Express gets there in time, and can unload the armies and the Avatars, yes, yes, perhaps so, but that's not the only battle being fought, Boodleberry, and it's not the most important one anymore, either."

Suddenly the Command Module shook and rattled. The sound of a harrowing, if muffled, howl, as if from far away lingered for awhile in the Command Module. When it had dissipated, Boodleberry said "What was that?"

"Like I said, it's not the only battle being fought, and it's not the most important one." said Fugue, looking back at Clancy.

The Command Module rattled a little more, as if to underscore the point.

"What do you mean?" Boodleberry said, following Fugue back to the seat where Moebius was held fast and Clancy busily preparing some mechanisms and instrumentation attached to the thin wires that Fugue had attached to Moebius' head.

"Very long story, Boodleberry. Another time, perhaps, we still have work here."

Clancy looked up at Fugue and said "It's ready when you are."

Clancy backed away, zipping up his tool pouch while Fugue sat down next to Moebius.

"You will likely be familiar with this technology, Dr. Noblechuck the Third. It's an improvisation on one of your Memoress machines. It hooks directly to the Implausible Chip and the stored experiential data of the entire, vast hypothecation. You will now be treated to a full download in your mind, directly into your very cerebral cortex, of all the anguish and pain that was experienced, just as if you were experiencing it yourself, of the last living moments of all the inhabitants of ProbablePolis. Remember the CloudTree Shane, you knew Shane, didn't you? He was the Avatar of EverLast, loved by all the creatures of his Kingdom"

Fugue pulled a switch and Moebius shivered and shook like a tree in a hurricane.

"Incredible, eh? And that's just the beginning, my friend. Next is the King of EverLast, Andironé. You nailed him to the Black Harp and he rode it right up until the very end, with broken limbs and a heavy heart, watching his own Kingdom go up in smoke. Here you, go, Doctor Moebius Noblechuck, second course coming up."

Again, Moebius shivered and shuddered, and began to cry.

Fugue's face still betrayed no emotion, and he said to Moebius, tears streaming down his chubby cheeks-

"This is just the beginning, Doctor. Clancy has perfected a perpetual loop for this program with a random vector. We intend to leave you here, through all eternity, to experience all the pain and misery you have caused every living thing in ProbablePolis, all down through the Ages…over and over…forever."

Then Fugue smiled. It was the first he'd had in many years.

Clancy decided to leave Moebius and Fugue alone for some quality time and walked over to the view screens next to the Teddy bear. Boodleberry had been watching the battle on All-Sorrows closely the whole time, and quipped to Clancy – "They're outnumbered; you know…they didn't have enough Sky-vessels to keep the troops pinned in the Castle during the initial attack. All three armies are surrounded and giving ground."

Clancy seemed unperturbed and switched one of the view screens to a long range display.

"They won't be outnumbered for long, Agent Boodleberry. Look! The Dwark Express is almost there, another five minutes at most."

Fugue called to Clancy suddenly "Bring me the detonator, will you Clancy?"

Clancy handed a large gray box with a very big red button to the Teddy bear.

"Here, would you take this to Fugue? I want to radio the Emperor and let him know that the Dwark Express is bringing reinforcements. It will raise their morale"

Boodleberry used the Teddy bear's eyes to look at the contraption, a mess of wires and gadgetry with a gray top and an ornate red button marked DO NOT PRESS. He ambled over to the chair and handed it to Fugue. Moebius, tears still gushing out of his eyes- looked over and down at the Teddy bear and whimpered –

"Et tu, Poopsy?"

Fugue did not take the box but merely hooked one end of one of its cords to the observation chair that Moebius was strapped in and looked back at Moebius, saying - "Or, if you like, Doctor, before we leave, the Teddy bear will bring this device within your reach. At anytime you can end your own misery, if you are actually able to experience such an emotion anymore, since you will be so distracted by the misery of all the poor souls you have tormented over the hundreds of thousands of years you have been here in ProbablePolis…all you'll need to do is simply depress that big red button and BOOM, all done, all over."

He looked at Moebius, who was now beginning to shudder and shake from the experience of some other poor creature his war had destroyed.

"Do you understand, Moebius, all you will have to do is to depress the red button at any time, and the resulting explosion will end the whole affair- it will come down to your choice, old boy."

Moebius suddenly became very lucid, and volatile.

"This is sheer NONSENSE! This is WRONG, it's patently UNFAIR! This whole thing…ProbablePolis…it's JUST A SIMULATION, SHARD! IT'S JUST SIMULATED SUFFERING!!!"

Fugue showed no emotion, but sat down again next to Moebius, barely inches from his face, and responded with –

"I have a few things to tell you, Doctor Moebius, and I might as well do it now. First, I am no longer Shard. I am a part of Shard, a small part that was separated from him a very long time ago, apparently by the Logos…and I have spent my WHOLE life following the cues and clues of the Logos…watching you, Moebius, waiting and watching your every move, shadowing you…and figuring out…how to take you down. I have gone to every length, made every sacrifice…and stopped living my own life…a very long time ago, JUST to TAKE YOU DOWN… so, I am simply no longer Shard, Doctor Moebius- I am Fugue, I am…your nemesis, I am your final downfall INCARNATE, and if I have become only a shadow of the man I was once a part of… with this…I am content, because right now, the moment I've waited for is finally here."

Moebius just stared at him.

"Oh, and one other thing, Doctor…simulated suffering…is STILL SUFFERING!!!."

Agent Fugue was smiling for the second time that Clancy had ever known him.

*

Back at the Plain of All-Sorrows the final counter-offensive of Castle DeepSteel was going very well, for the enemy. Once all stops had been pulled out, with nothing more to hold them back, the denizens of DeepSteel had erupted across the blackened moors and dark meadows with frenzy and fury.

Giant black metallic Furies, creatures the size of dinosaurs with steel heads shaped like women, screamed and hurled cannon fire against the hulls of the Sky-vessels. Stainless steel toads the size of bulldozers with tank treads for legs roared into the ranks of the battle armored giants and elves of EverGreen while Ambrosian Minotaurs fired lasers at flying Fire-Glooms, ogre sized synthetic creatures that morphed from smoke to fire and back to steel as required. Cascading Crystal Rectomancers, coils of sentient light as hot as an oven, were bouncing everywhere from sky to land and back again, ripping soldiers to shreds. The Koradgian Generals had indeed released every black vicious semi-robotic thing still lurking in the dungeons of DeepSteel, and their own shock troops, six foot tall, drooling reptilian gladiators were sallying forth with screams and weapons of every kind, from shotguns and spears, to hatchets and machine guns.

Bric was still on the SS Tenacity, which had just been caught by one of the giant Furies. After a rapid blast of fire a series of explosions began to rip into the command deck. One of the elves manning the command sequence control panel for the cannons slumped over in his chair as it exploded beneath him. Bric, realizing that the ship was heading down into a spiral dive, still in the clutches of the Fury, grabbed Elberonor and screamed -

"Abandon ship Elberonor! Get the BRAC out of here!"

"I'm not leaving you, Emperor." Elberonor yelled back as he pulled Bric from his chair and lurched through a portal into one of the escape pods. An ogre captain held the door open until the rest of the command deck crew could get into the pod. They all watched the Fury take what was left of the Tenacity down to the ground where it gave a final belching explosion of flames. The Fury stomped and stamped in the flames exulting as several rectomancers danced here and there around the entire scene.

The Furies had brought down all but seven of the Sky-Vessels.

As the pod came down to rest on a hillock a good hundred yards from the battle lines, a Minotaur handed Bric a nasty looking piece of equipment. He took a moment to show Bric how to use a high-powered rapid-repeating laser blaster with incendiary grenade-launching capabilities, and Bric thanked him ceremoniously for the quick on-the-job training. He turned to Elberonor and barked-

"Alright, soon as these doors open, we hustle back behind this hill and up that hill there to the Sky-vessel hulk- doesn't look like there's anything more going on there now. We'll set up communications equipment and re-establish communications with the rest of the commanders."

The pod doors opened, and just as Bric turned around, something long and tendrilous, like a forty foot long metallic serpent with the head of a TV, lurched into view. From behind the TV screen a dozen large lasers erupted and prepared to fire.

But Bric was ready, and he and the Minotaur, as well as the Ogre, open-fired on the thing, cutting it down to ribbons in a heartbeat. The Ogre had to get Bric to stop firing after it was quite apparent that the thing was in pieces.

"I'm sorry, bud, I've just always hated TV."

The Ogre Captain grunted and smiled, and helped escort Bric away from the fray. The battle line was advancing rapidly again. They all made for the crashed Sky-Vessel and Elberonor and an elvish helper went to work on setting up the communications rig. The first missive was from the SS Shrike to the SS Kaheela.

"We're down to five vessels. Tenacity just went down and there's no word from the Emperor. We're done for, you and the rest of the fleet do what you can, I'm headed for last reported coordinates of the Tenacity to see if any one got out in the pods."

Bric grabbed the mike from Elberonor and yelled "Don't you dare, son! We're fine, we got out and we're at a safe location behind our own lines…such as they are. Stay up there and keep giving the ground troops cover. We can't afford to lose anymore air superiority, understand."

"Got it. Glad you made it, Dad." There was relief in Shard's voice. The Shrike fell back into attack formation, firing away into something that looked like a huge black helicopter with a very ugly human face.

Elberonor went dialing for communications channels. Two more Sky-vessels were going down in flames, and one of the brigades of EverLast was failing morale as their ammo was running out. Looking out across the fiery smoke choked battlefield, Bric watched the skirmishing going on around the colossal carcass of the SkyWhale and said aloud, to no one in particular-

"At one point, someone had mentioned that there might be reinforcements coming. I don't really remember who or what told me that, but if they're coming, they need to let us know, and soon."

"They're here, Emperor." Elberonor took off his ear piece and stood, pointing up to the sky above.

Bric squinted, and then the Minotaur handed him a pair of binoculars. Still squinting, but squinting with a longer range, Bric looked where Elberonor had been pointing. He let the binoculars down from his eyes and could not shake a perplexing look of dismay. He looked at Elberonor and said-

"That's a train, Elberonor. That's a flying train. What on earth is a flying train going to do for us?"

Elberonor smiled and said "You'll see, Emperor, you'll see."

A few minutes later, the Dwark Express was tearing its way through the smoke and grime, colliding with creature and beast and even a

Fury, knocking them all out of its way without moving from its course one little bit. Heading down for a landing on the ground, the Dwark Express was still firing its fuzion engine full power, and it bounced several times back into the air before it finally settled on the ground, not far from the fallen SkyWhale, but it did not slow down.

Lil Bonsai Rex was hooting and hollering, too, entirely alone in the control room, and having entirely too much fun. He was hollering because they had only been here for twenty seconds, and they'd already put the smack-down on several large aerial targets, and he was hooting because he had no idea of what to do next, other than land the thing, but he was so enjoying the thrill of the speed and his own hooting, that he couldn't bear to slow down the Dwark Express.

The Walrus had long since taken his place in his Hardly Bathing-soon Dwark chopper, back with an army of rowdy faeries in one of the cabooses. He was putting on his helmet, and he'd already donned his full combat suit. His fiery lance was ready for some action, and resting on one of the throttles of his steering bars. Using his little communication pod in his helmet, he called up Bonsai.

"We ready to lay down de can o whoop ass, lil buddy. Go ahead and release de cabooses, an' we'll take it from here, ok?."

"Hokay Boss, here goes nothin'!" Bonsai pressed a lever on one of his control sticks, and ten seconds later, every one of the cabooses, nearly three dozen in all, uncoupled from the Dwark Express with their tops firing off in every direction.

In less than a heartbeat, the Koradgian Storm Troopers and still teeming minions of DeepSteel were harried and hurtled every which way by thousands upon thousands of creatures, both large and small; Rowdy Faeries, Arthropodicans, and countless warriors of nearly every page of ProbablePolis rolled like a wave over the Plain-of-All-Sorrows. There were bangers and smashers, lasers and lassoes, catapults and crochet needles, missiles and metal mugs wielded by an unimaginable variety of strange and wondrous creatures from all the Kingdoms of ProbablePolis. Things with wings of many colors, creatures with a dozen legs and bird-like heads, beasts that looked half-human and part

Praying Mantis, others that seemed to be combinations of spider and jelly fish, or cheetahs wearing Tudor clothing and wielding long swords with daggers- and everywhere there were gigantic beasts of might and magic, the Avatars themselves, jumping into the fray with equally wild abandon.

Hiram Kaine had flown into the sky and grabbed two furies, knocking them so hard into each other that their heads and gears flew off in every direction. Deb-o-rah Craine was right by his side, fending off rectomancers swirling around in the air. Herr Leuchtkäfer, a Firefly the size of a jumbo jet with a long wispy white beard and very thick spectacles, flew off above Kaine and Deb-o-rah Craine and shone a light so bright across the Plain of All-Sorrows that many of the synthetic nasties of DeepSteel had to recoil for a few seconds before their optical sensors could re-adjust, giving the Resistance extra seconds to pound away at them.

Madame Kotoridayori, a hummingbird the size of a tractor trailer was busy hurtling herself full force through Koradgians like a lawn mower over a summer yard. Lady Fucale Kombu followed her, pulling an ocean wave along with her that took out Koradgians that Kotoridayori had missed. Lord Theopolis, the multi-colored Octopus led a whole fleet of flying multicolored squid here and there, picking up the DeepSteel beasts and lobbing them into the black poisonous sea-without-waves that was just behind DeepSteel. Lord Amphion and Lord Zethus, a Cheetah and Lion, both as big as two twenty story buildings, waded through the ranks of the DeepSteel machines, leading their feline followers in every direction they could, making for the Gates of the Fortress.

The Walrus was flying high, leading a great horde of rowdy Dwarkchopper riding Faeries from one fray to another, shadowing Amphion and Zethus, crying as loud as he could: "COO-COO-CA-CHOOWIE!" and laughing as he mowed down one batch of Koradgians right after the other.

Back on the hill, Bric was jumping up and down like a little kid, whipping his helmet up into the air. Elberonor continued to watch the

Dwark Express and said quietly to himself "I wonder what the engineer is up to?"

Bric looked over his shoulder.

"You're right. He's not slowing down…in fact…he's speeding up!"

Lil Bonsai Rex was having tears of joy. As he mowed through the ranks of the Koradgians, he saw the great gates of Castle DeepSteel approaching him at meteoric speed. Gritting his teeth, he pushed the throttle and the fuel input levers as far as they could go, increasing to maximal speed, but not pulling up the flaps for take-off.

"FOR ERNIE AND CLYDE!" he screamed, and then "BONSAI!!!"

The Dwark Express hurled, roaring like thunder, into, and quite through, the left gate, which had still been in one piece, somewhat, but was now shattered everywhere. As the Dwark Express hurtled into the dark interior of Castle DeepSteel, the sound of lil Bonsai Rex echoed over the plain-

"BONSAI! BONSAI! BONSAI!"

Flames and billowing smoke erupted everywhere from the tops of Castle DeepSteel. The sounds of cheering and jeering began to replace the sounds of grunts and death cries.

The Resistance was winning. Koradgians were beginning to flee the battlefield. Most of the really big cybernetic nasties were in flames and barely moving.

*

Clancy turned away from the view screens overhead and said –

"Looks good, Fugue. Maybe it's time we left Moebius to watch the end of his empire in privacy."

Agent Fugue was still sitting next to Moebius. "Alright, Clancy, I guess you're right. Boodleberry, I suppose you can have Poopsy do the honors."

As Fugue leaned across Moebius with the detonator box, Moebius, with tears still in his eyes, but hatred in his heart, vowed he would not be murdered by a teddy bear, and lurched his leg out to the side as far and as hard as he could, tripping Agent Fugue, hurtling him down to the floor where he landed with his whole weight

…on the detonator.

The explosion was catastrophic and devastating.

The Command Center had been built with an enriched plasma fuel core and an extra layer of thick shielding outside the interior latticework structure. The result was that the explosion immediately generated its own field of incredible internal pressure, and along with all of that special fuel, well, the explosion did not stop, but consumed itself under its own weight, ripping from one implosion to the next, growing brighter and brighter inside the command center cage.

Point of fact, for those of you who don't care for the physics involved, let it just be said that all the unique characteristics of the Command Center had allowed the explosion to become a kind of perpetual furnace not unlike the Sun that burns in your own sky.

All across the plain of All-Sorrows and across the Kingdom of Koradgia, the sky turned from night into day. The Koradgians continued to flee, even more panicked than they had been before; the creatures and Avatars of ProbablePolis one by one dropped their weapons and stood staring up at the orb in the sky.

ProbablePolis now had a sun, a moon, and a star.

*

Nowar was now nearly completely covered in black tendrils and tentacles. The mélange of memories of hate and arguments had weakened her attempts to keep stabbing at this thing, and her heart was barely working. The strength in her arm and her whole body was nearly gone, just a numb stinging across her skin as memory upon memory of her parents and her friends and her family fighting with one another rang through her head.

But again the voice was in her head…the voice of the Twinkler, saying once more "…remember this one thing, please, that the seed of Charity lies in forgiveness."

Summoning all her will, Nowar said to herself "I forgive you, each and every one of you…I forgive you…you didn't know what you were doing, you just didn't know…and I forgive you."

And the pain began to flow away and out of her, like a river. The memories, the nightmares, ceased.

And then, suddenly, there was light. Searing and bright, it illuminated the whole of the Dwarkopologue with a bright yellow glare like a welder's torch, and with it, showed the scene she was in with an incredible, brilliant clarity. It was as if a tiny sun had erupted into being on the far end of the Dwarkopologue.

She looked around wildly and saw that she was nearly trussed up like a turkey, with this black things tentacles and tendrils over most of her body, her spear and spear arm were totally covered with this slimy black thing, and a great deal of the right chest, and most of her right body as well. It had started to slowly pull her up and closer to its hundred tiny mouths, quivering with delight in anticipation that in just a few more minutes they would feed, that the body could grow again.

But the light of the birth of this new little star seemed to hurt this thing, and even though it seemed to have no eyes, it ever so slightly loosened its steel-tight grasp on her.

With her left hand, Nowar flawlessly pulled the Utility of Fidelity from her belt and not knowing what it might possibly turn into, plunged it towards the Slithery Tove. She missed, soundly, but as she did, she saw that it had turned itself into something that resembled a giant can-opener, and, furthermore, she had hurled it at the Slithery Tove so hard that, as the Utility hit the wall of the Dwarkopologue, it gashed a deep hole into it!

Suddenly, air was rushing past her, an incredible hot torrent of air was everywhere, but clearly it was rushing past her into the hole she had made in the Dwarkopologue itself! In fact, the air was rushing with such speed and ferocity that it was beginning to suck the tendrils and tentacles of the Tove right into it. This had the result of slowing the speed of the outrushing air somewhat, but it also had the result of sucking the Tove into it with even more power and force.

Struggling with every last bit of energy left, Nowar used the Utility to hack and slash at every tendril and tentacle she was caught with, eventually freeing herself nearly entirely of the thing as the last great mass of it got sucked up into the hole, and SHLOOP! -pulled through, to heaven only knows where.

But the wind rose again, and quickly Nowar brought the Utility of Fidelity to bear once more, and as she did, it flawlessly became a hot trowel, simultaneously melting the surface of the Dwarkopologue as she smoothed it to patch and cover the hole.

Working as quickly as she did, though, she had not noticed that the great sucking winds had drawn the little Sun of ProbablePolis right behind her head. Turning to see where all the heat and light was coming from just then, she nearly had it in her face and flailed as hard as she could with the Utility of Fidelity, which had instantly become a sword. The little Sun was hurled away from her in a shower of sparks.

Somewhere, somehow, someone seemed to say "The Work is… Perfect!"

When Nowar opened her eyes, the Utility had returned to its normal state, a humble rod with the symbols of a bird, an anvil and a butterfly- but the little Sun she had struck had fathered a hundred other even tinier suns, all very much tinier than the original, but hovering and floating everywhere- rotating slowly, with the original Sun, orbiting the tiny book of ProbablePolis.

The Dwark would never be as cold and dark as it had been.

Nowar slumped to her feet with her back against the cold Dwarkopologue wall behind her. The light and heat of all the little Suns began to make her feel very sleepy, and she felt a deep longing to just lay down and go to sleep.

Blast-off!

"Roots and branches shall change places and the newness of the world shall be a miracle"

The Prophecies of Merlin

When Nowar awoke, she realized immediately that she had returned to her original size, and that she was drifting, slowly, downward, through a new, very ephemeral, very bright, gossamer-filled Dwark. Lights and sounds shifted and moved everywhere, like tiny newborn elementals, quivering with life and curiosity.

Far, far below her in the distance was ProbablePolis, still twirling ever so slowly. Everywhere around her was light. Here and there she could see creatures of all kinds, making their way to…where?

She even fancied a couple of them looked like Jajuma, those marvelous single celled creatures the size of elephants that the Morning Star had introduced her to…when? It seemed like so long ago…her sense of time had deserted her.

But none of the creatures ever got close enough for her to be sure, and still, she drifted, gaining in speed ever so imperceptibly. How long had she been out here, she kept wondering to herself.

"Not so long, Nowar." – came a reassuring voice beside her. She looked around wildly to see, a little boy, floating along side of her, drifting downward at about the same speed as she was.

"Who are you?" she asked. He was beautiful, with skin the color of snow, eyes the color of the sky, and hair the color of wool.

"Who do you think I am?"

"I think you are the Logos."

"And I think you are right." He smiled at her.

Suddenly she realized that all her armor, her shield, her spear, even her Remembrançarium, were all gone. Somehow it didn't bother her, and she asked. Everything changes, but nothing is lost…what an odd thought she thought to herself, and then asked-

"Did we do alright? Am I dead? Are we going home? Is Moebius defeated?"

"Yes, no, yes, and…mostly yes, all four in the order that you asked just now." answered the Logos.

Nowar got very quiet, looking around her again. The hundred tiny suns shed their light in competition with the one big sun, casting incredible shadows everywhere, but shadows of what?

"Those shadows are cast by all the shattered fragments and pieces of all the pages that Moebius destroyed over the many turnings of the great ribbon. They are all islands like Opus Delirious and Dangling Dow, with survivors of one war or another, eking out their survival on a shred of a Kingdom."

"What will happen to them now? Their world is so bright now, and they were all used to Twilight or less."

"Difficult to say, but why should it matter to you now, Nowar? You are going to go home soon."

"But it matters a lot to me… I love them."

"You…love them?" there was surprise in his voice.

"Yes, I love them. All of them. I love all the creatures and places in ProbablePolis, both the ones I got to see, and the ones I'll never get to see."

"I understand…completely." said the Logos, and he beamed, continuing with-

"You know, we have plenty of time to talk, but…I sense that your family would like to return home soon, so we shouldn't take too long."

Nowar thought about it all for a moment. It was almost too much to imagine. She hadn't even seen her Mother in years and barely remembered what she looked like. She hadn't seen her Father in at least two years. The Logos said, with measured tones-

"Before we go back to ProbablePolis, I thought I would give you a parting gift."

"Really? What would that be?"

"One…last…wish."

Nowar was stunned, and then she realized that the wish would only be good for her while she was here, and that wouldn't be for much longer. She thought on this for a good while, watching the Book of ProbablePolis get larger in her field of view. Suddenly it looked so sad, and page-worn, tattered, like a very badly-cared-for book, left out in the rain far-too long, missing most of its pages…etc.

And then, closing her eyes, she said-

"I wish for all the pages and Kingdoms and creatures and Avatars of ProbablePolis to be healed and renewed and restored, just as they were in the first days before Moebius, and that all the beings that lost their lives in the last War could be returned to life again! That is what I wish for!"

When she opened her eyes, the Logos was no longer a child, but a young man, and he gingerly took her arm, guiding and gliding her downward with greater speed.

"You wish…is…granted!" he said with a hearty and happy voice.

As they glided downward, they were picking up even more speed. He was guiding her along at an oblique angle, taking her now on a whirlwind tour over every one of the landscapes of every page in ProbablePolis. An incredible dazzling array of places, strange and wonderful, went rifling past her eyes. As they finished up this brief but incredible tour of all the restored Kingdoms of ProbablePolis, the Logos maneuvered to hover right in front of Nowar.

"All these worlds are yours, Nowar, they will never belong to Moebius. They can only belong to someone that loves them, just as they are."

As Nowar looked around, she realized that they were coming to settle down upon the ground of a very interesting place. The Logos continued, proudly-

"Behold your own handiwork, Nowar. Castle DeepSteel is no more. In its place is an Emerald Fortress."

Nowar scanned the beautiful blue skyline. Against the background of a beautiful ultramarine ocean rose a dozen Emerald Towers sprawling along the cliffs, encrusted with willow and cherry trees, shrouded with a mist rising from the beautiful cerulean bay. The Plain of All-Sorrows was now a lush meadow filled with song-birds, strewn with wild flowers and surrounded by apple trees.

"Behold the Plain of All-Joys. Do you like the statue in the middle of the valley? The Black Harp is now nothing more than a gigantic white piece of art. Hah! A Harp of Alabaster! Hahhahhah!"

Nowar stared at it and had a look of disbelief on her face.

"My wish did all of that?"

"That, and more, child! Look up there!" and he pointed.

Very high up in the sky, Nowar saw great structures, giant pieces of some kind of giant device starting to piece itself together. The Omega Ring was beginning to whirl itself into place, the whole thing humming louder and louder as it finished the last touches of its own self-assembly.

There were people running now from the hills down into the valley. Nowar could not see them, but now she noticed something she did not care for at all.

The Sky-Whale! There it was, in the middle of the Plain of All-Joys, but…

It was not healed.

Nowar began to run to it, and the Logos followed her. Nowar could not bear to look on her left side where she had apparently taken all the damage from the Black Harp. Amazingly, though, she was not dead yet, and Nowar could see her lungs rise and fall, ever so slightly.

"I thought you said that everything would be healed! She's not! She's dying!"

"It's her choice, Nowar." The Logos said. "Uhranitee Gnosticius Mare has chosen to pass on, for she has a very special secret that can only be released with her passing…go and talk to her now, her time is short."

As Nowar walked up to her, she saw that her breathing was indeed very heavy and labored.

Before she could say another word, Nowar was shocked to see Mandrake NeverSong walk up to her. She threw herself into Mandrake's arms without even noticing that he had two wings, and sobbing loudly said –

"This is not fair! She is so beautiful, Mandrake. Why won't she choose to stay, to live with all the other creatures of ProbablePolis? Why?"

"Good Queen Nowar, this is some of the oldest lore of all, from the beginning of all days- she has chosen this fate, but you may give her comfort. Go and touch her skin."

Nowar knelt next to her huge eye, and tried to touch her, but began to sob.

In her mind, Nowar heard a voice so deep and wonderful; she knew it had to be the Sky-Whale.

"Do not cry, child, do not cry for me…for there is beauty everywhere, even in a sea of pain…and…and you have redeemed all of ProbablePolis. Look around you."

"Why won't you stay, Mare? Why?"

"You will see, child, you will see. Just remember what the Twinkler told you…"

"What?" she was still crying "He told me so many things…"

"That the more childhoods you can live, the better…"

Mare exhaled deeply, one last time. For a second, the only sound that could be heard was Nowar crying on the Plain of All-Joys, but then, there came, a most peculiar explosion. All along the sides of the flanks of the Sky-Whale, one after another, came explosion after explosion, and with them, came hordes upon hordes of-

Little winged sky-whales, each of them no bigger than a puppy dog.

The air became filled with them, flying everywhere. Suddenly, Nowar was being pestered by one after another, each of them bumping into her face or arm, laughing and saying-

"Hello, I'm Benjamin!" or "Hello, I'm Patrick!" or "Hello, I'm Donald!" or "Hello, I'm Tyler!" and on and on and on for many minutes.

But after several minutes, the air around her started to clear, as each and every one of the little Sky-Whales was beginning to go off and explore one thing or another, swishing around an apple tree, or checking out the surf in the bay, or sniffing a dandelion.

Mandrake, still standing nearby, said "A SkyWhale can only give birth to her progeny by dying, Nowar. She died so that they might live. This is one of the mysteries of Motherhood."

All of them had all but vanished; all but one had all bolted off to parts unknown, headed for the heavens and the new skies of ProbablePolis- off to discover all the worlds that the Logos had shown her, that she had healed for them to explore.

But one did remain. She had stayed off at a distance for a bit, but now began to dance closer and closer. Cruising in closer and closer to Nowar's head, which was feeling like crying again, she began to laugh and giggle while the tears on Nowar's face were still fresh.

Nowar barely managed to get out the question "Why did they all leave?"

The little newborn SkyWhale said - "Oh, they're all boys, and that's just what boys do, you know."

"So, aren't you going to leave, too?"

"Oh, no, I'm not a boy. I'm a girl. I'm Sonya Maru, and I'd like to stay with you, if that's ok"

Nowar hardly knew what to say. She played with the baby SkyWhale for a few minutes, until they both giggled.

A moment later, the Logos had brought forth, from the crowd now assembling all around them, a number of people that had been running very hard to get out to the middle of the Plain of All-Joys.

Her Grandfather, her Father, and her Mother were all there.

They all hugged her and everyone started crying, including all the creatures and people that had escorted them all out here.

The Logos even seemed like he was about to cry, but only said –

"The time is at hand for you all to return to the Big World from whence you came. You have all saved the Little World, and your reward is a simple one. Join hands, my friends, and you may all go home."

They all enjoined hands, and there was a clap of thunder across the heavens, followed by a great and nearly indescribable shimmering that began to grow steadily in its presence and power, until the Rondells disappeared into a perfect halo of silvery white light.

*

Nowar opened her eyes.

She was sitting in the back seat of Grandma Brandy's Van!

She looked, with a wild-eyed look, to her right. Her Father was staring out at the trees passing them by. He looked at her, and smiled.

Nowar then looked, even more wild eyed, to her left. Her Mother winked at her.

Nowar leaned forward to see who was in the front seat. Pop Bric and Grandma Brandy were in the front seat. Pop Bric was driving, though, and fiddling with the radio.

At her feet was a very thick book. It had a Sun a Moon, and a Star on the cover.

ProbablePolis. It must have been nearly four hundred pages!

She picked it up and looked back again at her Mother with even wider eyes.

Her Mother said quietly-

"Life is but a dream"

Nowar looked back again at her Father who was still smiling. He said, just as quietly-

"There's no place like home."

The van was pulling into the circular driveway in front of the house. She and her family were finally all home. Nowar leaped out of the van and ran down the brick walkway to the bell in front of the house and began to ring it loudly, over and over, thinking to herself-

"Life may be but a dream, but there is definitely no place like home."

She could not stop laughing.

Epilogue

Conceive of a young boy, perhaps ten or eleven years old, running through the snow on a tall beautiful ridge. Behind him are several mountains and an ocean. He is running, he is laughing, he is free and he is alive. He is in love with everything he feels, with everything he sees and hears, the cold snow under his feet, the whistling wind on his cheek, the sun twinkling in his blue eyes and making a sheen on his black mop of hair flopping about in the breeze.

He finally arrives at a strange and small hovel with an odd entrance framed by roots in the ground underneath a huge old oak tree. Inside he puts up his cloak and hangs his breeches by the fire, and runs into a small dining room where an Angel sits at the table.

The Angel watches the boy eat his soup without a word. After a time, when the boy is nearly done, he says-

"Today is a special day, young lad."

"Is it? What day is that Mandrake?"

"Today you are eleven years old. Today is the day I promised you that you would get a very special choice presented to you."

"I get to choose my name!"

"That's right!" and he leans forward. "But even more importantly, you get to choose whether you will face the past or return to the future. You may choose to be given back the name you wore in your last life, or you may choose to take a new name that you will wear in the life to come."

The Angel waits to see if the boy is absorbing all this.

"If you choose the name you had, you will be given back all the memories of that life, for ill or good, and you may discover all the mysteries and secrets of who you were, perhaps spending your life making amends or even reuniting yourself with the people you cared about in that previous life."

The boy remained quiet and still, taking it all in.

"But if you choose a new name, you will be given a blank slate, to make new mistakes, to discover untainted joy, to relearn the gravity of love. This is your choice. You can make it now, but you must make it today…"

The boy thought hard and long about his choice.

"So which will it be?" the Angel asked.

"I choose a new life."

Mandrake smiled and said- "And what will you be called?"

"I am Enigma."

Acknowledgements & Inspiration

Credit comes where credit is due. All of these authors and their good works have at some point influenced and inspired my daughter, myself and our families as we have crafted ProbablePolis.

- C.S. Lewis
- Madeleine L'Engle
- Edward de Vere
- Mary Shelley
- J.R.R. Tolkien
- Marion Zimmer Bradley
- Jorge Luis Borges
- Margaret Atwood
- Lewis Carroll
- William F. Buckley Jr
- Frank Baum
- Eileen Gunn
- Ursula LeGuin
- Robert Heinlein
- Lord Dunsany
- Franz Kafka
- Ray Kurzweil
- Gwyneth Jones
- Diane Duane
- Tanith Lee
- John Smart
- Patricia Anne McKillip
- Andre Norton
- Arthur C. Clarke
- Richard Adams
- Joseph Campbell
- Erin Hunter
- Carl H. Claudy